A Contemporary Romance by Lily White

If you are interested in reading additional books by Lily White or would like to know when new books are being released, Lily White can be found on:
Facebook, Instagram and Twitter

Join the Mailing List!

If you are interested in receiving email updates regarding additional books by Lily White or would like to know when new books are announced or being released, join the mailing list via this link.

http://eepurl.com/Onoeb

Join the Facebook Fan Group!

If you are interested in receiving exclusive previews for upcoming novels, or to

participate in giveaways, join the fan group
for Lily White Books.

FAN GROUP LINK

Follow Lily on BookBub!

https://www.bookbub.com/profile/lily-
white

OTHER BOOKS BY LILY WHITE

MASTERS SERIES:

Her Master's Courtesan
(Book 1 of the Masters Series)
(Available on Smashwords and lilywhitebooks.com)

Her Master's Teacher
(Book 2 of the Masters Series)

Her Master's Christmas
(Novella in the Masters Series)

Her Master's Redemption
(Book 3 of the Masters Series)

Her Master's Reckoning
(Book 4 of the Masters Series)

STANDALONE NOVELS:

Target This

Hard Roads

Asylum

Wake to Dream

Four Crows

Crazy Madly Deeply

Rules of Engagement

Wishing Well

The Five

ILLUSIONS DUET

Illusions of Evil
(Book 1 of the Illusions Duet)

Fear the Wicked
(Book 2 of the Illusions Duet)

DARK EXCLUSIVE - Available only on LilyWhiteBooks.com:

The Director

Table of Contents

PART ONE

CHAPTER ONE

Perspective.

It's a simple word with three syllables that means nothing to the residents of the small, suburban town of Tranquil Falls.

On one side of town, mansions and elegant estates reach up to scratch the sky with their gaudy turrets nestled behind electronic gates and lazy, winding driveways, the grounds covered by manicured lawns, shrubs clipped and shaped within one inch of their lives, and dainty little flowerbeds that were currently buried beneath a foot of snow.

Following the streets away from those stately manors, one can mark their trail by the ridiculously cheerful holiday decorations from three decades before, the creep-factor of those reindeers and snowmen, brightly lit snowflakes, and colored bulbs marking the path until you reached Tranquil Falls High where it sat like a bastion of hope in the center of town, the buildings desperate for a few coats of new paint while the football field was immaculate.

It was on that field that the lumbering brain-dead jocks ran into each other while spirited by the shouts and screams of a town that had nothing better to do on a Friday night, where the darlings daughters wore their practically pornographic cheer costumes beneath the proud, practiced smiles of their mothers who were busy reliving their own glory days.

The wealthy owned that field during the day when the players would practice, and at sundown when the games were held, but I owned it during the midnight hours when I would lay in the center and watch the stars.

Perspective.

I had it. They didn't.

They were all the same, and when the overhead lights shut down at night to reveal the stars that belonged to me, those wealthy kids would retreat home or to their raucous parties after stopping on the other side of Tranquil Falls where I lived.

You see, by following those gross decorations with their weird eyes and colored lights past the high school that was a dividing line, you'd find the train tracks that cut the town into two unequal halves, the stately mansions holding court on the right while what was referred to as the *servants' quarters* plagued the left.

Nothing more than run-down houses that had once belonged to those poor saps who considered themselves middle income, my side of town had fallen hard during economic crashes, the white picket fences crumbling to dust, the reasonably priced SUVs sold and replaced with mid-sized sedans. As more people lost their jobs, my side lost half its residents, the modest, foreclosed homes standing empty except for squatters. Now, you could walk through the center of my side, turn right to score your next fix, or turn left to find my house which still had running water, electric light and a freshly painted white picket fence that did nothing to keep the vagrants out.

And while my parents resented the sixty hour work weeks they slaved and labored to give their children the semblance of a normal life, I had every desire to march over our small manicured lawn and rip out the fence that was a freshly painted *lie*.

I couldn't blame my folks for trying to give us something better, even while we studiously ignored the sad truth that our lives scraped the bottom of the barrel. My father was a yes-man to one of the big wig investors who lived on the other side of town, my mother a maid who scrubbed and polished a few of those stately

4

mansions, attempting like hell to be included. And while the wealthy women mostly ignored her and laughed about how far she'd fallen, one woman had thrown her the smallest of bones by sponsoring a shy, delicate dancer who had the face of an angel and the grace of natural born ballerina without the wallet that could afford it.

Delilah, my sister with long legs and a megawatt smile, had a spirit that matched her angelic face. Her long, blond hair was up in a ponytail as she swept through the cafeteria following Michaela Paige around like a puppy.

I hated to see my little sister subvert herself to the whim of the popular crowd. Michaela seemed slightly more human than her bully of a quarterback boyfriend, despite her status as homecoming queen two years running. She always had time to mentor Delilah on the dance team Michaela's mom owned.

For that, I couldn't hold Michaela's perfect smile and brightly polished nails against her, couldn't hate her for her pompous jerk of no-neck boyfriend, couldn't seem to stop watching her from my shadowed corner where I held court as the King of Freaks in the lunchroom where we all were now gathered.

Tucked behind a ragged copy of whatever bullshit drivel the teacher assigned me to read by the end of the week, I turned the page and shoved my black hair from my face to glance up and monitor my kid sister. Deli, as I liked to call her, climbed over the bench seat with her long, graceful legs to sit beside Michaela. Michaela, in turn, laughed at something another person said, but flashed Deli a smile.

It made me happy to see my reputation as the freakshow recluse hadn't polluted the waters for my kid sister. She desired the limelight, the wealth, the esteem, the friendships of the popular kids who'd gathered together in their exclusive group that believed being worshipped had been their birthright. She was also a year younger than Michaela and I, a junior while we were both seniors.

Technically, we'd all grown up together, but while Michaela had the simple life tucked behind the dividing line between wealthy and poor, Delilah and I were two of a handful of students that crossed the train tracks to attend Tranquil Falls High. We'd known each other since we were children, but until Delilah joined the dance team, we were considered outsiders. I was still the outsider among the wealthy and elite, but Deli had managed to find a place among the popular, a fact that concerned me more than it should.

It was the last week of school before the long winter break, and while skimming the pages of a classic novel I'd read too many times already, I glanced up every so often to keep watch over Deli. Although she trusted that group to keep her best interests in mind, I knew at least three of the players seated at her table had been a little too handsy with several girls, and if they even looked at Deli the wrong way, I would destroy them.

And that's what I mean when I talk about perspective, about points of view and why they matter. Because whereas the majority of the sheep who flood this school look to those bastards like they were royalty in a world full of peasants, I saw the truth of their lives, their roaming hands and rushing fingers, the drugs they purchased from my side of town so they could take advantage of the girls at their parties.

There was one such party tonight at a parentless house that had everyone talking, a party Deli had begged mom and dad to let her attend. It was fortunate my parents still considered her too young to go to a late night shindig and had declined her request. Because if they'd given her permission, I would have had to put my foot down and locked her away, just so I knew she wouldn't be one of those perverts' next victims.

Clive Stanton, a particularly questionable running back, was eyeing Deli a little too closely. Every so often, he'd run his meaty palm over his short clipped brown hair, a snide smile tugging his lips while his eyes dipped down to study her shirt. Turning another page, I kept careful watch, pretending to read a line of words that taught some moral lesson about non-violence, while I was actually imagining all the things I would do to Clive should that hand get too close to my sister.

Michaela laughed at something her boyfriend, Jack Thorne, whispered, his hand reaching to slide over the small of her back, the ends of her long brown hair she left loose brushing his fingers. I'd stopped lying to myself about a year ago that I wasn't jealous he could touch her and I couldn't.

Shaking away that dangerous train of thought, my eyes crept back to my sister. She had no clue what Clive Stanton was thinking, no idea that he was leaning closer to reach across the table to touch her in ways that I deemed inappropriate. I would have given the guy a pass if something he'd said hadn't caused her to lean forward just a little too close. And I probably would have stayed in my seat if I hadn't noticed the way his fingers reached out to brush her breast from over the thin material of her shirt.

Crossing the cafeteria on a long-legged stride, I caught Clive's gaze before my sister knew I was coming. Scowling my direction, Clive straightened in his seat, the tension in his shoulders rallying the rest of his meathead friends to straighten in theirs and turn to eye me.

It was game on before any of the girls knew what was happening, and I genuinely felt bad that Deli would have to witness this, but I didn't worry it would dampen her reputation at the table, because to each person sitting beside her, I was just a loser freak with a bad attitude that most considered crazy.

Perspective. I hated them, and they hated me. They thought I was a nut-job, and I thought their faces would look a lot better with some black and blue coloring.

Clive stood from his seat knowing he was the man of the hour, the feet of his chair scraping the floor like an alarm bell alerting the rest of the student body that a fight was about to go down. Rounding the table, he tipped his chin in defiance, purposely ignoring the fact that, in this particular squabble, I was the biggest predator around.

They may have spent their hours in the weight rooms and on the field, but I had a naturally stocked physique, standing two inches taller with shoulders five inches wider than even the largest player on their team.

"Holden!"

My sister's sweet voice rang out over the low din of the cafeteria, the rush of whispered comments and excited murmurs, the students jostling about trying to get the best view of the scene that was about to explode in front of them.

"Touch her again, asshole! I dare you!"

Clive rounded the table smirking at my taunt, his fists moving into position before we collided, and his friends moving to surround me knowing it would take three of them at least to stop me from shattering his face.

"Holden! Stop! He wasn't doing anything!"

It was too late, Deli's complaints falling on deaf ears as Clive and I came within reach of each other. Not that Deli had any clue was was happening at this moment, because whereas she believed Clive was being the utmost of gentlemen, he and I both knew he wasn't.

We were on the floor within seconds, my fist slamming into his face while he did what he could to block the blows, and by the time I'd helped both the left and the right eyes swell up and water, three sets of hands were latched to my shoulders to drag me off him.

Surging forward as much as I could, I only stopped struggling when Deli was in front of me, her expression serious, her palms pressed to my chest, and her mouth opening on a plea that I reconsider killing the guy.

"Holden, please!"

Tears sprang from her radiant blue eyes that were the same shade as mine, the lower rims stained red by her panic. Where I was naturally tan, Deli was pale, and where I had dark hair, hers was light. I was big and she was pixie sized, but her touch was the only thing powerful enough to stop me from surging forward again, even with the three clowns clinging to me from behind.

I guess that's where I was different from Jack Thorne. While Deli was doing her best to stop this fiasco, Jack was rounding the table to join in, his face set in an angry mask, Michaela jumping in front of him to stop his forward progress. But whereas I stopped moving to keep from knocking Deli over, he practically shoved Michaela to the ground, not caring that the girl who'd been with him for over three years cried out in pain, her head snapping back as her body went tumbling over. Another rush of anger flooded me, my sights set on that son of a bitch as my hands clenched back into fists, the knuckles already busted from their impact with Clive's face.

"Deli, move."

I tried to keep my voice calm with her, tried to move her gently as Jack came barreling at me, but he was moving too quickly, his jaw set in rage. "I mean is, Sis, MOVE!"

A feral grin stretched my cheeks as I picked Deli up and set her aside, she tried to lunge to stop me, but I was already two steps ahead, my feet set in a battle stance, my eyes glued to the only guy in the entire cafeteria that had any chance of standing against me.

Before Jack could reach me, another voice boomed from behind us, a voice that stopped Jack in his tracks, but had absolutely no effect on me.

"This stops NOW!"

Coach Granger's poor imitation of a superhero peacekeeper had the desired effect, halting Jack and Clive in place while giving me the perfect opportunity to get in one last jab before I could be dragged off again. Blood burst from Jack's face, the telltale crunch of a broken nose echoing over the now silent cafeteria just before I was grabbed again and Coach Granger roared out his discontent.

I understood his frustration. This wasn't the first time I'd taken on his star players and embarrassed them in front of a school full of slack-jawed kids and teachers.

Technically, I'd started this fight, which to most would make me look like I was the out of control freak, but I had history with these guys, years of putting up with their bullying, both physical and verbal. I'd learned to ignore it, to keep my cool while they took turns taunting me with jokes about my mom being the 'help' and taking every opportunity available to make my life a living hell. It didn't matter to me, their snickers and jeers whenever they trashed my locker or spit at me as I walked down the hall.

They had a reason to hate me. Their coach has been after me to join the football team since the minute I stepped into the school as a freshman. Not just after me, the guy had been promising the world on a silver platter if I would just give it a chance. But I wasn't into it. Not then and definitely not now. I was fine with the abuse I took from the team as a result. Laughing it off as jealousy, I never cared much when they made it a point to come after me. But I drew the line when it came to my sister. Had Clive kept his hands to himself, this never would have happened.

"Holden Bishop!"

Jerked from behind, I was spun in place, my eyes locking with Coach Granger's. "Front office! Now!"

Snatching my bag from where it had been dumped on the floor, I shot a look of apology at Deli before storming out, Coach Granger still yelling at Clive and Jack as I passed through the cafeteria doors into the hallways. Reaching the front office five minutes before Coach Granger, I took the time to plant my weight in a rickety plastic chair, my knuckles bleeding as the elderly receptionist watched me, her expression filled with disapproval. She tossed a few tissues my way, but that was the limit of her concern for my injuries.

The coach stormed in finally, his lips twisted into an angry snarl, the bald spot on his head red with anger, the vein pulsing at his temple letting me know I'd pushed him a bit too far this time.

Opening the principal's door, he canted his head to the side silently ordering me to follow him. The feet of my chair screeched over the white tile floor, my booted steps heavy as I made my way inside the small office.

"Take a seat, Bishop."

Lowering myself into a seat, I cast a quick glance between Coach Granger and Principal McGrath, a no-nonsense blonde that had intimidation down to a science despite her small size. Pinning me with her light grey stare, her forehead stretched taller by the severity of her tight bun, Principal McGrath cut a scathing look down at my knuckles. "Let me guess: Was Mr. Bishop fighting again?"

She said it like I was always fighting, but in truth I'd only been in two other scuffles, and both times had been self-defense. I said as much only to be shut down immediately by two sets of eyes that made it perfectly clear my days at Tranquil Falls High were numbered.

The problem in this school wasn't fighting, it was winning, especially when you sent the glorified football players onto the field with black eyes and broken noses.

Pinching the skin between her eyes, McGrath leaned back in her seat, blowing out a long breath filled with frustration. "Holden, I thought I made it perfectly clear last time you were marched in this office that I wouldn't tolerate violence in my school." Pulling her hand from her face, she pinned me again. "We took a risk allowing you to enroll for your senior year at Tranquil Falls, and as I can now see, that risk wasn't to our benefit."

Her gaze shooting to Coach Granger, she asked, "Who was involved in the fight and how much damage occurred?"

"Clive Stanton and Jack Thorne. We may be dealing with a broken nose. And Clive should have matching black eyes by tomorrow."

Principal McGrath not only had intimidation nailed down, she also had an iron will. Somehow preventing the flood of swear words I knew she wanted to spill, her unwavering gaze swept back to me, her eyes narrowing with disapproval. "How's your family going to pay for the damage, Mr. Bishop? Did you even think about that before breaking the faces of two of our most valuable players?"

"The season is over," I offered weakly, as if that would excuse the damage caused.

Both their stares locked on me. Coach Granger attempted to ease the tension, but his question only added fuel to the fire. "Why did you attack those two boys, son?"

I hated when people called me son, as if affixing some familial title would make me feel more relaxed so I could spill all the pain and frustration inside me, and we could all cuddle and cry afterward. I wasn't his son, and I never would be. But now was not the time to bring it up. "Because your players have no respect for women. I can't stop them from drugging and molesting the girls that are stupid enough to show up at their parties, but if they lay a hand on my sister, you can be damned sure I'll rip that hand off and slap them with it."

Both McGrath and Granger stilled in their seats, their expressions careful and practiced. It wasn't a secret what the team did to many of the girls that attended their parties, but most parents and administrators were willing to look the other way as long as one of those girls didn't end up pregnant. Sadly, the lack of concern in the adults taught those girls that what was being done to them was normal.

"I'm going to speak with your parents," McGrath said, her voice tight and controlled. "but I think it's safe to assume you won't be graduating from Tranquil Falls High after this incident, Mr. Bishop."

My face shot in her direction. "What? You can't do this. Clive Stanton was fondling my kid sister. Are you going to mention that to my parents as well?"

"As far as I can tell, she's not a kid anymore. Your sister is able to tell him no, Mr. Bishop-"

My voice grew louder as I interrupted, "She's sixteen and he just turned eighteen! Isn't that statutory rape or something?"

Sighing, McGrath swiped a pen from the surface of her desk, clicking the end of it several times before answering, "In this state there must be a five year age difference until anything as untoward as statutory rape can be charged. I'd appreciate it if you'd stop accusing my star students of crimes."

Star students. Of course those perverted jerks got a pass. It was nothing new in this shithole town where money talked and the rest of us could learn to live with it. "Are we done here?"

"Yes, Mr. Bishop, I believe we are."

I didn't wait to be formally excused before shooting out of my seat and storming from the office. The halls were empty as I made my way out of the school, the parking lot a ghost town as I pulled out of my spot and gunned it away from Tranquil Falls High.

This is where perspective slid in again to show me how the world was different through my eyes.

While Principal McGrath thought her punishment would ruin me, I saw it as a cutting of strings, a moment where I would finally be set free to leave this shithole town.

CHAPTER TWO

"Expelled? Tell me you're kidding, Holden. You can't be expelled. How will you graduate?"

My pencil sketched across the paper, a soft scratching sound, the feet of a mouse running over the floor. *Scritch, scritch, scritch.* I loved this sound, craved it, and the silence that came with it.

The image came to life through the shading, eyes watching me, the soft angles of a gentle face, smiling.

Sitting on my bed, hunched over paper, I brushed away the lead dust, not caring that it stained my skin. "Guess I won't graduate." A negligible shrug of my shoulder. "Not that it matters. I can get a diploma from one of those adult schools. I'm eighteen now."

The mattress dipped with Deli's weight, not that it was a lot of weight. She was tiny compared to me. Maybe that's why she could jump and twirl, spin and move like she was fluid and boneless. She'd always danced, always wanted to join gymnastics or cheerleading. Our family never could afford it, at least until Michaela's mom offered to sponsor her.

"Is Michaela mad?"

I didn't know what I would do if Michaela's mom kicked Deli out of dance. It would my fault, but for a good reason. I kept reminding myself of that. Clive had no right to touch my sister. I'd break his hand if he did it again. But still, Deli lived for her dance squad. All she talked about was the upcoming competitions. All she did was practice, even to the point where exhaustion rode her body, dark circles bruising the skin beneath her eyes when she'd pushed herself too hard.

"No," Deli finally breathed out. "Michaela doesn't like Clive. And she's mad at Jack for shoving her down. But, she's mad at you, too."

Soft laughter shook my shoulders, my pencil tracing another long line through my sketch. "Why would I care if she's mad at me? Michaela and I haven't spoken two words to each other since we were kids."

Deli scoffed, the small sound causing me to laugh a little more. "Michaela isn't a bad person, Holden-"

"I never said she was," I argued. My eyes peered up at my sister. Sometimes it was so hard to see her all grown up. Every time I thought of her, I saw her as the small five year old that would chase after me constantly. She always wanted to do what I was doing, even if she didn't have the strength to climb the same trees, or the talent with a pencil and paintbrush. But what she lacked in that particular talent, she made up for with her ability to move as if gravity itself didn't apply to her. "She's not the best person, either. And I don't trust her to watch out for you around the football team. Especially Clive and Jack."

Deli grew quiet, her expression thoughtful. When I met her eyes, she averted her gaze, her head bowing down, her hair falling into place as a curtain to hide her eyes. Absently, she picked at a pulled string on my comforter. "What happened today-"

"Will never happen again. Clive is bad news, Deli. Probably the worst of all of them." My hand stopped, the soft scritch of lead against paper dying off. "Why did you let him touch you? Especially like that. Where everybody could see what he was doing. You're smarter than that."

Her shoulders shrank together, her tiny body huddling over itself because she knew I was right. With a voice as tiny as her, she admitted, "I just want to fit in. You know how hard it is for us. Without money and

16

everything that comes with it, we're nothing but the *help*. Nobody took me seriously until I joined the dance team. But now..."

Her voice trailed off and all I wanted to do was pull her into my arms and hug away all the pain and self-doubt inside her. Yes, I knew what it felt like to be invisible. I knew how kids like us were treated by the wealthy kids who had no clue how hard it was for people not born into the same power and influence as their families. But unlike Deli, I didn't care much. I never cared.

As far I was concerned, graduation was a line of demarcation, a moment dividing what my life had been and what my life would become. I had no plans to stay in Tranquil Falls. And now that I was most likely expelled from school, that line moved closer. I could jump in my car and haul ass finally. The only problem was that I'd have to leave Deli behind. Without me here to watch, what would those bastards do to her?

My voice softened to see her so insecure. She, of all people, shouldn't feel that way. She was a shining star in a sea of the same boring faces. Almost every student was a carbon copy of the other. But not Deli. She had a bright future. Brighter than all of them. And brighter than me. Maybe that's why I felt the need to watch out for her, to protect her even if it hurt my chances to succeed. "You need to stay away from them, Deli. I've already told you what those guys do to girls. And don't think I don't know you asked mom and dad to go to the party tonight. Even if they had given you permission, I would have stopped you. I'll kill every single one of them if they hurt you like they've hurt a lot of other girls."

I heard the sniffle before I saw the tear fall to her lap. She tried to hide her pain, but I could always see it. I hated that pain, wanted to rip it out of her and absorb it into myself, take it as my own, shoulder the burden so she could be lighter on her feet and dance free.

"I know Michaela is your friend, but when it comes down to a choice, she'll choose them over you. She'll let them hurt you if it means she doesn't get hurt in the process. She's weak, Deli. And although I'm happy she's nice to you, I don't trust her. She's another carbon copy. Another facsimile. Another one of them, just with a friendlier smile. Don't forget that."

Another sniffle before, "She would never hurt me."

A sigh escaped my lips, my own shoulders withering in response to hers. "Maybe not directly, Deli, but she wouldn't stop them from hurting you. She's not strong enough."

"She has her own problems," she argued.

"I know." And I did know, I'd watched Michaela get pushed around since she was a kid. Not just by her friends, but by her parents, her teachers, anybody she deemed to have influence or authority over her. Michaela was so afraid of losing her status that she went along with whatever crowd gathered around her. She was another sheep, a black one within a sea of white, maybe, but still a sheep.

Dropping my pencil on top of my sketchpad, I shoved both aside and reached for my sister. I would have pulled her in for a hug, the size of my body swallowing hers, but an angry voice boomed from the living room, the sound of the front door slamming causing both Deli and me to flinch.

"Holden Bishop! You get your butt out here this instant, young man!"

Mom's voice screeched at about two octaves higher than her normal tone. Hearing how mad she was, I had no doubt my father was on his way home. He was her back up, the strength behind her, the man who gave me my dark hair and broad shoulders. Only problem was, he didn't have my strength. He was a yes-man, a coffee fetcher, another sheep like Michaela that depended on the scraps offered to him by those who were stronger and more powerful. I wished I respected him, but I didn't. He wasn't strong enough to protect my mom...to protect Deli.

"Mom sounds really mad," Deli whispered. "I don't want to see what happens when dad gets home."

"You have nothing to worry about," I promised. "I won't tell them why I started the fight. As long as you promise never to let Clive touch you like that again."

Her voice was barely a rush of breath in the quiet room. "I won't let him touch me again."

Nodding, I pulled my lip ring between my teeth, playing the metal over the enamel as a nervous habit. It wasn't that my parents scared me, I just hated being the disappointment again. I knew they worked hard, knew they struggled to give Deli and I everything they could, but I still couldn't find it within me to respect them.

We should have moved away a long time ago, left this town and the pompous elite behind with it. But they'd stayed thinking that something might change eventually. I knew it wouldn't, but that's what you deal with when you're the only smart one in a sea of stupid - you see the end coming while everybody else smiles and drools, too dumb to know when they're being led to the slaughter.

"Holden!"

"I better go."

Getting up to leave, I was surprised when Deli reached up to wrap her arms over my shoulders. I could easily pick her up with one arm, easily carry her through life if I had to. She was the only person that mattered to me. Regretting that I had to peel her away, I gave her a wan smile. "Don't worry, little sis. It's not like mom and dad are going to kill me. I'll still be here tomorrow."

"You better," she whispered, a small smile tugging at her lips beneath the tears.

I gave her one last look, sticking out my tongue like when we were kids. She stuck hers out in return, crossing her eyes just to be funny. I loved that girl and didn't care that siblings should squabble. There was no reason to fight when your sister had a heart of gold.

Breathing out, I walked down the hall to find mom. Knowing what was coming didn't make it any easier. But I was willing to take the hit for what I'd done, and I'd do it all over again, rage day in and day out to protect Delilah from the world.

Stepping into the living room and seeing mom's face made me wonder if my days were numbered. Her blond hair was a messy bun on her head, her normally bright blue eyes dull with exhaustion and grief. Still wearing the black pants and green shirt that was her typical work uniform, she scowled in my direction, the lines of her forehead razor sharp. "Do you want to tell me why, after everything we've done to keep you in that school, you thought it was a good idea to fight?"

Her voice grew louder, her small frame appearing larger as she put her hands on her hips and craned her neck to look up at me. My mother wasn't a weak woman by any means, she'd labored and slaved to get where she was in life, but she still found herself bowing down to the status quo, still considered herself inferior to the women who employed her and treated her like a second class citizen.

"What are you going to do now, Holden? Where are you going to work and how are you going to earn money without a high school diploma? I spoke to your principal and they're done with you! Do you hear me? Done! Why in the name of everything that's holy did you attack those two boys? Are you crazy?"

If there was one word in this world that drove me to rage, it was crazy. I'd been called that for most of my life, been told I was somehow wrong because I didn't see the world the same as everyone else. I was a big guy, strong. I'd had my share of girlfriends. But I was different.

Instead of wearing the standard clothes preferred by most of the preppy jocks in my school, I preferred black. Black shirts, black jeans, black jackets, black beanies, you name it. With my dark hair and piercings, most people referred to me as a Goth. And maybe with my choice in music and my love of art, they were only slightly right. I didn't sit around mourning my existence, and I wasn't the great intellectual that sat on my perch looking down at the rest of the fools who didn't know better. I wasn't Goth, or Emo, or whatever title it was they used to describe me. I was just me. Myself. A man who wanted nothing more than to forget this bullshit town and find my way elsewhere.

But if you asked anyone else, they would tell you I was insane. Crazy. Deserving of a padded cell. Just because I refused to bow down, refused to fall in line with what was expected of me.

I was the King of Freaks because I wasn't like everyone else.

Screw them all.

"Don't call me that," I warned.

Crossing her arms over her chest, her scowled deepened. "Well, maybe if you didn't act like a lunatic, I wouldn't have to say that word! You could have been arrested for assault, Holden! You're lucky those boys chose not to press charges. You broke Jack Thorne's nose!"

That pleased me to hear. The bastard deserved it after shoving Michaela down, but I didn't vocalize the thought. It would only piss her off more.

"Why, Holden? Tell me why!"

"They looked at me funny," I lied. Refusing to drag Deli into this mess, I held my tongue, bit the inside of my cheek to keep from telling mom everything Clive was doing, was most likely planning to do to ruin my sister. Yeah, she was old enough to make decisions on her own, but she was innocent in mind. Not stupid or slow, just overly trusting. She was such a good person, she believed other people were good too.

My mom's scowl deepened, our screaming match interrupted when my dad came through the door and slammed his briefcase down on a table. "Turn around, Holden."

His tone of voice was off, the deep growl spinning me in place just before he surged forward, his fist raised as if to hit me. Caught by surprise, I couldn't dodge the blow in time. Guess breaking the nose of the son of his employer was enough to make my father violent. He'd never hit me before.

"Dylan, stop!"

My mother attempted to jump in between us, but the damage had already been done. Rubbing at my jaw, I stared at my dad, my eyes shading over with red, my violence coming to the surface to be caught off guard. If mom hadn't been standing between us, I would have lunged back at him, would have shown him that I may be younger, but I wasn't smaller, and I wouldn't put up with any person thinking they could hit me and get away with it.

Spit flew from my father's mouth as he screamed at me, his face red with anger, his shoulders trembling with

22

the rage he couldn't contain. I smiled, the feral expression pushing him further into his loss of control.

"I am sick and tired of having a freak for a son! We've been embarrassed by your bullshit long enough, Holden, and as far as I'm concerned, you can get the hell out of my house and find somewhere else to live. I was almost fired today because you can't control your urges. You're out of control and I'm not putting up with it. If you want to stay in this house, you'll apologize to those boys tomorrow while gathering your stuff from school now that you've been kicked out."

Apologize? For what? Defending my sister? I'd apologize the day Hell froze over. "I'm not apologizing."

My dad swung again, knocking my mom aside so he could get to me. Dodging the blow, I laughed when he stumbled. He may have thought he was big and bad, but he wasn't. Losing his balance, my dad fell to the floor, his face twisted in rage as he screamed, "Get out! You can take your freakshow ass on the road and sleep in your car for all I care! Get out of my house!"

He didn't have to tell me twice.

Snatching my keys from the table, I stepped around him and headed for the front door. My mother was kneeling down beside him, my sister standing at the end of the hall watching the entire fight with tears in her eyes. I hated that I couldn't comfort her, but if I didn't leave now, this would only get worse.

I winked at Deli before walking outside, a quick gesture between siblings, a silent promise that I would be fine. Her worry saturated the air around me, making life feel heavier, this moment more significant than it should have been. I didn't understand it at that moment, but Delilah must have known this would be the end of what had been our *normal*. She must have intuited that what we had known and what we'd loved would be turned upside

23

down so fast that we both would be left drowning beneath the surface of circumstances and tragedy.

Anger has a way of blinding you to intuition, to what's important, to what has been and what could have been.

Slamming the door, I marched to my junker of a car, climbed into the driver's seat and peeled out of my parent's driveway. Fishtailing as I took the turn off our street a touch too fast, I ignored the ice on the road, the slickness beneath my tires, the danger of winter's wrath. All I cared about was getting away, getting far, and getting there as fast as the car could carry me.

I should have known escape could never be that easy.

I was on the main road through town, traveling over the train tracks toward the school. The twenty-four hour diner passed by, a blur of lights that were dim and drab compared to the holiday decorations tied to lampposts and strung through trees. Hitting a slick patch of ice, I almost lost control, my car spinning, my headlights flashing against the buildings and shops that were closed for the night. But it wasn't the spin that stopped me. That mistake was easy enough to correct. It was the sputtering of my engine that locked me in place, the smoke billowing out like an omen from beneath the hood.

My car wasn't something I would ever call reliable.

Pulling to the side, I threw the car in park, cussing and raging as I climbed out of the driver's seat to kick the tires several times. The least this piece of junk could do was get me outside of Tranquil Falls far enough to hitchhike down the main highway. It was like a force field had gone up, trapping me in this town, in this life, in this miserable existence.

Rounding the front end, I opened the hood, fanned my hands to drive the hot smoke away, and looked down at an engine that should have been replaced when I first bought this clunker.

I didn't know that fate was heading toward me at a speed not safe for icy roads.

I should have looked up in time to see the headlights heading straight for me.

I should have made a lot of different decisions that day - decisions that wouldn't have permanently altered the entire course of my young life.

CHAPTER THREE

Michaela

It's anybody's guess how my night ended up this way. Perhaps the decision had been taken out of my hands, the sympathy I felt for Jack's pain and broken nose making me weaker than I should have been. I always hated the servants' quarters, hated the streets stretched out with dark, empty houses where any type of monster could be waiting inside.

This part of town wasn't so bad when you first crossed over the tracks. There were still a few houses down the first street to the left where normal families lived. Delilah lived in one of those houses...and Holden.

A sigh blew out of me, the breath a plume of white in the cold night air. Jack hadn't taken a left down the road where the families lived after crossing the tracks. He'd kept going until reaching the parts where the neighborhood turned dark, taking a right on some other road where the houses were full of vagrants, drug dealers and squatters. He claimed he needed help because the pain of his nose was unbearable, but I knew differently. We always came here before one of his big parties, always stocked up so Clive and the rest of the team could have their fun.

I didn't see it as fun, but not many people care about what I have to say.

Normally, Jack took care of this part of the evening before picking me up from my house. He knew these streets scared me, always teased that I was too much of a spoiled snob to give his *friends* a chance. But I didn't think they were healthy friends to have. Their clothes always stank and their hair was always greasy. Half of them were

26

passed out on old couches and the floor by the time we arrived here on the nights I was forced to tag along. And the ones who were still awake, who weren't too zoned out to notice that we'd walked inside, they always stared a bit too long, their eyes reaching for places that sent chills down my spine and forced bile up my throat.

Jack would never let them touch me, he was too possessive for that. I was his alone. His girl. His toy. His warm body that kept him entertained while the team went off into their separate bedrooms with whatever girl they'd chosen for the night.

None of this was normal, but I wasn't going to be the only person who spoke up. I didn't want to be an outcast. Didn't want to be labeled a freak. Just like they'd done to Holden.

While sitting on a dirty couch with my arms wrapped around my abdomen and my breath beating out of me on white, puffy plumes of hot air colliding with the cold, I watched as Jack bumped fists with Jimmy Parker, a known dealer who was twenty-seven, but looked like he was in his forties. I guess that's what drugs do to you after a while, age you as if someone had pushed the fast forward button on your life. It leaves pock marks on your face, and turns the light off behind your eyes until you're walking death just waiting for the day your heart stops beating and your lungs can't draw in another breath of air.

Jimmy slid his eyes my direction, smiled to show me his brown, broken teeth. I almost gagged just to look at him. Turning my face away, I hid behind my hair, my thoughts drifting back to the fight that happened today in the cafeteria. I wanted to be mad at Holden for starting it, for pissing off the entire team and making Delilah even more of a target, but I also understood why he was angry, why he struck out at Clive.

Delilah was a beautiful girl, both inside and out. She was just a little too sweet for the sharks that circled our school, a little too naive to keep from falling down on her ass every time someone took advantage of her. That's why I took her under my wing as soon as she joined the dance team - to keep the other girls away from her, to keep her spirit from being crushed beneath the pressure of having to be a certain type of person to fit in. I really liked Delilah...and Holden, if I were to be honest. There was something about him that drew my attention, but it was his reputation that kept me from being his friend.

"Hey, Michaela, I'm going to go in back with Jimmy real quick. Will you be okay out here alone?"

Glancing around at the two drugged out losers asleep on the other couches, I shrugged in response. Jack didn't even wait for my answer before walking off with Jimmy to leave me alone. The anger that flashed through me was nearly as forceful as the pain radiating up from my hip. He'd told me that knocking me down during the fight had been an accident, but I didn't believe him. Jack had a habit of being a bit too forceful, just like everybody else in my life.

A sigh blew out of me. I should have had my hip looked at while I'd been at the hospital with Jack for his nose. A dance competition was coming up in four weeks and I needed to be in shape for it. If this pain didn't stop in time for practice next week, I'd have to make up a lie to give my mom about what happened to me. Not that the truth would cause her to do anything about it. She'd simply roll her eyes and tell me I'd done something wrong.

I wanted out of this life, but I knew it would never happen. I was the princess of Tranquil Falls, the Homecoming Queen, the Prom Queen, the pretty doll my parents could dress up to flaunt in front of their perfect

28

friends. All the girls at school wanted to be me, and all the guys wanted to be with me. It's too bad none of them realized my entire life was a lie.

Holden didn't have to lie.

I respected him for it.

"Thanks, man! I'm sure I'll be feeling all better in no time." Laughter chased after Jack's rushed voice, he and Jimmy stepping out from the dark hallway. Jack's nose was taped up and bandaged, both his eyes swollen and dark, but it wouldn't stop him from partying tonight. Not Jack Thorne. Never.

"Just take it easy on the road tonight. Shit's slippery and I don't need you doing something stupid and getting caught with those. The last thing I need is the cops asking too many questions."

Jack smiled at Jimmy's warning like it meant nothing. "I don't fuck up, man. You know that. I'll see you around."

They bumped fists and Jack inclined his head toward the front door, his silent instruction for me to follow him. I resented being bossed around, but I jumped up anyway. Following after him meant I could get away from the crusty couch.

"You have a good night, Michaela." Jimmy's voice slithered behind me and when I turned to look at him from over my shoulder, he smiled again to reveal all his rotten teeth. Bile flavored the back of my tongue in response.

"Damn, it's cold," Jack grumbled as soon as we were outside and exposed to the wind. "Hurry to the car."

Slipping on the icy concrete, I collided with the door of his car, my bruised hip screaming in pain again. Like a shot straight up my nerve endings, the pain flared then radiated out, a spreading explosion along the right side of my body. Gritting my teeth, I opened my door to climb in the passenger seat of Jack's ridiculously priced two-seater sports car. He scared the crap out of me behind the wheel of this thing, but I had enough to worry about tonight without adding my fear of his driving on top of it.

By the time I was shutting my door, Jack was already nestled and warm in the driver's seat, his brown hair messy around his face and his green eyes bloodshot from whatever he'd done in the back room with Jimmy. Even with those bloodshot eyes, he was gorgeous, the most desirable senior in Tranquil Falls High. Sometimes it made my heart flutter to think that out of all of the girls, he was with me - and other times it made me want to cry. Being Jack's girlfriend wasn't easy.

Reaching for my seatbelt, I tugged it down just before he grabbed my wrist to stop me. Turning to look at him in question, I saw mischief sparkle behind his eyes. He leaned over the center console to cup my cheek with his hand and kiss me, his tongue slipping inside my mouth in a rushed bid for control.

Pulling away, I smiled, "Slow down, Jack. We have all night to make out."

His smile matched mine, but it was a touch too wide, his white teeth a hair too big. "I can't wait that long. I need you to do me a favor."

A groan escaped my throat. Needing a *favor* was Jack's way of saying he wanted me to go down on him. "Not here, Jack." I glanced around at the dark houses, knowing that in each one there was one, if not several, shady people lingering about. "This place gives me the creeps."

He cupped my cheek again. "You know I won't let anybody hurt you, baby. But I need this so bad. It'll only take a second. I can't help myself when I'm around you. I'm in pain when I can't feel those lips," his eyes dipped down to my crotch and back up to my mouth, "or those

30

ones wrapped around me. You do this to me, so you could at least help me out. Especially after I fought and got a broken nose for you."

"For me?" My eyebrows shot up, my eyes narrowing on him in disbelief. "You didn't get in that fight for me. You were sticking up for Clive."

Yanking his hand away from my face, his fingers curled into his palm. Not knowing what the hell he'd taken with Jimmy, I backed up to the window as much as I could, just in case the drugs made him violent. It wasn't anywhere near far enough to be out of reach.

"Is that what you think? Clive can take care of himself. I jumped into that fight to help your charity case of a friend. Who knows what that freak of a brother does to her? Holden was a little *too* pissed off about seeing Clive touch her. Especially since Clive wasn't doing anything she didn't want him to do. Don't you think it's creepy how Holden always has his eye on her like she's his property or something? Poor girl probably has to lock her door at night just to keep that crazy son of a bitch off her."

His explanation was bullshit and we both knew it, but there was no point arguing. Jack was getting angrier by the second and it would only get worse if I didn't do him the *favor* he needed. My stomach rolled with anger, but I smiled anyway. The last thing I needed was for Jack to do something cruel to me at school just to teach me a lesson.

"Fine," I breathed out, rolling my eyes at the grin that stretched across his face. I used to love that grin, but now it rubbed me all the wrong ways. From birth, it feels like, it had been decided that Jack and I would get married. Our parents were best friends and practically owned Tranquil Falls. If I were to leave him and set out on my own path, the fallout would be enormous. I wouldn't be

31

surprised if my parents disowned me for breaking up with him. We were even destined for the same college after graduation.

Jack unbuttoned his pants, and poured absolutely zero romance into grabbing my head and shoving my face into his lap. My hair flung forward and wrapped over my mouth from the quick movement. Shoving it out of the way, I ignored the welling of tears in my eyes. He wasn't like this at first. Jack actually waited a full year before trying to have sex with me, but now that three years had passed, I was a means to an end, a plaything and nothing more.

But, still I played. Only because it was expected of me.

Jack was a quick blow, the throaty groan of his release filtering over my head as I sat up to wipe my lips over the sleeve of my jacket and finger brush my hair back into place. He didn't even bother with a thank you before starting the car, the loud roar of the engine echoing through the nearly abandoned streets, the purr of the engine growing louder as he picked up speed down the main road that led through the small stretch of woods between the train tracks and the servants' quarters.

I breathed easier when we crossed the tracks back into the center of town, the brightly lit holiday decorations catching my eye like shooting stars as we flew past. Several times, Jack's car swerved over a slick patch on the road, but he maneuvered over them without losing control, and I kept my mouth shut, not wanting to distract him while he drove.

It was too bad the silence didn't stretch longer.

"Why aren't you more appreciative that I stuck up for your friend?"

Jack's eyes darted my direction, his voice low and throaty. I pulled my gaze from the outside landscape rolling past the car to see his knuckles had turned white where he clenched the wheel, tension rising up his arms and over his shoulders. I hated it when he did drugs with Jimmy. It was always a crapshoot on whether he took uppers or downers, sometimes both. Tonight looked like an uppers night, which meant Jack could turn violent with one wrong word.

"I don't know what you mean?"

Deflection. Ignorance. Confusion. They were the only weapons I had in my arsenal when Jack was becoming enraged. I should have let out a brainless giggle and twirled my hair, it might have saved me from those glossed-over eyes that narrowed in aggravation and rage.

"You don't know what I mean? How about when you jumped in front of me to try and stop me from knocking that thug freak out? Do you have a secret thing for Holden? Do you want to explore what it's like being with a crazy fuck?"

The volume of his voice ratcheted higher, his accusations becoming more disgusting and pronounced. No I didn't have a thing for Holden...except for jealousy maybe, respect, or even approval. Holden may have been a freak among the students of Tranquil Falls, but he was the only person among us who genuinely didn't care. I often wondered what it felt like to not want to fit in, wondered if the freedom that came with it was worth the stupid taunts and contemptuous pranks.

Although the guys hated Holden, wanted to hurt him and chase him out of town, I knew the girls secretly watched him. If he weren't so different, he would have been the hottest guy in school. Especially with those blue eyes of his, the kind of eyes that were like neon bulbs blazing out from beneath his dark hair and in contrast to his tan skin. He had the shoulders of a linebacker and the arrogant stride of a man who owned whatever space he

33

occupied. He never cowered beneath another person's stare, never allowed the judgment of a crowd to bend his will. But it wasn't just his strength, both mental and physical, that made him unique. Beneath his bored expression and hypnotic stare, Holden was different in other ways.

Lead dust always stained the side of his hand since we were kids. He sketched all the time, his pad of paper always tucked beneath his arm while a pencil was tucked behind his ear. I'd never seen any of his work, but Delilah had snapped a few pictures on her phone when I'd expressed interest. She showed me the shots in dance practice one day and I gasped aloud to see the beauty of his work.

It wasn't just sketches; Holden painted as well. Why he never let the public see his gift with pencils and paint was beyond my understanding. He belonged in some artsy hub of New York or another big city, not here in Tranquil Falls where he was labeled the town freak.

As if that weren't enough to make Holden stand out in a crowd, Delilah had also secretly recorded one other talent - Holden played guitar and could sing.

She told me at the time that he would kill her if he found out she'd taken the video on her phone, but while I remember her saying the words, I had been too entranced by his voice to absorb what she'd said. Deep and gritty, he sang low and soft, as if his soul wanted to burst from his throat to fill a room, but he was too shy to let it.

Delilah cherished her brother, and I believed he cherished her, too. That's why I hated it when Jack or the other players on the team suggested he was a freak who abused her. None of them had enough integrity to stick up for the female members of their family. None of them cared much about the lives and hearts of any of the girls they knew. Who were they to judge?

"No, Jack. I don't have thing for Holden," I lied. Playing the part was important, especially now as Jack's foot was heavier on the gas pedal. The car's engine grew louder, the curves coming up dangerous at the speed we were traveling. Ice glistened on the road, small patches that could catch a tire and cause Jack to lose control. "Please slow down," I murmured.

He sped up instead, his eyes darting between the road and me. "Just be honest, Michaela. Tell me the truth that you want to get boned by a freak."

Anger filtered through me, muted by fear as he took the curves without concern for the weather. I had to calm him down before he caused an accident. "Holden is gross, Jack. You know that, so please calm down. He's a disgusting freak who deserved to get expelled from school. Just look at what he did to your nose."

I'd inwardly cheered when Holden took that last shot at Jack in the cafeteria, but I wouldn't let a single soul know it.

As we took another curve, a dark mass was visible in the distance. Once Jack's headlights reached to illuminate the mass, I realized it was a broken down car. A person climbed out of the driver's seat, kicked the tires a few times before lifting the hood to release the smoke from its engine. Both Jack and I recognized who the person was at the same time. Jack smiled and my heart sank into my stomach.

"Speaking of freaks," Jack murmured, his fingers tightening over the steering wheel as his foot sank heavier on the gas pedal.

"Slow down, Jack. I mean it!"

Laughter poured over his lips, his eyes locked to Holden where he stood staring down at the engine of his car. "I'm just going to scare him. The freak deserves it after breaking my nose."

"Jack! Slow down!" My fingers tightened over the handle of the door, my heart thumping painfully beneath my ribs as the engine roared. "Please slow down!"

"I'm just going to kick up some sludge and snow as we pass him. Shut up and let me drive."

"Jack!"

My scream tore through the still night air, the ice that caught Jack's tire spinning the car until the crunch of metal and sharp tinkle of breaking glass were the only sounds I could hear. My body was jostled around the interior of Jack's car, pain shooting down my neck and spine, my eyes closing as we continued sliding over ice and snow.

When we stopped, I didn't want to open my eyes again, but I forced them apart regardless, to see that Holden's car had been shoved further along the shoulder, to see Holden's legs hanging limp from beneath the hood of his car.

I couldn't sit up, couldn't move beneath the seatbelt to get a better look at Holden. The only thing I could do was turn my head to see Jack's body leaning forward against the steering wheel, his skin split from the glass that shattered, his eyes closed from where he was knocked out by the impact of his head against the wheel.

A scream tore from my throat, never ending until sirens cut through the night, the flash of emergency lights brightening the scene around us to reveal that Holden was still pinned between the vehicles, his upper body lost beneath the twisted hood of his car.

CHAPTER FOUR

DELILAH

When people throw out words like black and white, angry or sad, large or small, I'm not sure I envision the same meaning as the majority of society.

Not with all of the words, at least. Not after the meanings he taught me.

Perhaps if I hadn't been raised with a unique soul like my brother, I would have seen things the same way, believed the same way, idolized and coveted the same way as every poor person that came before me. But it's impossible to see the world the same when you've been shown how reality and circumstances always come down to a person's perspective.

Black isn't black when it comes in shades. Angry isn't angry when it can grow into fury or rage. Large and small don't simply mean the physical size of a person or object, they also describe the magnitude of what's inside them.

My freshman year of high school was the worst for me, the feeling of being lost, of being insignificant, of not being *seen* by my classmates and peers because I didn't have what they had, or very much of anything to offer them. I had me. I had my friendship. I had a listening ear and a friendly smile. I had the *small* things in life, the forgettable, the cheap or free. Eventually, I made a few friends, girls who only gave me a chance because they felt sorry for me, but it was like a domino effect. Once they spoke to me, somebody else did, and before too long, I wasn't an outcast anymore, a girl forced to be alone because she wasn't worth it.

The original friends - those girls who did something nice because they felt sorry for me - they didn't like my tenuous popularity. They turned on me, and they were vicious.

Within a week, I was a pariah at Tranquil Falls High, an untouchable to anyone who didn't want to be cast out themselves. I don't know what those girls said about me because no one would tell me, and I broke down as soon as I got home, my tears a lazy river of pain that would never stop flowing.

Holden - my brother, my protector, my rock - he was the one who fixed me.

He appeared in my doorway with his standard dark presence, the black hair and black clothes hiding the light that existed inside. It drove me nuts to see him purposely exclude himself, it angered me to see him take the potential of being a big man on campus and so carelessly crush it beneath his boot. He had no concern for anything or anybody.

Anybody, except me.

As soon as he saw the tears, the corners of his mouth tipped down, his eyes softening with genuine sympathy. He cared when nobody else did, and I repaid him for that steadfast devotion by screaming at him and calling him a freak. By calling him crazy.

Yes, even me. His own sister.

Rejecting Holden ensured you were accepted in school because people love to join forces in hate, as if having the biggest team somehow validates your ugly opinion. I'd refused to reject him before that moment, but I was so desperate to fit in that the pressure of it all broke me.

Holden had every right to hate me, and I didn't miss the sharp slice of pain cutting through him, the flash of betrayal behind his blue eyes. Walking toward me instead, Holden took me in his arms, rested his chin on the top of my head and held me while I cried and raged.

My fists beat on his chest, my feet kicked at his shins, but he held on.

It's okay, Deli. I already knew this would happen. I knew this was coming.

Having experienced high school already, Holden knew the kids would judge me, he knew they would hurt me because they'd already tried to hurt him. Sitting me down on the side of my bed, he knelt in front of me and talked about being large and small. At first I didn't understand, but that's how it was with Holden. He didn't think like everybody else.

"Stop being small, Del. You're letting them crush you by taking away your size, they're making you small like them. Just chipping away until there's nothing left of you."

My brows had pulled together, my mind trying to digest what he was saying to me. I was a petite girl, five foot two and didn't weigh a hundred pounds soaking wet. *"I don't know what you're saying. I can't grow bigger."*

He laughed. Holden always had the best laugh. It surrounded you and hugged you. Comforted you if you felt alone.

"I don't mean large like that. These wealthy kids think they're large. They think they're more valuable, more worthy, and more entitled. But the truth is that most of those kids are small. They're empty. They've had it so easy that there aren't enough memories and tragedies and victories inside them to fill them and make them bigger. They see you walk by and you shine. You have so many victories that you are large. You're genuine so you overshadow them. They don't have what it takes to get large, so to win against you, they have to steal your size, make you small like they are. But they'll never roar as loud as you can, their lives aren't as magnificent, large and loud."

His speech helped me get through that day, but there was something I knew that he didn't:

39

Holden was the one who was large. He was the good person. The strong person. Holden didn't have to make other people small so he could be larger than them.

But he wasn't large now. Not in a hospital bed with a net of small tubes running everywhere, with a thick one running down his throat, with his head shaved and bandaged, his eyes closed, his life silent. This wasn't right, wasn't real. Holden should have been roaring instead of quiet because Holden was never small - he was large.

"Where are the doctors? I want to know what's wrong with my son. Is there anybody here who can help me?"

Tears burst from my eyes as my dad paced and complained at the end of the bed. My crying made my mom cry harder, her hands fluttering over Holden's face too afraid to touch anything. Taking his hand, I was careful not to touch the IV. His fingers were limp and lifeless.

"Can I please talk to someone who can tell me about my son?"

Dad was angry, every festering drop of it directed at himself. He blamed the fight on Holden's accident, believed that if he hadn't kicked Holden out, we wouldn't be here now. He was right. But that didn't make the accident, itself, his fault.

Deep down, in a place I didn't want to admit was there, I blamed my parents for this, too. I blamed my dad for hurting Holden. I blamed my mom for stopping me when I tried to chase him and bring him back inside. I'd broken free of her and reached the door by the time his taillights were blazing red down the road. "Holden, come back!"

He kept going.

The phone was ringing and a police officer was knocking on the door an hour later.

The hospital was twenty minutes outside of Tranquil Falls in a larger town that was more of a city. When we arrived, I wanted to run to my brother, to feel his warm hands in mine, to see him wink to tell me he would always be all right. But he wasn't, not this time. I didn't know that for four long hours. He was in surgery when we'd arrived. He was in a coma. There was swelling on his brain and they didn't know when, or if, he would wake up.

How do you look at a person who had always been your superhero and not shatter to see them broken?

So while my father raged at himself, at the hospital staff, at anything or anyone because the anger and guilt were too powerful to hold inside, Holden lay quietly. Tranquil Falls had stolen his size. They couldn't be as large as him, so in their hate, they'd made him small like them.

I understood it now, saw it so clearly it might as well have been one of Holden's beautiful paintings staring me in the face. The naked, raw truth revealing the way Holden looked at life, the way we would all look at life, if we weren't so damn small.

All three of us had stayed in his room that night, my mom and I taking turns talking to him, hopeful that our voices would bring him back to us, would show him that it was safe, that nobody could hurt him while we became the superheroes.

Holden didn't wake up at first, he stayed in his dark space for over a week. I was there every day. I missed my last week of school before winter break because I fought tooth and nail to convince my parents I needed to be by his side when he first woke up again.

Sitting beside him, day after day, hour after hour, I didn't care about what was occurring outside the room, didn't want to hear the details of the accident, didn't care that my father lost his job because it had been his employer's son that almost ruined my brother. My father had demanded the medical bills be paid by the Thorne family, and they were, but my father would never be allowed to return to work again.

I didn't care what happened to Jack, didn't care that Michaela felt so bad that she'd begged to be allowed to see Holden at the hospital when she was here visiting Jack.

She was small. Holden was right about that, and beside his bed I wouldn't let a single small person come into the room for fear they would scrape away what was left of him so that they could win.

I became large so I could protect him.

Nine days after the accident, nine long days that made me feel like life would end, Holden opened his eyes. I'd jumped up to see him staring at the ceiling. I'd whispered his name. I'd squeezed his hand. I'd danced inside myself to discover that Tranquil Falls hadn't destroyed him.

But he wasn't the same.

The doctors said it would take time. It would take rehab and a bunch of testing to determine the extent of permanent damage. But I didn't care if he wasn't exactly who he'd been before the accident. I didn't care if it would take years before he was whole again. Because that's the other truth about people who are large. No matter what happens, no matter how much you whittle them down, they will grow large again.

Holden wouldn't be contained by prognosis or diagnosis. He wouldn't be relegated to some box where strangers told him if he would succeed. I knew my brother well enough to know that the light inside him was so warm and pure, it would cure all the damage inside him.

Confusion held him firmly in the first days he was awake, but eventually he was smiling again, laughing and making jokes. My parents had spoken to him and cried, my father apologizing for every mean word he'd said, and Holden had forgiven him.

That's what large people do. They're so big and so deep and so wonderful that grudges and resentment and anything deemed ugly are crushed beneath the weight of their virtue.

Three weeks out, and my brother was my brother again. Until that night. The last night. The night after we had been told that Holden would recover fully.

We were eating dinner at the kitchen table, the winter wind outside howling its discontent, when the phone rang from where it hung on the kitchen wall, a corded device Holden and I both had called ancient.

Normally, Mom would ignore the call if we were eating dinner, but with Holden at the hospital still, she'd jumped up, her fingers had tightened over the receiver, the color draining from her face in response to what she was hearing.

Holden had a seizure. A full one, the nurse had said. He'd stopped breathing, he'd bitten his tongue, he hadn't needed resuscitation, but the event was scary enough that the hospital felt the need to call.

They'd told us to wait.

They'd said there was no rush.

But when it comes to family, when it comes to someone you love being in pain, there is always the need to drop what you're doing and run to be beside them.

History has a screwed up way of repeating itself. Just like fear has a way of reviving intuition while panic sweeps in to prevent you from hearing what intuition has to say.

Maybe we should have sat back down to finish our meal. Maybe we should have waited an hour, a minute, five seconds before grabbing our coats and racing out the door. Maybe we shouldn't have left our plates full of food sitting on the table for when we returned.

We would never return.

Not the same.

Not as the people we had been before tragedy struck.

Maybe is a word every person can regret for the rest of their natural life. It's a heavy word filled with vacillation and indecision, of what could have been and what will never be. It's another word I'm sure Holden would have given a new definition if circumstances had been different.

But maybe was what we were left with after jumping in the car to rush to my brother.

Maybe.

And I love you.

I'm sorry.

And goodbye.

CHAPTER FIVE

HOLDEN

Being sick was a lesson in patience. Not sick, I guess, but injured. The swelling on my brain had caused a small amount of damage, the pressure of the blood killing off a few brain cells I guess I didn't need that much because I didn't feel different.

The doctors had explained to me what injuries the accident caused, the bruises and bumps on my body that were nothing compared to my head. They'd said I was lucky for surviving an accident as bad as the one Jack caused. Anger had filtered through me to know it was his car that came careening at full speed in my direction despite the inclement threat of weather.

Regardless, I was the same. I was healing and getting better. But then everything went black. I don't remember the seizure. I just knew that in one minute I was sitting on my bed wondering when they would finally release me, and in the next I was surrounded by nurses in colorful scrubs and concerned doctors in white coats.

It's fortunate how the brain protects you from remembering the pain of your body when everything threatens to shut down.

I wish it would have protected me from remembering what came next.

Dr. Lucas Silva was a good guy, not too old for being a neurologist, with just a tinge of silver peppering the brown hair at his temples. He had a wife and three daughters, all of which were older than me, two of whom were becoming doctors like him, while the third wanted to be a stay at home mom. We'd spent a lot of time talking to each other over the weeks that I'd been stuck in bed, several weeks that made him believe he should be the person to tell me.

When he walked into my room, I didn't even realize it had been twelve hours since I'd had the seizure, and I hadn't seen or heard from my family. Seizures can do that to you, leave you confused and struggling with the concept of time. Dr. Silva told me the confusion was normal. It was everything else he told me that wasn't.

"Hey, Holden. How are you feeling?"

Wrestling my way out from under the covers, the tubes and hoses and monitors, I smiled as the good doctor grabbed a seat and dragged it to sit beside my bed. Normally, he wore a smile, was always ready with a corny dad joke or some other ridiculous comment that would make me grin. However, this moment was anything but normal.

"I'm okay," I answered, "ready to get out of here if you'll just sign the damn papers."

Laughter was painful beating up my chest and throat, but not as bad as it had been when I first woke up from the accident. Every day, I'd begged Dr. Silva to sign off and discharge me home, and he'd been so close to doing it before the seizure.

He didn't laugh in return.

Wringing his hands over his lap, he cast his gaze down to the floor, mentally preparing himself to meet my eyes again so he could tell me the news. "Listen, I have something I need to say to you and I wish I could tell you to stay calm when you hear this, but I can't. Typically something like this would be done by social services, but I couldn't let you learn this from a stranger."

I would have sworn my heart stopped beating in my chest if the heart monitor hadn't kept beeping steadily above my head. "What's wrong? Did the seizure cause more damage?"

He shook his head, regret pulling at his lips until they were a thin line of sorrow. "No, Holden, this isn't about your health. It's about your family."

I saw all of them in that moment and in response to that one word. I saw my dad tossing me up in the air when I was just a kid, heard my mom laughing loudly and singing out of tune as she drove down the highway with me in back before life and money altered our existence. I saw my sister the most. I saw her dancing, and smiling, I saw her crying and getting mad. I saw her chasing after me with chubby legs back when she was so tiny we couldn't believe she would ever become big and strong.

"What about my family?"

"There's no delicate way to say this, so I'll just be blunt," his eyes tracked up to me, asking for permission, begging me not to fall apart at his words. "Your family was in an accident last night. After your seizure, after they heard -"

Sometimes being blunt is just as hard as dancing around the point. There's never an easy way to give bad news.

"I'm sorry to tell you this, Holden, but your parents didn't survive."

Sobs should have poured out of me to hear the words, great gasping wails that shredded my throat and tore me apart from the inside out. But instead of the pain that should have taken hold with punishing fingers, I felt cold numbing claws clenching my throat, a question frozen to the tip of my tongue that I was terrified to ask.

Don't let her be...

Dear God, tell me she's okay...

She was dancing in my head again, sunbeams radiating down to where she was so light gravity couldn't contain her.

"Deli?" I whispered, the sound broken and without weight. Dr. Silva's brows pulled together, confusion clouding his gaze.

Clearing my throat of the shards of glass shredding it apart, I spoke louder. "Delilah. My sister. Is she okay?"

Dancing.

Spinning.

Twirling.

As large and bright as those sunbeams, until tragedy came down in a crash of clouds to smother her.

The doctor's expression shadowed. "She survived the accident."

My body melted against my pillows, relief rushing in to massage away the tension, the flood of gratitude a heavy blanket warming my bones.

"She's here, Holden. But, she's in critical condition."

The tears finally spilled down my cheeks, tiny drops of soul-crushing sorrow leaking out to dot the sheets beneath me. "What happened?" I croaked.

"They were in a car accident on the way to the hospital. That's as much as I know. Trauma surgeons are working on your sister now. She sustained internal injuries. They have to stop the bleeding before I can assess her for brain injuries. Before a team of doctors can run her through tests and determine how badly she was injured."

While my mind processed what he was telling me, another question crawled up my throat. "My parents? Did they suffer?"

Reaching out, he touched my hand. I pulled away, too cold, too shaky to accept that small comfort.

Sighing, Doctor Silva answered, "They died on impact. They didn't suffer."

It was another small gust of relief, a gust that blew the panic away and carved a channel through me wide enough to allow the torment of loss to come flooding in.

My parents were gone.

I would never speak to them. Never hug them. Never prove to them that I could make them proud. That they had been *enough* to raise a good man, despite not being wealthy like the rest of Tranquil Falls.

It was all my fault.

If I'd made different decisions that day.

If I'd controlled myself and hadn't fought.

The channel of pain stretched wider, scraped away until it was as wide and deep as the Grand Canyon.

Another thought hit me, as heavy and out of control as a bolder bouncing through that channel, wrecking the walls and splitting me wider. "Delilah's legs," I breathed out. "Her spine, her arms, her body. How broken?"

All I could imagine was a baby bird fallen from the nest, her wings twisted and without feathers. She couldn't dance without her legs. She wouldn't be able to fly with broken wings.

I couldn't draw in enough air to formulate a complete sentence, to ask him an intelligible question. He understood what I was asking regardless. I assumed doctors were used to comprehending the incoherent ramblings of terrified family members.

"The orthopedists will assess the damage to her bones and muscles as soon as the trauma surgeons are finished stabilizing her. We're doing everything we can, Holden. We're fighting to save her life."

The words were meaningless in that moment, sand escaping through the fingers of my clenched fist, the images sweeping in and blowing out before I could grasp on to them to make sense of it.

"I need to see her," I breathed out, each word becoming harsher, more firm, more powerful. Sitting up, I started pulling the blankets away from my body, reached for the IVs to rip them out of my arm. Panic had grabbed ahold of me once again and it was crushing me within its skilled fingers.

"I need to see her!"

Dr. Silva surged forward, his hands gripping my arms to keep me from freeing myself of all the medical equipment that had turned into a hunter's snare, trapping me in place.

"I need to save her!" I begged, my voice practically screaming, my emotions so out of control that thought had dissipated into meaningless whispers, the adrenaline pumping through me taking hold, refusing to let me go.

"Holden, I need you to calm down."

His voice was broken through by the alarms on the machines, the rate of my heart climbing too high, too fast. A nurse rushed in, her face stricken when she saw me struggling against Dr. Silva. He said something that sent her away, but I didn't hear the words spoken.

"Please," I begged, "you have to save her. You have to go in there now and make sure she's okay. I can't lose her. I can't lose everyone."

I would deal with the loss of my parents later. At that moment, every drop of energy I had belonged to my sister.

The nurse came rushing back a minute later, a syringe held in her hand. Looking at Dr. Silva in question, she received some silent instruction and ran to stick the needle into the port on my IV. The alarms on the machines were still screaming, my heart rate, my blood pressure, my vitals a chaotic mess.

Pushing me back against the pillows, Dr. Silva spoke softly. "We're giving you something to help you relax. This panic isn't good for you."

A floating sensation was instantaneous, but I fought it. I raged against it. I wouldn't let it take me under while Deli needed me. It plucked at my ability to move, stole my ability to think, but still I fought it, for my dancer, for my sister, for the baby bird who was twisted and broken, who needed me to lift her up from the tall grass and teach her to fly again.

The drugs were too strong, the current too swift as I was dragged under, my muscles relaxing, my body becoming boneless. "Please, Doc," I pleaded, my words slurred and soft, "please save her. I don't care what she needs. If it saves her, you can take it from me. My heart, my lungs, my kidneys, whatever she needs. Just rip it out if it will heal her. I don't care what it does to me."

The last thing I remembered was Dr. Silva's face, a blurry image that came into focus before going out again. The last thoughts in my head reached for my sister, for that broken bird, for Delilah.

· · ·

They must have kept me unconscious the entire time they worked on Delilah. By the time I came to again, the sun was rising over the horizon outside my window, a new day being born despite the fact that my parents were no longer alive to see it. The reality sunk deep inside me, but I shoved it aside, promised to deal with it later. Just as soon as I knew my sister was alive and safe.

Dr. Silva must have known I'd come around and instantly panic. He had a nurse stationed in a chair near my bed, her friendly eyes peeking away from the crossword she was doing to stare at me as soon as my eyes were open. I recognized her instantly, a pretty younger woman with skin the color of coffee. Her black hair was pulled back into a bun, her cheery yellow scrubs a pretty color against her skin. She'd always been nice to me.

"Good morning, Mr. Bishop. How are you feeling?"

My voice was hoarse. "Delilah?"

The nurse's lips pulled into a grin, her head shaking with mild disbelief as she stood from her seat. "Dr. Silva knew she'd be the first thought on your mind and he gave me permission to wheel you down to see her if you promise to be a well-behaved young man and not rip the IV out of your arm."

Happiness surged through me, the cold fear disintegrating beneath its warmth. "She's alive?"

Rounding my bed, the nurse helped me escape the tangle of my blankets. "Yes, Mr. Bishop, she's alive, but she's in the critical care unit and she's not awake. We can't disturb her, but if you promise to keep your voice low and gentle, you can talk to her and let her know you're there with her."

I would promise her anything to get to my sister. She was alive. She was breathing. Who cared if she was awake yet? Deli was strong like me. She would wake up like I did.

Although it only took a few minutes to wheel me between my part of the hospital and Deli's, it still felt too long. The hallways looked the same, long corridors with the same equally spaced doors, a nurse's station set in the middle of each, the staff waiting and ready to begin their rounds or jump into action for an emergency.

The temperature inside this place was frigid, always frigid, and the antiseptic smell grew stronger as we rounded the corner from my wing to approach critical care. What had been hallways with small windows and large brown doors became hallways with large windows and larger glass doors, small desks set outside each room where a nurse could sit and watch monitors, could look inside the room and keep an eye on the patient while giving them some sense of privacy, too. I remembered being in this hall in the weeks following my accident. I wondered if my parents and Deli had run through here feeling panicked and scared much like I felt now.

Deli came into view, and if not for the nurse shoving me down by the shoulder when I tried to stand, I would have run in that room, shoved my way past the two doctors, just to be by Deli's side.

She was tiny in that bed, itty bitty, and she was bruised, battered, covered in all the same tubes and monitors they'd used on me. Was she as scared when she saw me as I was to see her? Did she cry as easily? Did she fall apart while staring wide-eyed at a swollen face, a bandaged head, at the machines above my head monitoring the beat of my heart and the rate of my breath?

Was she scared when she saw that a machine was breathing for me?

I knew I was.

"She looks bad, Mr. Bishop. I know that. But you have to remain calm for her. I can't let you run in there with the IV dragging behind you. Especially not with Dr. Silva standing inside."

The thought came and went that I should rip the IV out and tell them all they could go to Hell. Deli was my sister. She was all I had left. But Dr. Silva turned just then, his eyes locking to mine, exhaustion riding his shoulders. Walking out, he approached us on unhurried steps.

"Holden, I'm sorry, but your sister hasn't woken up yet. She's going to be here for a while. We stabilized her, but we still need other specialties to examine her. I have a battery of tests I want to run, and -"

"Is she going to live?" I interrupted, none of the other stuff mattering to me as much as the end result. "Just tell me that."

His expression fell. "We're hopeful. But it will take time."

Time. He needed time. I had all the time in the world at that moment. Whatever he needed, just as long as Deli would be okay. But he would also need something else: money.

Panic gripped me again, the realization that my parents weren't here to help me. I had a sister in critical care, no income to speak of and two people to have cremated or buried. I was the adult now. Just me.

"I'm checking myself out."

In chorus, the nurse and Dr. Silva objected. "No, you're not."

Closing my eyes, I took a breath, opened my eyes and met Dr. Silva's gaze. "The Thorne's paid my dad enough money to cover my hospital bills in here for two months. And that's all I have. I'd rather it go to Deli. I'm alive. She's the one who needs it now."

"Holden, no. You need to be watched a little longer. You just had a full seizure-"

"I'm checking myself out. I'm not changing my mind. You're going to save my sister."

Glancing back at the nurse, I asked, "Am I allowed to go in and see her?"

She nodded and wheeled me in, Dr. Silva following in behind us, still angry I wouldn't stay. His anger meant nothing to me. I was doing the right thing. I was taking care of Deli.

She didn't move the entire time I was with her, she didn't respond to my voice, didn't open her eyes. They wheeled me out again when I stopped whispering finally and laid my forehead on the side of the handrail and cried. Dr. Silva followed us back to my room, giving me one more warning before I checked myself out against his advice.

"I'm going home," I explained again, trying not to raise my voice because I knew he was doing what he believed was the best thing.

After looking at me long and hard, he relented, his shoulders withering with defeat. "If you leave, you can't stay here, Holden. Not while she's in critical care. They have strict visiting hours."

I hated leaving her, but I would if it meant I could afford everything she needed for them to save her life. "I'll go home and come back for visiting hours."

"How are you going to get there? It's freezing outside and you don't have clothes."

"I'll walk in this stupid gown. Whatever it takes."

His expression soured more. "At least let me call you a cab. And we can get you some scrubs to wear home."

"Whatever it takes," I repeated.

Giving me a clipped nod, he left. I was unhooked from the IV within the hour. Once the papers were signed and the warnings were given, I stopped by Deli's room one more time. She was being prepped for a test, so I couldn't go in.

The cab ride home was silent.

So was my house when I walked up the sidewalk that cut through the lawn. It was bright like my family was waiting at home. But I knew it would be empty. They hadn't taken the time to turn off the lights when they left to come see me. They'd left too quickly.

Using my spare key that we kept hidden under a pot, I let myself in, dropped the key on a hallway table and turned the corner to look in the kitchen.

Their dinner still sat on plates on the table.

My fist met the wall beside me, my desolation complete with the sight of what they'd left behind.

I hit the wall five more times, and the scream that poured out of me was insane and unholy.

PART TWO

CHAPTER SIX

Michaela

The holidays are always tough for me, especially Christmas, especially when those awful holiday decorations will be strung up in Tranquil Falls, reminding me of that night - the night that everything came crashing down around our small town, the night that I learned life wasn't always perfect when you had everything handed to you on a silver platter.

Sitting on the side of my bed in my college dorm that was dressed up to look like it was as close to superior as a small dorm could be, I rolled my eyes at the custom wall paint, the ornately carved furniture, the rugs my mother spent thousands of dollars on to make it look like I was a step above the rest of the freshman and sophomores at my college. In six months, when I was in my junior year, I'd be allowed to live off campus per the college rules. I had an apartment already, bought and paid for by Jack's parents and mine.

Jack was overjoyed to finally see a light at the end of the tunnel, thrilled to know that, soon, we wouldn't be bound to the dormitory rules set in place to keep the younger students from partying too hard. He wanted to join a fraternity, but he also wanted to live with me.

Not because he loved me. But because he wanted to keep an eye on me, trap me like his little mahogany feathered birdie in a gilded cage. I was still his property, even after that night, even after he destroyed a family who had never done anything to hurt him.

Christmas was in two weeks, and in a few hours I would be climbing into the passenger seat of Jack's car to drive four hours back to Tranquil Falls to spend those weeks with our families. It would be our second return since that night, the second time I had to walk around the town and wonder what really happened to Holden and Delilah Bishop.

There were rumors, always rumors, and from what my mother told me, Holden had been seen working at the small twenty-four hour diner closer to his part of town. She'd scoffed at the absurdity that they'd allow a crazy man like him to handle other people's food, especially since he had a reason to hate the town we'd grown up in. Nobody ever saw him come and go from work. And only a few had briefly glanced at him where he worked in the kitchen. They said he washed dishes. They said he cooked food. They said he hadn't spoken a word to anybody since that night.

Delilah never returned to school after the accident that killed her parents. In truth, nobody really knew if she was dead or alive. We'd graduated without hearing a word about what happened to her. The Bishop family hadn't disappeared the night Holden was run down by an out of control car, but they did after the night Holden's family was struck in an intersection by a semi that had lost traction on the ice.

We knew what happened to Holden's parents only because one person saw Holden standing alone in the graveyard while the coffins were being lowered in the ground. They said a black beanie covered his black hair. They said his hands were tucked inside the black jacket he wore. They said he looked like a punk, like a freak, like an outcast as he watched his parents disappear beneath the frozen earth. They criticized him even then, couldn't give him just one single moment of solitude so that he could mourn the destruction of everything he'd once been.

There were two small markers showing where his parents were laid to rest. I left flowers on those graves the

59

last time I'd visited Tranquil Falls. I'd done it in secret because I was still too afraid to step out of line and reveal that I didn't want to be like my parents and friends. I wanted to have a heart.

Rumors placed Delilah in a home somewhere for cripples. Rumors had her dead body tucked away inside Holden's house where he kept her because he'd lost his mind. Rumors had her working the streets in another town because she'd become a junkie addicted to pain pills after her recovery.

Rumors.

They were a staple of life in Tranquil Falls.

My last memory of her was from the day I stopped by Holden's hospital room to see him, to apologize to him, to tell him that Jack was a bastard who didn't deserve the easy life. Delilah had practically chased me from the room, her eyes swollen from tears, her spirit ferocious as she took on the task of protecting Holden from anybody she believed wished him harm. Even me. Her only friend from the dance team. The only girl in the entirety of Tranquil Falls that genuinely felt bad for what had been done.

I hated Jack for that accident. Hated that his family replaced his car with nothing more than a shrug at the expense. Hated that despite being caught with drugs on him and being blamed for an accident he caused by being a relentless bully and jerk, there were no consequences other than a slap on the wrist. He was still the big man on campus, still the smug prick that skated through life on his daddy's dime. Still the pompous bully that outgunned every decent person who dared speak out against him.

Even now. Even in college. Jack Thorne was still King. And I was his Queen. The Queen of hearts. The Queen of diamonds. The Queen suffocating beneath the weight of her thorned crown.

His knock on my door dragged me away from my thoughts of Tranquil Falls.

"Come in."

The door slid open, Jack's cocky smile wide and excited. He loved returning home during the holidays, loved reuniting the team so they could continue their stupid parties. He loved rushing to see his new friends in the servants' quarters that supplied him now that Jimmy had died from an overdose.

I wasn't sad to hear about Jimmy. I blamed him for what happened to Holden and Delilah as well.

Scrubbing his hand over the back of his neck, Jack's smile faded, his eyes narrowing in concern. "I came to see if you're ready. Is something wrong?"

"No, I lied, "just feeling a little gross. Guess my stomach didn't like what I ate for dinner last night." If I told him I didn't want to go home, there would be hell to pay for it the entire ride there. He'd call me a freak-lover, a whore to rejects. That's what he always said when I brought up either of the Bishop kids.

"*I guess Delilah wasn't all that bad. She, at least, looked like she would be a fun time. But her brother? He deserved what he got.*"

Those were his exact words the first time we went home for Christmas break and I brought it up. The words he spoke before he and his friends got high and got right back to business destroying the hearts of high school girls. Jack didn't stick close to me anymore during his parties. It was a crapshoot who he'd take to bed once the festivities wound down. Me or some oblivious girl that didn't know better.

If I did something like that, Jack and both our families would destroy me. Jack's family and friends would run a smear campaign on my reputation. My parents would most likely disown me.

61

All for money.

Money.

Money.

Money.

The only thing those assholes had that made them believe they were superior to everybody.

"That sucks, but do you have your bags packed? We need to go."

Glancing up at Jack, I let my gaze trail over his hair that had grown out, the stronger cut to his jaw that appeared when the last of his childhood had faded away. He was more handsome now than he'd been in high school and it wasn't fair. There were moments when he could be sweet, and I grasped on to those moments, clung to them like small islands in a turbulent sea because I'd hoped they meant Jack was turning over a new leaf, that he would finally understand the evil that he'd done.

But just like everything I actually enjoyed in my life, those moments were fleeting. They were a tease, a small window showing me exactly what I was missing.

"I'm packed. My bags are by the door." Jutting my chin in their direction, I had a flash of stupidity to think Jack would actually pick them up and carry them to the car. Instead he smiled again, jangled his keys and opened my door to step into the hall. "Awesome. Grab them and come on. It's a four hour drive back to Tranquil Falls."

Rolling my eyes, I stood from my bed and sighed as the door slammed shut. He couldn't even be bothered to hold it for me. When it opened again and he poked his head through, I was taken by surprise. Maybe he realized he was being an intolerable prick. Maybe he was going to help me with the bags after all.

"Oh, and when we're in the car, try not to breathe in my direction. Keep your window cracked or something.

Just in case your stomach pain is a virus and not bad food. I don't want to get sick."

The door slammed shut again. I picked up a book from the desk and tossed it at the wood. The book thud hard and slid down, but the door didn't open again.

Another sigh burst out of me, one filled with regret, anger, torment and bitter strife. I had no one to blame but myself. By going along with him, I was letting this happen. Yet, I still picked up those bags like a good little girl and dragged them down one flight of stairs to where Jack was waiting by his car. Hitting the key fob, he opened the trunk for me. The biting cold was nipping at my cheeks, my jacket not thick enough to keep my body from trembling. While I rounded the car to tuck my bags away, Jack climbed into the driver's seat to escape the weather.

At least one of us was toasty and warm.

Fog rolled over the surface of the parking lot, dissipating beneath the light sprinkle of freezing rain that wasn't quite snow yet. The dorms were deserted already because most of the students left yesterday when the weather was still slightly nice. I wanted to go, too, but Jack had a party to attend at a frat house he didn't belong to. Always a party. Always.

Sliding into the passenger seat, I was about to buckle up when Jack grabbed my wrist to stop me. Déjà vu flashed, another time he'd stopped me from putting on my seatbelt that led to the destruction of an entire family.

"What?" I asked. "I thought you wanted to go."

His expression twisted with annoyance. "Can you take off your wet jacket, at least? You'll ruin the leather seats."

My eyes narrowed, but I shrugged out of the jacket anyway. Thankfully the seats were heated and I would be warm eventually. The engine purred as Jack pulled out of the campus parking lot, his foot a little too heavy on the pedal as we shot like an arrow down the highway towards home.

I've heard that all over the world circumstances had a way of changing from day to day. Life had a way of changing, for good and for bad. It wasn't the same tired story being told over and over again, never changing, never evolving, never giving you the opportunity to actually learn something about life.

Not in Tranquil Falls.

In my small town, nothing changed.

It always stayed the same.

CHAPTER SEVEN

Holden

Damn, the wind could really grab hold of you when it skated past the side of a building, blindsiding you as it came on like a whip to knock you off your feet. I tucked deeper into myself, a cigarette hanging between my lips while I took a break out back from the constant noise of the diner. The glorified next generation was returning home to visit from college, and they all gravitated to the diner for an early meal before they went out to raise hell.

I just wanted the hours to pass and for my shift to be up. I needed to leave and get home to Deli. Needed to convince her to go visit our Uncle Scott for the holidays because two years was too long to be cooped up. The first year wasn't her fault, she was still recovering, but now she was back to normal and still refused to leave the house. To step outside. To go back to school or make new friends. To accept the awful truth that our parents were gone and would never return home again.

Delilah had stopped dancing. She'd stopped twirling. She'd stopped spinning and laughing and grinning. Not because her body prevented her from doing so. It was the pain in her heart and the hatred in her mind that did that. All day, she waited inside that house, the injuries to her head having caused damage to her brain. She believed mom and dad would come home. She told me she knew she would see them soon.

I didn't know how to help her, but I was trying. That's why I was working at this run-down grease trap. It's why I was still in Tranquil Falls and why I hadn't yet abandoned what my life had once been in order to carve out a path of my own. Somebody had to take care of her, and since my parents were six feet under, that someone was me.

Dragging a cloud of slow death into my lungs, I watched the smoke blow out past my lips to collide with the cold night air. It twisted and turned until spinning in circles like my sister used to do. A voice called out to me from the back door, Kaley Smith peeking her head out to warn me my time was up. Tendrils of her blond hair had fallen loose from the long braid running down her back, her brown eyes twinkling beneath the exterior security lighting.

"Better get back inside. Angela's going to tear a new hole in your butt if you're late."

Winking at Kaley, I dropped the cigarette down to the ground and stubbed it out with the toe of my boot. "Come here."

Her lips pulled into a wry grin, her head turning so she could look over her shoulder and make sure nobody was around. Sneaking out, she closed the door quietly and ran into my arms.

Kaley was a good girl. She had a vibrant spirit and she was friendly despite her circumstances. Living in the servants' quarters like me, she was three years older than I was.

We met when I first took this job, and I liked that she'd never attended Tranquil Falls High, that her house sat behind the district line that split my neighborhood between Tranquil Falls and Benson Ridge High. She had no ties to the town I couldn't stand to live in, to the people who had destroyed my family and wandered off without uttering a word of apology for what they'd done. Kaley wasn't my girlfriend, by any stretch of the imagination, she didn't want labels or commitment, but she liked taking me home with her some nights to waste away a few hours.

Never longer than that, though. I wouldn't spend an entire night away from home and leave Deli all alone.

My hand slid up to cup her breast from over her shirt. She giggled and kissed my neck. "Holden, stop. We're going to get caught and then Angela will be gunning for us both."

My lips slid along the line of her jaw, the tip of my tongue pushing out to taste her skin. "But it's cold outside and you help me warm up."

She laughed again, low and throaty, her hands clenching my hips as she pushed up to her toes to let me run my lips down the line of her neck. Biting softly where her neck met her shoulders, I appreciated the way she trembled. It sucked that I'd have to stop now before walking inside became uncomfortable.

"What are you doing after work tonight?" she asked, her voice breathless.

"Meeting up with you, I hope. But I work the late shift. What time do you get off?"

"As soon as you get to my house."

My chest rumbled in response to her answer, my growl like rolling thunder as my cotton work pants suddenly became tight and restrictive. Nipping at her jaw, I lifted my head just enough to press my mouth against her ear, my breath hot against her skin chilled by the night air. "I mean, what time are you leaving here?"

Shivering at the depth of my voice, or maybe from the wind, she snuggled in closer to me, stealing my heat and using me as a wall to block her from the bitchslap of winter. "I know that's what you meant, but I thought I'd take advantage and confirm that's what we'll be doing tonight."

My hands took possession of her ass, tugging her closer, I showed her the answer to that question. "Yeah, if I'm able to walk there. Look what you've already done."

A husky laugh shook her shoulders. "I leave here at eight. It'll give me time to get cleaned up before you arrive."

"Do whatever you need to do. I'll just get you dirty again." My mouth found hers, but she dodged away before I could lock down.

Slapping my chest, she pushed away from me and yanked my arm in the direction of the back door. "Dammit, Holden, you are a big, strong, beautiful body full of trouble, but no sense. We need to get inside before Angela starts yelling."

Laughing, I replied, "I don't care if Angela yells."

"Yeah, I bet you don't. You don't care about anything." Shaking her head, she turned to smile at me. "I don't know how your mom survived raising you."

Flinching at the comment, I pulled away from her. Kaley's expression fell, her smile fading. "Shit. I'm sorry, Holden, I didn't mean it like that. Come on. We need to get in there."

Yeah. Back to work. Back to the place where I scrubbed and polished, flipped burgers and dropped fries in a vat of boiling oil that would block the arteries of all the spoiled kids who ate there. Often I envisioned them in forty years. Fat. Ruddy skin. Balding and unhappy. Just like their parents. It helped pass the time. Helped me choke down the fact that, in a way, I was working for them by cooking their meals and scraping their plates. Working for them, just like my mother and father.

A wave of greasy heat collided against my face as I walked in. Kaley disappeared around the corner of the right hallway, while I ducked left to stalk back to the dishwasher. A pile almost as tall as me was stacked up and I was glad I hadn't been stuck cooking on such a busy, chaotic night.

Tying the black, vinyl apron on that did nothing to keep me dry, I slung plates and bowls, cups, forks and spoons through the machine, stacking them into their trays and shooting them down the conveyor belt that pulled the dishes through the hot water. Sliding over the floor mats, I caught them on the other end and stuck them on the next belt to dry. The cooks and servers would pull them from the racks on a night as busy as this, saving me the time of stacking them into orderly piles.

I heard Angela's heavy feet stomp in behind me. She was checking to make sure I was on time returning from break, ensuring that every penny she paid me was for work and not messing around. I wanted to resent her for it, but there had been times I slacked off, especially when the confusion crept in carrying the darker thoughts alongside it.

Turning my head, I winked at her and smiled. She was an older woman with silver hair, huge breasts that could probably swallow a small child, and a sarcastic sense of humor that shone during the times she let it out. Always quick with a warning about timeliness or slacking, Angela was also a grandmother of three that insisted on mothering me when I was being a pain in her ass. She loved me, and I appreciated her for it, but that didn't make working for her any easier.

"Hey, beautiful," I called out. "Looks like you didn't catch me this time." Another wink had her blushing through her fake scowl. She never could stay mad at me.

I dropped the dishes from my hands and grabbed a hand towel to dry my fingers. Stepping over to her, I took her into a hug and squeezed.

Her fists beat on my shoulders with no strength. "What are you doing, Holden? Have you lost your mind?"

"I lose it every time I'm near you. When are you going to leave your husband for me?"

Laughter burst out of her mouth, loud and free, just like I loved it. Because laughter is one of those parts of life that should be free. It should be unrestrained and wild, with no rules or shadows to contain it. Laughter is never polite, it's never prim and proper, at least not the kind of laughter that is worth a person's time, the kind that sears a memory into your mind and makes your eyes water.

"Holden! Put me down and get back to work." She tried to sound angry, but there was the residue of laughter still coating her words. "And don't think I didn't see you out back kissing on Kaley. You can't have both women."

A wolfish grin stretched my lips. "She's just keeping me warm until you come along, the real prize."

"Dammit, boy!" Her cheeks were bright red. "Get back to work. I'm not paying you to flirt with me."

"You should. I'm a natural at it."

Shuffling back to the machine before she could smack me on the shoulder, I was still chuckling when she walked off, probably in route to find somebody else who was slacking in their duties. Despite her iron rule over the diner, its employees and patrons, Angela Barrett was one of the people who helped save my life after the accidents happened, after the holiday season that gifted me with burials, hospitals and soul-crushing agony.

It took three months for Deli to recover enough for me to feel comfortable being away from her, two of those months laid up in the hospital, and one of them recovering from home.

At four months, Deli was getting around again, not laid up in her bed where I brought her all three meals of the day and played guitar to entertain her. I was an oldies person when it came to music, a guy who could always count on the classics, but Deli loved the modern pop songs, the kind sung by boy bands that had more talent prancing around stage in their choreographed dances than they ever would carrying a tune. I'd refused to learn the songs she loved before the accident, but afterwards I learned them all just so I could see her smile. I never knew if she was smiling because she loved the song, or if it was because she was laughing inside to hear me sing them.

Pop music and I did not get along.

After those four months, money was tight and there was nothing I could do to get more money out of Jack's family. I'd wanted to sue, wanted to hurt them for everything they'd taken from me, but lawyers are a nasty bunch, which can make life convenient for the rich while singlehandedly destroying the poor.

The paid off cops lied and claimed my car was blocking the road. Jack's attorneys were able to suppress the drug evidence. Jack walked away with a slap on the wrist for speeding, while Deli received what was left of the insurance money from my parents' accident. Unfortunately, that was just enough to cover the medical bills and money to live on for a few months because my parents had run a red light trying to get to me.

When our money ran out, I'd set out on foot on a clear night that quickly crumbled, rain pouring down, drowning me as I sludged through a shortcut in the strip of woods outside my neighborhood. I'd crossed the tracks and walked up the main drive to apply at the diner. Water was dripping from my hair, my boots squeaked on the clean linoleum floor, my black t-shirt and black jeans clung to my body.

Angela had looked up from where she was standing behind the counter and tsked at me in disapproval. *"Look what the weather dragged in. What can I get for you?*

Something to eat? To drink? A blow dryer and a towel? Don't you have enough sense to carry an umbrella?"

It didn't matter if you were a patron or employee, she told you exactly what she was thinking regardless.

"No, Ma'am," I'd answered with chattering teeth. *"I'm here looking for a job."*

Her eyes had narrowed on me, she tsked again, and then snatched an application from beneath the counter. While I was filling out my personal information, she watched me closely, questions lingering between us that took three minutes for her to ask.

"I don't mean to pry, young man, but aren't you the boy that just lost his family?"

My teeth grit together, but I nodded. It had been all over the news, my face, Delilah's and my parents' plastered on television and on the front page of the paper, a tragedy worth the pens and voices of their highest paid reporters.

She'd snatched the paper away from me. When I looked up in question, my heart sinking because the diner had been the only shot at a job I'd had, she'd said, *"You're hired. When can you start?"*

The rest was history, and during holiday and summer breaks when the kids I'd known were back in town from college, Angela made sure to tuck me in back just so those people couldn't heckle me, shout insults, or cause problems. Tonight was one of those nights, the rich and entitled returning home to brag and compare notes about the next step in their lives that Deli and I had never taken.

Knowing they were out there didn't bother me much, as long as I didn't have to see them, but when I heard Angela come running back into the dish area, her steps hurried, her hands waving to get my attention, I had a feeling something bad just happened.

"Holden, make sure you stay back here and out of sight for the next hour or so, okay? There's some people in the dining room you won't want to see."

She might like hiding me in back, but she'd never asked me to stay put before. Which meant...

"Jack Thorne is here, isn't he?"

Angela nodded. "Him and Michaela Paige. I love you, Holden Bishop, but I don't need trouble in my diner, so I want you to promise me you'll stay back here."

Her words hurt. I thought I'd proven myself over the last two years, that I had shed the reputation of being a crazy freak. "I won't do anything to him."

Something in my voice must have given away the hurt. Angela's expression softened, her hands coming up to rest on my shoulders as she craned her neck to look up at me. "I don't think it's you that will cause the problems. He's the problem. I have no love in my heart for that boy out there, and if it did come down to a fight in the middle of the diner, I wouldn't stop you from beating him senseless. He deserves it and much worse. But I don't *need* that, you understand? I can't afford it."

My eyes darted to the window looking out over the main floor from the kitchen, my fingers curling into my palm as I breathed deeply. Hatred coursed through me, my shoulders tense beneath Angela's nervous hands. But I wouldn't cause trouble.

I wouldn't.

I would just watch. I would listen. I would stay out of Jack's way as long as he didn't cause trouble first.

Those are always the famous last words, aren't they?

CHAPTER EIGHT

Michaela

We hadn't been in Tranquil Falls longer than an hour before Jack was itching to get his night started. Arriving a few minutes after two in the afternoon, Jack and I had gone to his house first to say hello to his family and chat about college. Jack lied about everything, claimed he was studying all the time, which was why his grades were so high. The truth was I was writing his essays and other written requirements while he'd found a way to obtain all the tests prior to class, and after I was finished figuring out all the answers, he would cram that information and waltz into class like he was a genius.

The truth also was that Jack had developed quite the drug problem, and on the four hour ride to Tranquil Falls, we'd stopped three times so he could use the bathroom, each time returning with a sniffle and some white powder beneath his nose. I'd kept quiet, but I could tell when he was getting itchy again, could see the small tremors in his hands or hear the way his words slowed down like he would pass out without another bump. After the third time, I'd offered to drive the rest of the way, but Jack refused because *nobody touches his baby*.

His baby was another two-seater sports car much like the one he'd used to destroy the lives of the Bishop family. I hated the thing, wished his parents would buy him a tank just so I would feel safer when he was driving fifty miles over the speed limit and weaving between cars.

After leaving his family's house, we went to mine, my parents delighted to see us while my siblings just nodded their heads in our direction before running upstairs. My brother and sister were twins that were born two years

74

after me, and they were now the kids to know at Tranquil Falls High, the top of the food chain, the opinions that could make or break another student's reputation on a whim. I didn't know either of them very well, and I regretted that they'd turned out to be more like Jack than me.

Not that I was someone to be admired. My life was a sham, a pretty picture painted with blurred lines between right and wrong. People loved to look at me and covet my life, but if they looked deep enough they'd discover I was spineless and empty. There was nothing there worth coveting, nothing to desire or want.

Giving my family only a third of the time, he'd given his, Jack started itching again, his red rimmed eyes glassy when we made the drive to the servants' quarters to find Jack's new friend. Walking into the abandoned house, my nose wrinkled at the smell of piss and mildew, my head throbbing after breathing in the haze of smoke that lingered like low lying fog throughout the house. The sun was setting outside the dirty windows, streaks of it breaking through the grime and thin, ragged curtains to paint the inside of the house a putrid orange, the same shade as nicotine residue that stained the walls or a person's fingers.

Taking a seat on a couch, I groaned at a wet spot that soaked into my jeans, not heavy or flooded, just slightly damp like someone had passed out here recently and drooled. A disgusted shiver coursed up my spine as Jack disappeared down a hallway in search of the man with his next fix.

I never knew what types of drugs he was doing, and most of the time I didn't care. But I hated the uppers the most, especially now that Jack's mood changes were coming on faster, especially now that his violence wasn't just reserved for strangers. It shamed me to know he'd hit me three times and I still didn't have the strength to walk away.

That's the problem with lying and telling yourself that you somehow caused the violence. After a while, you begin to believe it.

Noise crept out from the back of the hall, deep laughter, a high pitched voice, the slap of skin as hands met for a high five, or some other greeting. The chemical smell came after, floating on a cloud of noxious fumes that mingled with the lingering cigarette smoke in the living room. Willing myself not to throw up, I breathed as shallow as possible hoping to avoid a contact high.

The voices died off, but came roaring back a few minutes later, the thud of footsteps approaching from the hallway. Jack and the man who'd replaced Jimmy turned the corner to stand near me. One look at Jack told me he was high enough to touch the moon as he floated past it, his friend who I wanted to call Jimmy, Jr., tracking his eyes over my body like I was some prize to be won at a used-car lot or a county fair. He had the carnie motif just right with greasy brown hair and beady brown eyes, stained clothing, and fingers that wouldn't stop drumming on the side of his thigh. He didn't smile so I couldn't see if his teeth were rotted too. With a simple stare, he conjured a need in me to get up and run, the intuition that what looked at me was an abyss of sorrow, slow death and pain.

This guy would probably die just like Jimmy, which meant it was a waste of time to learn his name. Thankfully, Jack was too high for introductions.

"Let's go. I need food."

His bark of a command was enough for me. Moving fast, I pushed up from the couch, twisted my body so as not to brush against Jimmy, Jr. and half walked, half ran to the front door. The wind slapped at my face as soon as

I stepped outside, but I gulped it down because it was fresh and clean, not a swirling mass of smoke and chemicals.

Tucked inside Jack's car, I wasn't paying much attention as he flipped through songs on his iPod, chose one and blasted the volume. The car lurched when he hit the gas pedal too fast, the engine roaring but not loud enough to drown out the music. Leaving the servants' quarters, the train tracks bumped below our tires, my head snapping left when Jack turned the music down and said, "Did you know Clive stopped into that all night diner yesterday?"

Hesitation filled my gut, a sharp concern of why he'd mention the diner, and dread to think I knew the answer. "Why would I know that? I don't talk to Clive." My voice dropped lower, my eyes turning away to look at the holiday decorations flying past. "Why would I even care?"

Jack's voice was strained, more curt and broken, the drugs taking effect, wrapping their claws into his brain so they could dig deeper. "Because your freak lover works there. Clive saw him."

The dread rolled and stretched, filling me with urgent concern. Not for the fact he was talking about Holden, but because he'd found him. In Jack's current state, there was no telling what he would do. I needed to diffuse the situation. Needed to cut it off before Jack did something stupid. "Who cares? He was a loser in high school, and I'm sure he's even more of a loser now. He's crazy. Why are you wasting your time thinking about him?"

"I went through a lot of shit because of that crazy fuck. Don't you care about that? Or are you too in love with him to think about me?"

A lot of shit? He was fined, given a few hours of community service and forced to take a driving course to

77

knock the points off his license. If anything, Jack lost a few hundred bucks and twenty hours of his life, while Holden had lost his family. "Yes, I care. Which is why I want to go somewhere we can have fun and not stop at that grease-pit. Let's go to McDougal's instead. Their burgers are better."

"Oh, we'll have fun here," Jack murmured, his expression tight as he cut a quick left into the diner parking lot.

Driving past the building to find a spot, I glanced inside those large windows to see the place was busy, almost every booth filled as light spilled out to bathe the parking lot in yellow. A neon sign beaming *OPEN* just beside the set of double doors leading you in, a counter with stools in the back, while on the main floor of the dining room there were tightly packed tables surrounded by the booths. I didn't see Holden. I prayed he wasn't here, that Jack would get bored quickly and want to leave.

Finding a spot, Jack threw the car in park, the chassis rocking as he climbed out and bent over to look at me where I still sat on my seat. "You coming or what? Afraid to see your crush?"

"He's not my crush."

"Whatever you say, freak fucker," he mumbled back, slapping his palm on the roof of the car before slamming his door shut. Mine was jerked open a second later, his fingers bruising my bicep as he yanked me out. Following behind him, I tucked my hands into the pockets of my jacket and let my long hair fall forward to hide my face. I didn't want to be here. I didn't want trouble.

I'd be a liar to say I didn't want to see Holden. That I didn't want to confirm he was in one piece. The last time I'd laid eyes on him, he was broken atop a hospital bed, his little sister red faced as she demanded I leave.

Jack opened the door and strolled in ahead of me as a waitress with blond hair in a braid down her back peeked over and held up a finger to tell us to wait a minute to be seated. Glancing around without making it obvious, I breathed out a sigh of relief (and disappointment) to find that Holden was nowhere in sight. Hopeful that Clive had been lying, that he was just going along with the rumor of Holden working here to have something to say to Jack, I smiled politely once the waitress approached us, the name tag on her shirt reading *Kaley*.

An older woman watched us from behind the counter, her eyes widening in recognition just before she ran off and disappeared around back.

"Table for two, I assume?"

Kaley's voice wasn't friendly. Curt and professional, the words were a touch sharper than they should be, like hidden razors that nipped at your skin to slice you apart slowly. She recognized us too, and she didn't like what she saw.

Jack nodded his head, his hands clenching into fists at his sides. He was probably angry that the waitress hadn't dropped to the ground to kiss his feet. She showed us to our table, swiped a pen from behind her ear and stood ready to write down our orders. "What can I get you?"

"How about a menu since this is the first time I've stepped foot inside this rundown grease trap, and a little bit of respect for your betters would be nice, too."

My eyes darted to Jack where he sat glaring at Kaley, a sheen of angry red staining his skin. Embarrassment and revulsion flowed through me.

"My betters?" she mumbled, more to herself than us. A bark of humorless laughter shook her shoulders, her eyes darting to the back of our table. "Your menus are right there. I'll return in a few after you've had a chance to look them over."

79

Spinning on her heel, she marched through the main dining area and stalked into the same hallway the older woman had run down earlier.

"Why do you think they keep running around back? Think the crazy freak is behind there spying on us?"

Keeping my voice low, I groaned, "Just leave it alone, Jack. You're being rude."

Jack wasn't as discreet in the voice department. Instead he spoke loud enough for everyone to hear. "I'm being rude? What the fuck ever. These fuckers should learn whose ass to kiss. If it weren't for our families, this town wouldn't exist and this shithole for a diner wouldn't be here."

Other patrons turned to look at us, but they were mostly kids who lived on our side of Tranquil Falls. Laughing at what Jack had said, they returned to their own conversations, the buzz of noise more excited than it had been a few seconds ago.

"Let it go. He didn't do anything to you."

Wrong words. Damn it, I couldn't have spoken worse words, even if they were true. Jack's eyes narrowed into slits, his jaw ticking as he ground his teeth. The drugs were taking hold and his anger was drifting to the surface.

"He didn't do anything?" he asked, keeping his voice low for once. "How about breaking my nose, huh? How about that? How about costing my family money?"

"You hit him with your car," I hissed, too pissed off to do the sensible thing and agree with him just so he would calm down and shut up.

God, I hated it when Jack got high.

The waitress returned, her pen poised over her pad of paper, her expression politely professional. "Have you decided?"

Jutting his chin toward the hall, Jack grinned and spoke loud when he asked. "Yeah. Why don't you tell the crazy freak in back to come out and talk to me? We're old friends."

Laughter burst from some of the tables, naked anger filtering through Kaley's brown eyes as her lips pulled into a thin line. "I'm sure you were." Pointing between us with her pen, she said, "You two need to leave. As in now. As in right this minute. We don't want your kind of trouble in here."

Jack was growing louder, angrier, his eyes bloodshot so badly that the green shone neon. "We have to leave? Why? Because you have a crazy freak in back? You need to do you job and serve me, you understand? I was just trying to be friendly by inviting him to my table-"

"Kaley is right, Mr. Thorne. You need to leave my diner right now and without another word. Nobody is going to be serving you here."

Marching up to the table, the older woman looked as if she would pick Jack up herself and toss him out. Murmurs burst through the room, the patrons turning in their seats to watch the show. Just as quickly as the noise level grew louder, it quieted, everybody's eyes turning to the back hallway as those murmurs turned to faint whispers.

My eyes locked on the hallway next, seconds before Jack turned to look. I'd only experienced time stopping once before. I'd only felt this chill course through me during one other event. That time involved Jack and Holden, as well.

Holden...

My breath froze in my lungs to see him.

Holden Bishop had grown in the past two years. Not just in height or width, but in presence, in magnitude, in strength. I wasn't sure how to explain what my body was

81

feeling, what my heart was doing to look at him, why I hadn't yet taken a breath since my eyes connected with his neon blue stare radiating cold, raw hatred.

In high school he'd been a shadow, a wisp of darkness that tore down the halls with his shoulders folded in on themselves, his head lowered, his mind trapped by whatever he was reading, or whatever image captured his thoughts. But now, Holden stood with his head high, his broad shoulders rolled back, the darkness about him no longer a shadow but a black hole that absorbed and licked at the light all around him.

I took a breath.

"Well, there he is! The freak of the hour. I was wondering when you'd stop hiding and come out to say hello."

Jack's voice boomed above the whispers hissing through the room, venomous snakes of gossip and rumors. The older woman moved to block Jack when he stood up, the waitress waving over a few other men who wore chef pants and aprons. They stepped out of the kitchen and took a place behind the older woman but in front of Holden.

"You need to leave my diner right now, Mr. Thorne. And if you're not out within the next five seconds, I'll call the cops and report you for trespassing."

Jack's gaze slid between the older woman and Holden, a grin stretching his lips in challenge. "Did you hear that Holden? I have to leave. All because you're a scared, little crazy freak who can't take care of himself. Not so big and bad anymore are you?"

Laughter rolled like soft thunder across the tables, snickers and jeers. I don't know how Holden stood so still to hear it, his expression blank, his eyes daring Jack to come closer despite the people standing between them.

"Come on, Jack. We don't need the cops called. Especially not with-" My eyes flicked down pointedly to his pocket where I knew his drugs were stashed.

Jack hesitated.

"Listen to your girlfriend, Mr. Thorne. At least she has enough sense to know where she's not welcome."

His eyes narrowed on the woman, his hands clenching and releasing. If I didn't get him out of here now, he'd start a fight with someone. Stupid fucking drugs. They make people insane.

"Come on, Jack. I want to go." Grabbing his arm, I ignored the way his bicep flexed beneath my palm. He was high as a kite and wound up by whatever uppers Jimmy Jr. had given him. Thankfully, he was sober enough to realize he couldn't take on all the employees of the diner to get to Holden. Shooting me a scathing look, Jack wrenched his arm from my hand, stormed out of the diner without bothering to look back. Tucking my hands into my jacket, I shuffled out behind him, aware that the older woman was following me as far as a few steps outside the door.

Turning, I peered over at her, my cheeks heating with embarrassment. Keeping my voice low, I apologized. "I'm really sorry about that. I didn't want to come here and cause trouble."

Her eyes studied me before she shook her head and scowled. "You seem to have some sense. A girl like you can do a hell of a lot better than that jackass. Money isn't everything, sweetheart, and you'll do better in life when you learn it. I know my advice is beneath you, but I'm giving it to you anyway: You need to drop that guy like a bad habit. He's not right in the head."

With that, she spun and stormed inside. Jack was pulling out of the space before I even reached the car. Stopping just long enough for me to climb inside, he didn't give me time to close my door before peeling out of the parking lot.

Keeping quiet, I refused to look at him as we tore down the main drive taking all the curves at a dangerous speed despite what happened last time he was driving like this on an icy night.

"Please slow down," I finally whispered, too afraid to add any strength to my voice.

His jaw ticked. "Slow down. You want me to slow down?" His foot pressed the pedal harder, the needle of the speedometer shooting higher.

Hitting the brake suddenly, he turned the wheel, the car's tires sliding over slick asphalt, my hands clenching to whatever I could find to hold myself in place as we spun to go back the other direction.

"No, I'm not going to slow down. Not until I'm in a nice little hiding place where I can wait for that bastard. He owes me for what he did to my nose, and I'm going to break him a little as payback."

His car was speeding through town again, back toward the diner, toward Holden. Panic erupted in my chest, my heartbeat erratic as I held on to the handle of the door, praying I'd find a way to turn him back around and away from the diner. "Jack, this is ridiculous, we're going to be late to the party." Trying to sound bored rather than petrified, I leaned his direction, put my hand on his knee and smiled. He didn't bother looking at me, but at the speed we were going, I was fine with that. I'd rather his eyes remain on the road.

"We'll still go to the party. I'm sure once that freak gets out of work, it'll only take me a few minutes to get even for my nose. Just one bone, that's all I need to break. One."

The panic spread to my stomach causing bile to roll over itself, to push its way up and burn my throat. "But you have the party favors, Jack. Clive and the other guys-"

"Will understand," he barked. "They hate that crazy freak as much as me. We wanted to get even for that last fight, but he never came back to school."

Probably because you almost killed him with your car, I thought, too afraid to voice the words. *Probably because he lost his family.*

Jack passed the diner and kept driving until we were near the train tracks. Pulling into a small empty dirt lot masked by shadow, he parked. His words were slowing down, his hands shaking. He needed another bump as the itch surged through him. While he angled his hips to reach in his pocket, I continued arguing, desperate to get him to the party and away from Holden. "This is gross, Jack. Aren't you worried about your car in this lot? There could be razors and used needles, broken glass or other things that could pop your tires."

If I'd learned anything in the five years I'd been with Jack, it was that playing to his own interests was better than defending whatever target he'd set his sights on. I knew better than to tell him to leave Holden alone for Holden's sake. Jack would only accuse me of being a freak fucker for doing so. "Plus, it's an all night diner. You don't know what time he gets off work. We could be sitting here for hours in the cold."

Jack wasn't paying me much attention, not with the plastic baggie in his hand filled with white powder, not with the tiny spoon he was dipping down into that powder before bringing it to his nose. He inhaled it harshly, sniffing over and over to make sure he got it all. After closing the baggie, he rubbed his nostrils, his head falling back against his seat. "Shut up, Michaela. Stop complaining about everything."

I couldn't shut up. Not when we were sitting here waiting to jump a man that hadn't done anything wrong. Not when I remembered back to the diner and Holden's presence. While Holden had grown in the past two years, Jack had become softer. He was still tall, still muscular, but nothing like he'd been in his senior year of high school. Since starting college, he'd stopped playing football and wasn't working out anymore. Add how the drugs had been eating away at his physique, and I doubted Jack was an equal match for Holden.

The shaking in Jack's hands stopped a few seconds after he snorted whatever the powder was, his eyes wide open as he stared out the window toward the tracks. "I'll wait for as long as it takes," he finally said, his voice gritty, his throat moving to swallow. Turning to look at me, he allowed his gaze to travel down my body. "If you want to pass the time you could always do me a favor."

Deja vu came flaring back. History repeating itself. This night mirroring the other. Decisions being made that would affect our lives in tragic ways. The bile crept further up, coating the back of my tongue with its acrid flavor. "I'm not doing it. Not here. I want to go."

The sound was sharp, so sharp it ricocheted through the car, the burning pain across my cheek bone trailing behind that sound. By the time my mind could catch on to understand that Jack had hit me, his fingers were gripped in my hair, the strands snapping from my skull with how hard he gripped. I was being shoved down toward his lap, his words bellowing to fill the small space inside the car and chasing away the remaining echo of the strike to my face.

"You'll do what I fucking tell you."

Tears welled in my eyes, dripping down my cheek to dot his jeans, my unfocused gaze watching as he unbuttoned his pants to force the favor from me. He was too strong, too dangerous when he was like this.

He wasn't giving me another option.

I was being stripped of my choice.

I was sick and tired of a life where I was forced to behave, forced to smile and pose, forced to swallow the lie that being born into privilege was somehow a blessing.

If anything, the privilege I was born into was smothering the life out of me, stealing the soul from my body and forcing me into an early grave.

CHAPTER NINE

Holden

A pall had fallen over the rest of my night after Jack made an ass of himself in the diner, a bad feeling crammed so far in my heart that I couldn't shake the hatred, the rage, the need to work the aggression out in some way that wouldn't hurt anybody. Normally when I felt like this, I would lock myself in my studio and paint. I would work myself until I was bleary-eyed and exhausted, only to wind down with my guitar in my lap, softly singing whatever song came to mind while I strummed the remaining tension away. Nights like that would leave paint smears on my skin and on my guitar strings. I didn't mind the smears, didn't mind the dabs of color added to brighten the drab, monotonous black and white.

It was unfortunate I didn't have the option to lock myself away once Angela had forced Jack and Michaela from the diner. After breaking a stack of plates and damn near shattering a rack of glasses, Angela pulled me aside, ignoring the dirty dishes piling up as she dragged me out back for a smoke and a pep talk.

Wrapping her arms across her body, she stared up at me with concern etched in her expression. "So that kid, he's a bully, Holden. A no good jerk that would be nothing without his daddy's wallet. Don't let him get to you."

Pulling a drag from my smoke, I tilted my head to the sky and blew it out, watching the smoke swirl and stretch across the cold winds sneaking around the side of the building. "He's a lot more than a jerk, Angela. You and I both know that, but I won't worry about it. I won't do anything about it. He just pisses me off, that's all."

"Not just you. He pissed off everybody in that diner."

Soft laughter shook my shoulders. "Not everybody." Not the people sitting at their tables, not the bratty rich kids who were slumming it in my half of Tranquil Falls before heading back to their end to have fun. Those kids had laughed. They looked up to people like Jack, thought speaking out and saying whatever you felt like was something to be admired. They'd crowned their king of hatred and greed because it gave them the go ahead to be just as hateful and petty as him.

Breathing out in a huff, Angela rolled her eyes. "He pissed off everybody that matters. Who cares what those dumb kids think as they gobble down the heart attacks on a platter I serve them each night? They're dumb. They've never been taught any better."

"He doesn't matter," I drolled, mindless repetition of her words that would get her off my back if she believed I actually meant them. Angela knew better. She knew Jack mattered, that if anybody on the entire planet mattered, it was him. He may not have been the direct cause of my parents' deaths, but he was a catalyst. And for that, he mattered more than anybody would ever know.

"You don't mean that and don't try to play me like I'm an idiot."

Her tone of voice brought a smile to my face. Angela was a mother to everybody, but especially me. I felt sorry for her that she'd decided to take on that role. I wasn't an easy child.

"I know you hate Jack Thorne for everything that happened to your mom and dad. And I wouldn't be surprised if you've thought of a thousand different ways to break him apart and leave the husk out as carrion. To be honest, I just thought of a hundred ways to kill him after that show he put on in the dining room, but I'll keep those thoughts to myself because I'm not giving you any ideas." Her voice softened, the anger dissipating into concern. "But you still have your sister, and that girl needs you right now. She can't survive on her own. Not until she can come to terms with what happened."

Taking another drag, I eyed the smoke tumbling over my lips as I answered, "I'm not going to do anything to him."

"Damn straight, you're not. You're too good for that, Holden Bishop. And you're also going to stop murdering my dishes. I don't have the money to replace my entire kitchen because you're in a bad mood."

Her hand clasped my shoulder. "You're also going to quit that nasty smoking habit, but I'll let you have this one in peace because you deserve it. I know it wasn't easy for you to stay put in the hall when that spoiled rotten waste of skin was screaming all those things at you. But you did stay put, which tells me you're stronger than him. Better in every way that matters."

An unintentional smoke ring burst of my lips, stretching and growing until the perfect circle was torn apart entirely. "It'll be fine," I breathed out, the tension bleeding from my shoulders because Angela had been right in everything she'd said. Especially about Deli. She needed me and I wouldn't let myself do something that could take me away from her.

Deli mattered more than Jack, but in a different way.

"And I'm sorry about the dishes. I slipped on the mat."

"Sure you did," she replied, "we can go with the word 'slipped' even though we both know it was more than that." A breath poured out of her. "You have two more hours before your shift ends and I know you're meeting Kaley at her house after. You can work out your issues with her in a more constructive way, in a respectful way. With a condom."

Angela pointed her finger in my face, her eyes narrowed in warning. I laughed. "Did Kaley tell you that?"

More laughter now, Angela's shoulders relaxing, the worry bleeding out of her expression. "No, she didn't. The girl thinks nobody in the diner knows about you two, but we aren't stupid. The instant she went bouncing out of this place with a stupid smile on her face, we knew you two had plans to meet up. When are you going to make an honest woman out of her?"

"She doesn't want to be honest. Kaley's perfectly content with keeping things casual. I don't have time for honest, anyway, not with Deli to look after."

"Well, that's between you two. The point is to let all this drama with Jack go. It's not worth your time or your energy. And let's face it, if something did happen and you hurt that boy, the circumstances wouldn't matter. The cops would cart you off and lay the blame on you just so they could avoid dealing with the team of lawyers his family could afford. It won't matter, Holden. They'll blame you." After eyeing me and confirming I understood, she nodded her head and jut her chin in the diner's direction. "Finish your cigarette and get back to work when you're done."

Stepping away, she stopped short, twisting back to look at me. "And if I hear another dish break back there, I'm going to shove you through the dishwasher myself. I'm not down with the shenanigans, you hear me?"

Smoke filled laughter blew from my lungs, the sound chasing after her as she made her way inside. After a few minutes, I returned to the dish station and spent the remaining two hours mindlessly doing my job without breaking another dish.

My shift was up, so I straightened up the dish area as best I could for George who would be taking over for the rest of the night. Stripping the vinyl apron off, I shrugged back into my hoodie and jacket, tugged my beanie down low over my head and made my way to the back door. Angela intercepted me before I could make it.

Grabbing my arm, she asked, "Are you going to be all right?"

My smile beamed. It felt good to know someone genuinely cared. "I'll be fine," I promised, but my voice turned into a tease when I added, "but I'd be a whole lot better if I was leaving here to meet you."

Wiggling my eyebrows, I slipped an arm around her to squeeze Angela tight, to feel the way her body shook with laughter. The freedom of it extinguished the last of the dark feelings inside me.

Pulling away, she smacked my shoulder. "One of these days my husband is going to come down here and whip your butt for flirting with me. But until then, take care of yourself and have fun with your casual sex. I'll see you in two days for your next shift."

"Sounds good."

Turning to leave, I was halfway out the door when she shouted, "Condoms, Holden Bishop. The world isn't ready for little Holdens running around flirting with random people."

Shaking my head, I let the door slam shut behind me, my breath coming out in great, white plumes, my boots crunching over the gravel path. Rounding a stand of trees that sat out back, I stepped onto the main road through town, crossed it and hung a right toward the tracks. It was only a mile between the diner and my house when I took the shortcut through the woods. Normally, I didn't mind the walk, except for on nights it was so cold that the dampness on my pants from the dishwasher turned to ice.

The night was quiet. Not quite midnight yet, this side of town had gone to sleep, the drugged out losers tucked away in their squatter houses, the families tucked away as well, but behind deadbolts and chain locks. The servants' quarters had degenerated more since my parents died, the vagrants and meth-heads attempting to break into houses when desperation for money had them in its grasp.

With my hands tucked into the pockets of my jacket, I kept my head low to prevent as much wind as possible from stinging at my eyes, making them water and then freezing those tears to my skin. I wasn't paying attention to my surroundings, was lost in thought by the time I approached the tracks that divided Tranquil Falls. My plan was to go home and shower, then check on Deli. As long as she was fine, I'd leave for a few hours to have some fun with Kaley. But plans have a funny way of changing at the drop of a hat. They have a way of disappearing when you hear something odd and turn to look.

It was the sound of a car door clicking shut that had first drawn my attention. But it was the figure moving out of the shadows that forced my heart rate to pick up speed, my body to tense with anger. I heard another voice call from the shadows, fear and urgency riding Michaela's tone. "Jack! Please don't do this!"

Breath poured out of me, hot with rage, but I eyed Jack from a distance, decided he wasn't worth the trouble of a fight. Not when it would threaten my ability to take care of Deli. There was enough space between us that I could dip into the woods before he reached me, could outrun him if I really needed to. Not that Jack scared me. From what I saw at the diner, his body had lost mass and he had the shakes common to drug users.

But I didn't need the trouble, so I ignored him and stalked off.

"Come back here, crazy freak! Are you scared of me? Is that it?"

Jack sounded amped, his pitch higher than normal, his words coming out on a rush of furious breath. I kept walking, kept going, kept hoping that he wouldn't follow me beyond the tree line once I passed it. I wanted nothing more than to cave his face in with my fist, but Angela was right. They'd blame me. I'd go to jail for it. Even if he had been the instigator. Picking up my pace, I could hear the argument occurring behind me, could hear the hurried steps following me.

"Jack, I mean it, stop!" Sobs tore from Michaela's lungs. She sounded panicked, afraid. Terrified, really, which made me wonder if Jack had a weapon I hadn't seen.

"Shut the fuck up! What? Are you worried I'll beat the shit out of your freak boyfriend? Because that's exactly what I plan to do!"

Boyfriend? Had the drugs messed with his mind so much that he actually believed something was going on with Michaela and me? I hadn't seen her in two years. That was insane.

My hands clenched into fists in my pockets and it took every drop of self-control I had in me to keep moving forward. Turning around and destroying him would be so much easier, but look what happened last time I laid a hand on him. I lost my parents. I almost lost my sister. Decisions have consequences and I wasn't willing to play with fate just to work out the fury inside me toward Jack, the raw, undulating need I had to rip his body apart.

Urgency pushed my feet faster. I was practically jogging by the time I reached the line of trees. My hope that Jack would retreat was futile. His steps pounded behind me, his mouth shouting out the most ridiculous statements. "You can run, but you can't hide, freak! Afraid you won't get a sucker punch in this time? Why don't you turn around and face me?"

Pulling my hands from my pockets, I broke into a full sprint. But I was exhausted and didn't have drugs pumping through my veins, pushing me harder and faster. Not like Jack. The old high school quarterback, a guy who could run much faster than me apparently.

Michaela's voice cut through the quiet night sky. "Jack! Stop!"

It was too late. He'd caught up to me, slammed into me from behind and tackled me to the ground. Adrenaline poured into my veins the instant our bodies made contact. Falling forward, I was launched to the ground, my knees and hands bracing for the impact, but his weight and speed had been too much. My forehead hit and scraped along a downed tree, my arm was gripped and my body jerked over until I was on my back, the tree beneath my head not giving way. Jack straddled me while stars were still bursting behind my eyes from the hit. He yanked me up by my shoulders and slammed me down again. The back of my head impacted against the tree. My vision hazed red.

"Jack! Please!"

A figure ran up behind Jack, the scant moonlight lighting Michaela's face as she reached to grab him and attempted to pull him off me. His fist flew back, the knuckles catching her face, knocking her sideways.

Everything went black as pure, undiluted rage poured through me.

. . .

When I came to, I was leaning against a tree, my chest beating with labored breath, my knuckles flaring with

95

pain, the skin burning in the cold wind howling past me. Confusion held me in its grip, my mind racing back to remember where I was, how I got here, what happened. I could feel hot blood dripping from my nose, could taste the copper flavor of it in my mouth. The night was quiet except for my hard breathing.

Images rushed past me, memories of...something.

Raising my hands to my face, I winced at the torn skin over my knuckles, looked down to see blood covering my ripped jacket. My pants were stained and wet, my hair in my face because my beanie was gone. Blood dripped from my lip and when I followed a hot drop of it down to the ground, I froze in place, my mind begging for this moment to be a hallucination and not real.

Both Jack and Michaela lay on the ground, their bodies still, their silence lifeless.

Alarm overwhelmed me, the force of it tight and explosive within my body.

Oh, God...

Please let them be alive. Please let them be alive. Pleasepleasepleasepleaseplease.

I got to Jack first and almost vomited. A puddle of blood expanded beneath him, both eye orbitals of his skull crushed in, his jaw hung slack and out of place. Closing my eyes, I sucked in a breath, opening them again to reach out and check his pulse.

There was nothing. Not even a slight flicker.

His eyes were as open as they could be with the damage, unblinking.

Jack was dead.

Jack was dead.

Jack was dead.

This couldn't be happening. I didn't do this.

Judging by my busted knuckles, I did.

Angela's voice was a whisper in my mind. *"It won't matter, Holden. They'll blame you."*

Another spike of panic drove through me, my head aching with it, my body pulsing with the pain of it, my senses screaming with it, my body frozen in place, unable to crawl forward and check on Michaela.

She hadn't moved since I came to by the tree.

Fighting against the frantic rhythm of my heart, willing myself to breathe evenly before I passed out on top of them, I swallowed hard, trying to force down the screams crawling up my throat, the incessant question thundering in my head:

What will happen to Delilah if I'm gone?

How did this happen? Why couldn't I remember anything? Why couldn't this stupid son of a bitch just let go of the past and leave me the hell alone?

I was nothing to him. A nobody.

But now, I was the man who took his life. I was the last moment he had before he stopped breathing.

Another surge of panic crashed over me like a tall wave, the undertow of denial and disbelief dragging me under. My thoughts were a jumbled mess, my vitals at a level far above healthy, but I crept forward regardless to see that blood covered Michaela's cheek. Reaching out with hesitant fingers, I pressed the tips to her neck and found a pulse.

Oh, thank God...

The thought raced through my head before I took a second to understand what her being alive meant:

I'd murdered Jack Thorne, and Michaela Paige had witnessed it.

Pushing to my feet, I paced the ground beside them, my fingers tugging at my hair, my palms wrapping over the back of my neck while I screamed every obscenity in the book.

I had to think, had to move, had to fix this somehow.

I couldn't fix this.

There was no bringing Jack back to life. And Michaela would wake up eventually to tell the cops what I'd done.

They would interview me. And I would have no answers, so I couldn't even claim self-defense because I didn't know what happened.

FUCK!

I had to think, had to think, had to...I didn't think. I reacted. Stepping up to Michaela on one long stride, I knelt down and took her limp body into my arms. Cradling her against my chest, I tried kicking leaves over Jack's body to camouflage him. Nothing I did helped to disguise him from view and I knew it would only be a handful of days before someone came through here and saw him. But those people wouldn't see me as long as I got the hell out of there right that second.

Shoving him with my foot, I knocked him away from the small foot-trampled trail, leaving him like trash among the drug needles, plastic baggies, used condoms and empty styrofoam cups.

I didn't have a damn clue what I would do with Michaela, but I knew I couldn't leave her lying there, couldn't run back home and hope like hell she wouldn't wake up and go immediately to the police. I needed time and that's why I kept running down the road holding on to her even when I had absolutely no idea what I would do with her once she was inside my house.

I wasn't thinking straight. I was reacting. And sometimes, quick reactions during an emergency aren't always the best. Mine certainly wasn't. I was only complicating the problem, adding kidnapping onto murder, heaping all the possible felonies onto the pile so I could face them at the same time when the cops finally found me.

But I'd panicked. And taking Michaela was the brilliant plan I came up with.

What would I tell Deli? Where would she go if I went to jail? How would I get Michaela in the house without Deli seeing me? Where would I put her once I had her there?

Instinct and intuition took over. I was on autopilot as I ran up the walkway to the front door, autopilot as I snuck inside and ran to my room without Deli seeing me, autopilot as I laid Michaela down on my bed, stepped back and wondered how I would keep her quiet, autopilot as I grabbed rope from the garage, tied her hands together, and whispered an apology against her ear.

Autopilot as I bound her completely.

Autopilot as I gagged her to make sure she didn't scream.

Autopilot as I went out in search for my sister to beg her to go spend time with our uncle.

Autopilot as I found Deli sleeping, returned to my room and then slid down the door to sit on the floor while staring at a major, life-altering problem.

CHAPTER TEN
Michaela

Hammers were beating on the inside of my skull, the thunderous pulse traveling down my temple to slide along my cheekbone that felt hot and swollen. I wished it was one of those moments where you wake up from something terrible, but your mind shields you, erasing all the scary parts so you don't panic when your eyes open.

But it wasn't one of those moment. I remembered all the scary parts, they were playing behind my eyes like a movie, over and over.

Blinking the space around me into view, I knew instantly that my hands and feet were bound because I could feel the pinch of rope on my skin. My mouth was gagged. I wasn't outside. It was in a bedroom instead. Not mine. Not Jack's.

Holden's.

I recognized it from the video Delilah had shown me of Holden playing guitar. Tears stung my eyes, the nagging fear that Jack had been right - Holden was crazy.

Only a crazy man would lose it the way Holden did. Only a crazy man would carry me back to his house and tie me up. Only a crazy man would be sitting on the floor with his chin resting on his knees, covered in dirt and blood while staring at me. There wasn't a drop of concern in his stare, either. Only pure, naked hatred.

"Did I do that to you?"

The question took me by surprise. Not just the question, but the depth of his voice, the fluid baritone that I knew could sing softly. I assumed he wanted me to answer the cryptic question, but being gagged made it impossible. Mumbling behind it, I tried to point out the obvious to him while he continued glaring in my direction, his blue eyes beaming.

A disgusted grunt rolled off his lips, but he got up, approached the bed, ripped the gag from my mouth and then went back to where he was sitting before. "Did I do that to you?"

Fear was heavy on my words, the weight causing them to shake and tremble, causing my voice to pitch higher in anxious fits. "Do what? I don't know what you're talking about. Are you the one who tied me up?"

His head cut left. "No. Your face. Did I do that to you?"

I wanted to reach up and touch my face, evaluate the damage, determine if the bone itself had shattered when I was struck. But being bound made it impossible for me to move. And maybe that was a good thing. Holden looked like he was only barely clinging to control. His body shook, his jaw ticking furiously. Any quick moment or one wrong word could send him careening over the edge of control into violence.

Keeping my voice soft, calm despite the circumstances, I answered, "No. You didn't do this. Jack did."

Relief flashed in his eyes just before the hatred returned, but he didn't say anything in response. I decided to fill the silence for him. I needed to convince him to let me go. Not knowing whether Jack was alive or dead, I needed to get out of this situation one way or another.

Thankfully my life had taught me to be complacent, had taught me how to deal with strong men who'd lost their damn mind. "Why am I tied up, Holden? Will you please let me go?"

Holden stared, the shaking of his body stopping as he went perfectly still. The silence returned, ticking by on anxious beats, the tension so thick it was drowning me. Fear trickled through my body, drip, drip, dripping until it was a puddle, a pond, a lake, an ocean churning beneath a turbulent storm.

"I can't do that," he finally answered, his tone curt, the words clipped and forced.

Swallowing down the dread crawling up my throat, I forced the calm tone to remain in my voice, added some sweetness, hoping like hell it would settle him down. "Why not?"

He was so big, massive when you were close to him, a man that looked like a runaway train heading toward you that could break you faster than you understood what he planned to do. Even folded over himself with his arms wrapped around his bent legs and his chin resting on his knees, he was as tall as the doorknob, his shoulders stretching as wide as the frame of the door. Black hair hung limp in his face, dried blood caked beneath his nose and on his knuckles. His jacket was ripped at the shoulder, dirt smeared over the knees of his pants. A nasty scrape made the skin of his forehead look raw and broken.

But his eyes, they were gorgeous, even with the hatred glittering behind them. I'd always noticed his stare growing up, had always been caught in the hypnotic pull of a set of eyes that truly saw me, that looked right through me until every last bit of my truth was revealed.

Holden knew my life was a lie. He saw past the prim and proper exterior.

"Because you couldn't let things go," he answered, his tone matter of fact. "You just had to make it worse, didn't you? Had to take everything that was left."

There was no fluctuation in his voice. Dead. Monotone. In shock. Holden spoke robotically, answering my question with whatever words filtered into his head, but not really talking to me. He was somewhere else.

"Where's Jack?" Whispering because I was terrified to ask the question, I studied every muscle twitch in Holden's arms, stared at the disgust and rage rolling behind his eyes.

Holden moved suddenly, which caused me to flinch in response. But he didn't get up, didn't do anything beyond stretching his legs out on the floor in front of his body, lean his head back against the door and cross his arms over his chest. Fear had mutated into something else, the shock still present, but fading. A grin stretched Holden's lips. Feral. Unfeeling. Insane.

"He's dead."

My terror overwhelmed me, a curtain of dread falling down to distort reality. My heart was beating so fast and hard it must have been a drumbeat that even Holden could hear. My lungs were so frozen that I could only manage short, shallow breaths. My head fell heavier against the mattress and I closed my eyes, tried to stop the room from spinning. Tried to deny myself the truth that I'd just learned my boyfriend of five years had died and I didn't care.

Not about him, at least. Jack Thorne deserved it. He'd asked for it by refusing to let his hatred of Holden go. It was sad that his life was over, but I didn't pity his fate.

"You're not crying," Holden commented in observation. There was still no life to his voice. No warmth.

On a tremulous breath I answered, "Because I'm not sad."

"He treated you like crap," he barked out, "and you let him."

"I know."

As his voice grew in strength, mine softened and became weak. Silence swept in again, a tidal wave slapping over the earth, smothering the life that failed to outrun it.

"Why?"

My pulse was an imperfect rhythm fluttering non-stop beneath my skin. A butterfly trapped in a jar, bouncing and bouncing in search of freedom. "Because I'm not strong. I - I'm a-"

"You're small," he answered for me, "but that's not what I meant when I asked why."

His words sent me back two years, to another time I'd been called small. Delilah had screamed it at me over and over again while chasing me out of Holden's hospital room, her voice so loud for such a tiny girl. I never understood what she meant by it. I just assumed she was so heartbroken and terrified for her brother that it was the only word she could think of in the moment. But judging by how Holden repeated it now, I wasn't so sure.

Tears welled in my eyes, the cold in the room combining with my fear until every muscle in my body was painfully tight across my bones. "I don't know what you're asking me."

"Why did you have to take it all?" He roared, his voice sweeping to fill every crevice of his room, booming from wall to wall, floor to ceiling, shaking the tears free from eyes that wouldn't stop spilling. Curling into myself in terror, I sobbed, reality finally pulling the curtain of dread aside to shine brilliantly in its danger and torment.

"Why?" He bellowed again, not giving me time for an answer before he added, "Was killing my parents not good enough for you? Destroying my sister until she doesn't know one day from the next. Was that not enough? Why couldn't you just leave me alone and be happy with what you already have? I'm nothing to you!

104

Nothing! I own nothing. I am nothing. You already made me nothing!"

His fist slammed against the wall and I flinched, expected him to jump up and storm over to hurt me, but he didn't move. My eyes were clenched shut, but I didn't hear the rolling thunder of his steps approaching.

Settling enough to gain minimal control over my voice, I forced out, "I didn't do this. I didn't want to do this. It was Jack."

"It was Jack," he repeated quietly, his words tumbling forth on a whisper of disbelief. "That's funny because every time *it was Jack* doing something to destroy my life, you were the one right beside him."

Sobs wracked me, my entire body shaking over the mattress as pain spilled from my heart, beating and pulsing just as bad as the burn along my cheekbones and the hammers still pounding against my skull. "I didn't want to be there. Jack was shitty to me, too. He was a bully. Not just to you, Holden, but everyone."

"That still doesn't answer the question. Why, Michaela? Why come looking for me at all? There was nothing in life I had left to give. Just my sister. Just her. And now you took that away, too. I don't know where she'll go without me. I don't know what will happen to her. Why? Why did you have to do this?"

His words broke apart as soon as he mentioned Delilah. She was alive. He'd said as much. But where was she? She couldn't be in the house right now. She would have heard Holden yelling. Wouldn't she come in here to check and see what was going on?

Without an answer to give him, I reverted back to a captive begging. "Please let me go."

"I can't. Don't you understand that? I know you're used to skating by in life, protected by your money and your expensive lawyers, but I don't have that. So before I get carted off to jail for *defending* myself against you, I need to buy enough time to figure out what to do with my sister. I need to figure out how I can take care of her from prison. Do you have any suggestions for me, Michaela? What would you do if you were me? Go running to mommy and daddy? Let them make it all go away?" He barked out a humorless laugh, his voice softening, "I can't even do that. You took them from me two years ago."

Gaining control of myself wasn't easy. My willpower was a slippery noodle bending and sliding to keep my hands from getting a good grasp on it. My strength was ebbing and flowing, there one minute, dragging me out to sea the next. I was trapped in place, the silence buzzing against my ears as static and white noise. "I can help you, Holden. I saw what Jack did. I know he attacked you first. I can tell them what you did was in self-defense."

Another bark of sound. "Yeah. Sorry, but that's not something I can rely on. You didn't have a voice to protest when Jack was alive, what would make me think you'd have one now? As soon as you're safe and sound, hiding behind your family's power and money, you'll go along with whatever they want you to say. You're weak as fuck, Michaela."

"I know the truth," I pled.

"The truth doesn't matter. It never does for men like me. We're disposable. An easy answer to lock away so the police look like heroes and Jack Thorne will be remembered as the helpless victim against a crazy freak who wanted revenge for an *accident*. Your truth is meaningless. It's as weak as you. To everybody that matters, it's an inconvenience that will be shoved aside and forgotten."

Holden wasn't yelling anymore, he was rambling, talking so fast that I had to focus on each word just to ensure I didn't miss one and lose track. It felt like I was spiraling right beside him, a picture being painted in front of me that revealed the ugly reality of life, the differences between people born into different types of families. While he ranted, I cried, absorbing every word, every insult, every heartbreaking truth he was shoving down my throat.

"And now, now I get to add a few more felonies to the pile. But hey, I guess it comes to me naturally. A trashy guy from a trashy neighborhood who was lucky enough to sit in the same classrooms as people like you. So while you lie there and cry, I'll be out dealing with this problem before the sun comes up tomorrow morning. I'll be figuring out what to do with a sister who can't take care of herself. I'll be coming to terms with the fact that you succeeded in taking it all. You broke me down until I was small like you. Does that make you happy?"

"No!" I cried out. "I'm not happy!"

"Good! At least I'm not the only one this time. I'm sorry to inconvenience you, princess, but I need time to make some last minute arrangements before I get hauled off and stuck in a prison cell to rot away the rest of my life."

Standing up, he pulled the ripped jacket off his shoulders, dropped it to the floor and kicked it away. His hoodie was next, the stained garment deserted as he stood in a t-shirt and dirty pants. My eyes widened at the size of him, the sheer force of him, buckets filled with terror being poured inside me until I was saturated and bloated, my tears soaking the blanket beneath me. "Please don't hurt me!"

His head snapped my direction. "Hurt you? Why would I hurt you? I'm not your psycho boyfriend."

With that he stalked over to tie the gag back over my mouth before disappearing into his closet. Emerging from

107

the shadowed interior, he carried a clean pair of jeans in his hand, a clean hoodie slung over his shoulder. He didn't look at me or say a word as he left his room, slamming the door shut behind him.

Unable to move, I was left to swallow down my fear, to simmer in the cold anger Holden had left behind in his wake.

There was nothing I could do in this situation, so I just buried my face into his blanket and cried.

CHAPTER ELEVEN

Holden

I've always found it odd how emotions could beat on you harder than another man's fist, could weigh on you heavier than a thousand large stones, could tear you apart faster than a hundred scraping claws digging deep beneath the skin.

Emotions should be weightless, something without mass, a non-entity that doesn't have shape or form because they are a subjective idea. They can't be measured or appropriated. They are a figment of a human's imagination that pours into our veins as chemicals and hormones, making us *feel* something that isn't actually there. Emotions are ghosts, incarnations that overpower us when we can't even see them to fight back.

Walking down the street at two in the morning, I sank beneath the weight of those emotions, was knocked to the side by the force of them, was being hollowed out by their cruel, punishing fingers. My hands were tucked deep inside the pockets of my black hoodie, my head hanging down despite the sharp tension in my neck. Dragging a thousand pound bolder behind me would have been easier than what I was strolling down the street to do. Two more felonies: hiding a body and getting rid of a car.

While Michaela was passed out on my bed for over an hour, I had time to think about what I would do, my mind spinning through every scenario and coming to the ultimate conclusion that I had to buy time. Delilah would shatter completely if she saw me carted off in handcuffs, she'd lose what was left of her fragile mind because she would know, deep down, that she was helpless and alone. I had no choice but to get her somewhere she would have help, even if my Uncle Scott was old and feeble. Maybe his adult daughters could take care of Deli. Maybe one of them would know what to do.

My jaw ached from how hard my teeth were clenched, my frustration pouring out of me with each heavy step down the road. By the time I reached the woods where I knew Jack's lifeless body lay, I wanted to rage against everything around me, wanted to knock down trees and set fire to this life that had done nothing by shred me from the inside out.

Pulling a flashlight from my pocket, I swung the beam in Jack's direction to find him exactly where I'd left him, lying limp like the trash and debris that surrounded his body. The woods weren't thick, but they were long, and only two paths had been trampled down, the rest of the area was wild with overgrown bushes and untrimmed trees. Breath billowed out of me as I stomped toward him, his hands cold and limp in mine as I dragged him farther from the trail and dumped him near a grouping of bushes that would conceal him from easy sight.

He wouldn't stay hidden forever, the smell alone would prevent that from happening, but I hoped the vagabonds that traveled this path would ignore the obvious, that they would go about their way and mind their own business because calling the police wasn't an option.

After searching the grounds and finding my beanie, I patted Jack's pockets and heard the crunch of keys. I pulled them free and went in search of his car, thanking God that I actually knew a guy who could take care of it.

Leonard Cramer wasn't a bad guy, per se, but he was shady and he ran a junkyard twenty miles outside of Tranquil Falls. I'd worked odd jobs for him in my tenth and eleventh grade years. He'd sold me the junker car I'd scrounged and saved for in high school and I was pretty sure he would know what to do to scrap a car that nobody wanted found.

I won't lie and claim driving Jack's car wasn't fun, and I would have floored the gas pedal to eat the twenty miles between my town and the junkyard if I wasn't scared to death of getting caught. Making sure to drive at the speed limit despite the way the car wanted to be opened wide and driven as it was intended, I pulled into Leonard's yard at a little past three in the morning, his three Rottweilers charging the front gate, snapping and snarling for the unexpected visit.

Lights flicked on inside his small trailer, the door bursting open just before he yelled at the dogs to calm down. Obedient, they sniffed in my direction one last time before sauntering away to go back to their doghouses.

Wrapped in a robe, Leonard slowly meandered his way to the front gate, a gun in hand just in case I was a stranger lurking and attempting to steal something.

"Who's out there?" He peered into the darkness, his eyes widening a fraction when he recognized my face. "Holden?"

"It's me," I called out in response as I tucked my hands into my pockets and walked against the freezing wind that was whipping through the junkyard.

With a voice laced in suspicion, he asked, "Do I want to know why you're at my front gate at three in the morning with a car that costs more than one hundred thousand dollars?"

"No, sir. You don't. But I was wondering if you want the car."

Brows rising up his head, he puckered his lips and whistled. "I take it this isn't your car and you have a good reason for it to disappear?"

"Something like that," I answered with chattering teeth.

He rocked back on his heels and eyed me for a few minutes, but the dollar signs he saw in a car like Jack's must have shoved his curiosity to the side. "I can take care of it, and since that implicates me, you know I'll keep my mouth shut."

Relief flooded me. "That's what I was hoping for."

"Toss me the keys, Holden, and we'll pretend this night never happened."

Approaching the gate, I flung the keys over the top of it, Leonard easily snatching them out of the air with one hand, his hairline much farther back than I remembered. "How are you getting back home from here?"

I blew out a big breath, resignation settling inside me as I scrubbed the back of my neck with my hand to ease some of the tension. "I guess I'm walking."

"In this weather? I don't think so. Give me a minute to get dressed. We'll stow the car and I'll drive you back in my truck."

The drive back to Tranquil Falls was silent, and by four thirty, Leonard dropped me off at the border into town. He waved as he drove off, the hour or so he'd given me worth every penny he made off the encounter. I trudged down the dark streets, keeping to the shadows, not too worried that anyone would see me and remember. In this area of the neighborhood, people had learned to ignore other people's business and were good about keeping to themself.

I walked inside my house at a few minutes past five, the sun just beginning to rise over the horizon to cast the sky in streaks of color, a sunlit fire in the distance as the Earth continued to turn through time and space.

The first place I went after slamming the front door closed was to my room to check on Michaela. With the hit

112

she'd taken to her face, I was worried she could have a concussion, but not enough that I was willing to seek out medical help just yet. She stirred when I opened the door, her swollen eyes blinking open.

Seeing that she wasn't dead was enough for me. Closing the door, I walked down the hall to Deli's room and found her awake and sitting on the side of her bed. "Hey," I called softly, "why are you up so early?"

Deli's hair fell down her back as she turned her head, big blue eyes staring up at me with confusion rolling behind them. "I feel like there's something wrong."

Sighing, I moved to sit on the floor in front of her, my back leaning against her wall. "Nothing's wrong. Why would you think that?"

Shaking her head, she blinked her eyes, the corner of her mouth curling down in concern. "I don't know. Maybe it has to do with mom and dad. Have they come yet?"

I didn't think it was possible for my world to shatter apart more than it already had that night, but hearing Deli's question crushed me into dust, scattered me on soft winds until I was nothing more than a speck lingering on a dirty floor. "They're not coming, Del. I've told you that."

Tears shimmered in her eyes. I wanted to take her in my arms and protect her from the world, wanted to comfort her and sing to her, but I couldn't bring myself to touch her because I was too dirty after killing Jack. I was tainted. I was dangerous and not sane enough to touch someone as fragile as her.

She didn't answer, just sat quietly watching her fingers braid together in her lap.

"Deli, I've asked you before and I'll ask again: Will you please go see Uncle Scott for Christmas? I think

113

getting out the house will be good for you. It'll be healthier than sitting here."

"How long do you want me to stay away?"

A knife twisted in my heart to hear her say it that way. "It's not that I want you to stay away. It's just that you deserve a good Christmas and I can't give it to you with my work schedule. I'm working doubles that entire week. We need the money for the bills."

Seconds crept past becoming sandspurs that scratched my skin with every silent tick tock. "I already called Uncle Scott. Yesterday after we talked and you left for work. He's picking me up this morning."

The relief that flooded me was the same as being doused with cold water after walking for days in the grueling sun. "Thank you," I breathed out.

Her voice was tiny. "What about you, Holden? What about your Christmas?"

"I'm working, Del. I'll have people around me, even if it is a whip-cracking boss and three grumpy guys cooking burgers."

Laughing softly, she pinned me with her eyes. "I need to pack up if I'm going to be ready by the time Uncle Scott gets here."

I was thrilled she was finally getting out of the house, and if I didn't have the events of the night weighing me down, I would have jumped up and danced through her room. This was a huge step for her. Since she came home from the hospital, she hadn't stepped foot outside the house. I wanted her skin to feel the sunlight again, wanted her to remember there was a life outside the tragedy that wrecked us. I'd tried to help her as best I could, but it's hard to hold a person above water when you're drowning beneath the surface yourself.

"It's kind of early for him to pick you up. What time is he supposed to arrive?"

114

She rolled her eyes and laughed again. I clung onto the sound, wanted to beg her to keep laughing because it might be the last time I'd ever get to hear it. Two years ago, all I had was time to give her and now even that had run out.

"He's old, Holden. He gets up before the crack of dawn and goes to sleep at five in the afternoon when the sun goes down again. You know that."

I did know it, but Uncle Scott had kept those hours even before he was officially old. The man had a circadian rhythm so in tune with the sun and moon that he didn't need a watch to know what time it was. Looking up in the sky, he could tell you it down to the minute.

Silence fell between us again, but I wanted to fill it with endless conversation, wanted to tell her I loved her and that I was sorry I'd let other people ruin our lives. I wanted to spill all my horrible secrets, reveal them to her just so she'd understand why I had to say goodbye, but I couldn't force that weight on her. Not now. Not at the same moment she was taking the first step forward to reclaim her life.

How do tell someone goodbye without actually saying it?

"I love you, Deli. I hope you know that."

Her lips tipped up into a smile. "Of course, I know that, stupid. You've been saying it since we were little kids."

Smiling back, I answered, "I know. But I thought you needed to hear it one more time."

"Dork," she chided me through her laughter. "I'll be back after the holidays. Stop acting like I'm leaving forever."

In truth, it would be forever, she just didn't know it yet. Murder was a crime deserving of capital punishment. The death penalty. A life incarcerated and caged until the day came that they stuck a needle in my arm and told me to sleep tight. With as young as I was, there was a chance I'd get life without parole, but I was sure that Jack's parents and his fancy, bulldog lawyers would push and push until they were certain I'd lose my life for this.

Even if it wasn't my fault.

Even if their son was such an unrelenting bully that he caused the fight that got him killed.

He was the prized Prince and I was the commoner, my life not worthy of his.

"I know you're not, Del." I hated to lie, but I did it anyway, just so I didn't have to see her face when the truth came out. I wanted to remember her smiling. I was selfish like that. "I'll be here when you get back."

Shaking her head in disbelief, she stood from her bed and walked inside her closet to pack. I leaned my head against the wall and sat watching her, soaking in the last minutes I had as a free man taking care of my sister.

This was the hardest moment I'd ever faced in my life. Harder than losing my parents. Harder than seeing Deli broken and damaged in her hospital bed. At least, back then, I'd still had hope in my heart that everything hadn't been lost.

That hope was gone now, scorched and shredded, the minutes ticking past within the sad reality that when the police found Jack's body, it would be the end of me.

The end of me.

The end of every dream I had of leaving this place and finally carving out a life of my own.

The only prayer I had left when this was all said and done was that it wouldn't be the end of my sister.

CHAPTER TWELVE

Michaela

Being bound and gagged has many disadvantages. It's something you never really think about in life, a situation you never fully consider. Sure, you see it in the movies and think how much it would suck, but you don't appreciate the practical aspects, like the inability to get up and go to the bathroom when you need to.

The sun had risen outside Holden's window several hours before, the house as quiet as a tomb outside his door. He'd woken me when he peeked inside earlier, but since then I'd been alone and miserable, my bladder was screaming for relief.

Another fact I'd never considered about being bound and helpless was that every small movement caused the ropes to scrape your skin raw, the burning sensation crawling up my arms until I wanted to scream in response. I would have done just that if I wasn't terrified that Holden had lost it and would come charging in to shut me up once and for all.

It must have been mid-morning by the time he came through the door, his hair a mess and the skin beneath his eyes bruised and darkened. He was dressed in clean clothes and he'd washed the blood from his face and hands, but the scrape was still obvious on his forehead, his knuckles wrapped in gauze.

"Do you need to use the bathroom?" he asked.

Yes! Oh God, yes! I would have yelled the answer if I weren't gagged.

He shuffled over on exhausted steps, his hands gentle as he worked at the knot binding my ankles. Once they were free, he examined the skin, my breath hissing against the gag from the burn.

"Damn. I didn't mean for that to happen."

Mumbling from behind the gag, I hoped to grab his attention. There was actual regret behind his eyes when he turned to look at me. "I have a first aid kit in the kitchen. We can bandage you up when you're done using the bathroom." He held up two fingers. "How many fingers am I holding up?"

Confusion pulled my brows together and I mumbled again. Shaking his head, he ripped the gag from my mouth and tossed it aside. "How many fingers?"

I had to clear my throat to answer. "Two, why?"

Grabbing my arm, he pulled me into a sitting position, his eyes averted when he guided my legs over the side and explained, "I'm just making sure you don't have a concussion."

"I'm not sure that's how it works."

He shrugged a huge shoulder, "I'm not a doctor."

I must have weighed nothing to him because he gripped my arm and lifted me to my feet one handed, balancing me in place until he was sure I was steady on my feet. "Are you going to untie my hands?"

"We're not to that point yet."

"How will I wipe?"

"You'll figure it out," he said, walking me to the adjacent bathroom and pushing open the door. Tucking me inside, he flipped on a light and shut the door. His presence lingered just outside, a shadow spilling across the floor from beneath the door. I guess he would have to listen to me pee, because he hadn't moved far enough away to keep from hearing everything I did in here.

After finishing my business and getting inventive to use the toilet paper, I walked the short distance to look at my reflection in the mirror. I looked like hell, my skin mottled and red over my cheekbone, the beginning of a nasty bruise. Droplets of blood splattered my face, but I couldn't determine where they came from. My skin wasn't broken.

Turning on the water, I did my best to splash some over my face to wipe away the dirt that smudged it. There wasn't much to be done about the leaves and twigs clinging to my hair, not with my hands bound.

Stepping out of the bathroom, I almost collided with Holden's chest, my neck craning so I could look up at him.

"Are you hungry?"

Normally, my stomach would have been growling by that point in the morning, but I couldn't think of food with the ball of dread tumbling around inside it. "Not really. I'm too scared to eat."

His eyes met mine. "Scared of what? Me?"

Taking a chance with my life, I nodded. "You kind of kidnapped me."

The skin wrinkled between his eyes. "You kind of left me with no choice. You jumped me with your psychopath for a boyfriend."

"I didn't jump you. I tried to stop him."

Recognition filtered through his gaze, a memory bubbling to the surface then floating away again. Noticing the confusion, I asked, "Don't you remember what happened?"

"Not really," he answered absently. Gripping my bicep again, he walked me out of the room, through his house and to the kitchen, shoving me down into a chair by the table before walking away to look through a cabinet.

"What do you mean 'not really'? If you can't remember anything then how do you know Jack is dead?" A glimmer of hope shot through me, the feeling mixed with disappointment that Holden may have been wrong about Jack. On one hand, I prayed there was someone out

119

there who knew Holden had me, and on the other, I dreaded the thought that I would have to go back to Jack again as his miserable, perfectly complacent girlfriend.

Holden pulled a first aid kit from the cabinet, flipped the lid and fished around in it to find the supplies he needed. "I know Jack is dead because I saw the body. I hid the body, in fact, nestled it among the other stray trash where it belongs." His eyes lifted to study me. "Why do you ask?"

He didn't wait for my answer. Turning away, he opened a drawer, pulled a plastic baggie from inside and went to work filling it with ice from the freezer. It didn't matter that he turned before I could respond. I didn't have an answer to give him. How could I admit openly that I preferred Jack was dead? It was a horrible thought, but yet I found myself thinking it.

Stalking toward me with his supplies in hand, Holden set everything on the table beside me, offering me the bag of ice. I was still eyeing it when he barked out, "It's for your cheek. Just take it so I can stop feeling so bad about the swelling."

Taking the ice, I held it to my cheek with both hands. "You didn't cause the swelling. That was Jack."

"He wouldn't have hit you if you weren't trying to pull him off me." Genuine regret filtered through his expression. It shouldn't have shocked me, but it did. I wasn't used to people feeling sorry for the way I was treated.

Whispering, I said, "You didn't do this, Holden."

He kneeled down in front of me, his fingers gently probing the rope burn on my ankles. His skin was warm against mine, rough like he worked with his hands often. "I know it's not my fault. It's your fault for waiting by the tracks to jump me. I've never done anything to either of you, and you've taken everything from me."

Peering up, the hatred had returned to his tired gaze. "I've done nothing to you. Not a damn thing. I've barely spoken two words to you since we were kids."

Swallowing hard, I breathed deeply. "Jack was waiting for you because he's still mad you broke his nose in the cafeteria. He wanted revenge."

Holden's shoulders shook with a bark of humorless laughter. "Hitting me with a car wasn't enough revenge? Was he upset he didn't kill me along with my parents?"

Shame blanketed me. "I'm sorry about your mom and dad. Nobody meant for that to happen."

He was smoothing a salve over my ankles by the time he muttered, "Yeah, well, decisions have consequences."

My thoughts wandered back to the events of the night, each soul-wrenching detail sharp and in focus. "My cheek wasn't damaged when Jack hit me in the woods. Well, I mean, that probably didn't help, but-"

My voice drifted off when his blue eyes lifted to me again. Even kneeling down and hunched over, he was intimidating, a sleeping dragon that could open its eyes at any time while you searched for the hidden treasure. I was haunted by those eyes, always had been, even in high school.

"But?"

"But, he hit me the first time in his car. I was complaining and trying to get him to leave you alone."

Brows pulling together, he returned to bandaging my ankles. "Why would you put up with a guy like that? I would think with all the prim and proper rules of hoity-toity etiquette in your world, respecting women would be a rule for the men."

"Apparently Jack missed that rule. As well as my dad, or my brother." A sigh blew over my lips, sorrow crashing against me. "Maybe it's not a rule after all. Nobody seems to know it."

His head shook in disbelief. "Deli was jealous of the kids on your side of Tranquil Falls. I always told her not to be, always reminded her that the grass isn't necessarily greener on the better manicured lawns. What you're telling me confirms I was right to say it."

Finished with the bandages, he packed up his supplies and moved away. I hated the distance, hated the loss of his presence close by. Although fear had held me in its wicked grasp for the morning hours, Holden had a way of muting it - even when he was the one who had tied me up in the first place. It was an odd realization, one I tucked away to consider later.

"Delilah's really alive? She made it? Is she here?"

A feral smile stretched his lips, there one second, gone the next. It wasn't a friendly expression, wasn't exactly sane, but I didn't sense he meant any harm by it. "Delilah is alive, no thanks to you or Jack. But there are different degrees of alive, aren't there?"

Planting his hands on the counter, he stared at me. "If you mean alive in the sense that her heart is beating and her lungs draw in air, but she's too broken to step outside, and believes her parents are coming home one day, then yes. She's alive. If you mean, she dances and smiles and enjoys the same hobbies she used to enjoy, or if you mean she goes to school and does stupid girl sleepovers, or goes to movies or even out to dinner once in a while without fear of missing her parents and not being around when they return home, then no. In that case, Deli died two years ago. Very much *thanks* to you and Jack."

Turning his eyes away, he sorted the items in the first aid kit, his voice low when he added, "Not that we can afford all those fun activities for her. I'm a horrible caregiver."

My heart dropped to my stomach, the harrowing truth of Delilah's life slapping me in the face. Delilah was such a pretty girl. I liked her more than all of my friends. She was real, not some fake persona she tugged on each morning along with a shirt and pants. She was also the best dancer I'd ever seen. Better than all the girls on the team, though nobody would dare admit it. "She doesn't know your parents are dead? She's never been to their graves?"

"She doesn't go outside, remember?"

"Is she here now?"

His shoulders withered, the tension melting away before my eyes. "No. She left this morning to go see our uncle for the holidays. It's the first time she's been away from the house since she returned from the hospital. I'm proud of her for it."

"I'm sorry, Holden. I didn't know. The last time I saw her, she was screaming at me."

His stare pierced me. "When did that happen?"

"When you were in the hospital. I tried to come see you, but Delilah chased me out. I'd never heard her scream before, had never seen her so angry. She kept insisting I was small. I didn't know what she meant. But you called me small, too."

Grinning, he replied, "That's because you're small."

I knew it was an insult, knew he was smiling to throw it at me. But despite his joy to call me some derogatory term that only he and his sister knew, I couldn't help liking the way he smiled. "Are you happy to insult me?"

"No," he answered, leaning against the counter at his back and crossing his arms over his chest. The material of his t-shirt stretched taut over his biceps. "I'm happy that Deli used the term correctly."

I gave him a few seconds to explain, but he remained silent. "Are you going to let me in on the secret?"

"Not now. We're not there yet."

Not there yet...

Our unfortunate circumstances were slammed to the forefront of my thoughts, trepidation creeping along my spine with tiny icy fingers. "How long are you planning on keeping me, Holden? We can't stay like this forever."

Holden flinched as if slapped by the same circumstances, by the reminder that our being here together wasn't normal. Rubbing at the back of his neck, he averted his gaze, focused those hypnotic blue eyes on the counter in front of him. "I'm not sure. I want to take care of a few things. Make sure Deli has somewhere to go. That she has someone who can take care of her."

"Why?" I asked, genuinely confused as to why he felt the need to make the arrangements of a dying man.

Slowly, his gaze lifted, raw truth revealed in the way he stared at me, in the tone of his deep voice. "I killed a man, Michaela. I killed your boyfriend, Jack. And I don't remember doing it."

Tears welled in my eyes, but not for Jack. Never for him. "I can help. I can tell the police what I know, that Jack was waiting for you-"

"Did you see me kill him?"

Shaking my head, I admitted, "No. He hit me when I tried to help you. I don't remember anything after that." I remembered what happened before Holden walked home, remembered what Jack had done to me in the car to amuse himself while we waited. I wished I didn't remember those details.

Holden's silence dragged my attention back to him, to the dark hole of a man that was the same, yet different, than the person I'd known when we were kids, than the person he'd been in high school. Our eyes locked, the weight of our situation settling over my shoulders as heavily as it rode him.

"That's as much as I remember, as well," he confessed on a soft voice. "But the moment he hit you, I must have snapped. Must have lost it. Because I can't remember what happened later, not until I was leaning against a tree and Jack was lying at my feet, dead."

"Maybe if we just told them it was an accident-"

"The front of his skull was caved in, Michaela. His face was caved in. Do you understand? That wasn't an accident. I may not remember doing it, but I could tell by looking at him that I hit him over and over, probably kept hitting him after he was already dead. The police won't look at that as an accident. Jack died painfully. And I don't regret that fact."

My gorge rose, my hands pressing against my stomach in response to the pain. "Can I have some water?" Something. I needed something to fill the emptiness of my gut, to ease the dread still spinning and tumbling down in there.

Snatching a glass from a drying rack, Holden pulled a bottle of water from the fridge and filled it. His steps shook the floor when he walked to hand it to me. I swallowed it down, my eyes closing at the instant relief of cold liquid traveling down my throat. Pulling the glass away, my eyes widened to see Holden studying me.

"Feel better?"

Nodding in response, I handed the glass back to him. "Yes. Thank you."

He was placing the glass in the sink when I offered to help. "Maybe if I tell them what I know? He went to that diner specifically to mess with you. Clive called him the day before and said he saw you working there. It wasn't a coincidence that Jack and I showed up. After we were kicked out, we were headed to a party on our side of Tranquil Falls, but we reached the same curve where he hit you two years ago and he spun the car around, sped back to hide near the tracks so he could wait for you. The police have to see that for what it was. Jack caused this fight. You were only defending yourself."

"It won't matter."

Anger flared through me, not at Holden. Even if he had taken me from the scene and tied me up, I wasn't angry at him. I knew he'd panicked, and I was oddly thankful that he hadn't left me lying there in the freezing cold, in a path traveled by the homeless and the drug dealers that lived in the abandoned houses. It hadn't occurred to me until that moment, that by taking me, Holden most likely saved my life. I couldn't simply let him go to jail for something that wasn't his fault. "It will matter because I'll tell them what happened."

The flash of a smile stretched his face again. It was a nervous expression, a tiny hint of his thoughts spilling out into the open before he could hide them again. Not happy. Not in a situation like this. "I can't trust that, Michaela. Not you. Not ever."

"Why?"

His eyes pinned me. "Let me ask you this: Two years ago, when Jack hit me with his car, did you tell the police he intentionally gunned his engine toward the curve? Did you happen to mention he was racing toward me on purpose?"

My argument died in my throat. No. I hadn't said a word to the police about it because Jack had threatened me. His family, and mine, had told me in no uncertain terms what would happen if I said anything.

"That's what I thought," he said, filling the heavy silence. "You didn't tell the truth when he almost killed me back then. What would possibly make me think you'll tell the truth now?"

Slamming the lid closed on the first aid kit, he almost ripped the cabinet door from the hinges when he opened it to put the kit away. With his back to me, he spread his

126

arms to the side, planting his palms on the counter to hold his weight. His head hung low, his broad shoulders taking up too much space. "It doesn't matter anyway. Justice doesn't exist for people like me, Michaela. I can't afford it, and the system is designed to throw people like me away because we can't pay for the fancy lawyers with their fancy legal pads and fancy pens. I'll get stuck with some wet behind the ears public defender who doesn't give a damn what happens to me. Someone who will bend to the will of Jack's family because he is the golden boy when it comes to the law."

"That's not fair," I whispered.

"Nobody ever said life was fair. You have to purchase fair. And if you don't have the cash, well..."

"What are we going to do, Holden?"

He twisted to glance at me from over his shoulder. "There's no 'we' in this. As for what I'm going to do, I'm going to make arrangements for my sister and try to earn as much money as I can for her before the police come knocking on my door. You are going to stay here until they come. The last thing I need is for you to go running off and telling everybody what happened before I have a chance to do what I can for Deli."

Blinking in his direction, I couldn't find my voice to respond.

Holden pushed away from the counter and moved to stand next to me - above me - his size so much more apparent when he was standing practically on top of you and looking down. "I'm sorry for the inconvenience, but I think you owe me at least some cooperation when considering the circumstances and the part you played."

Grabbing my arm, Holden hauled me up from my seat and walked me to his bedroom to sit me on his bed. He didn't say another word before stalking out and shutting me inside to think about everything he'd said.

CHAPTER THIRTEEN

Holden

I wasn't lying when I told Michaela that life isn't fair. Not for me, not for anyone, really. Maybe that's where my statement had been dishonest, in the moment I'd applied the phrase only to those unlucky enough to be born into poverty.

In truth, fair doesn't exist no matter the size of your bank account, the size of your heart, or the amount of years you'd lived fighting to do everything right despite your circumstances. Fair is an ideal, a utopian distinction, a theory that can only exist in vacuums where bad things can't happen to good people.

Fair hadn't happened to my family, not to my parents, not to Deli. Perhaps I deserved what was coming to me, and I could even argue that my parents had done something in their lives to deserve the fate that destroyed them, but Deli? Deli was a perfect angel. She'd never hurt a fly in her entire life. Yet she still pulled the short straw, and now her life would be ruined again because of it.

Sadly, I was the short straw, and every time Deli relied on me, she was let down.

Even this morning, I'd let her down. So exhausted from a night piling felonies one on top of the other, I'd fallen asleep on her floor watching her get ready. I'd curled up on the soft, fluffy, pink rug I always thought was ridiculous, but she loved, and I'd slept through the moment she took her first step back into the world - into a life beyond me, beyond tragedy, beyond all the horrible consequences of my actions that day in the cafeteria.

I wanted to see that step, wanted to paint a picture of it in my mind that I could dedicate to canvas, recording it and memorializing it because it was a vision of strength in a woman so tiny you would never think her body could contain a soul as fierce as hers. But I'd slept through it. I hadn't been standing there beside her as she faced a nightmare from which she may never wake. And Deli, my sweet, kind, innocent sister, had taken that step regardless. Maybe she'd tried to wake me, or maybe she'd let me sleep, had accepted the burden onto herself, even while knowing I would do anything, be anything she needed, just so she wouldn't be left to fight alone.

I didn't know what would happen to her when she learned that coming home was as futile an option for her as it had always been for our parents. With that thought in mind, I'd picked up the phone several times to call Scott, to beg him to make sure she was safe when I was gone, but I'd hung up each and every time because I was too afraid he'd tell her what was going on, ruining the first real Christmas she had since returning from the hospital.

Promising myself to call later, once everything was arranged and I had some answers to give, I scrubbed my palms over my face, pushed up from the dining room chair and paced the living room just to ease the frustration crashing through me with the force of a tornado.

All I could do was wait at that point. There was nothing more to arrange than finding Deli a place to stay, and leaving what money we had and the deed to the house where Deli and Scott could find it. It's all we had left in this world - a few hundred dollars and a house that sat on the wrong side of the tracks, worthless.

Pacing wasn't helping to bleed the tension from inside me. Storming in the direction of my studio - of my parents' old bedroom that I'd emptied and converted three weeks after they'd been lowered in the ground - I let myself inside and breathed deeply. The smell of paint always soothed me, the canvases sitting on their easels waiting for me to finish whatever image had been assigned to them. It was a mix of subjects, but mostly people. Some were random strangers that had caught my eye, while others were of Deli and my parents. The landscapes and still objects were always easy to complete, but the people, the souls filled with memory, tragedy, victory, and remorse, those were always the ones that took the longest.

Even now, I had seven canvases lined up side by side, the empty eyes staring at me from empty faces, begging to be brought to life. One was the face of an angel glancing to the side, a blonde girl with pigtails in her hair looking toward a future that wouldn't be there. Another was of a silver haired woman, her arms crossed over her large chest, her mouth opened as she scolded an employee for slacking off, the hint of amusement gleaming behind her eyes. The one next to that was of a father and son, the father's arms in the air ready to catch the child who laughed above him. There was a random drug user after that, a vagrant that wandered the neighborhood. A vibrant woman who was tough as nails came after, her expression caught at the moment she laughed the loudest. Canvas after canvas after canvas just waiting for me to fill them.

I was safe here, among memories, among slices of time frozen in place, never advancing to the day that I lost everything.

Drop cloths were a sea of paint-dabbed white, color splashed and smeared across virgin snow, the floors protected from the moments I became so lost in what I was creating that cleanliness was a second thought. Crossing the room, I selected a CD of my favorite songs, a playlist I'd made years ago that represented these images, their lives and losses, the lyrics flowing through me as I brought brush to canvas, the tempo and beat pulsing beneath my skin as I transformed the photographs in my mind into a picture that others could see as well.

Each picture is a message, a lesson, a viewpoint that delves into the heart of what life is all about. They reveal truth, illustrating clearly how when I look at the world through my tired eyes, I see it unmasked, unpolluted, a monochromatic collage of epics and stories that have paint smeared throughout to highlight the parts I found the most beautiful and intriguing. Nobody sees the world like me. And where my words fail to convey what I'm seeing, my paintbrush becomes the vehicle for my voice.

Hours passed as the music played, as I got caught in a trance of chaos and pain, every drop of it bleeding out through the colors I pulled across canvas. With the CD on repeat, I found myself revolving, a shadow beneath the eye drawing my attention before the music picked up pace and I was painting a sky. I was lost, you see, hypnotized, hiding. And the frustration and tension and gradual decay poured from my body to be absorbed by the paint-dabbed floor.

Eventually, just like every manic moment when truth explodes out onto the faces and snapshots I'd frozen in time, my energy waned leaving me exhausted, in need of my guitar.

I hit a button to stop the music's endless loop, grabbed a towel to wipe as much paint from my fingers as I could. It was never gone completely, always a stain, just like the lead dust from when I put pencil to paper.

Leaving the studio, I shuffled across the house, my bones weary, my muscles exhausted, but my mind was quiet, so quiet in fact that I didn't mind filling the silence with the strum of a guitar string, the complicated intros and flowing melodies that brought a song to life.

Opening my bedroom door, however, brought all the tension roaring back to the surface, a sleeping woman with hands bound, her mahogany hair like silk where it splayed across my blanket. *Click.* A snapshot frozen. *Click.* A slice of time that will forever exist within the confines of an abnormal mind.

If I had to give Michaela credit for one thing, it was that a word as simple as beautiful could never reveal all there was to see in her when she dropped the pretenses of her shallow life, and left herself exposed.

Michaela was never a shallow child, but then youth doesn't feel the need to pretend. It wasn't until she was eleven or twelve that she hid her true self from the world, disguising herself beneath fake smiles and pretty clothes. Though, her truth comes out when she dances. I only knew that because I'd taken Delilah to a practice, my eyes climbing from whatever picture I was sketching to watch Michaela spin.

She'd mesmerized me in those moments, and I'd be lying to claim I didn't have snapshots of her I wanted to paint.

Green eyes opened to stare back at me, the haze of sleep still clouding the color. Full lips opening on a small yawn, those eyes rounded wider when she remembered her hands were bound.

"Hey," she whispered, her voice gritty and tired. Attempting to push herself up, she fell over, exhaustion still weighing on her, thick and heavy.

Staggered by the sight of her, I'd stood frozen by the door, but moved when it became apparent she needed help to sit. Leaves and twigs were still stuck in her hair from the woods where Jack hit her, dirt still smudged along her jawline where she hadn't been able to completely wash it away. Guilt rode me for the first time that I was treating her poorly, that I'd stripped her of the

133

ability to see to her needs all because I was afraid she'd take off and go to the police.

I couldn't hold all of Jack's actions against her, she wasn't the person prodding him along. But what I could hold against her was the weakness that had kept her from being honest about what happened in the past, that kept her next to a man that treated me as horribly as he treated her. Her weakness wasn't deserving of being made to live as less than a human, wasn't deserving of having her basic needs denied.

"You need a shower," I commented softly, my finger tracing over the rope that bound her wrists. Kneeling in front of her, I lifted my gaze to see concern etched across her features.

"Do I stink?" she whispered back.

Her question tugged at the corner of my lip, the grin small, her eyes tracking the movement of my mouth to trace the shape.

"No. Not yet anyway, but you look like you've been rolling around in the woods."

Holding up her bound hands between us, she pointed out the obvious. "It's kind of hard to take care of my hair like this."

"I'm sorry," I breathed out.

"For what?" Genuine confusion flashed through her expression.

Chuckling, I answered, "For kidnapping you."

Working at the knot, I felt another sting of regret when she winced at the pain. "Sorry," I muttered again.

Leaning close, the floral scent of her perfume wafted beneath my nose. I liked the scent. It bothered me that I liked it. "It's fine. Stop apologizing."

The knot came loose, the skin beneath scraped raw. "Damn. I'm going to need to bandage these."

"Maybe I should take a shower first."

Suspicion flooded me. Peeking up at her, I realized how close her face was to mine, so close that I could see the brown and gold flecks in her eyes. "There are no windows in the bathroom, if you're hoping to escape."

"Actually," she replied, straightening her posture so that our lips weren't noticeably close, her breath colliding with mine. "I've been thinking about that."

"About escaping?" Brows drawn together, I was about to commend her on her honesty, but she laughed, cutting off my thoughts.

"No. Not about escaping. About staying."

"Okay," I said, stretching the word out longer than it should be. "What are you talking about?"

"After we talked this morning, after what you told me about Delilah and everything you've gone through because of Jack, I feel guilty. I'm sure you could have received a lot more money if the truth had come out about the auto accident. Enough to help more with the medical bills and daily expenses, or whatever. Part of what you and Delilah have gone through was my fault."

"Michaela-"

"No, listen to me." Spilling out the words harshly and with no patience at all, she looked pained and surprised both, as if she'd never asserted herself before. "Nobody ever listens to me. It's always me doing or saying whatever they want. But I need to say this, and I'd really appreciate it if you would just listen."

"Okay, I'm listening."

"Really?"

"Yes, really. Say what you need to say."

The poor girl was flustered, completely out of her realm to have the main floor in a conversation, and it made me wonder about her life, wonder if there wasn't more to her than I realized.

"I think I owe it to you to stay here as long as you need me to. For the past, for what happened last night." She shrugged. "For everything, I guess, even high school."

Standing, I backed away from her, leaned against a wall and crossed my arms over my chest. She wanted to stay? Was she insane? I killed her boyfriend and abducted her. I tied her up and shoved her in a room. What could possibly be going on inside her head to even suggest voluntarily staying?

She was nuts. She had to be. There was no other explanation.

"Micheala-"

Holding up a hand to silence me, she argued, "No, just listen. I know you need to make money, and, honestly, I think if we combine our heads on this, we might be able to get you out of it. We just need time, maybe? A few days to think and then we can come up with a plan to make sure you don't go to jail. You don't deserve it, Holden, and I'm not willing to just sit by and watch your life be ruined because of Jack."

Her expression tightened, her eyes narrowing, but not on me. "I hate Jack. I HATE him."

Michaela's words, I realized quickly, weren't spoken to convince me of her hatred, they were spoken to convince herself of their truth. Remaining silent, I simply listened like she'd asked, but I already knew my response would disappoint her. This wasn't just about Jack's death anymore. I'd added way too many crimes to the pile for there to be any hope I wasn't going to prison. But she was working something out inside herself, something that needed to be exorcised. My silence would allow her to do so.

"I think if we go to the police together and explain, if I can get to them and give my statement before my parents or Jack's family step in to intervene, then it'll be too late. They'll have the truth and nothing anybody says or does will be able to change it. I want to stand up for someone else for once. I'm tired of always doing what everybody else demands of me. I want to do what's right for a change."

Her gaze met mine, her stare hopeful. "What do you think?"

Maybe the kids at Tranquil Falls High had been right after all. Maybe I was crazy, because I found myself feeling sorry for a woman who was a symbol of everything that was wrong in my world. I should hate her. I should lock her away and not give a damn what happens while I set as much as I can to right. Yet, there I was, staring at her, wondering what had been done to her in life that made her so timid and tame.

Careful with my response only because I didn't want to be that tiny gust of wind that knocked her off this newfound course, I answered softly. "I think it's a nice idea on your part, a hell of a lot better than what you've done in the past. But I also know it's hopeless."

"It's not hopeless, Holden. Nothing is hopeless."

"This is."

Giving her no wiggle room with my impassive tone, I continued, "Had we gone to the police straight from the woods and told them, then maybe I would have had a chance. But that's not what happened. I panicked. I took you. I got rid of his car-"

"You got rid of his car?" Her eyes rounded. "How?"

"That's not important, what's important is that it has been eighteen hours since I killed a man. I also hid the body. I hid his car. And I kidnapped his girlfriend. This is looking really bad for me. I made some extremely stupid decisions. But this is where we are. You can still tell the police anything you want when they finally find me, but don't get your hopes up that justice will prevail. I'm going to prison."

I've seen a million surprising sights in my life, moments where I'd underestimated some danger, or a friend reacted in a way I would never expect to a joke or some other thing I said. I'd seen miracles happen, and tragedies. I'd witnessed comical events and depressing ones. But nothing surprised me more than the tears running down Michaela's cheeks. Either this woman was an accomplished actress, or she was truly upset that I was going to jail. "Why are you crying?"

"Because it's not fair."

We were back to that word again.

Michaela needed some comfort in this, she needed someone who would lie to her and say everything would be okay. But I couldn't be the person to provide her that comfort. She was still a symbol of my destruction, and I wasn't a liar.

"Maybe you should get that shower. Then we can bandage your wrists."

Nodding, Michaela pushed up from her bed and walked to the bathroom. Reaching out, I stopped her just before she could move through the door. She didn't look at me.

"If you're serious about wanting to help me for the next week or two, then I'd prefer it to tying you up. I want to trust you're not screwing me. But when it comes time for me to go, do not tell them you volunteered to stay here. It'll only get you in trouble, too."

The slow trail of tears down her cheek shimmered beneath the light. "Are you asking me to claim you held me against my will?"

"That's exactly what I'm asking you."

Her jaw tightened, her lips pulling into a thin line. "Can I get my shower now?"

"Will you tell them that, Michaela?"

An angry gaze shot to mine. "I'd like to think about it."

Remembering what she'd said about other people always telling her what to do, I didn't want to be like the rest of the assholes who barked commands at her. I didn't want to be another Jack. Giving her this time wouldn't hurt me, even if it would drive me up a wall not to know. Nodding my head once, I answered, "Yeah, you think about it. But I'd like an answer by tomorrow."

Michaela inclined her head, her eyes staring at my arm in silent request for me to let her pass. Slowly, I pulled it away, watching her move further into the bathroom and close the door.

CHAPTER FOURTEEN
Michaela

There was no way in hell I was thinking about it. Holden may have already accepted the fact that he was going to jail for what happened, but I wouldn't. There had to be a way to fix this, had to be a way to make the police understand that Jack was the aggressor, the bully, the person that should have been locked up a long time ago for all the crimes he'd committed since we were sophomores in high school.

The fights.

The drugs.

The parties...

Jack Thorne was never a good person. Since the moment he learned what he could take from the world, he took, and he took and he took. Never giving back. Never caring who was hurt in the process.

I was one of Jack's victims. Not at first, not when he still felt the need to don a mask of concern when it came to me. But after the accident with Holden, Jack's mask had fallen aside, and if I said anything he didn't like, if I questioned him, if I didn't mindlessly follow him, he hurt me as much as he hurt the others.

Never more than Holden, but then pain doesn't always come in degrees, at least not the kind that rips your feet out from under you and leaves you tumbling through a life you never asked for.

If any crimes had been committed last night, Jack had been the criminal. For the drugs. For stalking Holden. For starting the fight. For what he'd done to me in the car while we waited.

Finishing my shower, I dried off, wrapped the towel around my body and wiped the steam from the small mirror above the sink. My face was swollen on one side where Jack had struck me. Bringing my fingers to the skin that was deepening in color, I pressed softly along the length of the bone. It wasn't broken, but the bruise would take weeks to heal. The examination of my face also revealed that my lip was split. Not enough to bleed heavily, but enough to cause the skin to swell, to look fuller than the rest of my mouth.

It was an odd feeling to be the person who was abused, and yet to also be the person who felt shame for the beating. Jack should have been the one carrying the burden of shame, and yet here I was, the victim, carrying it for him.

Perhaps I could have forgiven myself for the pain inflicted without my permission, but the shame, that was something I took on myself, and I wouldn't carry it any longer.

Helping Holden wouldn't just be what was right for him, it would be what was right for me.

Smiling despite the bruises, I reached for my dirty clothes when a knock sounded at the door. "I left some clothes for you on the bed, Michaela. They're Deli's, but I think they should fit. I'll be in the living room so you have privacy to get dressed."

My head turned toward the deep voice. "Thank you."

He didn't respond, but I could hear his footsteps fading as he left his room and shut the door.

The clothes fit, sort of. Deli and I were the same size in chest and hips, but I had a few inches on her, which made the legs of the sweatpants ride up to my calves. Still, they were warm and clean, a rainbow of color in contrast to Holden's room. I found it funny that an artist's room would be nothing but black and white. If not for the pencil sketches pinned to the walls, the guitar sitting on a stand in the corner of the room, I would have never guessed Holden considered this his space.

I wanted to take my time, now that I wasn't bound, to walk and look closely at the images he'd sketched, but I felt like doing so would be intrusive. Holden had never been an open person. Even as a kid, he was reserved and quiet, a significant presence that hovered over the rest of us, but was always trapped in his head. The other children made fun of him for it, and it was his silence that was the beginning of the labels they assigned him in school.

Crazy.

Freak.

Goth.

Loser.

Hundreds more. So many that I couldn't keep up with them all.

Yet, none of them fit.

Holden never reacted, unless it came to his sister. He'd said Delilah had been jealous of us, when, in truth, we should have been jealous of Delilah. How many people can say they have one person in their life that is willing to give up everything just so they can be happy? I could never say it, but Delilah could.

Another knock. "You okay in there?"

My head snapped to the sound. "Yeah, sorry. I was just -"

Just thinking about what a good person you are. Just spinning in a slow circle wishing I could touch, observe, smell, learn everything there is to know about you.

"Just getting dressed," I lied.

Crossing the room, I opened the door to find Holden leaning against the wall beside it. His black hair was a disheveled mess framing his face, his clothes and hands spotted with paint in an array of color. When had he been painting, and where was the art? I wanted to see it, but I didn't feel comfortable asking.

"I cooked some food. I know you weren't hungry earlier, but-"

"I can eat," I admitted, my stomach no longer pained by the dread I'd felt earlier.

He simply nodded his head and led me to the dining room table. Two plates of pasta sat on its surface, the smell heavenly. It was slightly embarrassing how quickly I devoured the meal. Within ten minutes, I'd practically licked my plate clean while Holden was still twirling the spaghetti around on his fork.

"Not hungry?"

His gaze lifted to mine. There one second before dropping back to the twirl of noodles on his fork. "Not really," he breathed out.

Something was riding him, and I didn't need to think hard to figure out what it was. "Are you scared?"

"More like annoyed," he admitted. "Not by you, just by this entire situation. I'm not scared of prison. It is what it is. Just worried for Del."

"I wasn't lying to you, Holden. I want to help. And if staying here helps, then you have me for as long as you need."

His fork clattered onto his plate. "By tomorrow, your family will be looking for you, if they're not already. No matter what, this gets worse and worse."

Sad laughter burst from my lips, the truth of my life depressing. "My family won't be looking for me until after I don't show for Christmas. Neither will Jack's. Every time we come down here during school breaks, we always stay at Clive's house or wherever the parties are being held."

Anger flashed behind his eyes, his jaw ticking once. "Yeah, the parties..." he mumbled beneath his breath.

143

Eyes meeting mine, he said, "If it hadn't been for those damn parties I wouldn't be sitting here right now. I'd be in another state doing something other than washing dishes or cooking at a diner."

Brows pulling together in confusion, I opened my mouth and closed it several times, my thoughts taking time to catch up with the need to speak. "You never went to any of the parties. Why do you blame them?"

Holden leaned back in his seat, the wood creaking beneath his weight as he pinned me with blue eyes that saw everything. "Deli wanted to go to those parties, but knowing what I knew about them, there was no way in hell I'd let her. It's what caused the fight in the cafeteria that day. Clive reaching for my sister with hands that had taken advantage of so many girls."

"I wouldn't have let anything happen to her."

He barked out a laugh. "Yeah, sure. How many of the other girls did you help?"

Holden's glare pinned me in place, the weight of it as heavy and truthful as his question. I didn't respond, couldn't with the shame choking me. Jack's shame. Clive's shame. The team's shame. My shame for never saying a word about it.

"That's what I thought," he mumbled. Standing, he took our plates from the table and dropped them on the kitchen counter, his palms pressing against the counter holding his weight, his head hung low. "How could you stay silent knowing what those guys were doing to so many girls? Why have all of you stayed silent?"

"Fear," I answered honestly. "Everybody knows what happens at those parties. It wasn't some big secret. I never understood why the girls let it happen to them, why they kept showing up and swallowing whatever pills one of the guys gave them. But they did. They still do. I think they all want to believe that they'll be the one that snags the heart of whatever creep they're allowing to use them. But when the sun rises the following morning, it's always the same. Tears followed by the girls leaving, drowning in the shame of it all."

Our eyes met when he glanced up. "So, what happened was consensual?"

I shook my head. "Not always. Not after the girls passed out and were...shared," I admitted, the knot in my throat breaking the word apart. "But saying something would have destroyed their reputations. They would have been torn apart at school, labeled with all sorts of horrible names. Nobody took on the team, Holden. You know that. Not even the teachers, administrators or the police would go against the team. They held the power and influence."

Snatching one of the plates from the counter, he turned to scrape the food into the garbage. "That's disgusting, Michaela. I hope you know that."

A tear slipped from my eye, hot and guilty. "I know."

Tossing the plate in the sink, Holden didn't react to the clamor, but I did. After staring at the plate for far too long, he finally looked at me again. "I work a double tomorrow, which means I'll leave here by ten in the morning and won't return again until ten at night. So, you'll be free to go. I won't tie you up again."

"I'm not leaving. You need time. It's the least I can do for you."

Eyeing me with suspicion, he shook his head. "If you say so."

"I mean it."

He simply shook his head again and went to work cleaning the dishes.

The silence between us was awkward. Holden and I weren't friends. We had never really known each other beyond school and our shared connection through

Delilah. We were complete opposites in everything. I didn't know what to say, or how to act. So I did what I did best: shut up.

The minutes ticked past as he cleaned the kitchen, his eyes darting to me every so often, absent of friendliness or affinity. It wasn't like I could blame him. I would have been suspicious of me, too. But, I wanted to prove myself, not just to him. To myself. Staying here and figuring out how to save him from prison would be my first sojourn into a life I'd always wanted, but was too afraid to live. Jack wasn't around to knock me back in line. I was free. I just had to decide how I would hold on to that freedom.

Saying as much while Holden continued cleaning, I wasn't sure how I expected him to react. With praise, maybe? Support? All he did was glance at me every so often, the suspicion still firmly in place. But as I told him more about my desire to move beyond being a tiny little mouse running her maze, pity filtered into his gaze.

Pity.

Holden Bishop pitied the woman who had always lived a life more fortunate than his.

He pitied me when he was the one facing prison for everything this town had done to him.

I had no other choice than to swallow that pity, no matter how bitter it tasted.

It was the first time I encountered a person who wasn't jealous of me. The first time I didn't have someone falling at my feet wanting to be me. I wasn't sure what to do with it. My desire for Holden to approve of me was outside my realm of understanding. But I did want that approval. I craved it.

Unable to take how he said nothing, how he didn't react, how he simply kept glancing at me like I was some annoying fly buzzing past his ear, I asked, "Why aren't you saying anything?"

146

A single brow lifted above his eye, silent thoughts lingering in his head that I wanted to hear but feared would never be spoken.

"What do you want from me, Michaela?" His stare finally met mine. "To cheer for you that you've decided to be a decent person? To jump up and down and dance across the floor because you think you have it in yourself not to be weak and fake as fuck? Do you want applause? Lives have been ruined. Not just mine, not just my family's, but all the lives of those girls that were used while you sat back and watched. This entire town is just like you. I wouldn't believe a place like this could exist if I didn't live in it. And now that you've decided to turn over a new leaf, I'm supposed to breathe out in relief and smile? Congratulations on discovering that you're a selfish bitch. I'm proud of you. But from where I stand now, I'd like to see you actually live up to your decision. I'd like to see how your epiphany will work to repair the damage that has been done. Because that's what your silence has accomplished. It's *damaged* people. And some of us can't be repaired."

Slapping the towel down on the counter, he stalked away, ignoring the tears dripping down my cheeks, unconcerned for the bucket of reality he'd just dumped down my throat. Turning to look at me from over his shoulder, he said, "I'm going to bed. You're welcome to sleep on the couch or in Deli's room. We'll see if you're still here in the morning."

With that, he disappeared into his room, the door clicking shut quietly.

I'd never felt more alone in my life. Never felt so exposed and naked.

Not knowing what to do with myself, I sat in my chair for a while, my thoughts always returning to what Holden had said. It was painful, the criticism, the sharp edge of his words echoing endlessly, but I absorbed those words, tasted them, rolled them around in my head and over my tongue. There wasn't a single one of them that was dishonest or vengeful. Holden had bluntly stated the sad truth, and I was left to learn how to make up for it.

Finally standing from my seat, I padded barefoot along the floors, took a left down a short hall and found Delilah's room. On the outside of the door was a placard that had her name scrawled in a rainbow of colors. I wasn't prepared for what I found when I pushed the door open.

I nearly crumbled after taking two steps inside.

Time was frozen within these four walls. A wash of girly color with pink paint, pink rugs, pastel bedding and photo collages framed with ribbons, small ornaments and dried flowers, Delilah's room wasn't what you would expect to see in an adult's bedroom. I'd never visited her house when we danced together, had never witnessed what her tastes had been, but what I saw now was a young teen's room that hadn't aged or grown in the time since the accidents that stole the lives of Delilah's parents.

"If you mean, she dances and smiles and enjoys the same hobbies she used to enjoy, or if you mean she goes to school and does stupid girl sleepovers, or goes to movies or even out to dinner once in a while without fear of missing her parents and not being around when they return home, then no. In that case, Deli died two years ago."

I'd heard the words when he'd spoken them, but apparently, I hadn't understood how true they were.

Stepping up to look at the photographs in their frames, I grieved for the girl smiling back at me. Many of the photos were of Delilah and Holden together, and the others were of Delilah in the costumes she'd worn for our dance competitions. Every pose was different and I wondered who had taken the photos. They caught her at her best, captured her in the moment when her talent far outshone mine. The girl was boneless when she danced, she was no longer human, she became the music. But for all the photographs displayed proudly, none of them were taken after the year her parents died. Nothing in this room was dated after that fateful night. Not a book. Not a photo. Not a magazine, a poster, a calendar, or a movie.

For Delilah, time itself had stopped moving.

Tranquil Falls had done this to her. I had done this to her. The evidence of what my silence could do to other people becoming a ton of bricks sitting on my chest, crushing me.

I had to make this right. Not knowing how, I promised myself - promised Delilah - that I would fix this so that she wouldn't lose her brother, too. And with thoughts racing through my head, ideas and pain and promises, I lay down on her bed and pulled the covers over me.

I didn't sleep well that night. The guilt was too pervasive.

CHAPTER FIFTEEN
Holden

Waking up the next morning wasn't easy. My eyes peeled open, pulling me away from dreams. My past was a source of comfort, my breath coming to me easier when I could pretend my life hadn't slipped from my fingers to fall in a gutter beneath my feet. But reality has a way of slamming into you the minute you open your eyes and remember present circumstances, it has a way of pouncing on your chest like a hungry cat, mewling in your face to be fed, or petted, or scratched. Unfortunately, the cat pouncing on me now weighed a thousand pounds, had fleas, and mange, and was feral. I won't even mention how sharp its claws were.

Regardless of the pitfalls I'd been forced into, I still had a few weeks to work and earn money. That was if Michaela was still here and I didn't leave my bedroom to find the police sitting on the couches, twirling cuffs around their fingers, grinning to drag me off and lock me up. There was only one way to find out.

Climbing out of bed, I scrubbed my palms over my face and went to the bathroom. After showering and getting dressed, I held the knob of the door in my grip for a few minutes while attempting to put on a brave face and stalk out to find Michaela gone. I was sure she was down at the station now, crying and playing the victim, her parents fluttering behind her with their sharply dressed lawyers. Jack's parents were most likely on the news talking about their golden boy child who had been found nestled among the garbage littering the ground once you crossed the train tracks into my part of town, his pretty face crushed and broken.

The only question was: Why hadn't they dragged me out of bed to slap the cuffs on me yet?

Pulling the door open so hard wind gusted against my face, I stepped out into the living room and stopped dead in my tracks. Michaela was lying on the couch, a throw pillow tucked beneath her head, a light blanket pulled over her body. The shock of it rattled me to my core.

"Hey," she whispered, her eyes heavy with exhaustion.

"You're still here?"

The corner of her lips tilted up. "I said I would be."

"I didn't believe you."

"I know." Sitting up, she brushed the hair away from her face. "I wouldn't have believed me either."

Feeling out of place, and still staggered by the fact Michaela hadn't run from the house the instant I went to bed, I shifted my weight between my feet, reached up and rubbed the back of my neck with my palm. "I'd cook you breakfast or something, but I need to get to work."

She smiled. "No worries. I know you have to go. I'm sure I can scrounge up something. I'm not completely helpless."

This moment was surreal. "Um, yeah, that's cool. There's a remote for the television on the table beside you and Del has a bunch of movies in her room you can watch. Unfortunately, I don't have much more to offer-"

"Holden, it's fine. I can manage. I'm not here as a guest that needs to be entertained. Go to work. I'll see you when you get back."

"Really?"

Her soft laughter whispered across the room. "Yes, really. Now go."

Shaking my head, I moved toward the front door, her voice calling out before I could reach it. "Would you mind if I cook dinner for us tonight? I can have it ready for when you get home."

Maybe I hadn't woken up after all. This had to be a dream because none of it was making sense. Turning, I explained, "I'm not getting back until late. Probably ten thirty or so."

"That's fine. I'll see you then."

Yeah. Definitely a dream. Not only was Michaela voluntarily staying at my house when it did nothing to benefit *her*, she was also offering to cook a meal for me.

"Okay," I muttered, not able to make sense of it enough to say anything more intelligent. Leaving as quickly as I could, I welcomed the slap of freezing cold wind against my face. The weather was the only thing I could believe or rely on anymore.

The walk to the diner was quick, the woods still smelling like woods and not a hidden body. It was dropping below freezing every night, so I hoped that it would conceal the crime long enough for me to get a decent amount of money saved up for Del. As usual, greasy heat slapped me in the face as soon as I let myself inside. What wasn't usual was Angela running up to me with anger written across her face, the lines also etched with worry.

"Are you okay?" she snapped.

Still dazed by Michaela being at my house, I blinked a few times and found myself unable to utter an answer.

"What happened to your head?" Angela looked down, her eyes narrowing. "What happened to your hands?" Her gaze met mine, "Why are you walking in here with head injuries and busted knuckles?"

If she didn't stop rattling off the questions so fast, I would need a pen and paper to take notes.

"Hi," I said, "it's nice to see you, too."

"That doesn't answer my questions." Scowling up at me, Angela crossed her arms over her chest, the tops of her breasts shoved up and out by the position. Red colored her face, the shade traveling down her neck. She wasn't just mad. She was pissed.

"I tripped over something the other night walking home and busted ass on the ground. But I'm fine."

Eyes narrowing more, she didn't believe a word I'd said. "Then explain why I have a waitress stalking around my dining room snapping at customers and dropping dishes."

My expression fell. "Crap. Kaley. I never made it to her house."

Kicking myself for having forgotten her, I knew she must have been hurt. She hadn't received so much as a phone call. She hadn't called me either. At least, I thought she hadn't, but then again I wasn't exactly listening for the phone.

"Yeah, Kaley. Except that woman's broken heart isn't my concern at the moment. We all have tried calling you since she came in yesterday alternating between cussing and crying. You didn't answer, and now you come in with a busted face and busted knuckles. Considering who was in here the other night making an ass of himself, I'm asking you to get real honest with me right now, Holden Bishop, and tell me what happened to you the other night."

Although panic was flooding every cell in my body, I couldn't let it show on my face. Forcing my expression to remain neutral, I did the other thing I was becoming an expert at other than committing felonies: I lied.

"I tripped over a root or something in the woods..."

Lie.

"...and I hit my head on a downed tree..."

Not a lie.

153

"I scraped up my hands on the same tree."

Lie.

"And then when I got home. Deli needed me, so I stayed home with her. She finally left the house, Angela. She went to spend the holidays with our Uncle Scott. I guess with all of that happening, I got caught up and was out of touch."

Half a lie, but not one I felt sorry about.

Angela's eyes widened, the tension draining from her shoulders as her lips tugged into a hesitant smile. "Delilah left the house?"

Relief surged in to douse my panic. "Yeah, she left yesterday morning to go see family we haven't spent time with in several years."

Angela was the only person who knew all the details of Delilah's problems. While mothering me in the moments when I questioned whether I could keep going, Angela had always somehow known and pulled me aside. It was easy to dump everything out for her to see, easy to spill the details if for no other reason but to ease the pain of feeling so alone. Although Angela had never met Deli, she gave me advice and worried about my sister because she'd adopted Deli right along with me.

"How's she doing?"

Shrugging, I tried not to notice Kaley glaring at me from the hallway behind Angela, tried not to notice the hurt in her eyes, the feeling of rejection obvious in her expression. "She's better, I hope. This is a big step for her."

"Yeah, it is. I'm happy for her, Holden. I really am." Reaching up, she touched my cheek and directed my focus back to her. Meeting my eyes with as much sincerity as she could manage, she said, "I'm happy for you, too. But if you're lying to me right now, about anything you just told me, I'll kick your butt for it. I've been worried

154

sick thinking I needed to get you a new identity and ship you off to some foreign country that doesn't extradite. Amsterdam, or something like that."

Well, actually, Amsterdam did sound nice. I considered it for a moment, but then decided it was in everybody's best interests that I kept Jack's death to myself. Telling Angela would only drag her into the problem, it would only make her culpable if she didn't go to the police with what she knew. I refused to do that to her.

"You don't need to ship me off into hiding. Everything's fine."

Biggest lie.

Giving me one cynical and sharp nod of her head, she glanced back to see Kaley standing in the hall. Angela's eyes rolled, but she knew I needed to talk to Kaley if she wanted her best waitress to stop scaring off the customers. Darting her gaze to me, she snapped, "You have five minutes, then back to work for the both of you."

Grinning down at her, I asked, "Is that an order?"

Her expression twisted with warning and humor. "Boy, don't try me or I'll break your nose to go along with your scraped forehead and busted knuckles."

She stalked off, moved past Kaley while issuing the same warning, and then disappeared down the hall in search of another employee to harass.

Kaley moved closer to me on measured steps. Normally I would flirt with her, take her into my arms while saying something dirty or suggestive, but I couldn't do that tonight, not to her, not while knowing I was going to prison and it would only hurt her all over again.

Although she claimed she wanted our relationship to stay casual, I'd known in the last few weeks that Kaley had changed her mind. Her voice was softer when she spoke to me. She blushed more. She spent more time

155

kissing me than ripping off my pants. Emotions had leaked into the arrangement we'd had for months, and now I would have to step on those emotions, stomp them out and let her know that she and I could never be more than what we'd been.

"I'm sorry I didn't call and cancel," I whispered as she drew near. "Something came up and..."

I forgot all about you... I didn't say. Saying it out loud would only hurt her worse.

"It's cool," she lied, her eyes swollen and rimmed red from crying. "I was just worried about you." Her expression grew hopeful when she craned her neck and met my gaze. "I overheard what you told Angela. Your sister. She's okay?"

Nodding, I stuffed my hands in my pockets. "She's good. She left to go see family."

You could have inserted an entire ocean between us and it wouldn't have increased the distance I was feeling. Kaley wanted to close that distance. I wanted to shove out and make it wider so I could protect her from being hurt.

"Five minutes is up!" Angela screamed from the hallway. I'd never appreciated her micromanaging more than in that moment.

Giving me one more sorrowful look, Kaley turned to move out into the dining room where she belonged. Brushing past Angela, she increased her pace, a cloud of disappointment stretching behind her. Angela stared in my direction, a question arching her brow.

"It'll be all right," I promised.

Thank God Angela had a one track mind. She simply shook her head and ordered, "Get to work, Holden. Today's going to be busy."

CHAPTER SIXTEEN

Michaela

Being left in a person's home unattended is a lesson is restraint. After Holden walked out the door, I caught a few hours of sleep on the couch - making up for the hours I lost in Delilah's room - but once I woke again, I could barely contain my curiosity.

Holden had always been a mystery. The same couldn't be said for his sister, but if anything, he was a closed book, a leather bound journal secured with a padlock, the exquisite detailing of the cover drawing a person's eye while mocking them that they'd never get a peek at the inside. Many girls had tried to pick that lock regardless of Holden's reputation around school, and while some had claimed he'd taken them to bed, none had claimed he'd told them even the smallest detail about himself. I'd always wondered why he was so closed off to the world, why he refused to give in to pressure and become one of us.

That same refusal had made him a target, but even with the names he was called, the pranks that were played against him, the fights that he'd never started until that day in the cafeteria, Holden had never buckled. I tended to think it was the main reason the guys on the team hated him so much. Holden could have surpassed them in sports, in intelligence, in looks and everything else, but he'd turned his nose up at it, making it clear he didn't admire or envy the only qualities those guys had that made them feel special and worthy.

In truth, I'd secretly admired him from afar, wished I could be like him, wished I could know him better than all those girls he'd taken to bed. If it hadn't been for Jack, I would have been one of those girls, and I would have cried just as hard when I realized that, with Holden, there was no guarantee of a relationship.

It wasn't that he used the girls. Each one of them admitted he'd been perfectly clear from the start - sex and the respect they deserved. But never anything more.

Sitting in his living room, the same question came to mind that I'd wondered every day in high school: Who was this gorgeous shadow? This person who had grown past the demands of youth and carried all his frustrating secrets into adulthood.

The answers were available to me now. In his room. In this house. All I had to do was walk around.

The need to explore was overwhelming. But I fought. Several times I turned on the television, the soap operas and legal shows doing nothing to curb my curiosity. Turning it off, I'd explored Delilah's room again because Holden had given me permission to be inside it. Every time I stepped in was more depressing.

It was as if Delilah never grew older than she was on the day her parents died. Holden had been on his own for two years doing his best to take care of her.

My family would have never done that for me. They would have stuck me in a home, sent me flowers on my birthday and maybe a postcard from wherever they were traveling.

They wouldn't have stayed by my side.

I respected Holden more. Hated myself more for being part of the town that hurt him.

Circling the room several times, I caught myself glancing at the door, struggled against the desire to walk through that door, down the hall and into another room that was black and white instead of rainbow. To the room of the artist instead of the dancer.

158

My gaze flicked to the clock. Seven after ten, he would be home at any time. I still needed to put the finishing touches on dinner, but it could wait a few short minutes.

Temptation won.

Traipsing to his room, I rested my hand on the knob, stopped, listened; turned the knob and let go. The door opened on its own, or at least that's what I told myself. It wasn't like he said I could never be in his room. He'd tied me up and left me in there. That's an invitation, right? A strange one. Initially, a terrifying one. But still an invitation.

I won't lie. I actually tiptoed in. It was like walking into enemy territory, or possibly dodging lasers on the way to the precious diamond I was attempting to steal. Only the diamond wasn't a multi-million dollar stone, it was a spattering of sketches pinned to his wall with no pattern or symmetry in the way they were hung. Tiny windows into Holden's thoughts, scattered without rhyme or reason.

The first was a set of doors I recognized from school. The cafeteria, I realized. Inside, the tables were filled with students, all of them identical. Peering closer, I saw that their faces were actually masks with cartoon smiles, their bodies positioned equally spaced and exactly the same. The image was disturbing, but oddly fitting. I peered closer to see the intricate details, noticing how each student had a knife in their back, a turnkey attached to the hilt as if to wind them up like tiny tin soldiers.

"Okay, that's creepy," I mumbled, moving on.

A second sketch was hung to the right of first, but several inches higher. Delilah laughing in dance practice, her body seated on a bench seat, her soul dancing above her, endlessly spinning.

159

My breath caught at the third. Another dancer, but this one had brown hair flowing down to her hips. She wasn't in costume, not a formal one anyway. Standing in front of a set of mirrors, she stretched her leg on a rail, her head turned toward the mirror, her face absent.

No mask. No fake smile. Nothing.

This girl was empty.

"I drew that one a little over three years ago. It was boring sometimes when I brought Del to practice."

My heart was in my throat as I spun on my heel at his voice, my cheeks flaming red to have been caught. "Oh! Hi. I was just -"

The corner of his mouth tipped up. "Snooping?"

Shoulders deflating, I tried to speak around the rapid beat of my heart. "Not snooping, it's just that I saw these yesterday when I was locked in here, and I wanted a closer look. You're talented, Holden. It's hard not to look."

Not just at his sketches. It was hard not to look at him as well. Even now while he was bundled in a jacket and hoodie, his head covered with a black, slack beanie pulled down to just above his eyes and over his ears, his work pants stained with grease, his boots scuffed at the toes and heels, he stole my attention much like he'd done in school. No longer wearing the small ring on the right side of his bottom lip, his blue eyes were bright bulbs against his tan skin and black hair, glowing as if lit by an inner fire much warmer than anything I'd known in another person.

His hands were tucked into the pockets of his jacket, his broad shoulders rolled forward in response to the cold wind outside, he studied me from where he stood, his body perfectly still, but not his gaze.

I felt shy in his presence, regretted that the only clothes I had were a t-shirt and sweatpants that were too

160

small. My hair was a knotted mess down my back, my face swollen and bruised. But, I had a strange feeling that when Holden looked at me, he didn't see the superficial details, he saw something hidden deeper inside me, something that all the mirrors I'd looked at in my life were unable to show me. If his drawings were an indication, then I was right to believe that Holden didn't care about the outside of a person as much as he did the parts that were hidden beneath the flesh, the muscle and bone.

From the kitchen, the scent of food wafted into the room just before the timer buzzed. He turned to look between his door and me. "Is that dinner?"

Nodding, I hated the sudden shyness. "Yes, I just need to add the topping and we can eat."

The skin between his eyes wrinkled. "You really made dinner?"

A smile tugged at my lips. "I told you I would. Is that okay? I asked and you said-"

"No, it's fine. Of course, it's fine. I'm just surprised is all."

"Surprised?"

His smile stretched wider, two dimples at the corners of his lips indenting in. "I had no idea you could cook. I thought you probably had fancy chefs and all that, or ate out. I don't know," his voice quieted, "just whatever the people on your side of town do to eat or whatever."

Laughter burst from my mouth. "Well, we have a cook, so you're not all wrong, but I like Penny. She's worked for us since I was little and she taught me a few things."

He didn't move or answer, just stared at me with eyes that saw too much.

"I should probably go pull it from the oven before it burns."

161

Holden nodded, stepped aside, his eyes tracking me as I moved past him to leave the room. A tendril of his cologne reached out to wrap around me as I snuck past, the scent drawing me so much that I had to fight the instinct to turn and move closer to its source. Thankfully, my stomach was helpful in pushing me along, a grumble sounding as soon as the scent of food collided against me, the room warm and filled to every corner with the promise of a meal.

Behind me, heavy footfalls were a slow beat, Holden's long-legged stride eating the distance with fewer steps than it had taken me.

Grabbing the potholders, I pulled dinner from the oven, a tuna casserole that I'd gotten creative to prepare. Holden's house didn't have all the ingredients I'd needed, but he did have enough to improvise. Crushing a bag of potato chips, I added the topping and found two plates to dish out the food.

I almost dropped them when I spun to find Holden standing right behind me, a dark shadow that took up way too much space. His hands locked to my shoulders to steady me. "Sorry," he said, his apology spoken softly.

Nervous laughter rattled through me. "No need to apologize, I just don't understand how you sneak around so quietly with as big as you are."

"Lots of practice, I guess."

"Practice to be a ninja?"

He smiled again and I damn near melted right there at his feet.

"Something like that. I'll carry those to the table." His fingers brushed mine when he took the plates from my hands, his large body moving away, stealing the heat that I hadn't noticed when he stood close. Now that it was absent, I shivered against the cold that crept in, the increasing distance between us making me feel lonely somehow.

Setting the plates on the table, he didn't take a seat. He simply turned to look at me. "Aren't you eating with me?"

Startled out of my daze by the question, I grinned and padded over on bare feet. We took our seats and ate quietly, Holden's empty plate scraping against the table when he pushed it away. "That was awesome. Thank you. Normally, I just eat cereal or whatever is easy when I get home after a double."

"Delilah doesn't cook?" I asked, glancing up to see a stricken look on his face.

Shaking his head, he explained, "Deli suffered a head injury in the accident that killed my folks. I've tried to get her to seek treatment beyond what they did for her at the hospital, but until yesterday, she refused to leave the house. Maybe now, she'll go, as long as my issues don't-"

His expression was pained, his voice drifting off for a few seconds before his eyes met mine again. "Anyway, she blanks out, just pauses like someone turned off a switch. Sometimes for a second or two, and other times for several minutes. I don't feel safe with her cooking when I'm not home. I usually prepare meals she can pop in the microwave on days I'm working long hours."

My guilt was suffocating, a heavy, toxic cloud that wrapped over me, stealing every last bit of clean air and good feelings. Even though I wasn't directly responsible for the tragedies his family suffered, my part was indirect - a silent mouth, a person watching as a bright soul was dragged down and shredded by the jackals of Tranquil Falls. "I'm sorry."

"For what?"

"For never speaking up. For never defending you against the kids that called you-"

"Crazy?" he interrupted, stealing the word from the tip of my tongue. "A freak?"

Shame choked me so thoroughly that my next words were a whisper. "I never called you that. Not once."

He should have been angry, should have raged to have been treated so badly by people who attacked when he'd never done anything to deserve it. Instead, he laughed. "I wore those titles like a badge, Michaela. It meant I wasn't like the rest of you. Don't feel bad about it."

Peering at him from beneath my lashes, I shook my head. "Of course I feel bad. Those kids targeted you. Jack and Clive targeted you, and for stupid reasons."

"They were jealous."

Locking my gaze to his, I grinned. "That's what I think, too. You never bowed down to them. Not like the rest of the school." Pausing, I remembered more about our years in high school. "Delilah, however, was proud of you. She didn't have many people to brag to, but she bragged to me about you."

Breathing out heavily, he reached to run his hands over his head, tugging the beanie off and dropping it to the floor. Braiding his fingers together, Holden rested his hands on top of his head, his arms folded out at the sides, stretching his shoulders apart, making him look bigger. "Do I even want to know what she bragged about?"

Swallowing to ease the attraction I had to him, I asked, "Promise not to get mad?"

His grin was the only answer I needed. But he vocalized the thought, confirming exactly what I already knew. "I could never be mad at Del. Annoyed? Frustrated beyond belief? Yes. But mad? Never."

"She bragged about your art...and your music. She recorded you singing once and showed me the video at dance practice."

His eyes clenched shut and opened again. "Okay, maybe a little mad." Groaning, he cursed under his breath. "She's just as sneaky as me apparently."

"You shouldn't hide your talent, Holden. Those paintings were beautiful. I thought they belonged in a big city gallery somewhere. And your music, it was-" My voice trailed off, adequate words lost to me. I settled on a description that was far too simple. "It was beautiful. Soulful. I've never heard someone play like that before."

In that moment, I saw pride in his expression, but like everything I'd noticed in Holden, it was there one second and gone the next. The bubble bursting. The walls coming down again as his thoughts sped off to some unknown place. Sorrow replaced the pride and I wanted to reach out to smooth away the lines of it from his face.

"I need to grab a shower," he announced. "I smell like a greasy diner." Standing, he reached for the plates to take them to the sink. From behind the counter, he said, "I'll clean since you cooked."

"I don't mind cleaning," I offered, "it'll give me something to do."

Holden eyed me, his stare locking to some secret part of me that I doubted I'd ever seen. "Suit yourself," he answered with a shrug of his shoulder before stalking off.

The loneliness settled over me again, the knowledge that I'd missed years of knowing someone as amazing as Holden all because I was as shallow and fake as the people who'd made it their life's mission to abuse him.

CHAPTER SEVENTEEN
Holden

For as much as life is unfair, it's also sadistic and confusing. We have all these concepts and beliefs, views shared by the majority as part of a collective unconscious, the landscape always changing as to what is shunned and what is accepted by people who dare to step outside the box.

Not that the box ever existed for me, the walls failing to rise and close me in like they should have done when I was born. I've existed so far outside those expectations of normality that encapsulate most people that I've never suffered the loss of companionship or similarity because it had never existed in the first place.

If the world were a crowd of people moving in an endless circle, I was that one outlier you'd see when viewing us from above - the one soul shuffling in the opposite direction, always on the outside, always alone.

I didn't mind it, not until this moment anyway, when I had to wonder if, for once, I'd been wrong about one of those marching people endlessly circling.

Stripping off my clothes, I climbed in the shower to blast my body with scalding water, the ice from the walk home melting from my nose, the blood returning to my cheeks as pins and needles. Snow was supposed to fall tonight, heavy and thick, the potential of getting trapped inside, a looming threat. Angela had given me another double tomorrow, per my request, but if I couldn't get outside, it meant I was trapped with a woman who'd managed to surprise me with many of the things she'd said and done.

Had I judged her wrongly all these years?

My head dipped beneath the spray, my eyes watching the falling water as that question echoed inside my head.

I've never been a true genius, never had the ease with math and writing as I did with visual art, but when it came to understanding people, I would have put myself above the rest, would have sworn I couldn't be wrong about a person because I looked *beneath* the surface.

Michaela, however, a woman I'd watched grow from a girl, an open book I'd read for years on end, was proving to be a mystery. I thought I'd seen beneath the facade, but the more she revealed in her behavior now, the more I wondered if there weren't additional defenses she'd constructed beneath the superficial demeanor, hiding places that no other person had breached. I couldn't stop staring at her, couldn't stop trying to pick apart the puzzle and understand what made her tick.

Not that staring at her was difficult. It had never been. Michaela checked all the right boxes when it came to appearance. Tall and curved in all the right places, dancing had done well to tone Michaela's physique, her long dark brown hair flowing down her back where the ends brushed her hips.

I used to watch her walk the halls of Tranquil Falls High, used to memorize the way her hair swayed back and forth as she moved, reaching but not quite touching her heart shaped butt. In dance class, I'd snapped a few mental images of her as well, had sketched them out, but could never get the angles of her face just right, could never catch that *something* in her eyes that was more akin to pain than happiness. So I simply left the face blank, as empty and shallow as what I'd believed was her true self.

It's not unheard of for people to change. Time, age and maturity come into play as we grow, experience coloring the pages of a person's life - joy, heartache, love and hate a liberally sprinkled glitter to highlight the moments that matter the most, sticking to our skin, scratching us when we least expect it because you can never get all of it off.

Had she changed so much in the past two years, or had this always been who she was beneath the practiced smiles, the complacent behavior, the desperation to fit in?

I didn't know. I wasn't even sure I'd find out. Time was being snatched away like sand caught in the wind, the minutes scattered until nothing remained but my view of the prison cell as I was being walked to it.

Turning off the water, I stood dripping, my skin pink, my forehead pressed to the tile wall. There were moments when I forgot my present circumstances, tiny slivers of time where the crimes I'd committed weren't crushing down on my chest making it impossible to breathe. Oddly, those moments occurred the most when Michaela was around.

That thought bothered me.

Climbing out of the shower, I dried off and got dressed, my head so clogged with chaos that I needed a release before bed. I hadn't even noticed while selecting my clothes that I'd grabbed my old pair of tattered jeans, the legs spattered with paint in all colors. My t-shirt was a plain white, but I would take it off before working. It was easier to wash the paint from my skin than to wash it from my clothes.

Michaela was sitting on the couch when I stepped out, her eyes darting to me as soon as I entered the living room. I'd never seen her look so lonely. The need to comfort her was a pulsing warmth inside me, but I shoved it away, scrubbing my palm over my neck before glancing down the hallway to my studio. Awkward silence lingered between us, her full lips parting to say something when I blurted out my words instead.

"I'm going to go work on some stuff for a little while. Will you be okay by yourself out here?"

Her mouth hung open for a few seconds, her eyes widening then narrowing again, disappointment apparent in the lines of her face. "Yeah, I should be fine."

"Awesome. I'm just going to go."

Disappearing from view as quickly as possible, I didn't slow down until I was tucked behind the closed door of the studio, my back pressed against the wood, my eyes clenched shut because everything inside me when it came to Michaela was becoming a frustrating contradiction. I felt like a jerk for running and leaving her in there alone. It also didn't escape my notice that I'd literally bolted to get away from her like a scared little boy with a crush.

What was wrong with me?

Brushing it off, I crossed the room on two long strides, slipped my favorite CD into the player and relaxed a touch as the music blared through the speakers. This was my place, my sanctuary, the church that I ran to when I needed to pray. Within these walls, there was no need for words, and reality bled away as I transferred the snapshots in my brain to canvas. Tugging off my shirt to avoid dousing it in paint, I grabbed my brushes and absorbed the music, my eyes scanning between the paintings that were incomplete, none of them calling to me or drawing me close.

A new image had captured my mind, a sleeping woman, her veil slipping away to show me who she was inside. The details of her face becoming clear for the first time since I sketched her years before.

Fighting against the need to paint it, I dabbed some details onto one of the seven canvases already on their easels, but still I was unsatisfied, unable to enter that space where the art flowed freely, where it wasn't my

169

thoughts directing my brush, but my soul. After several minutes passed and the urge expanded until it filled me, I removed the last canvas from its easel, grabbed a blank slate, and set it up to begin assigning this new image to the canvas.

As soon as the first line dragged down the white background, I dropped the brush knowing the angle was wrong, my fingers itching for a sketch pad and pencil where I could rework the memory over and over again until I had it just right.

Gathering the tools of my beleaguered trade, I dropped down in the center of the studio to sit on the drop cloths and pull the memory from my mind, the quiet *scritch scritch* of lead over paper lost to the beat of music filling the room. Within minutes, the outline was complete, but the shading was the detail that would bring it to life.

It was wrong. Something was wrong. I couldn't quite grasp what I was missing, the snapshot not quite complete in my head. Flipping the page, I attempted it again. Wrong. I flipped another page, drew another line. Shaded. Traced. Wrong. Another page. Another. I couldn't get it right.

Lead dust blackened the skin of my hand, my lip caught between my teeth, my focus so acute, my frustration so overwhelming that I almost missed a soft knock at the door.

Head snapping up toward the sound, I waited for it to come again, wondering if in my trance I'd imagined it.

The knock came again.

A breath poured out of me, the need to ignore the knock and keep sketching holding me in place, but the knock came again, only harder.

Dropping the pad face down onto the ground, I pushed to my feet and stalked to the door, wrenched it open to find Michaela on the other side looking panicked.

"I didn't want to bother you but somebody is knocking on your front door."

"What?" Eyes wide, I shot a glance over her shoulder as if I could see the door in question, which I couldn't.

"Maybe they'll go away?" I mused.

Her lips pulled into a tight grin. "That was my thought. I ignored it the first three times, but whoever is out there isn't going away."

This was not good. In fact, this was very, VERY bad. Racking my brain to remember if the trail through the woods had been disturbed on my walk home, I couldn't think of anything out of the ordinary. If they'd found Jack, that entire area would have been taped off, police cars and a medical examiner's van blocking the path. There was no possible way whoever stood outside was here to haul me off to jail.

"What should we do?" Michaela asked.

Reaching out, I pulled her into the room. "Stay in here. Don't make a sound. Don't come out."

So concerned with who would be at my house this late at night - in weather that had dropped below freezing, no less - I wasn't thinking straight when I closed the door behind me locking Michaela inside a room that nobody had seen since I'd converted it.

Eating the distance between my studio and the front door with a rapid, pace, I waited to hear if the person would knock again. Within seconds, there was a rap of knuckles against the wood. I pulled the door open and froze in place.

"Hey, I was wondering if we can talk?"

"Uh..." It was insanely difficult to formulate words at that moment.

171

Kaley stood just outside the door, a thick jacket covering her body, the hood pulled over her head. White plumes of hot breath poured over her lips, her brown eyes looking up at me, pleading. Shaking myself of the panicked shock, I pulled the door open and angled my body to give her room to step in.

"Why are you here, Kaley? Is something wrong?"

She stepped in and was shivering beneath her jacket, her teeth chattering loudly as I closed the door against the wind racing in with icy fingers. Kaley looked up at me with the same swollen eyes she'd had at the diner. "Nothing's wrong. I just wanted to talk to you about...us."

Crap...

'Us' was the last thing I wanted to talk about. It wasn't that I didn't care about Kaley - it was that I had a secret that would tear her apart if I didn't let her down gently now, and unfortunately the time and place for that discussion was not here where I had the ex-girlfriend of the man I killed hanging out, a girl Kaley would recognize because she despised her as much as I used to.

"It's not a good time," I muttered, my arms crossing over my chest that I just now remembered was bare to her eyes. Music blasted from the studio at the back of the long hall, Kaley's eyes darting in the direction of the noise just before suspicion rolled in to mix with the brown color.

"Do you have somebody here?"

My heart stuttered. "No. Why?"

"I thought I saw someone move past the front window when I knocked."

"Yeah, no," I lied, adding yet another one to the pile of lies I'd been building since two nights ago. "Let me go take care of the stuff I was working on in back real quick, and I'll throw on some clothes and walk you home. We can talk on the way."

Pivoting on my heel, I stepped toward the hallway, Kaley's hand gripping over my wrist before I could escape. "Actually, I was hoping you'd invite me to stay the night."

Twisting to look at her, I locked my gaze on the hesitant smile pulling at her lips.

She shrugged. "I thought with your sister being gone, it could be the first time we stayed an entire night together."

Floored by the amount of hope that dripped from her words, I struggled to think of a way to tell her no. If Deli were around, I'd ask her what to do. She was always quick with girly advice, always my savior when it came to avoiding the pitfalls that left a trail of broken hearts in my wake.

But Deli wasn't here.

Only Michaela.

It wasn't the best idea, but it was worth a shot.

"I really need to get back to my studio and take care of some things real quick. Can you hold on for a second?"

Kaley hadn't finished nodding 'yes' before I was racing down the hall. Opening the door to the studio, I slipped inside, and turned to find Michaela staring at a painting of Deli I hadn't yet finished.

Her head swiveled to look at me, genuine admiration in her green gaze. "Holden, these paintings are amazing."

It irked me to have someone in my space, to have my work exposed to new eyes when they weren't finished. There was nothing I could do about it at the moment. Crossing the room, I turned down the music, my mouth running dry when I forced myself to ask the question.

"Michaela, listen, I need your help."

She stood silently, her brows arching above her eyes.

"If you were sleeping with a guy and it had been casual at first, but you suddenly had feelings for him,

173

what would be the best thing he could say to let you down easy?"

Her expression relaxed, a grin tugging at her lips before she shook her head and smiled brighter. "Oh dear. It sounds like you've got a slight problem on your hands, Holden."

Nodding emphatically, I couldn't have agreed with her more.

Soft laughter shook her shoulders. "How much time do we have to work this out?"

"Like three minutes," I admitted.

"Okay. Then tell me the details as quickly as you can and I'll give you my advice. But, in all honesty, I'm not sure there's anything you can say or do to prevent hurting her."

That's not what I wanted to hear. Taking a deep breath to steady the erratic beat of my heart, I leaned against the door behind me and spilled the details.

CHAPTER EIGHTEEN
Michaela

After listening intently to everything Holden had to tell me about the problem that had just knocked on his front door, two thoughts were front and center in my mind:

One, I now understood exactly why the waitress at the all night diner hated me the minute she laid eyes on me. And two, there was no way in hell Holden would be able to let this girl down without breaking her heart.

Especially not a girl who was willing to walk over in the freezing cold with the hope for an overnight invite.

Sighing, I pursed my lips, and tried to decide whether I should find a delicate way to tell him, or just be blunt. "Well," I said, going with delicate, "my first bit of advice would be to put on a shirt."

Holden glanced down, confusion wrinkling his brow.

Smiling, I explained, "It's kind of hard for a girl not to want you when your abs are all exposed and asking to be stroked, and stared at, and licked. Those are pretty much rational mind kryptonite, so putting them away would be in your best interest."

His blue eyes met mine and I could feel my cheeks flare red. Shaking his head, Holden moved to grab a t-shirt from a nearby table and pulled it on to cover his chest and stomach. Disappointment filtered through me to have such a beautiful sight hidden from view.

"Okay, what next?"

"Next," I said, going with blunt, "the only thing you can do is be honest with her."

His expression fell. "That's it?"

Nodding, I flashed him an apologetic grin. "Sometimes honesty is the best thing you can do. If you beat around the bush, she might cling on to hope that she can change your mind. And believe it or not, women are a lot tougher than they look. She'll appreciate your honesty, maybe not at first, but eventually."

Swallowing hard, he nodded his head and glanced at the door. "I hate to do this to you, but I need you to stay in here for a little while longer. I know its boring-"

"I'll be fine. Go. Do what you need to do and I'll play captive until you release me from my prison."

Giving me a sharp look, he growled, "Not funny."

I held up my wrists and grinned. "I have the rope burns to prove it."

Turning between the door and me several times as if he wanted to respond but couldn't decide, Holden finally locked his eyes to mine and did something unexpected. He laughed, the sound low and soft. "Try not to get in too much trouble while I'm gone. I'd hate to have to tie you up again."

"Yes, Sir."

A quick shake of his head and Holden was leaving the room on his way to break some poor woman's heart. Staring at the closed door for several seconds, I listened as voices carried down the hall from the living room, several minutes passing before the front door opened and closed, the house returning to silence.

I returned my attention to the unfinished paintings on their easels, my mind unable to comprehend the amount of talent hidden in a man born into a town that took everything from him, including his freedom. Piece by piece, we'd broken him down. Chained him. Enslaved him. Kept him living a life that was so far beneath him. Holden didn't belong on the wrong side of the tracks in Tranquil Falls. He belonged in New York. In Chicago. In some big city where his art could hypnotize and entrance, where the tragic bindings holding him to this place could be cut away to let him fly.

We'd called him crazy, when in truth, we were the crazy ones.

Crazy for not recognizing a good person among us.

Crazy for judging him when we were the ones who should have been judged.

Crazy for so needlessly hurting a man that wanted nothing from us but the respect to let him live in peace.

Crazy for not seeing that he had more raw talent in his pinky finger than any of us had in our entire bodies.

But maybe that's the way it is for shallow people. Maybe we do recognize those souls among us that are special, and out of jealousy and spite, we tear them down.

Stepping back to get a better view of all his paintings at once, my heel hit something lying on the drop cloth. I turned to see what I'd stepped on and found a sketchpad lying face down, a pencil hastily abandoned beside it. Remembering the black dust staining his finger and hand when he'd opened the studio door, I thought that whatever was on that pad was what he'd been focused on when I knocked.

It would be invasive of me to flip it over and take a peek, but I couldn't help it. The need to know what was pressing on Holden's thoughts was too strong, too compelling to ignore.

Would it be another memory of Delilah? Another thought of the parents he'd lost? Would it be like the art standing at my back on the easels illustrating how Holden saw the people that surrounded him?

Sitting down, I pulled the sketchpad toward me, lifted a corner as if to flip it over, but paused. I hated invading his privacy like this, hated taking advantage of Kaley's interruption.

I flipped it over anyway...and froze.

A woman lay sleeping on a bed, her head facing one direction while her dark hair splayed over a pillow behind her. Delicately folded, her hand lay near her face, her lips parted, her nose coming into view. But her eyes were missing, only the top half of her body fully completed.

Even halfway done, I recognized the angles of my face, the line of my jaw, the length of my dark hair. Turning a page, I saw myself again, the image hastily drawn and abandoned. Five more pages were the same, each abandoned, each one revealing less of the woman I'd seen in the first sketch.

He was creating me from an image in his mind, but something was missing, something that had driven him to attempt it over and over again, the outlines and shading shifting and darkening with each new attempt.

Setting the pad down on the drop cloth, I stared at the image he'd attempted to bring to life, my heart beating harder as sorrow filled me. Why couldn't I have known this person before his life became so complicated? Why hadn't I been strong enough to reject the hatred everybody had thrown at him so that I could stand by his side?

I was an awful person, and I was being torn apart inside by the fear that there would be nothing I could say or do to fix the present situation we were in.

Flipping the sketchpad over, I moved away from it to sit against a wall. My legs were bent in front of me, my arms wrapping around my shins to tug them closer to my body. Resting my cheek against my knees, I breathed out a heavy sigh.

There was no way in hell I'd let Holden be destroyed completely. I just had to find a way to correct the wrongs we'd committed against him and set everything back to right.

CHAPTER NINETEEN
Holden

Snow had started falling while I'd walked Kaley back to her house. It was the perfect complement to the conversation we were having, the frozen flakes freezing to our faces as quickly as her hot tears turned cold. Following Michaela's advice, I was honest with Kaley. I'd explained that I'd assumed from the beginning that she wasn't looking for anything beyond casual sex, that her heart wasn't ready for the emotional toll a relationship could take from two people. Casual had been fine for me, but given my situation, a relationship wasn't feasible. I'd used Deli as an excuse only to protect Kaley from the truth of why I wasn't in a good place in life to have a girlfriend.

So, why was it that after walking one woman home with the rationale that I was very much emotionally unavailable, I had another woman on my mind?

Tucking my hands deeper into my pockets, I curled in on myself in as desperate a bid to avoid the cold as it was to avoid thinking about a woman sitting in my studio - a studio that *nobody* saw. Not even my sister. Those four walls were my space, those paintings were my thoughts. That sketchpad...

I quickened my pace, almost busting ass on the slick roads several times. That sketchpad had Michaela all over it. Reaching the house, I was half frozen, but I brushed the ice and snow from my body as I walked inside and practically slid down the hall. Bursting through the door, I half expected Michaela to be sitting in the middle of the room looking at the drawings I'd dedicated to paper moments before she knocked, but instead, she was sitting against the wall, her legs tucked to her body, her cheek resting on her knees, a tear slipping from her eye that she didn't wipe away fast enough for me not to notice.

"You look frozen," she said, attempting a laugh that wasn't quite believable.

"I feel frozen," I answered. "Is everything okay?"

Why was this happening to me tonight? Every female who came within five feet of me was leaking tears like a dam had broken somewhere that the male mind was forbidden from traveling. Walking over to her, I leaned against the wall and slid down to sit next to her, my position mirroring hers.

"Everything's fine," she lied.

"It doesn't look like everything's fine. Did I do something to upset you?"

She swiped at another tear, the tip of her nose red, her bottom lip puffed out where a tiny split in the skin was still visible. Sitting up to press her back against the wall, she swept out with her hand toward my paintings. "It's just those, Holden. Your art."

Glancing over, I quickly perused the half finished pieces. "I didn't think they were that bad-"

"They're not bad at all. They're wonderful. You're wonderful. And we-" Her voice trailed off, her expression darkening as her eyes closed and forced more tears down her cheeks. Resting her head against the wall, she admitted, "We treated you so horribly."

Her words stunned me, stole the strength from my voice when I asked, "Why does that matter enough to cry about it?"

"Because it's destroying you," she breathed out, still not opening her eyes to look at me. "If anybody in this entire town deserves a fair shot, it's you. But because everybody who lives here is a self-righteous prick, you're facing jail while we're flitting off to college to continue the same tired bullshit there. And once we graduate, we'll move on to our careers to be just as mean and nasty as we've always been. But you - the one damn person that never did a thing to hurt anybody else - you'll be locked up for the rest of your life when you should be standing in the middle of an art gallery somewhere being praised by whoever praises art. You should be making a mark on history, or culture, or whatever, and half the jerks who attacked you should be locked up instead."

Her forehead fell to rest on her knees, her arms hugging her legs tighter. "It's not fair," she mumbled, the sound muted by the position of her body.

Unsure what to do with her sudden epiphany, I stated the obvious. "I broke a guy's nose. And that wasn't exactly the first time. I killed someone, Michaela. So it's not like I never hurt anyone."

"Jack deserved it," she argued. Turning her head so that her cheek was pressed against her knees, she locked her green eyes with mine. "He deserved everything that came to him. But you don't deserve taking the fall for it. He attacked you."

Grinning, I had to blink a few times to believe this version of Michaela was real. "Try telling the police that."

"I will," she answered with more strength in her voice than I'd ever heard. "I'll tell them aliens came down and abducted Jack if that leads them away from you. The jerk deserved a good anal probe."

Laughter burst out of me, her eyes widening in surprise as an unsure smile tugged at her lips. For both of us, the tension had dissipated, our shoulders relaxing as we sat staring at each other. Despite the impossible circumstances, this woman who I'd always thought less of was somehow easing the load I carried. To say I was stunned would be an understatement.

"Why couldn't you have been like this in high school?" I asked, curious about this evolving creature that was proving to be full of surprises. Her spirit was starting to shine through the veil, making my fingers itch to capture it on paper.

Sorrow filled her eyes. "I've always been scared, I guess. Of Jack. Of my family. Of the people who expected me to be one thing when all I wanted was to be myself. I was afraid of being rejected, of being harassed, of being labeled as-"

"A crazy freak?" I finished for her.

Silence fell, heavy and pregnant with her guilt. On a whisper, she reminded me, "I never used those words to describe you."

"I know," I whispered back.

Wiping away the last of her tears, she straightened her posture to lean back against the wall. I straightened mine as well, both our eyes now focused on the unfinished paintings on their easels.

Changing a subject that had become far too depressing, Michaela asked, "How did it go with Kaley?"

A deep breath poured from my lungs, "Well, she cried."

"That's to be expected."

"And then she called me a selfish asshole."

Her laughter was soft. "That's to be expected too." Smile fading, she asked, "Did you ever promise her anything more than sex?"

"No," I answered, leaving out that I'd known Kaley was getting attached. I should have ended things then, but I didn't know how.

"You're not an asshole, Holden. The few girls you slept with in high school had good things to say about you, and all of them knew it was only sex. Even then, they said you treated them better than anybody they'd dated, both before and after you." Her head turned my direction. "The only thing they had to be mad at you for was spoiling them. They never could find someone else who showed them the same respect."

With my eyes still trained to the paintings, I was all too aware of the way Michaela was staring at me. I couldn't meet her gaze. I was too afraid of that odd pressure in my chest and catch in my breath that occurred when our eyes met. "You talked about me with people in high school?"

"I overheard the locker room gossip." She sighed. "Okay, and maybe I asked your sister about you whenever I could. She loved to brag about your art and your music. Now, that I've seen the inside of your studio, I can understand why. I'm not exaggerating about how talented you are. It's breathtaking, even if the paintings aren't finished."

Although, I knew Michaela was, in fact, exaggerating, I still felt a small spark of pride to hear the compliment. My art was my voice. It was my therapy and my solace. I'd never intended to do much with it other than create it, but it was uplifting to hear someone besides my family who appreciated it. "Well, I probably won't be able to paint for much longer, but maybe they'll let me design some artsy license plates in prison."

"You're not going to prison."

Finally giving up on the battle not to look at her, I swiveled my head in her direction. The look in her eye caught me off guard, a quick shot of *something* bursting inside my chest at the sight of her. Michaela was the most gorgeous woman I'd ever known - at least on the outside. It wasn't until tonight that I was beginning to learn the inside might be just as magnificent. The timing couldn't have been worse.

"There's nothing we can do."

"I'm not giving up. And I won't let you give up either."

184

Sad laughter shook my shoulders. "What would you like to do? Run away? Become fugitives? You can be my captive while I hitchhike across the country because I don't even have a car to use in my escape mission?"

Her expression fell and I wanted nothing more than to see her smile again. I just didn't know how to make that happen, or if I even should. Delving deeper into this alliance we'd formed would be dangerous for both of us. Going to prison was one thing. Going there after finally finding the woman that makes your heart jump into your throat and your mouth go dry was a whole other tragedy. I would be willing to take the risk just to have five minutes of knowing what it felt like to genuinely love a woman in the romantic sense. But, I would never do it to her. I would never risk a woman's heart.

"I'm not your captive," she whispered, her eyes narrowing on me in feigned anger. Damn if it wasn't the cutest expression I'd ever seen.

What the hell was wrong with me?

This was Michaela Paige of all people and I was sitting here imagining what a future would be like together, including naming the kids. I didn't even want to think of my other bodily responses. Didn't want to think how my pants were becoming painfully tight when she hadn't done anything but look in my direction.

I needed to get up. Needed to run. Needed to get as far away from her as possible.

Instead, I reached out to run the tip of my finger over the raw skin of her wrist. "The rope burns say otherwise."

Naked heat flashed behind her eyes and I thanked God for my loose jeans and long hoodie. Her knowing the way she was affecting me would have been just one more tragedy to toss on the pile.

Clearing my throat, I said, "We should probably get out of here. You can't possibly enjoy sitting on a bunch of old drop cloths in a room that smells like paint."

Lips curling at the corners, Michaela's gaze returned to my art. "Actually, I do like it in here. It's calm, you know? Nothing's happening except...I don't know. It feels different, like nothing going on outside that door matters. Not in here." Her head rolled over the wall, her eyes finding mine. "I know I sound stupid for saying that."

Not at all...

I definitely needed to leave.

"Well, *I'm* tired of sitting on a drop cloth so I say we head to bed. I have a double again tomorrow."

Pushing to my feet, I made the mistake of reaching down to help Michaela to hers. The second her hand touched mine, a current of *want* buzzed just beneath my skin, expanding and pulsing until I felt it everywhere.

Once she was balanced on her feet, I let go, immediately stepping back to place distance between us. "Goodnight," I said, leaping toward the door to escape like a fucking coward.

CHAPTER TWENTY
Michaela

I dreamed about him that night. I know, it's stupid, but I did. It was one of those ridiculously sweet dreams that leaves you with perma-grin the next day. The type of dream that makes you think about the *idea* of possibility until you find yourself doodling your first name with his last, like some lovesick adolescent girl.

But while I thought our talk in his studio that night had brought us a touch closer, Holden acted as if I wasn't there...most of the time, anyway. Yes, he was always polite, aggravatingly so. And yes, he loaned me some of Deli's and his clothes, including boxers, since I had one pair of underwear to my name. And yes, he made sure I was as comfortable as possible while spending day in and day out in his house that didn't have much in the way of entertainment. But most of the time, it felt like he was running from me, not because he disliked me, but because he was scared. Or, at least, that's the title I would assign it. The question became: Was he afraid of me? Or was he so concerned about prison that he couldn't function like a normal human male when he had an interested female within easy reach?

Or, maybe, that was just Holden.

He'd never had a serious relationship from what I knew of him. Most people believed it was because no girl wanted to be with the town's 'crazy freak', but I was beginning to believe that wasn't the case at all. If I'd been asked to guess after the time I spent with Holden, I would say that he was the one avoiding emotional entanglements, the question then becoming: Why?

Four days had passed since the first time I saw Holden's studio. And in those four days, I learned that

Holden had a very predictable schedule. Every morning, he woke up, showered and got dressed (mostly black, of course), cooked breakfast and left for work. Ten hours later, Holden returned, ate dinner, showered and disappeared into his studio. The music would turn on and I'd lose him for another hour or two.

This was is *usual*, his pattern, his manner of navigating life that left very little room for complications. Often, I wondered if he was this closed off when Delilah was here, or if he took the time to spend with his sister that he was adamant not to spend with me. However, despite the standard, Holden had one hour every night when his walls came tumbling down.

Photographers also have that one hour, the *golden hour* as they call it, usually occurring just after the sun rises or just before it sets again. It's an hour when the light outside is perfect for capturing images that reveal the breathtaking beauty of a landscape, a human being, or whatever subject they happen to be photographing. Maybe it was an artist thing, despite the medium, because Holden, too, had this golden hour, always occurring just after he left his studio. It was an hour that he would come talk to me, he would laugh with me about stupid jokes, an hour in which the light inside him was bright enough and alive enough to reveal who he truly was inside.

Jokingly, I referred to it as the *Holden Hour*.

I not only adored that hour, I clung to it, waited for it, dreamed about it when the time came for us to part and go our separate ways. The next morning would always come, Holden would be sheltered inside himself once again, and I'd spend the next ten hours waiting for the hour I knew he'd grant me that night.

I wouldn't call it a miserable existence for me, just a boring one, an existence that gave me way too much time to think about all the mistakes I'd made growing up, including letting the opinion of a shallow town dictate my behavior.

If the time spent alone weren't bad enough, Holden's golden hour swept in to open him up and enlighten me as to all of his thoughts of the town of Tranquil Falls. In the past four days I'd learned of the wrongs committed against Delilah and him. I'd been schooled on the horrifying reality of what was being done and ignored at the team's parties. I'd learned that the lives of other people beyond the Bishop kids had been trampled on and diminished by my silence in watching it all go down without ever questioning what was occurring. And although our conversations during that one hour of the night weren't always about depressing subjects that made me feel like the world's most boring and silent villain, I still went to bed each night with a healthy dose of guilt to swallow down. Not because of my past mistakes, but because I got to know one of Tranquil Fall's most famous victims – I'd learned that he was exactly the type of man I could easily love, and that I'd watched without much complaint as the town tore him down.

Thankfully, on the fifth night, Holden's Hour wasn't started with discussions of prison, the past or tragedy, it began with a dab of paint smeared against the tip of my nose at a moment Holden had closed the distance he'd always kept between us and allowed himself to touch me. I felt that simple touch down to the tips of my toes.

After emerging from his studio with paint splatted over his bare chest, Holden had taken one look at me, shook his head and closed the distance between us so fast my heart actually leapt into my throat.

"You have flour on your nose," he'd said. "Hold still."

Holding still in his presence was easier said than done.

Realizing the flour must have dusted my nose when I was cooking dinner earlier that evening, my cheeks flared red with embarrassment at the thought that the flour had been there since Holden got home, since we ate dinner together, since he disappeared into his studio and I sat on the couch in the living room staring at whatever happened to be on television.

Reaching up, Holden wiped the flour off my nose, only to smile and laugh while pulling his hand away to show me his fingers that were apparently still wet with paint. "Whoops."

Closing my eyes and opening them again, I locked my gaze to his. "The tip of my nose is red now, isn't it?"

Soft laughter shook his shoulders. "Uh, yeah. You look like you should be leading Santa's sleigh on Christmas."

"Damn you and your reindeer games, Holden Bishop."

His laughter was louder this time, a genuine smile stretching his lips that revealed those shy dimples of his that only came out to play on rare occasions. I loved those dimples, wanted to see them more often, and briefly wondered what I could do to make them a permanent fixture on his face.

"We need to get you cleaned up," he said, the movement of his lips drawing my eyes away from those dimples and to his mouth, my gaze tracing the lines of it, the fullness. My thoughts...

Crap. My thoughts were all over the place and I felt absolutely ridiculous because never, and I mean *never*, had I reacted to a man this way. Not even Jack. Not even when we first started dating and he hadn't yet revealed the monster inside him.

"Cleaned up sounds good," I agreed, my voice breathless and robotic.

I'm not sure what happened in that moment, and I wasn't positive I understood how electricity had traveled between us, a pulsing, living thing that silenced our voices and froze time at a point where our eyes had met and neither of us were blinking. My heart was a thundering drum in my chest, my pulse a frenetic fluttering creature trapped just beneath my skin, my body temperature rising to levels I wasn't sure were entirely healthy. But there we stood, lost to whatever chemistry experiment had gone horribly wrong, the solution created by our mutual desires bubbling to the surface until we were drowning in it.

"Yeah," he practically choked on the word before clearing his throat and repeating it more smoothly. "Yeah, let's get that off your nose before it dries all the way. I have a solution in my studio."

He walked away without indicating whether I should follow him or not, so I padded barefoot behind him, taking his silence as an unspoken invite into the studio that I hadn't seen since the last time he shoved me in there to hide me from Kaley.

My curiosity had nagged at me over the last several days, my desire to see what he'd added to the unfinished paintings pushing me down that hall several times while he was at work. However, it felt intrusive to walk in without his permission, like I was invading a holy place that only he could use to worship. I'd turned around, never opening the door much less touching the knob.

He didn't turn around or tell me to wait for him to grab the solution and come back, so when he opened the studio door, I walked in behind him, my eyes immediately going to the paintings and my breath catching in my lungs.

"Oh my God. That's Jimmy."

Without thinking, I stepped forward for a closer inspection, my hand reaching out to touch a painting that was so accurate and lifelike that I didn't even stop to think that I shouldn't lay a finger on it. Luckily, Holden remembered for me, his fingers clasping over my wrist to stop the forward motion of my arm. "Careful," he warned. "The paint isn't dry yet."

Thoughts raced through my head, memories of the seedy drug den I was dragged to when Jack had forced me, the rotten teeth I knew were beneath those sorrowful lips, the scratchy voice I could still hear in my head. But while those memories crashed against my skull and forced my stomach to roll over itself in memory of the night I'd been there before Holden's accident, another thought came to me that was more disturbing.

"You knew Jimmy?"

Was Holden buying drugs from him as well?

"I knew of him," he finally answered, his voice careful and devoid of emotion. "He came into the diner late at night and would sit at the counter slowly eating whatever he ordered. That painting is of a memory I had of him the last time he came in. I haven't seen him since. Why?"

"He's dead," I whispered. "He died of a drug overdose six months ago. His body wasn't found for several days from what I heard."

Still holding my wrist, Holden spun me to face him. "You knew that guy?" Expression twisting with disgust, his gaze locked to mine. "Why would you know somebody like him?"

The obvious disapproval in both his voice and expression confirmed that Holden had never known Jimmy for the same reasons as me. I breathed out in relief. I couldn't stand it if I found out Holden was another loser scoring powdered death off Jack's dealer.

"Jack bought his drugs from that guy. Every once in a while he'd drag me to the house with him before driving back to my side of town for a party." Swallowing hard, I confessed about the memory that was banging against my thoughts, clenching my heart in its cruel fingers as images of Holden's body lying limp beneath the hood of his car flashed in my mind's eye. "We were coming back from his house the night Jack ran into you with his car."

Lips pulling into a thin line, he released my wrist, disappointment filling me to lose contact with him. It seemed like no matter how many steps we took toward each other, the past would come crashing in to push us apart again.

"He took you to this guy's house?" he asked, anger in his voice, his hand indicating the painting to our side.

All I could do was nod in response.

"Why?" Holden sneered, the word coming out on a soft growl.

Shrugging, I reminded him, "Because that's where he got his drugs."

"No, I mean why did you stay with a guy who would take you around people like this? Why didn't you demand more respect than that?"

Caught off guard by the sudden vehemence in his voice, I stared at him open-mouthed for several seconds.

Reaching, he closed my jaw with his hand, trapping my chin between his thumb and forefinger to keep my eyes locked to his. "I want you to promise me something. Can you do that?"

Nodding was a little difficult given the way he was holding my face, but I managed.

A sad smile pulled at his lips. "Promise me that, in the future, when you meet a new guy and start dating him, you'll demand to be treated as you should be treated. Make me that promise, because the little you've already told me about your life with Jack and everybody else makes me want to personally go around and kick all their asses before I'm hauled off to prison."

"You're not going to prison," I fought to say around my trapped chin.

Sorrow filled his eyes, matching his fading smile. "Yeah, Michaela, we can pretend that for a little longer, but that's not the point of what I'm asking you."

Tilting my chin up and stepping closer, Holden brought his face down to mine, our noses practically touching as the serious intensity in his eyes took me hostage. "Promise me, that from this day forward, you won't let people push you around anymore, and you won't go near guys like Jimmy again, and you won't stay so deafeningly silent when you know something around you is wrong. Promise me that."

I didn't want to lose physical contact with him, didn't want the connection lost again, for the distance to return that I know he'd place between us. But I pulled my chin away from his fingers to answer him, to question him, to understand why he'd become so concerned over learning I'd been around Jimmy. Barely able to speak louder than a shaky whisper, I kept my eyes locked to his and asked, "Why? Why does it matter to you?"

"Because if you had done those things years ago, I may have had a chance to know you before it was too late to-"

Shaking his head of the thought, he stepped away to dig through a bin of random bottles and other supplies, the silence infuriating me only because I was desperate to know what he'd intended to say. Impatiently, I waited for several seconds while he found what he wanted and grabbed a roll of paper towels.

Holden may have decided he was done speaking, that whatever unspoken thoughts lingering in his head wouldn't be voiced, but I was tired of the silence, of the distance, of the way he seemed to run from me every time we reached a point where we were communicating what was *real*.

"Too late for what, Holden?"

"Never mind. Just forget it." Shaking a bottle until the clear contents were mixed, bubbles forming at the top before he soaked a paper towel with the solution, he turned to me without meeting my gaze. "Come here. Let me get that off your nose...and chin."

I stepped back, purposely staying out of reach. "Too late for what?"

His expression hardened, his jaw ticking with annoyance that I wouldn't let the subject drop. But maybe that had been my problem all along...all my life, in fact. I'd always allowed other people to dictate what was said and what was done, and here I was being made to promise to stop remaining silent while Holden was forcing me into the exact same corner he'd asked me never to be forced in again. So I wouldn't. I would make the promise. And I would keep it. Starting now.

"I want to know what you were going to say, and I won't let you come near me until you say it."

"Michaela, just drop it-"

"No. I won't just drop it. You don't want me to be silent anymore, Holden. You just said that. So, fine, I promise you I'll push for what I want in life. I promise I'll speak up when I should. I promise I won't bow down to what other people want when I know it goes against everything I know is right. And this, whatever it was you were about to say, is important to me. It's right. So I won't just *drop it*. Tell me what you were going to say."

My eyes locked to his, determination holding me in place as I stared down a man that looked like he was ready to stalk away like he always did. "Too late for what?"

Breathing out, he crushed the paper towel in his hand. "Michaela-"

"Tell me," I demanded, refusing to back down for the first time in my life.

Holden's mouth opened and closed several times, a curse word muttered under his breath before he finally met my eyes again with indecision flaring behind his blue gaze.

I didn't care about his indecision, he was going to tell me whether he liked it or not. For the last time, I made my demand. "Tell me, Holden. Too late for what?"

CHAPTER TWENTY-ONE

Holden

Have you ever had a moment when words cling to the edge of your tongue begging to be spoken, but your mind knows, your heart knows, that once those words are given voice, you will never be able to repair the damage they cause?

I was in one of those moments with Michaela, my eyes caught by hers, my pulse jagged and sharp beneath my skin as silence surrounded us both.

How do you tell a person that you finally know who they are? How do you say sorry for having judged them harshly? How do you forgive yourself for wanting to scream from rooftops that you've finally found the one, while knowing you would leave that perfect person standing alone in the dark?

Speaking the words trapped by my indecision would eventually leave Michaela drowning in heartache. Not saying them at all was as good as lying without remorse, as good as denying what was true about a woman I had only just discovered.

It's too late for me to love you.

It's too late to admit I was wrong.

It's too late to tell you how wonderful you are despite everything this town has done.

Saying what was on my mind would only drag her into the same hell I was living. The same hopeless situation where something beautiful could have been born if I weren't facing going away from her forever. Despite how cruel my words would be, she stood staring at me with hopeful eyes, putting her foot down for the

197

first time, leaving herself open to be crushed by a truth that would only destroy us both.

I'm not a stupid man. My entire life has been spent observing other people. And except for this woman standing before me now, I'd never been wrong about what I knew existed beneath the lies that every person wore.

Everybody but her, a woman I'd watched for so long, a part of her calling to me since the moment I met her, a part I'd willfully ignored.

Her full lips parted just barely, her eyes searching my face. Her expression frozen in a moment I wanted to paint. This moment. Right now. When the veil had slipped to reveal a soul as abused as me who was just now learning how to gather her life to herself and take charge.

Forgive me...

"Too late for me to know you for who you really are, Michaela." My admission was spoken on a rush of regretful breath, but I voiced it regardless, dropping my own veil for her to see that the man who had been running from her for the past four days was really just a coward who couldn't face that his heart had been right for over ten long years to want her. "It's too late for me to know what it's like being with a woman I could have loved all along."

Greens eyes blinking, lips parting even more, Michaela's entire demeanor changed as soon as the words were released from the confines of my innermost thoughts. She transitioned from a woman asserting herself for the first time, to a woman weighed down by a confession she must have suspected, but never let herself believe could be real.

Disbelief saturated her soft voice. "You've known me since we were children, and you're just now telling me this?"

Shrugging, I admitted, "We barely spoke. We hardly knew each other beyond our connection to Delilah. It's like I said. I'm too late."

Clearing her throat of some emotion I wanted, no *needed*, her to deny, Michaela stepped forward, her fingers moving as if she wanted to reach out, to touch, to cross that invisible barrier I'd placed between us the minute I recognized I wanted to *feel* her inside myself.

People are so quick to throw the word 'love' around as if it were something distinct and separate from themselves. As if it were simple, basic, or exact. They confuse it with lust. They confuse it with romance. They confuse it with the simple interest they have to learn about another human being. But in that confusion, they lessen what it really means.

If you truly love someone, you feel them in every cell of your body. Whether they're right next to you, or a million miles away, that person is still the air you breathe, is still the first thought on your mind, is still so indelibly embedded in your heart that to lose them is to lose a piece of yourself. Love doesn't distinguish between a mother, a son, a sister, a brother, a father, or the woman a man eventually calls his wife. It's not interchangeable. It's not a word that has alternate definitions. It exists or it does not. And once it exists, *truly* exists, it never goes away.

Romance, lust, friendship, attraction, interest - those words carry alternate meanings, they can be applied and stripped away once the honeymoon is over, but love never falters, not in divorce, not in anger, not even in death.

It NEVER goes away.

And that's what makes it so dangerous.

I didn't need love with Michaela, she didn't need it with me, no matter how badly we wanted it, only because it would never disappear once I was sent to prison. It would linger on both of our hearts as a nascent phantom, forever calling to us, but never receiving an answer.

So why couldn't I stop myself from feeling the first spark of it now?

Shaking her head, Michaela trapped the bottom corner of her lip between her teeth, the movement dragging my gaze down to a set of lips that may as well have been dipped in poison. Releasing it so that the corners of her mouth could curl up into an unsure grin, she stepped forward. "I don't think it's too late."

Despite my heart pounding, my breath pouring out of me with the absolute *need* I had to touch her, I forced myself to step back and replace the distance she'd closed. "I'm going to prison. I know you don't want to believe it, Michaela, but-"

"You're not going," she insisted, stepping forward, closing the distance, forcing me to step back again.

"You can say that as many times as you want, but it doesn't make it true."

Another step forward. Another step back. This dance of ours ending once my body hit a wall, preventing me from maintaining the distance that was necessary to keep from committing my worst sin of all: the intermingling of two hearts that were doomed never to remain together.

Staring at me with expectant eyes that sparkled like priceless emeralds, Michaela stood still for several seconds that felt like minutes, hours, days and weeks, her mouth finally falling open on a question that was more dangerous than she understood.

"What would happen if I kissed you right now, Holden Bishop?"

Dragging in a breath, I released it slowly, my weary eyes never leaving hers. "We would both end up heartbroken."

"Immediately?" she whispered.

"Eventually."

A smile tilted her lips. "I can live with eventually."

I couldn't step away. Couldn't look away. Couldn't catch my breath enough to open my mouth and tell her how *eventually* meant forever. Couldn't explain that in a world full of chaos and heartache and tragedy, we didn't need to add to the pile by taking a chance that would ultimately end in failure.

The distance between us was lost. Her body softly pressed against mine. Our breath intermingling as she craned her neck to look at me, pushing up to her tiptoes to wrap her hands over my shoulders, this view, perspective, this moment captured and frozen in my mind.

My fingers twitched as I fought not to touch her in response. My heart pounded as if to expel that small spark of an emotion I didn't want to consider. My mind raced back to recall all the images of this woman I'd sketched through the years, empty and faceless...until now.

Now I saw her for who she really was.

Now I understood how wrong I'd been about her.

Now I couldn't deny that I'd watched her for years without understanding why.

And when she reached up to pull my head to hers, when her mouth pressed to mine, tentative and tender...

Now I *felt* her for the first time.

Once you feel a person who touches your soul, it's too late to deny that you can't live on for eternity without them.

201

My body reacted before my brain could catch up, my hands going to her hips, my fingers gripping down so that I could pull her against me tighter, so that I could lift her a little higher and deepen her tentative kiss until it was as destructive and violent as fire.

She tasted like heaven and hell all wrapped up in one, her scent like fresh flowers blooming over a field that had once been barren. The heat of her skin scorched my own, the sounds escaping her throat...

Damn. I'd lost the fight against her before I realized we'd even started battling.

My thoughts were cut off so completely that all the warnings stopped screaming, my hands lifting her legs to wrap around my hips so that I could turn and press her against the wall she'd trapped me against earlier. And the second our bodies connected in places that should have been left alone, the only warning that softly whispered was that if I didn't have her now, I would burst apart at the seams, I would shatter to the ground or implode.

This. This was the moment I'd been running from since the day I brought her into my house, and I realized quickly that the running had been futile because *eventually* would always come.

We kissed like two people who had never known true passion, like two separate souls waking up for the first time to discover there was a perfect fit staring them in the face, and once that kiss had left us both breathless until we were forced to pull apart, I pressed my forehead to hers while gulping down oxygen, my eyes locked to hers, our gazes wide and startled.

"I want to take you to my bedroom," I finally said once my lungs were no longer gasping.

"You should," she answered just as breathless as me.

"I really shouldn't."

"But you're going to."

I hated how simple her argument was. If she'd said anything else, maybe I would have stood a chance, but instead my fingers tightened over the cheeks of her butt, a growl rumbling from my chest because despite what my mind was telling me to do, my body wasn't hearing it.

"Yeah," I answered, "I think you're right."

"Stop thinking," she whispered.

So, I did.

CHAPTER TWENTY-TWO
Michaela

It was the abs. Had to be the abs. There was nothing else more powerful and mind-altering as three sets of muscles toned over the male body that could cause a woman's mind to go on temporary hiatus long enough for her to do something she might live to regret.

Not just abs, but paint speckled abs. Abs that carried the mark of an artist's trade, the hint of a beautiful mind, the knowledge that within the recesses of that man's body lay a soul that was far more brilliant and superior than mine.

The abs were his first mistake if he had been serious about keeping this from happening. His words had been the second mistake, the mistake that solidified every decision in my mind that I wouldn't allow him to keep running.

He should have listened to me when I warned him about those abs four days ago, should have taken my advice to heart and kept them covered. But instead, he'd forgotten they were rational mind kryptonite, and that's how we ended up pressed together as he carried me down the hall away from the peace of his studio and into a black and white bedroom covered by the sketches he'd created of his world.

I remembered his bed from being tied up on top of it, every detail of that day coming back to me in stunning colors that meant nothing now that I was learning what it really meant to be in this bed.

The locker room gossip I'd overheard in school didn't even begin to describe what it felt like to have Holden's full attention on you. This man that had captured my attention so many years ago was now showing me why I could never fully ignore him in the halls of Tranquil Falls High, why I'd felt shy and beautiful both during dance practice as he sat off to the side - why I'd cried for three straight weeks after Jack had almost killed him in the accident.

Holden was everything in this moment, all hands, and tongue and teeth, and I couldn't cling on tight enough, couldn't move against him hard enough, couldn't steal enough of his glorious heat fast enough to warm the places inside me that my life until now had turned cold.

We moved together as if choreographed, my fingers exploring the dips and valleys of his body, his mouth exploring every tiny place on my jaw, my neck, behind my ear that made me whimper and beg and whimper some more.

Damn him for being so patient, and attentive, and surprisingly gentle when all I wanted was for him to lose control.

"You sure about this?"

His question burst against my ear on hot breath that forced goosebumps to erupt over my entire body, my head shaking yes, my mind screaming, *I've never been more sure about anything, ever.*

But I couldn't talk, couldn't catch my breath enough to formulate a word on a tongue and lips that were desperate to explore every toned and tight muscle my fingers had already had the opportunity to discover.

Holden's forehead pressed to the side of my head, his chest beating with labored breath, his hands gripping on to me with far too much restraint. "Damn it. You were supposed to say no."

Except we'd passed the point when I could say no to anything having to do with this man. But instead, I whimpered again because it was the only intelligible sound I could manage, my hands sliding down his body to find his hips, my grip pulling his body so tight to mine that I could feel every square inch of his arousal against my stomach.

No was no longer a word defined by the dictionary, at least not the dictionary programmed into my brain at that moment.

My silence must have clued him in to my iron-clad refusal to stop this moment from happening. His hands loosened their hold on me, creating a moment of panic as he slipped off my body to escape the bed. I reached to drag him back to me, only to see the corners of his mouth dip down with regret before he started laughing. "I'm just pulling a condom out of the drawer in my bedside table. I didn't really need you to move with me."

Oh. Well. Yeah. Safe sex is always a good plan. I was glad he was responsible enough to think of it.

Crawling back my direction, he dropped the condom on the bed, ignoring the need for safety as our bodies collided back together, my shirt - or I guess I should say *his* shirt, since he'd loaned it to me - was no longer covering me, my bra the only barrier still preventing our chests from being bare against each other, his mouth aggravatingly thorough as he kissed every square inch of visible skin and avoided those parts still covered.

Don't get me wrong, I wasn't complaining. I just wasn't used to a man who spent more time turning me on than trying to get to the final act to satisfy himself. I now understood what it meant to be 'spoiled', why those girls in high school couldn't find anybody after Holden that didn't make them want to go running right back to a man who could only offer them casual sex. My mind drifted to the question of why he never seriously dated someone, but then...

Oh! Right there...

He was all over me at that point, his scent, his touch, his essence, his soul, all burning and teasing and tasting and maddening. If he didn't take off my clothes in the next five minutes, I'd roll him over, pin him to the bed and undress myself for him.

His mouth opened again, this time with words that sent me into a panicked overdrive because it meant he was running again. "Maybe we should stop."

No! No we should not stop. I wasn't able to utter the sharp refusal, not as breathless as I was, not with his hands still gripped over my hips, my legs wrapped around his body. My head fell back against his pillow, my eyes peeling open and blinking away the haze of lust that was blanketing me in heat and desperation.

"If you stop, I swear to everything that is holy, I'll find those ropes you used to tie me up and I'll do the same to you."

Laughter shook his chest against mine, the tone of his voice dropping so low that every syllable he spoke vibrated against my skin. Mouth pressed to my ear, he answered, "Maybe I'd like that."

"Next time," I breathed out, directing his hands to better places. He gripped down with his fingers, stopping me.

"I'm serious, Michaela. I'm not going to be able to give you anything beyond this."

Yes, he was. He just didn't know it yet. I still wasn't sure how I would explain Jack's disappearance once we failed to show for the holidays, but I'd worry about that later. Much later.

"You never gave anything beyond sex to anyone else, so I'm not sure how that's a problem."

His hand gripped my chin so fast, I gasped at the speed of it. Eyes locking to mine with anger blazing behind the blue, he stared at me for several seconds as the mood dissipated into hostility. "You are worth more than just a casual fling, and if I ever hear you settling for less than what you deserve, I will personally kick your ass for it. Do you understand me?"

Whoa...

At first, I nodded in acceptance of his demands, but then my eyes narrowed on him, my own anger drifting to the surface because I was tired of him making demands of me while settling for the bullshit life had handed *him*.

"And you are worth more than a prison cell, your life getting tossed aside because of the assholes in this town."

Holden flinched as if I'd slapped him, his body moving away until I reached out and stopped him before he could exit the bed. Let him run. Let him hide away as much as he wanted, but that didn't mean I couldn't chase him down, didn't mean I couldn't drag him out from beneath whatever rock he'd decided to crawl under and make him face reality.

"I will let you leave this bed if you can look me in the eye and honestly tell me that you feel nothing for me beyond wanting sex. If you can say that, and say it without blatantly lying, then I'll let you go right now and we can forget this ever happened. But if you feel for me the way I feel for you, then do me a favor and fucking SHOW me how a man treats a woman he's falling in love with."

His jaw dropped, pride flashing behind his blue eyes before heat swept in to replace it. "I never meant I only wanted you for sex, Michaela, but you and I both know there's a body out there just waiting to be discovered and when that happens, my time with you will be over. That's not what I want, but it's what will happen, so when I say that this is all I can give you, I'm not saying it's by choice. Not my choice, anyway."

My words were practically spoken on a growl. "Then I'll take whatever time I can, Holden, and if you try to deny me even a minute more of it, I'll be sure to personally kick your ass for wasting whatever time we might have left."

Game.

Set.

Match.

Not another word was uttered in argument. He was on top of me again in a second flat and this time my clothes were being ripped away.

Finally!

Of all the talents I already knew were born into this man, this beautiful soul, this person that had taken all of Tranquil Fall's crap and still managed to keep an arrogant smile on his lips, he possessed one other talent I hadn't considered...Holden could move.

I'd barely had time to catch my breath before his mouth was on me, his legs shoving mine apart, his fingers dipping down to places that had me moaning while he swallowed those sounds and worked me into a frenzy, never stopping, never slowing down, never giving me time to process how I was being pushed toward an orgasm that would make my head explode. And when that moment came, I wasn't ashamed to scream it into his mouth because for the first time ever I was the person deserving of pleasure, even before he'd made a move to take his.

It could have been like this for years if I'd just been stronger, if I cared about myself, my needs and my desires enough to kick Jack and my family to the curb and live my life like I wanted.

I knew what I wanted now. He was on top of me, all around me, crushing me beneath a strong chest and broad shoulders. He was devouring me slowly and I knew when the moment came that he pushed inside me, I would never be able to let him go.

Holden treated me like I was a planet and he was the moon, endlessly circling my orbit. His entire focus was on me, every movement intended for my pleasure, and when tears were leaking from my eyes because I'd never felt so good before, he kissed them away before grabbing the condom to make two bodies become one.

He thrust inside me, filling me completely, and then he began to move.

I didn't have words to describe what he was doing. I couldn't comprehend where I ended and he began. But like two dancers caught in the hypnotic pull of a shared, pulsing rhythm, we matched each other in the frantic sway of our bodies, each pushing and pulling, giving and taking, until a climax bowled us over that left us panting where we lay.

Holden's forehead fell against my chest, sweat causing our bodies to slide against each other, and I ran my fingers through his hair not caring that *this* moment had ended, because to me, *everything else* had just begun.

CHAPTER TWENTY-THREE

Holden

Lives aren't shaped by achievements alone.

My mother used to say that to Deli and me growing up. She used to pull us aside and sit us down when we'd failed at some test or project, when we fell off our bikes while learning to ride, or had broken a rule and were caught.

While we sat there crying, our mom would give us the typical mom speech telling us to try again, or study hard next time, or that she was disappointed we chose to break rules, but she would always follow it up with a reminder that to fail is to learn, even when we purposely chose that failure.

Her speech was one of the memories that was always clear in my head following her death, probably because I broke a lot of rules, but also because, despite my mother's anger or disappointment with me, she'd still taken the time to attempt to make me a better man. It was never just about how she was feeling, it was about raising me to understand that where most men measure themselves by achievements and successes, they make a vital mistake by doing so. Because lives aren't just shaped by the achievements we accomplish, our lives are also shaped by our mistakes.

It's when we're shaped by mistakes that we grow the most, because the true test of a person is not how they achieve a certain goal, it's how they pick up the pieces following failure and keep moving forward.

Sleeping with Michaela had been a mistake. Not the kind of mistake that I wouldn't do over again if given the chance, but the kind that left her alone to pick up the pieces. I knew where I was going. The course of my life

211

had already been decided. But Michaela's? She still had a chance to do something right in her world, and I'd been the selfish bastard to load her heart down with a love that could never be explored or fully kindled into the kind of soft rolling fire that consumes you while warming your body.

But even knowing what was coming, even being aware of the pitfalls we both faced once the holidays passed and I had to answer for my crimes, it didn't stop me from loving her.

My mistake had been her mistake, but only she would have the chance to prove what type of person she was by how she chose to move forward.

A full week had marched forward since the night I took Michaela to my bed, and in those two days, I'd learned what it meant to relax, to be happy, to stop dreading the next hour because, in my life at least, I'd learned that the next hour is never actually guaranteed. Everything changes from one moment to the next, and trauma had shaped me to remain on guard for the next disaster waiting around the corner. Sure I could smile, and I could joke around, and I could lose myself in a woman's body, or in my art and music, but my shoulders never lost their tension, my heart never stopped beating with worry - not unless she was around.

It was selfish, I know, but having Michaela at the house made it feel like a home again. Even though I was still working doubles every day, I looked forward to the few hours I managed to spend with her when returning to a house that had felt empty since the night my parents died. Even with Deli there, I'd felt alone, only because with her injuries, she'd been a ghost of herself, never quite growing or maturing beyond the night everything around us fell apart.

Speaking of Deli, despite my happiness that she'd gone to see family for the holidays, I couldn't get over the worry I felt that no matter how many times I called Uncle Scott's phone, nobody answered. The voicemail message was the standard robotic tone that comes with every phone service, and I left message after message with that fake voice, hoping for a return call. It never came and worry began to nag at me, my thoughts drifting back to the last time Deli had been out of my reach.

She had seemed so small in that hospital bed after her accident. Every day I'd sat at her bedside waiting her to open her eyes, to twitch a finger, to do anything that meant she was coming back to me. But no matter what I'd said, or what I'd done, she hadn't responded. I understood then what it felt like to be a parent, to have the duty to protect someone with the realization lingering at the back of your thoughts that there would be times when their life, their wellbeing, their fate was out of your control and out of your hands. With my parents gone, I'd taken over their role, begging to see the light shine behind Deli's eyes again. But I'd returned home each night feeling like a failure because I hadn't been strong enough to wake her up and bring her home.

That same feeling weighed on me now as I walked home from a long day at work. The snow was falling heavier with every hour that passed, and as I made my way through the woods, I paused just beyond the site where I knew a body lay just waiting to be discovered. The body didn't bother me, but knowing Delilah would be out of my reach once the crime was uncovered set my teeth against each other in a painful clench, my hands tucking deeper inside my pockets as my head tilted down to block the cold wind from slapping against my face.

I had to remind myself that where Delilah was, she was happy. She was with people that loved her and would take care of her when I was gone. I kept telling myself that as I made my way out the woods, emerging on the road and making the left toward my house. Shaking myself of the frustration of unanswered calls, I smiled to know who was waiting for me to arrive, a beautiful brunette who had managed to turn that empty house into a home.

Home...

I'd forgotten what the word meant until the last few days when I looked forward to walking through the door to the scent of dinner waiting for me and the sight of a wide smile on a beautiful face, passion shining behind a set of gorgeous green eyes.

Walking in the door, warmth enveloped me, loneliness stepping aside as soon as Michaela came into view, her body bouncing to the beat of some pop song Delilah would have danced to as well. I rolled my eyes at the sound of it, but smiled regardless. It had been so long since I was assaulted with music that made me grind my teeth, but I hadn't realized how much I'd missed it.

Spinning to look at me even though I hadn't yet made a sound, Michaela's grin beamed and warmed me more than the dry heat pumping through the house could manage.

"Hey," she called out, waving at me with a spatula in her hand. "Dinner's almost done. Why don't you jump in the shower and thaw out before we sit down?"

Click... Another image frozen in my mind, a picture many people had seen in their days arriving home, but hadn't stopped to consider. This was home. Not just a house. Not just an object, but a feeling. *Home...* Michaela had returned it to me without even knowing.

I smiled for the first time in what felt like forever, but really it had only been hours since she'd made me smile like this before. "Yeah, okay. I'll be out in a second."

214

The hot water against my skin felt wonderful, but not as heavenly as what I knew waited for me once I climbed out from beneath the spray. I'd well and truly fallen for a woman that had been here against her will initially, but had the strength to take a bad situation and turn it around. Over the past week, I'd marveled at the changes in Michaela, and although I wanted to take credit for the transformation in her demeanor, I knew the majority of it had to do with these past days being the first that she'd allowed who she really was inside to shine through. This town had held her down as much as it had me, but in different ways.

Where I'd been labeled as the King of Freaks and shunned by a town that couldn't tolerate my differences, she had been sat upon the throne of an exalted queen, her wrists tied down to the armrests by ropes made of demands and expectations. While drying my hair as best I could with a damp towel, I realized that being labeled 'crazy' had been much easier than the labels they'd forced her to carry.

The scent of food slammed into me again as soon as I stepped out of my bedroom, the table already set as I padded barefoot and famished out into the kitchen. Michaela spun around to look at me, another smile tilting her lips before she wiggled her eyebrows and motioned for me to sit down.

It seemed like she always knew I was there, no matter how quietly I'd snuck up on her.

Taking a seat at the table, I endured her choice of music while she danced, pouring two glasses of water. Carrying them over, she sat down and smiled. "We need more food. I'm getting creative with what you have left in your freezer and pantry, so I'm not sure how this experiment turned out."

Letting my gaze fall to our plates, I wasn't sure I could identify what she'd cooked, but it smelled good. "I can run up to the store tomorrow. Angela cut me back to only an afternoon shift. She thinks I'm working too hard."

"I can go with you."

My eyes shot up to hers. "I don't think that would be a good idea. If we're seen together-"

Michaela nodded, her lips pulling into a thin line. "Yeah, I'm sorry. I didn't think about that."

The mood was dampened by the reminder of our present circumstances. Reaching across the table, I hooked her pinky with mine. "I wish it could be different."

A hesitant smile tilted her lips before she shrugged off the difficulties we faced. "It is what it is. Let's eat before dinner gets cold."

It was a little impressive what Michaela was able to pull off with limited groceries and a lot of imagination. I devoured what was on my plate, shoving it away as I laid my hands over my belly, letting out a dramatic groan as if I would burst by eating one more bite. Michaela was still picking at her food, a shallow line creased between her brow that had been there since the minute we sat down. Every so often she would peek over at me, a question lingering on her mind that she still hadn't voiced. Now that my stomach was full, my curiosity got the better of me.

"What's wrong?"

Swallowing down the small bite she'd taken, she pointed her fork at me. "Shouldn't I be asking you that question?"

My brow arched over my eye. "Okay, I'm game. Why do you think something is wrong with me?"

216

"Angela gave you time off. She wouldn't have done that if something wasn't eating at you. Plus, you've been stomping around."

Laughter burst from my mouth. "I haven't been stomping."

"Yes, you have. It's how I know when you're behind me."

Well, damn. And here I thought I was being sneaky.

"So, fess up, Bishop. What's wrong?"

More laughter shook my shoulders. This new Michaela was turning out to be a lady you didn't want to mess with. "I'm worried about Deli. I've been calling Uncle Scott's place for the past week and they haven't picked up or returned my messages."

Michaela's eyes met mine, concern filtering behind her gaze that she attempted to hide with a smile. "When is she supposed to come home?"

"After the holidays, but I'm not sure how all of that will go down. We have three days left until your family notices you're missing. And given how many people saw what happened the night Jack and you showed up at the diner, I'm sure my door is one of the first places the cops will be knocking."

"So, don't answer."

Sorrow sliced through me. "They'll find me eventually, Michaela. You need to accept that."

"I'm not accepting anything, yet. Not until I figure out how to get us both out of this."

Standing up before I had the chance to argue, she grabbed both our plates and walked them to the sink, cutting off the topic of conversation. After dropping the plates down, she moved back over to me and grabbed my hand. "Come on."

Both my brows shot up my forehead. "Are we going somewhere?"

Flashing me a wry grin, she answered, "You're going into your studio since being in there calms you down. I've been taking up way too much of your time over the past week with my bedroom antics and you need to blow off some steam."

Raw heat filtered through me. "I wouldn't say my time with you isn't a way of blowing off steam."

One yank had her falling into my lap, a surprised shriek bursting over her lips. My mouth trailed down her neck, my teeth nipping at the skin. Whispering close to her ear, I argued, "in fact, what we've been doing these past few days has been quite helpful in blowing a lot of things."

"Damn it, Holden," she yelled, laughter coating her words. "That's not what I mean and you know it. Now, come on."

She shot to her feet and pulled me with her to drag me down the hallway toward the studio. Confused by the sudden direction we were going, I asked, "Are you coming in with me?"

"Yep. I like it in there. And I love seeing you work. It's relaxing."

"You're using me to relax? How dare you?"

Opening the door, she glared up at me. "Whatever. Just take off your shirt and get to work."

"Yes, ma'am," I answered, stripping off the t-shirt from my chest and tossing it aside. I'd never been forced into my studio before, so I wasn't quite sure I was mentally in a place to begin painting, but the minute the smell of the room wafted beneath my nose, my fingers itched to create, to draw, to bring to life the myriad of images endlessly circling in my head.

While Michaela took a seat on the floor against the wall, I went about my usual routine of choosing music to fit my mood and arranging my materials to work on the painting of Delilah that was close to finished. She had been on my mind the most that day and taking a brush to her image helped alleviate the loneliness I felt with her being away.

Seconds bled into minutes that bled into an hour while Michaela silently watched me work. Every so often I'd glance back to find her entranced by the art coming to life in front of her. Finding myself overtaken by the serenity of what I was doing, I didn't notice the soft rustle behind me, didn't bother to check what Michaela was doing until I heard her clear her throat to grab my attention.

Glancing over my shoulder, my entire body tensed with confusion mixed with pure *want*.

She didn't have a stitch of clothing on, her back arched just slightly off the floor, her shoulders and hips firm to the ground and her head turned toward me with a teasing smile gracing her lips.

"What are you doing? Trying to distract me?"

It was working. Dropping my paintbrush and palette to the floor, I memorized the sleek lines of her body, the shadows that traced the muscles down her calves, the perfect curve of her breasts.

"Paint me," she suggested. "Draw me like one of your-"

Holding up a hand, I silenced her. "No. Don't even say it. That is one of the most overused movie quotes of all time."

Laughter shook her shoulders. "Fine. Then use what you have in front of you, Holden. I'll be your model."

Oh. I definitely wanted to use what was in front of me, but not in the way she'd suggested.

"You want me to draw you?"

Head nodding slowly, she said, "I see all these wonderful paintings of people that caught your eye, and

I'm not in any of them." Shrugging, she added, "I figured a woman needs to take her clothes off to get your attention around here."

My lips twitched with humor. What this particular girl didn't know is that I had sketchbooks stored in my room with dozens of pictures of her. She'd had my attention long before I ever had the chance to know the woman she would become.

Stepping across the room I grabbed a sketchbook and pencil then sat down near her and raked my eyes over a body that was absolute perfection. Jutting my chin in her direction, I instructed, "Fold your hands together beneath your head, and spread your legs a little wider."

Sin was the edge of her smile. "This picture is becoming a lot more pornographic than I imagined."

My eyes met hers. "Who's the artist? And who's the model?"

Soft laughter. "I've been sufficiently schooled."

Her legs spread slightly, just enough to send a wave of lust through me that was so toxic holding the sketchpad on my lap became uncomfortable. My fingertips slid against the smooth surface of the pencil, my lips parting just enough to drag in a deeper breath of air, but when the lead should have scratched across the plain sheet of paper, I found myself dropping it instead, a startled cry tumbling from Michaela's mouth when I stood to my feet, closed the distance between us and lifted her to carry over my shoulder. I was halfway down the hall before she realized that particular modeling session was over.

"Holden!" She cried out, still laughing despite the way my fingers clamped over the cheek of her ass. "You're supposed to be drawing me, not taking me to your bedroom."

For that one moment, I believed everything in life didn't have to go wrong.

"I'm still going to draw you," I promised, "I'm just taking you somewhere to get a more thorough inspection."

We fell into each other's arms that night without worry of the future.

I should have known better than to forget that in the happiest moments we find in our lives, circumstances always have a way of changing.

. . .

It was around one in the morning when my eyes peeled open, my body lifting from the bed as my head turned toward a noise outside the door of my dark bedroom. The shuffling of feet. The screech of the legs of a chair over the dining room floor. The sound of a glass being set down on the table. Shaking my head of the sleep that still kept me hazy, I listened again, unsure if the sounds had been real or a figment of my imagination.

A cough.

The glass.

I recognized those sounds.

Shifting off the bed, I left Michaela sleeping soundly beneath the covers as I pulled on a pair of jeans and slipped from the room. The house was silent again, but I knew, I just KNEW, Michaela and I weren't alone.

Slowly, I crept down the hall, my shoulder pressed to the corner as I leaned past to look into the dining room.

What I found was both a relief and a shock.

"Deli?"

Seated at the table, my little sister turned her head in my direction, the quick movement causing her hair to slip over her shoulder to hang down her arm. "Holden? I'm sorry. I didn't mean to wake you."

Blinking away the remaining sleep, my body rounded the corner of the hall, stepping closer to a girl who should not have been sitting in this house. "Why are you here? It's one in the morning. Did something happen?"

Her expression fell, the smile slipping from her lips as if she'd expected a better reaction. Guilt wove through my heart, my weight settling into a chair at the table opposite her.

"Aren't you happy to see me?"

Reaching across the table, I rested my hand over hers. "Of course, I'm happy to see you, but I didn't expect you home until after Christmas, and I don't understand why you're here so late."

Deli rolled her eyes. "Did you really think I'd leave you, Holden? I don't want you to be alone for the holidays."

"Del," I breathed out, my forehead pressing down on the table as I considered all the serious complications my sister's presence created. The first and foremost being the woman presently sleeping in my bed that had no explainable reason for being here. "You know I'm working doubles-"

"I don't care, silly. It's the holidays and you shouldn't be alone."

I wasn't exactly alone, but she didn't know that yet. Admitting as much, my voice was soft for fear our talking would wake Michaela before I had a chance to explain everything to Del.

"I'm not alone."

Surprise shot her eyebrows up her forehead. "Is that girl from the diner here?"

Shaking my head, I breathed out slowly. "Uh, no. Actually, Michaela Paige is here."

Her eyebrows shot higher. "I - I'm not even sure what to say about that. How? Why? Are you dating Michaela?"

I nodded my head, fear squeezing my heart as hard as I was squeezing her hand. "It's a long story, but I wanted you to know before you wake up in the morning to find her here."

Confusion wrinkled her expression. Seconds of silence slipped past, worrying me and leaving me struggling for a decent draw of breath. Deli's eyes met mine when she asked, "Does she make you happy?"

That was the million dollar question, wasn't it? Taking my time to consider the question, I couldn't help the way my lips curled up at the corners. "Yeah, actually. She does."

Shrugging, she grinned, "Then I'm happy she's here. The more the merrier, right?"

Leave it to Delilah to simply accept a person based solely on my opinion of them. I'd hoped to break her of that habit over the years, but sometimes it was just the way things were between close siblings: the younger always looked to the older for their opinions and advice. "Yeah. The more the merrier. But, Del, you should have stayed with Uncle Scott. We don't have anything here to celebrate. There isn't a tree, or presents, or even food for a holiday meal."

"You're here," she reminded me. "And that's all that matters to me. We're family, Holden. We're supposed to be together at Christmas."

I opened my mouth to keep arguing, but Deli yawned so loud, I knew she was too tired for a long conversation. Exhaustion was weighing me down as well. I decided I could save my questions for the morning.

"We should both get some sleep, little sis. We can talk more later."

Nodding her head, Deli stood from her seat. "I think you're right, Holden. I'm going to go to bed. I'll see you in the morning."

A tired grin stretched my lips. "Goodnight."

She didn't say another word before turning to disappear down the hall. Left at the table, I held my head in my hands and took a few minutes to think about all the problems Deli's presence would cause. After some thought, I realized Michaela wasn't the issue that should have worried me the most. It was the concern I had about what would happen to my sister once the holidays were over and everybody in Tranquil Falls knew that Jack and Michaela were missing.

CHAPTER TWENTY-FOUR
Michaela

Waking up the next morning, I grinned at the soreness of my body when I stretched. Normally people would react badly to pain, but I welcomed the discomfort, only because it reminded me of the hours Holden and I had spent intertwined, exploring each other and making our *closer inspections*, my laughter rising up above his insistence that he had to see every intimate part to ensure he got the painting just right.

Something about his eyes staring down at me felt natural. It felt like he'd always been watching, even when he'd been nothing more than a shadow roaming the halls of Tranquil Falls High.

What grabbed my attention the most after I'd pushed myself to the side of the bed was the lack of running water. If Holden wasn't lying here beside me, he was normally in the shower, but given he had the morning off, perhaps he'd found something else to do. A loud clatter in the kitchen drew my attention next, a low voice cursing before another crash.

Oh, hell no. He'd invaded my kitchen apparently and after the week I'd spent rearranging everything where it could be easily found, I shoved myself to my feet to march out there and keep the damage he was causing to a minimum.

Rounding the corner of the hall, I froze in step, my eyes rounding to see Holden in a pair of loose jeans hanging off his hips, his chest and abs bared to my eyes, his hands running through his hair as he stared at the pots and pans he'd thrown on the stove only to discover we were down to the bare minimum when it came to food.

I considered sneaking up on him, but the poor guy looked like he couldn't take another surprise. Clearing my throat instead, a smile split my face to see him spin on his heel, his expression flustered, his hair sticking up and out from running his hands through it.

"Problem?" I asked, leaning a shoulder against the wall.

"We have no food. How in the hell have you been making meals out of -" Looking in the fridge, he listed, "sugar, a jar of pickles, a packet of ketchup and a half used block of cheese?"

The refrigerator door slammed shut before he looked at me again. "Are you magic?"

Laughter shook my shoulders. "I told you I had to get creative."

"Creative? Are you kidding me? I was tearing everything apart looking for the magic wand."

Walking into the room, I sat at the table and wondered what it was about him this morning that was different. I couldn't quite put my finger on it, but Holden seemed happier, more relaxed. There was an extra spring to his step, a lightness about him that made him more adorable than usual. "I hide the magic wand. It would be dangerous if it got into the wrong hands." Pausing, I asked, "What's going on with you this morning? I thought you'd want to sleep in since you don't have work."

Standing behind the island with his palms pressed the counter, he rolled his neck and answered, "Normally, I would, but I'm cooking for two this morning. I need to get to the store."

Before I could question him, Holden spun and grabbed a pencil and a pad of paper, spinning back before rolling his neck again.

"Cooking for two, as in you and me?"

His eyes flicked up to me, "You and Deli. She's home."

My eyes widened in shock, but he didn't glance up at me again, one hand writing a list while the other rubbed at the back of his neck. "Could you do me a favor? There's some ibuprofen in the medicine cabinet in my bathroom. Will you grab me two?"

"Sure. Are you feeling sick?"

"A headache. They happen every once in a while. Ever since the -" Holden's eyes locked to mine as his voice trailed off.

Ever since the accident... he hadn't wanted to say. It didn't matter if he said the words or not, they still hung between us, still sent a shot of guilt through my heart.

"They're infrequent," he explained softly, "I haven't had one in a couple months."

After retrieving the medicine for him, I returned to the kitchen. Holden was finishing his list, his eyes scanning the pantry to see what we already had. "It would probably be easier to make a list of what we have rather than don't have."

Head turning to me, he grinned. "Good point. Did you find the medicine?"

Holding out my hand, I dropped the white pills in his palm. He swallowed them without water.

"Delilah's here?"

Grimacing at the question, he tore the grocery list from the pad, but rather than turning to me, he paused. "Yeah, my sister's back. I don't know why, but we have to pretend like everything is okay around her."

His eyes finally met mine. "I told her about you already so it won't be a surprise, but the other stuff...please, just don't say anything. I don't want our last memories together to be sad. I just want her to be happy. Okay?"

Nodding, only because I was in too much shock to speak actual words, I stood in place as he stepped around me on the way to his bedroom. Before he turned the corner of the hall, he stopped. "This doesn't change anything, Michaela. If that's what you're worried about?"

His eyes met mine as the understanding settled over me that I wasn't as worried about Delilah's unexpected arrival as I was Holden's odd behavior. Although it was nice to see him lose the ever-present brooding, the happiness seemed wrong, somehow. Forced. Fake. There, but not genuine.

Shaking off the concern, I smiled. "I know."

"Awesome. I'm going to get dressed and catch a cab to the store." He walked around the corner, but then popped his head around again to say, "Del's asleep, but she might wake up before I get back. If so, maybe you two can talk about, well, whatever girls talk about."

And then he was gone again, his bedroom door closing, leaving me standing alone in his kitchen. Taking a seat at the table, I stared at the empty hall, worry blanketing me, a nagging feeling that something wasn't right. It was possible I was worrying for nothing. In conversations with Holden, it was obvious he adored his sister. All through school, the only time he'd reacted to anything the other students said or did was when it involved her, but the change in his demeanor was still startling, even given what I knew about their close relationship.

I was still seated at the table when Holden reappeared from the hallway, his body bulky from the hoodie and jacket he wore. With a black beanie covering his head, he gave me a small wave before saying, "I'll be back in a little while." He rushed out the door a second later, not even giving me a chance to respond.

My heart sank into my stomach, dread thundering in my head that I tried to excuse away as nothing. It was reasonable to think he was reacting badly to his sister's sudden presence. We were both facing the eventual storm that would come on the day Jack and I were discovered missing. People react differently to all sorts of situations, so it wasn't completely unbelievable that Holden was acting off out of fear of what was to come, but, even with that reasoning, I couldn't shake the nagging whisper that I was missing *something*.

Perhaps Delilah would know. She knew her brother better than anybody in Tranquil Falls and if she thought his behavior was normal, then maybe...

Staring at the hall, I considered going into her room to wake her up. Deciding against it, I opted for watching some television to wait for her to wake on her own. It didn't help to stop the incessant whispers. The only thing television helped to do was pass the time.

Two hours passed with no sign of Delilah. She was still sleeping in her room when Holden returned home.

Watching him from the couch, I said nothing as he carried in the groceries, making several trips back and forth to get them all. By the time he'd put everything away and had pulled food out to make breakfast, I was sitting at the dining room table again, watching him.

The silence between us was deafening. "Did you want me to go wake up Delilah?" I finally asked.

Glancing at me quickly before turning back to the stove, he answered, "No. She got in late last night. She's probably just exhausted. I'll wake her in a little while."

"Okay," I muttered, worry firmly holding me in its grip.

The remainder of the morning was spent in awkward silence, Holden's attention distracted, absent, directed at anything besides me. By the time he had to leave for work

229

that afternoon, Delilah still hadn't emerged, even though he'd taken her breakfast in her room.

Was it because of me? The question echoed in my head while Holden did everything to politely ignore me, and his sister refused to come out of her room. The silence was giving me a complex, my eyes tracking Holden as he darted through the house, pulling on his winter clothes as he prepared to leave for work.

My thoughts drifted back to the last time I saw Delilah. I remembered the anger in her expression, the rage in her voice when she chased me from Holden's hospital room, screaming at me that I was small.

Perhaps I was no longer welcome here now that she'd returned home. The breakfast in my stomach rolled over itself, settling into a firm ball that sickened me.

On his last pass as he headed to the door, Holden only looked at me as a second thought. "I'll be back at my usual time tonight. I think Del is still doing whatever, so I'll see you later." He didn't wait for me to respond before he was gone.

The ball of food threatened to shoot up my throat.

What had just happened? It was blatantly apparent that Holden was running again. It was the same behavior from a week ago, the same refusal to acknowledge what was standing right in front of him. Cold had swept in to replace the warmth of the past week, worry overshadowing the progress we'd made, the past coming back to slap us in the face, reminding us that it had never gone away in the first place.

The old Michaela would have simply accepted the turn about, would have grit her teeth while other people dictated the direction her life would take. But I wasn't the old Michaela anymore, was I?

Holden had made me promise not to let people push me around. Had made me promise to stand up and speak out when something was glaringly wrong.

Well, this was wrong. And I refused to sit back and settle for whatever changes were taking place without at least fighting for what I knew was right.

Bravery washed through me, the determination to correct the mistakes of the past. Seeing as how Delilah was the only new piece to the puzzle of Holden's behavior, I assumed Delilah was also the only person I could go to in order to reverse this new course and turn it back into what it had been not even twenty-four hours before.

Decision made, I pushed up from the couch and moved down the hallway, pausing for a minute as my hand hovered over the knob of her door. Barging in would be rude and might lead to another fight, so I knocked first, waiting several seconds before knocking again.

Nobody answered.

I didn't care if she didn't want to talk to me. I'd knocked. I'd tried to be polite, but this silence and avoidance wasn't going to work if I had any hope of chasing Holden down again to stop him from running.

"Delilah?" I called.

No answer.

Turning the knob, I cracked the door, slowly pushing it open with the expectation that Delilah would yell at me. I knew she wasn't sleeping, Holden had taken her food before he left, but only silence filled the room as I edged around the door to peek in.

Freezing in place, I looked around as the door swung the rest of the way open, the room coming into view, unchanged from when I'd last seen it.

Confusion flooded me.

Everything was the same, except for the plate of untouched food sitting on the bedside table.

The bed was still made.

There were no bags on the floor or anywhere to show that someone had returned home.

The room was untouched from when I'd last come in to grab movies.

Despite Holden's insistence that his sister had returned home, the room was empty.

CHAPTER TWENTY-FIVE
Holden

I felt like a complete ass for leaving Michaela the way I did, but something wasn't right with Delilah. Even though she'd accepted what I told her the night before, she had woken the following morning and refused to come out of her room. Anger had filtered across her features at the mention of Michaela, and worse, she'd reverted back to wanting to sleep all the time, wanting to wait for our parents to return.

The entire walk to the diner was made in aggravating silence, my worries once again rushing back to suffocate every step forward I'd made with this new relationship with Michaela. All the happiness I'd felt, the hope I shouldn't have had, the belief that for even a brief stretch of days I could relax, was gone. Reality had returned when Deli had walked through the front door, the *home* I'd believed it was becoming returning back to the *house* it had always been.

Four walls. Silent. Empty. Crumbling down around me, trapping me within a town that had only treated me poorly.

More guilt flooded me because I understood that Deli's presence was the only thing left holding me to this town. A horrible thought filtered in to mingle with the rest:

If I hadn't stayed to take care of my sister, would I be facing prison now?

And if that thought weren't bad enough, the scene I walked into at the diner was the final nail in the coffin of my shitty day.

Cop cars.

Officers in uniform.

Angela standing in the center of the diner speaking to them as her eyes glanced out the window.

I should have gone around back. Should have snuck away silently. But running wouldn't hide me for long. And in truth, I didn't know why the cops were there. It could have been about anything. I walked through the front door, stepping out of the freezing cold and into a roaring fire.

"Holden," Angela called out, "could you come here a minute?"

Clenching my eyes shut, I ignored the spark of pain shooting down my jaw from grinding my teeth. Crossing the diner to where Angela stood with three officers, I kept my hands balled up in my pockets, my eyes scanning their faces with concern hazing my eyes. "What's up?"

The red color dusting Angela's cheeks was the first clue she was angry, the way her eyes locked to mine with disgust written behind them the second clue. "These officers are here asking about Jack Thorne and Michaela Paige."

Fear and anger traced down my spine, my muscles tightening over my bones to realize that the future I'd been dreading had arrived. "What about them?"

Glaring at the officers before returning her attention to me, she informed me, "I asked the same question when they came trotting in here, but they insist that those two kids are missing and that the last time they were seen in town was when they attacked you in *my* diner."

The oldest of the officers held up his hands as if to stop her tirade. A couple inches shorter than me, but with a belly that hung heavy over his belt, the officer had brown hair that was thinning on top, his eyes darting to me before locking on Angela again. "Ms. Barrett, if you wouldn't mind, we'd like to speak to Mr. Bishop alone. We'll get back to you once we've had an opportunity to get his statement. If you wouldn't mind giving us a list of the other employees who were on duty that night, we'd like to talk to them as well."

Angela huffed out a breath, her hands shaking as they balled into fists at her sides. I knew she was only trying to protect me, but I couldn't let her get in trouble as well. Not for this. Not for what I'd done. I was thankful my hands were still stuffed inside my pockets. I was shaking as badly as her.

It was typical of Angela not to take shit. Just like she did with her employees and her customers, she would give these officers a piece of her mind if she felt they deserved it. Pointing a finger in the face of the only man who'd spoken since I walked in, she suggested, "Maybe you should check those drug dens on the other side of the tracks you've ignored over the years. If we're all lucky, Jack Thorne will be lying dead in one of them from overdosing."

My jaw ticked at the comment, the woods coming to mind where I knew Jack's body lay waiting.

"Ms. Barrett. We've had enough of your comments. If you could please go get us that list, we'll talk to Mr. Bishop without you."

Another burst of air shot over her lips, anger drawing a line between her narrowed eyes. "I'll go get you the list. Not that it will help you any. I kicked those spoiled, rich assholes out of my diner and nobody here has seen them since."

"Ms. Barrett!" By the tone of his voice, nobody could miss that it had been his last warning. I stepped forward at that point, realizing that if I didn't prod her along, Angela would be leaving here in handcuffs.

"Angela, it's okay," I said softly. "They just want to talk to me. There's no need to get so upset."

Her lips were trembling, the anger filling her so thoroughly that she couldn't keep her body still. Thankfully, she took a second to calm herself and listen to me. Nodding her head once, she stormed off, slamming her office door behind her as she disappeared from view. The windows shook on that side of the diner.

The officers exchanged a look before focusing their attention on me. "Mr. Bishop," the oldest man said, "my name is Officer Timothy Shay. This is my partner Kirk McDonald and a new member on the force who's in training, Jerome Shelton. We'd like to talk to you regarding the whereabouts of Jack Thorne and Michaela Paige."

My stomach rolled with dread, bile creeping up my throat that I had no choice but to swallow. "Okay, what would you like to know?"

Officer Shay's brown eyes locked to mine, the other two officers watching me far too closely for it to be comfortable. I stood in place, too nervous to make a move they might misconstrue as evidence of my guilt. "When was the last time you saw Mr. Thorne?"

Thankfully, I could answer that question without outright lying. "The night he was in the diner screaming at me."

His eyes searched my face for any hint of deceit. "And what happened that night?"

I could still answer this without lying. So far, so good. "He came into the diner and caused a scene. He was screaming and attempting to start a fight. I never came into the dining room, and Angela forced him out the door. He took off after that."

"And then, what happened?"

Shrugging, I said, "I worked the last couple of hours of my shift and walked home." Still the truth.

"And did you see Jack Thorne at all after the incident at the diner?"

Damn. Technically I never saw him alive. He came at me from behind. I didn't remember anything until after I came to by the tree and he was dead. "No."

The officer's eyes narrowed on me. "You're sure?"

"Yes."

I wanted to ask why he was questioning me, wanted to point out that, for years, I was the victim of Jack Thorne, not the other way around. But rather than opening my mouth and giving them reason to look at me a little closer, I kept my answers short and to the point.

Thankfully, they hadn't yet mentioned Michaela's name.

After studying me for several seconds, the officer asked, "Aren't you curious as to why we're asking you these questions?"

"Because Jack and Michaela are missing, I assume."

His brows shot up. "And why would you assume that?"

"Because that's what Angela said when I walked in here."

Stepping back so that he could look me fully up and down, his lips pulled into a thin line. I didn't move, didn't flinch, didn't shuffle a foot or turn my head. I simply stared back at him without giving one indication that I was nervous. Technically, I was about to piss myself, but I refused to show it.

"Son..."

My hackles rose to hear the term. Nobody had called me *son* since Coach Granger on the day I was expelled from school.

"...are you telling me the truth?"

"Yes." Again with the short and simple. I'd save the panic attack for after they left.

Thankfully, Angela came storming back, slapped the list against the officer's chest, crossed her arms and asked, "We done here? I have a diner to run and I don't appreciate my employees being harassed because a selfish, entitled little drug addict thought he could come into *my* diner and attack one of *my* employees. And when you find the little shit, you should remind him that the next time he pulls some crap like that, I won't bother to open the glass door before throwing his ass out of it."

My eyes widened, as did those of the other officers. Officer Shay merely smirked. "Maybe I should be questioning you a little while longer. You seem to have a reason to make someone disappear."

Angela smiled. "Go ahead and question me all you want. While you're at it, why don't you cross the train tracks and question some of the drug dealers living in the abandoned houses. If you knew how to do your job properly, that would have been the first place you looked. I can tell you all of the rich and entitled around here keep those bastards in business. Also, while you're at it, why don't you stop in to one of those wild parties the kids like to throw? I can promise you that you'd have your hands full of underage children drinking and doing drugs. It's not a secret around this town and if you were worth a shit, you'd put a stop to it. Now, if you don't mind, I'd like to get back to doing my job and being a law abiding citizen."

Staring Angela down, Officer Shay's jaw ticked with irritation. But rather than cuffing Angela and hauling her to the squad cars, he nodded his head toward the door. Without saying another word, all three walked out of the diner, got in their cars and left. Angela and I didn't move a muscle until they were out of the parking lot.

A breath blew out of me as soon as they were out of sight. "Damn, Angela, were you trying to get arrested?"

Her eyes pinned me where I stood. "No. I was saving your ass from a prison cell. You know if something happened to that kid, they'll blame you. It doesn't matter if his bloated husk is found lying face down in vomit in one of those drug houses. So let them worry about me. I don't care. They'll look like idiots when they realize I was at the diner all night."

The mixture of relief and guilt was toxic in my veins. Angela had no idea how dangerous it was for the police to look in her direction, especially once they discovered Jack's body. Not responding to her because my throat was clogged with worry, I stood still, my expression blank, my heart pounding and my hands clenching into tight fists in my pockets.

"Now get to work. Dishes are piling up and I don't have time to be standing around staring at each other all day. I don't pay you to stare."

Hesitantly, I grinned, the tension easing inside me to be back to the usual. "Maybe I can't help staring at you. I mean, look at you. You're a goddess."

Her eyes rolled, but I didn't miss the smile that tugged at her lips. "If you don't get your butt in back in the next five seconds, you'll be the third missing person in Tranquil Falls. Now get!"

Walking away, I heard her soft laughter behind me and I knew if I turned to look, her cheeks would be blushing. Once I was in back, I stripped off my coat and hoodie, pulled on the vinyl apron and got to work. Unfortunately, running dishes through a machine wasn't enough to distract me from the fact that the stakes had just been raised in this mess with Michaela.

Wondering how long I had left before I was caught, I did my job while wanting to rage over how fucked up my life was about to become.

CHAPTER TWENTY-SIX

Michaela

After checking every room in the house three times to find that I was very much alone despite Holden's insistence that Delilah had returned, I spent the majority of the day sitting on the couch with my head in my hands, my thoughts completely scattered by the impossibility of the situation. There were two main exits in the house: the front and back doors, both of which would require Delilah to walk past or through the living room. It would have been impossible for her to leave without me seeing her, unless she'd crawled out a window. But really? The likelihood was slim to none. Even if she hated me, I couldn't imagine Delilah doing something as drastic as that.

Which only left one explanation for her absence: Delilah had never returned home in the first place.

I didn't like that explanation, only because it raised serious questions about Holden that I didn't want to consider. Unfortunately, that's exactly what I did during the course of the day. I considered, and it wasn't until Holden returned home that my worries for him were confirmed.

The front door swung open at ten thirty that night, Holden moving through as a dark mass in his winter jacket, hoodie and beanie. His boots tracked snow through the front entrance hall, his face a mask of concern when he took the time to look at me.

Dinner boiled on the stove. Nothing fancy. Just pasta. But it was warm, and it was almost ready. He didn't bother asking when it would be time to eat. As soon as our eyes met, a shadow flashed behind his gaze. Anger. Guilt. Worry. He looked away.

"Hey," I called out, my voice soft and unassuming.

"Hey," he answered, his eyes refusing to meet mine again. Shrugging off his jacket, he dropped it over a half wall that lined the entrance hall. "I need to get a shower and thaw out. I'll be right back."

Before he could disappear into his room, he called out, "Do me a favor and turn on the television. There's something you need to see." With that he closed the door, leaving me standing by the couch, the television screen black because I hadn't bothered to watch it all day. I was too busy...considering.

Now I had something else to consider, and by Holden's behavior, I didn't think I'd be happy about it. The remote was in my hand within the next second. The television coming to life. The reporter's voice an echo throughout the room as my own face stared back at me.

"Former high school football Captain, Jack Thorne was last seen at Tranquil Falls diner with Michaela Paige on Saturday, December eleventh. According to witness reports, Jack Thorne was accosted by an employee of the diner, Holden Bishop. Sources have confirmed Holden Bishop attempted to sue Mr. Thorne two years ago following a car accident that injured Mr. Bishop. At this time, authorities are asking for any information residents may have regarding the whereabouts of Jack Thorne and Michaela Paige. Police have not officially named a suspect, and at this time have only commented that this is an ongoing missing persons case. They would not confirm whether foul play is suspected..."

The reporter's face was replaced by a video of my parents and Jack's parents walking from the police station. Not a single tear was shed between the four of them, only matching expressions of concern. Reporters approached them and our parents turned to face the

241

cameras, their postures astute, their expressions professional. A barrage of questions were being asked and rather than appearing as concerned parents for the welfare of their missing children, they looked as if they were out for dinner, the reporters an annoying distraction more akin to paparazzi than anything else. I knew my parents didn't care much what happened to me. Like Jack's parents, they were more concerned with what happened to Jack. Their clipped answers to the reporters' questions proved as much. To the town, Jack's disappearance had already been pinned on Holden. I turned the television off.

"The truth doesn't matter. It never does for men like me. We're disposable. An easy answer to lock away so the police look like heroes and Jack Thorne will be remembered as the helpless victim against a crazy freak who wanted revenge for an accident. Your truth is meaningless. It's as weak as you. To everybody that matters, it's an inconvenience that will be shoved aside and forgotten."

Holden's words from the night I woke in his bedroom echoed in my head, the striking truth that Jack had always been the golden child in this town. He was the most popular at school, the star quarterback, the son of the richest man in Tranquil Falls. Even I couldn't hold a candle to Jack's importance, and Holden, in comparison, was nothing more than an afterthought, the *crazy freak* in a town where money, power, and popularity were all that mattered. He was garbage they wouldn't care to toss away. Only I knew the truth that, compared to Jack, Holden was a man to be admired, a man the town should have taken pride in, a man with so much talent that, given the chance, he would make a mark on history for his unique view of the world.

And maybe that's why this town had hated him so much. Instead of bowing down, instead of folding and giving in to the pressure of our demands, Holden remained true to himself and he was the only person who had the ability to see us for who we were beneath all the money, the expensive clothes, the makeup and perfectly practiced smiles.

Holden *saw* us, and he was never impressed with what he found. We'd attempted to destroy him because of it.

But not me. Not anymore. Now, more than ever, I was determined to speak out, to do what was right, to protect Holden from the entire world if that's what it took to ensure that his light would continue to shine.

"How could you stay silent knowing what those guys were doing to so many girls? Why have all of you stayed silent?"

I'd made a promise to him, hadn't I? And in this instance, just like everything else, I had a duty to stand up for what I knew was right, and to raise my voice in objection of what I knew was cruel and wrong.

The police would attempt to pin Jack's disappearance on Holden. And I would make sure that they looked for their answers somewhere else.

Epiphanies are startling moments. Like tennis balls lobbed in your direction by life, they come with a message scrawled across their surface, an answer that you can either choose to catch and read, or bat away in fear of learning some truth that may be painful or uncomfortable. I was catching that ball now, and when I turned it over in my hands to find the script scrawled across it, an answer came to my mind about what I had to do to help Holden, to save him, to put all the pieces back together that this town had slowly chipped away.

I would turn myself into the police in order to shield Holden, and I would give them a story as to what happened to Jack, a story that would take the spotlight off of Holden and turn it in the direction of this fucked up town.

But I couldn't do it on my own, only because there was one other complication I wasn't sure anybody but me knew: Delilah wasn't in this house, and I was beginning to suspect that she never was.

I had to find somebody to help me that Holden would trust, and I believed I knew just who that person would be. Getting to her without being seen would be tough, but I was determined to find a way.

Holden's bedroom door popped open. Our eyes met, his full of apology, mine full of resolve. The room came into sharp focus, the sound of a pot boiling on the stove drawing my attention back to the here and now. Frozen in place, I stared at a man I understood was worth everything.

"Hey," I whispered in repeat of our earlier greeting.

"Hey," he whispered back, the sound barely carrying across the room. "Did you see it?"

Nodding, I attempted a smile, but only one corner of my mouth was strong enough to curl. "I saw it."

"My time's up," he said, resignation settled into every syllable. "*Our* time is up."

Rolling back my shoulders, I grinned, not in sadness, not in defeat, but in fierce denial that time would end for us. Shaking my head just slightly, I argued, "Your time is beginning. You just don't know it yet."

Tucking his hands in the pockets of his jeans, he leaned back against the wall, his blue eyes locked to my face, his lips curling in sorrow. "Michaela-"

I held up a hand to silence him. "No. Don't Michaela me. I know what I need to do...for you, for this town and for myself."

Stepping towards him, I tried not to lose my mind at the sight of a broad chest and perfectly toned abs, tried to ignore the flutter of want deep down inside me. Holden and I had plenty of time left to explore each other, but at this particular moment, those desires would have to be set aside. I spoke as I approached him. "I have a plan to make this right, Holden. And all I need from you is a promise."

He didn't move from his position against the wall, instead staying in place so that I could trap him there, wrap my fingers through the belt loops of his jeans and tug his body close to mine. Pressed together, our hearts beat in tandem, both fear and want colliding inside me, my determination strengthening, my decision made.

Skepticism arched his brow. "A promise?"

Nodding, I answered, "Mm-hmm, just like you made me give you."

"And what is this promise?"

I stared at him for what felt like hours. "That when the time comes for all of this to come tumbling down, you'll claim to know nothing, you'll say nothing, you'll simply tell everybody that I showed up on your doorstep one night and you took me in."

"Michaela-"

Pressing my fingers against his mouth, I hushed him. "I already told you not to do that." Pausing, I waited until his eyes met mine again. "Holden, I know how to fix this, and in keeping with the promise I made to you, I need to speak out about something I know is wrong. But the only way I can do that is if you promise to keep your mouth shut and trust me."

His head fell back against the wall. I pulled my hand away. The pot continued boiling on the stove, the house still except for the food that was cooking. "Can you do that for me?" I whispered.

"I'm not sure," he answered honestly. "I won't let you take the blame for this."

My lips twitched. "I'm not taking the blame for anything. I didn't do anything wrong. I was a victim that night...just as much as you. And all you did was help me."

Concern etched his expression. "What are you planning to do?"

"I'm planning on finishing cooking dinner tonight, for starters. And then I'm planning on feeding you. What I have planned for tomorrow is a secret. But it won't work unless you promise me to never say anything about seeing Jack that night. When it comes to what you know, I showed up with a swollen face and bruises and begged to be allowed to stay. I'll take care of the rest of it."

Holden pushed away from the wall, thus pushing me back a step. He towered over me, forcing me to crane my neck to keep eye contact. "They've already interviewed me, Michaela. I told them I didn't know where Jack was-"

"Did they ask about me? Specifically?"

Shaking his head, he admitted, "No, it was mostly about Jack."

As usual, I was an afterthought, a girl trapped beneath the shadow of Jack Thorne. I'd always been that girl, so it wasn't a surprise. And I would use that knowledge to step out from beneath the shadow. "Promise me, Holden. Promise me that you'll tell them exactly what I said."

His eyes searched my face, defeat finally settling behind his blue eyes. "Fine. But the minute I hear they're blaming you for his death, I'm telling the truth."

"You don't need to worry. I know what needs to be done to fix this. I won't let this town hurt you anymore. I flat out refuse. It's about time Jack, and everybody else who think they rule Tranquil Falls, are brought to their knees and forced to answer for what they've done, for what they've been doing for far too long."

"Fine, I promise you. But that doesn't mean I'll let you go to prison for this."

"I know. Just ... trust me, okay?"

He nodded, swallowing hard because the promise went against every protective instinct Holden had inside him. "You said something about dinner?"

Soft laughter burst from my mouth. "Yeah. I'll pull it off the stove and make our plates."

"What about Deli? Has she come out of her room at all today?"

Heart squeezed to a standstill within my chest, I closed my eyes and opened them again slowly. Not knowing what to say or do, not understanding fully what was going on when it came to his sister, I answered truthfully, leaving my statement open ended just so I would know for sure. "No, she hasn't come out."

Because she's not here... I didn't say.

I had to remind myself to take this situation one problem at a time. "I'll go start on the food. You go check on your sister."

Nodding, he stalked off down the hall while I made my way into the kitchen. Five minutes later, he was walking toward me, a plate of uneaten food in his hand. Dropping it on the counter, he looked pained...worried. "She won't come out and she didn't even touch the food I took her this morning."

A frustrated sigh blew out of him as my heart lurched again to realize that Holden believed his sister was here. He saw her. He spoke to her. But, Delilah was nowhere to be found.

I had to fight to keep the tears from dripping from my eyes, to keep my expression blank while staring at a man who was far more broken than I'd understood. It was just one more mystery for me to solve. But one that would have to wait until the biggest problem we faced was handled.

"Maybe she'll come out tomorrow."

Running his hand through his hair, he answered, "Yeah, maybe."

Hating the pain I saw behind his eyes and in the lines of his face, I almost choked on the sobs that wanted to drive their way up my throat. Poor Holden. This beautiful, talented man that had lost everything and everybody, but still didn't know that, until I came into his life, he'd been very much alone.

Touching his shoulder, I drew his attention down to me. "Let's eat. Then we can go in your studio for a while. It's easier when you get lost in your art, isn't it?"

Blinking, his voice cracked with restrained emotion when he asked, "How did you know?"

"Because that room is the only peaceful place inside this house. It's the only room where you allow yourself to let go and just be you."

We ate that night in silence, and after, I watched Holden create his art. Tears had blurred my vision when he wasn't watching me, my soul shredded by the realization that a bubble was about to burst to allow chaos to sweep in and drown us both.

No matter how much a person prepares for the problems that were coming, those problems had a habit of showing up before you could take a last deep breath. It's exactly how it happened for Holden and me. Because that night, after Holden exhausted himself between his art and the love we made after, our worlds came crashing down faster than I'd expected they could.

CHAPTER TWENTY-SEVEN

Michaela

Three in the morning is a ridiculous time to wake up. When the night is still, the snow softly falling, and you're wrapped around a man who's existence had become your own, the sound of banging and shouting outside the warm blankets and thin bedroom door is a shocking annoyance that becomes terror after your mind is catapulted from dreams into reality.

Why three? Why not wait until eight in the morning? Why not ten at night for that matter? Why does everything horrible have to happen at the worst possible time?

Holden and I both sat up with a start, our eyes dragging to the window where beams of light attempted to break through the blinds.

"Police! Open up!"

"Fuck..." Holden muttered as he scrubbed his palms over his face. Throwing the blanket off his legs, he scooted to the edge of the bed and mumbled, "I guess it's show time."

My hand locked down on his wrist, holding him in place. "Not for you, it's not."

Where I'd found the strength to breathe, much less speak, was beyond me. My heart was thundering, my rapid pulse carrying every last drop of fear to my brain, but still I managed to function enough to stop Holden before he could make a mistake.

His head turned my direction. "Listen, I know I promised you I would play dumb in this-"

"And that's exactly what you're going to do," I bit out between clenched teeth. Three in the morning? Fucking seriously?! I hated the police.

It felt like chaos was erupting all around us, the potential for disaster staring us in the face if we didn't calm down and work together. "I know you don't want me getting myself in trouble," I whispered, my words coming out more like a hiss because the anger inside me was building far too quickly. "And I won't, Holden. But I can't fix this if you don't trust me."

"*POLICE!*"

My eyes darted to the muffled voices and banging, time counting down before they bust through the front door and screamed in our faces. I had to get Holden to agree with my plan. There was no other way. He HAD to agree. Otherwise it would come down to a fight over who actually killed Jack. Holden wasn't going to prison, and if I had to lie and claim I'd killed Jack for the fun of it, I would.

But if Holden would just trust me, it wouldn't come down to either of us going to prison.

"It's not that I don't trust you, Michaela. I know you'll tell them the truth."

"Who's telling the truth?" I hissed, still holding him in place while the cops outside were most likely bringing in the battering ram. "Neither of us killed, Jack. Do you understand me? Neither of us know what the fuck happened to him. Stick with what I told you. I showed up at your house, beaten and crying. I still have the fading bruises to prove it. I'll handle it from there."

What Holden didn't know was that I would be telling the police the truth about one thing - one thing not even Holden knew about what happened that night.

"*We have a warrant to search the premises! Open up now or we'll break down the door!*"

250

My fingernails were cutting into his skin from how firmly I held on. "All you know is I showed up and asked to be hidden. You have to stick with that story. I've told you nothing beyond that. Do you understand?"

"They interviewed me yesterday and I never mentioned you. How the fuck am I supposed to explain that?"

It's interesting how in times of crisis, the mind goes in one of two ways. Either it shuts down, leaving you frozen in a state of panic, unable to think clearly or remember your own name, or it slaps you across the face, clarifies the world around you and gives you such acute focus that the answers to all your problems start pouring in, begging you to take action.

Fortunately, my mind had gone into overdrive, every instinct waking up until I knew without doubt what I had to do.

"Tell them you wanted to come home and talk to me first. You can also tell them I promised to go to them the following day. Which is exactly what I would have done if they hadn't shown up at an ungodly hour in the morning. Just tell them that, okay? Promise me."

Indecision held him in place, and I made a choice I hated to make. But at that moment, I was willing to do anything to keep Holden from confessing his way into a prison cell for the rest of his life.

"Please, Holden," I begged, tears beginning to well in my eyes for what I would say next. "If not for me, then do it for Delilah. She needs you."

I choked on the words, hating myself for having used them. His confusion shouldn't have been a tool, especially when I didn't know how it started, what really happened to Delilah, or how badly he would react to learn that his sister wasn't here like he believed. But I'd used it as a tool

251

regardless, and I would regret it until the day I could fix that problem as well.

One problem at a time, Michaela...Breathe...

"You're right. Shit! I need to get to her before the police wake her up."

My hand gripped harder, our eyes locking as beams of light flashed through the blinds, brightening our panicked faces. "Do you promise me, Holden?"

His jaw ticked, his black hair a mess framing his head. Rolling back his shoulders, he cursed beneath his breath before answering, "Yes, I promise. But I hope whatever you have planned works, Michaela. I don't want you getting dragged down with me."

Reaching over, I cupped his cheek with my hand and kissed him while praying to God this wouldn't be the last time I had the chance. A million kisses weren't enough to satisfy the love I had for him. A million hours would never be enough time to time to bask in his light. A million heartbreaks would be worth it if it meant I could just have one more day by his side.

POLICE! OPEN THE DOOR NOW!

Breaking the kiss, Holden and I met eyes one last time before we both jumped to get dressed, leave the room and head in opposite directions. While he took off to help a sister who wasn't there, I ran toward the front door that was being pounded on so hard it shook against its hinges.

I took a deep breath in and released it slowly. My hand wrapped over the knob, the door shaking from the beating of fists on the other side. Closing my eyes and opening them again, I twisted the handle and yanked the door open. Bright lights blinded me, large bodies jostling against each other before rushing forward. Like a brick wall coming at me in full force, the police yelled orders so quickly, I couldn't process them all, but one voice rose above the others.

"Stop! That's Michaela Paige."

Movement stopped, my eyes blinking against the blinding lights as the sea of uniformed officers parted to allow one man through, his eyes stern as he stared down at me, his jaw tight. "Are you hurt? Has Holden Bishop been holding you against your will?"

Chaos erupted behind the men, the lights continuing to beam down on me, my throat clogged by so much fear my tongue felt swollen and I couldn't think to respond. Holding up a hand to shield my eyes from the lights, I swallowed hard and answered, "I can't see you. Can you please take those off my face."

The apparent lead officer raised a hand, bringing it down and saying, "Turn them down. We have one of the missing kids right here."

The lights were lowered, and I blinked away the remaining glare. The officer's face came into focus and I was able to see the stern set of his lips, the confusion behind his brown eyes. "Ms. Paige, is Jack Thorne here with you?"

"No," I answered, shaking my head. "I haven't seen Jack in two weeks. Not since the night at the diner. Listen, I know-"

Reaching forward, the officer dragged me outside while the other officers rushed into the house. I called out to stop them, but I was yanked back, my eyes following the men charging inside as the man who grabbed me continued asking questions.

"What happened to your face? There's a bruise over your cheekbone."

Turning to him, I narrowed my eyes on his. "Jack happened to my face. You all need to leave Holden alone. He was only helping me."

253

From inside the house, I could hear doors being slammed open, men calling out to each other as they cleared different rooms. My heart was beating in my throat as they progressed down the hall.

"I'll need you to come with me, Ms. Paige. We can talk in the car." His head turned toward more men standing farther out. "Can somebody bring me a blanket?"

"No! I don't need a blanket. I need you to listen to me. Please call your men back and ask them to get out of the house."

My requests were ignored, the yelling coming from down the hall grabbing both my and the officer's attention. I could hear Holden's voice, could hear the panic in his words as he demanded for the officers to get away from Delilah. Tears leaked from my eyes and I tried to run to him, but the officer wouldn't let me go.

"Ms. Paige, you need to come with me."

"No! You don't understand!" No matter how hard I tugged, I couldn't break free of him. Terror flooded me, the desperate need to escape the officer's hold so I could get to Holden. "You have to stop them!"

He was too strong, and despite the fight we could hear coming from Delilah's room, I was dragged away from the door, a blanket being wrapped over my shoulders as I was forced toward the cars.

"Get away from my sister!" Holden yelled, just before a crash sounded from the room.

I was being dragged in one direction, my head turned toward the house. "Holden, stop fighting!" I screamed, the tears pouring down my cheeks from the fear he would get himself killed.

"Is there another woman in the house, Ms. Paige?"

"No. It's not what you think. You have to let me get back to him! Please!"

"You're not going back to the house."

"Please!" I screamed, tugging as hard as I could, not caring that his hand was bruising my arm and my feet were being dragged over the icy ground. I had to get to Holden. Had to. If I didn't stop him from fighting they would hurt him. If I didn't admit that I never saw Delilah in the house, he would never believe the other officers. This was all my fault and I had to stop them before -

A gunshot blasted against the cold night air before I could finish the thought, a woman screaming so loud that the sound was piercing my eardrums. The world around me spun and shifted, the house going in and out of focus as the screaming went on and on, never ending, never decreasing in volume.

It was the sound of a heart shattering apart.

The sound of a happy future being shredded.

The sound of a soul being ripped from a woman's body as her world was torn apart.

It was my voice cutting through the chaotic night, my heart crumbling inside my chest, my soul being torn to shreds as I fell to my knees and tried to crawl toward the house.

Everything stopped and started at once. The house going silent as men rushed past. I was grabbed from behind and lifted from the ground before I could process what was happening.

I was still screaming for Holden as I was shoved in the car, left to watch helplessly through the window while every officer abandoned me to run inside.

My fists beat against the window, my throat burning from the sheer volume of my voice.

"HOLDEN!"

CHAPTER TWENTY-EIGHT

Michaela

"I get one phone call," I demanded, my arms crossed over my chest, my foot tapping against the ground incessantly.

Refusing to speak a word about Holden to the police until they let me call Angela, I stared over the exam table at an exasperated man, the legs of my chair rattling against the linoleum floor from the shaking of my body.

From the window beyond my interviewer's shoulder, I watched people rush past in white coats and cheerfully colored scrubs, each one potentially running in Holden's direction. My reflection stares back at me, a gray shape with wide eyes that is as transparent as me. Nobody would give me information on Holden, not the nurses or doctors, not Officer Shay with his receding hair and stern expression.

Head canting to the side, Officer Shay lifted one bushy eyebrow, impatience written into the severe arch. "I don't have time for this behavior. You will get your phone call *after* you tell me the whereabouts of Mr. Jack Thorne."

"I already told you, I don't know. The last time I saw him was when he was chasing me from his car. He didn't follow me after I ran into the woods." My eyes were still tracking the people rushing past the window. "Is Holden alive?"

Is this what Hell feels like? The not knowing, the inability to draw a breath as the heart threatens to collapse? Each fetid beat of the overworked muscle felt like its last, my pulse a weak flutter beneath my skin that somehow pounded against the inside of my skull.

Frustration had my fingers curling into my palm, the nails embedding in the skin until half moon circles filled with trace amounts of blood. I needed to know what happened to Holden, needed to see him, hear him, know he was okay, despite this bastard's insistence we talk about *more pressing matters.*

Jack being that pressing matter, because Jack was the golden child, and Holden was just an afterthought.

Tears stung my eyes.

"So, you're telling me that Jack Thorne assaulted you in his car while waiting for a drug deal in the woods? That you ran off and you haven't seen him since? That's what you're telling me?"

My head nodded robotically, my eyes searching for a gurney, a flash of bright blue eyes, a man being escorted past who was still breathing, whose heart was still beating, whose light hadn't been diminished even more by a town that never gave him a fighting chance.

Yes, I was lying to the police. But not about everything. Jack committed crimes the night we went missing. The drug deal and my rape, both of which I admitted to the instant Officer Shay asked. The only fact I was concealing was the *other* crime he committed by stalking and attacking Holden. I didn't feel bad for the omission. It wasn't exactly like I was holding back a detail that would prove Jack was innocent. I was merely lying about which crime he committed that night was the one that actually killed him.

"Jack didn't *assault* me, he *raped* me. And yes, that's what I'm telling you because that's what happened. I have the injuries to prove it." Holding up my wrists, my eyes met his as I asked, "If you found a dead girl with a bruise on her cheek and rope burns on her wrists and ankles, what would your conclusion be as to what happened to her? Would you think she was held against her will? Restrained? *Assaulted*, as you so willfully demand it be called?"

And maybe I was lying about where all my injuries came from, but still, I didn't feel bad. Jack hurt people. Lots of people. And I hoped some of those victims would be willing to step forward. "Now give me my phone call."

Ignoring my request, he leaned against the window, one foot crossing over the other at the ankle, his thick arms crossing over his broad chest. "If Jack attacked you as you claimed, why wouldn't you have reported him? Why run to Holden?"

It was infuriating that he refused to use the word 'rape.'

"For exactly the reason that you're showing me now! You want to believe Jack is innocent. You want to believe that something happened to *him*, instead of Jack being the criminal. You and I both know it. You would have just tossed me back to my parents and wiped your hands of it. And they would have just tossed me back to Jack. I'm tired of being his puppet. His father practically owns this town, which means you're on his payroll. That's why the police have never investigated the weekend parties. As long as the team is still scoring on the field, you don't care how else they're scoring. So how would running to you have done me any good?"

He opened his mouth to respond, but a nurse walked in with the most convenient timing ever. Sneering in Officer Shay's direction, I said, "Oh, look. They need to examine me. I guess that's your cue to leave."

Sneering right back at me, he surged forward as if to make demands that I answer his questions - to intimidate me, I assumed - but the nurse jumped in his path, her intimidation skills a lot more effectual with the finger she had pressed against a call button and her raised voice practiced and professional. "Take one more step toward the patient, and I'll have security in here to handle the situation."

It was immature of me, but I grinned. Being a patient apparently warranted more of a demand for consideration than being a victim. And what did *that* say about the town and its police force? It said exactly what Holden had claimed during the first nights I stayed with him: that unless you had the money to pay for respect, you didn't get it. Thankfully, the hospital wasn't bound by the Thorne payroll and they weren't willing to put up with mistreatment of their patients.

Officer Shay vacillated where he stood. It was obvious he wanted to jump across the exam table and pull me from my seat, but with the nurse scowling up at him as her finger hovered above the security button, he reconsidered his plan of attack. Pointing a finger in the nurse's face, he demanded, "Let me know when you're done so I can continue questioning her."

Storming off, he slammed the door shut, leaving me with a pretty nurse with black hair and purple scrubs. Turning to me, she cocked a brow at the fact that I was refusing to go anywhere near the exam table. Technically, I was fine. My injuries were healing. So I'd chosen to sit in a visitor's chair. "Are you planning on sitting there all day, or will you let me do my job?"

I didn't want to be rude to her. She'd just done me a huge favor by chasing Officer Shay out of the room, but I still had questions I needed answered. "I have no problem letting you examine me, but I won't let it happen until somebody tells me what happened to Holden Bishop."

She froze at the sound of his name, a medical chart in her hand, her eyes lifting to me in question. "Holden Bishop? What are you talking about?"

Apparently she hadn't heard why I was here. "He's my boyfriend and he was shot. The police won't tell me if he's alive or dead and I need to know."

The tears I'd been fighting the entire time Officer Shay was in the room finally fell along my cheeks, my body withering beneath the stress and fear I'd kept bottled up since I was driven away from Holden's house. "Please," I begged, "I'll cooperate with you completely if you can just find out what happened to him. They won't tell me anything."

Although the nurse had no clue who I was, she obviously recognized Holden's name. Her eyes narrowed on me just before she flipped through a few more pages of my chart, her lips pulling into a thin line before her head lifted again, her eyes locking to mine. "Are you telling me that poor man has been put through more hell by that town?"

Nodding, I swiped a tear from my cheek. "You know him?"

"Yeah, I know him. He broke my heart into a million different pieces two years ago. I've been worried for him ever since." Looking toward the door, she tapped the toe of her shoe against the ground, dropped the chart on the exam table, and glanced at me again. "I'm not supposed to do this, but let me see what I can find out."

"Wait!" I called, my hand locking over her wrist before she could get farther away. "I need to make a phone call. Holden doesn't have any family, so nobody has been notified about him being hurt. I need to talk to his boss, but the police won't let me."

Her expression softened as she glanced between the door and me. Lowering her voice, she whispered, "The phone is right over on that table. Make your call and I'll distract that asshole who was interviewing you. But make it quick."

The nurse left the room and I dove for the phone. Dialing zero for the operator, I begged the woman to connect me to the diner. The line was ringing a second later, a low din of noise in the background when a woman answered, "Tranquil Fall's Diner. Angela speaking."

"Angela? Hi, um, this is Michaela Paige-"

"Michaela Paige?" she barked in response. "Why are you calling me instead of the police? Because of you and that jackass of a boyfriend of yours, my employees are being harassed. You better have a damn good reason for bothering me after all the crap you've put me through."

"I'm at the hospital," I started to explain before she cut me off again.

"What happened? Let me guess: That entitled dickless prick you're dating turned his fists against you since he couldn't get to Holden? No woman deserves that kind of treatment, so I won't congratulate you on your ignorance for staying with a creep like that, but-"

I deserved her gruff demeanor, but I didn't have time to argue with her. "Holden's been shot," I blurted out. "And he doesn't have anybody besides you who can help him."

"WHAT? Girl, you better not be screwing with me right now."

"Please, Angela," I begged, my voice breaking apart on sobs, "I don't have time to explain, but you need to get down here. I don't know what's happening with him and you were the only person I knew to call."

"Does his sister know?"

My teeth clenched together. Taking a deep breath in an effort to keep my voice steady, I admitted, "No, his sister," my voice died off, my heart struggling to beat as panic and sorrow saturated every cell in my body. "Angela, I don't think Holden's sister is alive. I've been at his house for the past two weeks and she supposedly

261

came home two nights ago, but there's nobody in the house. Only Holden sees her."

If not for the hum of background conversation filling the line, I would have thought she'd hung up for how silent she became. A second passed, two, three, and then, "Oh, dear God, what is going on with that boy? Fine. I'm coming up there, but you and I need to have a long talk."

Relief flooded me. "Thank you. I'll be here. I won't let them take me back to town. I'll tell you everything, just hurry, please. I can't get to him and he needs somebody."

"I'm on my way." She hung up without another word.

I was wiping the tears from my face as the nurse walked back inside the room. Closing the door, she stared at me silently. My heart stuttered, my tongue refusing to ask the question that hung between us.

Shaking her head, the nurse patted the exam table and said, "You need to hop up here so I can take a look at you."

My body wouldn't cooperate, every muscle like jelly as I struggled to breathe. Unable to handle not knowing, I wrapped my arms around my abdomen and asked, "Holden? Is he okay?"

The nurse nodded, her expression sympathetic. "He was shot in the leg. It hit the muscle, but didn't damage the bone or any arteries. A through and through as they like to call it." Her hand patted the table again. "Come on, honey. Hop up here. Your boyfriend is going to be fine."

I ran to hug her instead. At first, I thought she'd shove me away, but her arms wrapped around me, her hand patting my back as I sobbed onto her shoulder. Minutes passed as she comforted me, but eventually she moved to hold me at arm's length, her warm brown eyes locking to mine. Speaking softly, she said, "Honey, I read in your chart that there is a possibility you may have been raped. Do you need me to do a test for that?"

Shaking my head, I wiped away the tears saturating my cheeks. "No. It's been two weeks since that happened. I think they brought me here because of the bruises."

Eyeing my cheek, she shook her head. "Was that from two weeks ago as well?"

I nodded, my breath rattling in my chest. "It was much worse when it first happened."

"It may be a fracture of some type. We should get an x-ray to see. Are there any other injuries I need to be aware of?"

"Yes," I admitted on a strained voice. "Old ones, so I'm not sure how well they can be documented."

"You'd be surprised. Even healed injuries from abuse can leave calling cards for us to find." She paused, her eyes searching my face. "Was Holden the one who did this to you?"

Shaking my head, I answered, "No! Holden wouldn't do this." A sob choked my voice. "Holden is wonderful. He would never hurt me. My ex-boyfriend is the one who hit me. He's been hitting me for a few years now. I just never told anyone."

She clucked her tongue. "That's more common than you know. Hop up on the table, honey, and tell me everything. I'll make sure we do what we can to help you get the truth out."

Doing as she asked, I climbed up to sit on the table, my body still wracked by sobs. "You're sure Holden is fine? They're not hurting him?"

More sympathy drenched her gaze. "Baby girl, I promise you Holden is fine. We've got him, and unless we give the say so, nobody will be touching him again."

I almost collapsed from the relief. "Thank you," I breathed out.

"We've got him. Now let's talk and see what we can do about helping you."

CHAPTER TWENTY-NINE

Holden

I'm not crazy. I don't care what I was labeled growing up, don't care what the police have told me, don't care that these voices keep insisting I attacked the men charging in Deli's bedroom for no good reason.

She was frightened beyond belief, balling up beneath her blanket so that when they finally burst through the door, her screams had filled the room and ignited every protection instinct inside me. Helpless to do anything to stop them from tearing her room apart in their mad dash for me, I'd charged them before they had the chance, and despite how loud my demands had been for them to stay away from her, they tore apart the room regardless, after shooting me, after dragging me away and lying that there wasn't anybody else in the room with me.

I didn't trust them. Didn't trust a group of thugs who were bought and paid for by the Thorne family. And due to my insistence that they were lying to me now like they had lied after the night Jack crashed into me with his car, they'd cuffed me and ignored the bleeding in my leg, they'd dragged me out and kicked me when I struggled. They'd tossed me in a car and driven me to a hospital where I was dosed with every tranquilizer known to man.

Waking up in a hospital bed had brought the past rushing back to my mind. Except this time, my sister wasn't sitting beside me, my parents weren't rushing down the halls to get to me after learning I was conscious. I was alone in a dimly lit room, kept company by the machines beeping above my head and the restraints holding me to the bed. No matter how hard I tugged, the restraints weren't letting me go.

The rage inside me was blinding.

And according to the voices filtering into my room from the hallway, I wasn't the only one planning to tear this place apart.

"Is he under arrest?" The voice was recognizable, a silver haired woman with the patience of a rabid dog. I couldn't hear the response to Angela's question, but they must have said something that irritated her. Voice notching a decibel higher, she asked, "Is he a suspect for something? Has he done anything to warrant being kept in a room by himself without being allowed to talk with anybody? What if I brought a lawyer with me? Would you let me in then?"

Again, they answered, but their voice wasn't strong enough to bleed through the door.

"Well, that's funny because yesterday one of your officers made it perfectly clear that I was a suspect as well. Is that your game, call everybody a suspect because you have a missing drug addict on your hands? Maybe you should be checking out the drug houses instead of wasting your time harassing good people who are just trying to live their lives. What the hell is wrong with you?"

The hallway outside my room became quiet, the door eventually opening as Angela slipped in. She rushed over to my bedside as quickly as she could. "We need to be fast about this conversation. I just sent that rookie off to go find his superior and I'm not supposed to be in here. What happened?"

"Angela? What are you doing? You're going to get in trouble." Still dazed by the drugs they'd given me, I was having trouble speaking around a tongue that felt like cotton.

"Don't you worry about me, Holden. I have a way of getting out of just about anything. But what I need to know is, are you okay?"

266

"I think so. My leg hurts like a wicked bitch."

She nodded. "That's what happens when people shoot bullets through it. I just taught you medicine 101. Why were you shot?"

My rage came roaring back, the heat of it driving blood through my veins and casting a red haze over my vision. "Those bastards were trashing Deli's room. She was screaming and crying for them to stop. I tried to stop them, but they wouldn't listen. They told me nobody was in the room, but she was under her blankets. They didn't see her and they wouldn't listen to me. I rushed to stop them and they shot me."

Flinching at my words, Angela's expression tightened even more, her eyes searching mine as her hand brushed softly down my arm. I could tell thoughts were racing through her mind, but she didn't voice any of them until settling on a question I wasn't sure how to answer. "Holden, where is your sister now?"

"I don't know."

My head was killing me, a steady pounding inside my skull that spread pain over every inch of my body. "I need you to find her. I'm not worried about me at the moment, but if you really want to help me, you'll find Delilah. She can't be alone. She's terrified of going outside or leaving the house. She-"

Angela patted my cheek, snapping her fingers in my face to stop me from speaking and pay attention to her. Once I was quiet, she glanced quickly at the door before saying, "I'll find your sister, okay? But you need to calm down. Those machines above your head are beeping so fast, they're about to melt down. So don't you worry, Holden. I'll handle this."

The door burst open behind her, Officer Shay himself storming in to roar out his discontent. "Who the hell said you could come into this room and speak to our suspect?"

267

Spinning on her heel, Angela planted her hands on his hips and barked out her response. "Oh? So he's a suspect now? For what? Getting in the way of the bullet your incompetent police force fired in his house? Is he under arrest? Have you done your job and read him his rights or told him he can speak to a lawyer?"

Officer Shay's face was crimson red. "I have the right to hold him for twenty-four hours, and in that time, if I find evidence that he had something to do with Jack Thorne's disappearance, then yes, he's under arrest."

"He wants an attorney," Angela screamed back, refusing to give ground to the man who now had his hand hovering over the butt of his gun. Panic shot through me, the machines beeping even faster now that the drugs they'd given me were wearing off.

"He can't demand one because he's not under arrest."

"Then you can't stop me from talking to him!"

They were nose to nose, as much as they could be. Officer Shay had several inches on Angela in height. Shay's voice coming out on a low growl, he scowled down at my boss, his hand still hovering over his gun, his eyes locked to the face of a woman who wasn't giving up. "I will arrest you if you don't leave this room in the next five seconds."

"For what?"

"For getting in the way of a police investigation."

"Oh? Now I'm just getting in the way of an investigation? Yesterday, you called me a suspect. It sucks to be downgraded."

She was going to get herself shot and be strapped down to a bed right beside me if she didn't stop. "Angela. It's okay," I called out. "Please, just go find my sister."

Both their heads snapped in my direction, Officer Shay's mouth pulling into an angry line and Angela's eyes filling with sorrow. Nodding her head, she ignored the officer still standing toe to toe with her. "I'll leave now, Holden. Don't worry. I'll find out what happened to Delilah."

Turning back to Shay, she snapped, "If you will excuse me, please. I need to go find out what you all did to another innocent person."

I was shocked when he actually stepped aside to let her pass. Nobody messed with Angela when she was in one of her moods. Not even the police, apparently.

She'd almost made it to the door, when Shay set his sights on her, calling his question out before she could place her hand on the knob. "How did you even know that Mr. Bishop was here?"

My brows rose at the question, only because it was one I hadn't thought to ask.

Turning back to face us, Angela smiled. "Well, you see, Officer, I happen to be psychic. And if you don't believe me, I'll be happy to pull the crystal ball out of my ass and read your future for you, too." Her smile became fiercer. "Actually, wait, how stupid of me. I don't need a crystal ball to know that you and your entire police force are about to be sued for shooting an innocent man. Now, if you'll excuse me, I need to go find what other victims to add to the lawsuit that's coming your way very soon"

Spinning back, she was out the door before he could utter another word. I didn't know whether to curse her for getting herself involved in my mess, or cheer to have her on my side.

The cheering would have to wait. Officer Shay leveled a glare in my direction, his large, stocky body taking up too much space in the room. "Do you want to tell me what happened to Jack Thorne now that you're awake?"

My first instinct was to admit the truth and save everybody the headache this entire situation had caused.

But remembering the promise Michaela had demanded from me, I stuck to the script, hoping like hell she knew what she was doing. "I don't know what happened to Jack. Have you checked with his drug dealers? Or asked around at the parties on his side of town? Maybe they know."

Shay smirked. "You know, it's really funny how you, Michaela, and your boss all want to paint Jack as some drug addict not worthy of your time, but I happen to know him as a talented and intelligent young man who has everything going for him. I also happen to know you have a bone to pick with him and no money to your name, so if I had to take a guess, I would pin his disappearance on you."

I shrugged. "Seems to me you've already done that. Did you happen to find him as you tore apart my house?"

"No, but I found his girlfriend, and isn't that all sorts of interesting? When we talked to you yesterday, you didn't mention Michaela was at your house. Sounds to me like you were hiding something."

"Yeah," I answered, wishing my voice could be a little stronger and clearer. The drugs weren't allowing it. "I was hiding a woman who was terrified to go to you about whatever caused her to show up at my door beaten and bruised."

Narrowing his eyes, he looked at me like I was scum he'd just scraped from the bottom of his shoe. "Are you trying to convince me that Michaela Paige showed up at your house unexpectedly on the night both she and Jack caused a scene at your restaurant, and you let her in without asking any questions about why she was at your door?"

"No, that's not what I'm saying. Of course, I asked her what happened. Her face was swollen and she was crying. But she wouldn't tell me why she was there, just that she needed help because she was scared and hurt. Given how Jack was acting that night at the diner, it didn't take a genius to put two and two together. So I let her in."

He scowled. "And what do you believe happened?"

Taking a deep breath, I let it out slowly. The pain meds were wearing off and my leg was throbbing as bad as my head. "Does it matter what I *believed* happened? That's just an opinion. All I know is that a woman needed help, so I helped her. She's a friend of my sister's."

"Let's talk about your sister, shall we?"

"My sister has nothing to do with any of this," I growled, anger balling my hands into fists.

He opened his mouth to respond, but the door opened behind him, a nurse I recognized from after my accident two years ago walking in. She had been the woman who sat beside me after Delilah was brought in, the same woman who had wheeled me to Delilah's room to let me see that my sister was alive. Seeing her brought all the pain back to me from that day, but I wasn't unhappy to see her either.

"You again?" Officer Shay angrily barked.

The nurse's eyes snapped up to him, her lips a thin line of annoyance. Crossing her arms over her chest, she reminded him, "As far as I can tell, this is a hospital and not a police station. I have every right to be in this room, even more than you."

"Are you planning on kicking me out of here like you did in Ms. Paige's room?"

"No," she answered calmly, "I'm here to tell you we have the results of Michaela Paige's tests that were run, and I think they might be of interest to you in your investigation."

A groaned rolled over his lips before he tipped his head toward the door. "Let's step outside to discuss it. I

271

don't need sensitive information being overheard by a suspect."

The nurse barked out a humorless laugh. "Suspect for what? Beating a woman for years? Because I can promise that you have the wrong man if that's the crime you're investigating."

Officer Shay wasn't amused. "Outside, now."

Rolling her eyes, the nurse stepped out, Officer Shay following right behind her. I was left on the bed to consider what I'd just overheard.

Resting my head against the pillow, I closed my eyes and thought about what the nurse had just admitted. Jack had been hitting Michaela for years, most likely leaving enough evidence behind for the hospital to verify the abuse.

My jaw ticked with anger at the thought of it, and I wasn't sorry for killing Jack. Especially not after what I had just learned.

CHAPTER THIRTY
Michaela

I had three healed hairline fractures. One on my cheekbone, one on my arm, and one on my hip. None of them had been severe enough to require casts or prevent me from moving, but their existence was proof enough that Jack had been mistreating me for far longer than I wanted to admit to myself much less anybody else. Shame enveloped me, but I had to look at it for what it was. The old injuries only helped to prove the story I was telling about a man so lost to the power that came with wealth and his drug habit, that he'd not only harmed his own girlfriend, he'd harmed other people as well.

I didn't know how many girls would be willing to come forward, but I did know how I would get the message across that I needed them to tell their stories. The only problem I faced was how to get the call for help out to the woman I knew had access to the girls in question.

Thankfully, the answer to that problem came walking through my door with a scowl on her face and anger written into the line of her shoulders.

"Spill."

Angela stood staring at me with her hands on her hips and a no-nonsense expression. How she'd sauntered into my room without someone stopping her was a question on my mind, one that would have to wait until I was done telling her what she wanted to know.

"Where would you like me to start?"

"From the beginning. When telling stories, that's usually the best place to begin."

Nodding my head, I weaved my fingers together in my lap. "The night Jack and I showed up at your diner, he hurt me."

"How hurt are we talking?" she asked, her voice careful.

I swallowed. "As hurt as a man can make a woman."

Sympathy softened her eyes and withered her shoulders. "I'm sorry that happened to you."

Shrugging it off, I decided against mentioning it wasn't the first time. The only information relevant at the moment was Holden. I'd become a new person since falling for him, a stronger person. The injuries against the Michaela of the past couldn't matter anymore. I wouldn't be able to run away from it forever, but for now, I had to roll back my shoulders and charge through it...for Holden, and for the person I wanted to be because of him.

"Thanks, but that's not what scares me right now." Pausing , I realized how it did scare me, even though I'd tried to convince myself otherwise. But it wasn't just me. It was all the girls used at the parties, the ones I failed to protect, the ones I'd failed to speak up for. I needed to change that.

"Anyway, after Jack did that, I ran off, and I ended up at Holden's house. I was friends with his sister. We were on the same dance team, so I knew where she lived. Holden took one look at me and said I could hide at his house and that's where I've been for the past two weeks."

Holding up her hand, she said, "Let me stop you there. How is it you were able to run on foot to Holden's house?"

"We were on his side of town so that Jack could buy drugs."

Understanding flashed over her face. "That's what I thought. Okay, continue."

"Holden and I..." My voice trailed off, the tears coming back again as sobs threatened my chest. "We're more than friends. He...I love him, Angela. He's an amazing person and his art..."

I could barely speak around the pain in my heart. "I want to help him. I want to make up for everything the town has done to his life. It's not fair. He's worth so much more than the bad luck he's been handed. It's like the universe is against him."

She barked out a laugh. "Yeah, I can agree with you on that. If that boy were a character in a book, I would swear the author hated him. I'd never let him buy a lottery ticket for me either. With his luck, I'd end up owing *them* money."

A sigh blew over my lips. "Angela, I don't think Delilah is alive. Or if she is, I don't think she's at his house."

Angela's eyes widened, pain and worry flashing across her expression. "Why?"

"Her room. I never saw it before the accident that killed her parents, but it doesn't look like a nineteen year old woman lives there. Her walls are still covered with pictures of high school. But, I thought that could be a result of her head injury, or some psychological trauma, so I didn't really worry about it until she supposedly came home two days ago."

"What happened then?"

My fingers tightened over each other, the tears I'd been trying to contain finally free to fall down my cheeks. "He swore she was in the house, and any time he went in her room, he saw her. He even took her a plate of food. But when I went in, the room was empty. She wasn't there."

Cursing under her breath, she looked up at the ceiling and back to me. "You're sure? She wasn't just in the bathroom? In the closet? Under the bed?"

I just looked at her.

"Well," she threw up her hands. "I would rather believe his sister has some strange love of hiding than believe that Holden has been imagining her for the past two years. He lives for that girl."

My voice low, I suggested, "He was shot trying to defend Delilah. If he is imagining her, it's severe."

"Yeah," she replied, swatting a tear from her face that had escaped her eye. "I know it. That's what he told me."

My eyes rounded. "You've seen him?"

Laughter shook her shoulders. "I snuck into his room same as I snuck into yours."

"Don't they have police posted outside?"

More laughter. "Yes. To get in Holden's room, I had to convince the rookie officer to go look for his superior. To get in here, I had to wait until he wasn't looking and just run past him. They really should fire that guy. He's a shitty cop."

My heart felt like it would tear from my chest. "How is Holden?"

"Drugged up and strapped to a bed, but other than that he seemed fine. He's worried about his sister and asked me to find her. Now, how the hell am I supposed to do that if she doesn't actually exist any longer?"

A thought occurred to me the instant she asked the question. "The nurse who went with me for the x-rays. She said Holden broke her heart two years ago, so I assume she worked with him after the accident. Maybe she would know what happened to Delilah."

She flicked a quick glance at the door before turning to me and saying, "It's worth a shot. What does the nurse look like?"

"Black hair. Pretty brown eyes. Purple scrubs. Tough as nails demeanor. Kind of reminds me of you."

A smile stretched her lips. "Then she should be easy to find. Bitch calls to bitch. We'll meet eyes and just know we like each other."

Nodding, I could hear noise out in the hallway, and I knew instantly that someone would be coming in the room, giving me little time to tell Angela the rest of what I needed her to do.

"There's one other thing," I mentioned, my voice soft for fear whoever was on the other side of the door would hear me. "I need to come clean about something that's been happening in town for several years now, and I'm afraid I won't be able to do it on my own. I need to get a message out." My eyes locked to hers, "Can you help me?"

"Whatever you need, Michaela. Personally, I'm sick of the way things are in Tranquil Falls."

Giving me a pointed look, she'd admitted she knew more about the secrets of the town without having to say a word.

Grabbing a scrap of paper and a pen, I wrote a name and phone number down. Handing it over, I said, "Call this person. Tell her I asked you to call. Then ask her to get in touch with the others. She'll know what it's about. Just tell her I'm not missing like the news says. You can also tell her what happened the night I showed up at Holden's, between Jack and me. She'll understand."

Brows lifting, Angela didn't ask any questions, she simply pocketed the scrap paper and inclined her head. Right on time, too. Officer Shay returned, his body barging through the door of my hospital room, his face set in a mask of irritation.

"You again? Who the hell let you in here?"

Angela smiled. "It's a busy night for fortune telling apparently. But you showed up too late. I just finished shoving the crystal ball back up my ass. Not that it's needed to know what'll happen to you."

"Get out!" he roared.

277

Angela simply chuckled before leaving, unimpressed with Officer Shay's booming voice. He slammed the door behind her, his face turning to me, the skin red from anger. "So, I hear you have some old injuries. You sure those aren't from dance?"

Anger filtered through me. Somehow, I already knew that would be his first response. "I'm sure. They're from Jack Thorne. And regardless of how badly you want to protect the criminal and paint him as the victim, I won't let you."

"Is this your official statement, Ms. Paige? That you ran off after Jack attacked you and have been hiding in Mr. Bishop's house for the past two weeks?"

"My official statement," I corrected him, "is that Jack *raped* me, and then when I got upset and tried to leave, he hit me and cracked my cheekbone. I ran after that and he chased me, but I managed to get away. I showed up at Holden's and have been hiding there ever since."

He scowled, his body practically vibrating with anger. "And you expect people to believe that?"

Regardless of his attempts to intimidate me, I wouldn't give ground. "What reason do you have not to believe me?"

"How about the fact that Jack is still missing?"

My brows lifted. "Perhaps he ran because he was afraid I'd go to the police? Or perhaps something went wrong with his drug deal? Or maybe he did too many drugs and he's in one of the abandoned houses? I don't know. I can't answer those question, because *I ran off.*"

Stressing those last words, I glared in Officer Shay's direction. He glared back, frustrated that I wasn't crying and offering some confession regarding Jack.

Pointing his finger in my direction, he snapped, "I'm holding both you and Mr. Bishop for twenty-four hours, and you better hope like hell we don't find a reason to hold you longer."

Knowing this man would dump me in a dungeon and forget about me if he had the chance, I made my demands.

"I want my parents notified that I'm here."

A bark of laughter shook his shoulders. "You're not a minor. We have no duty to contact your parents."

I grinned. "Fine, then I want to speak to an attorney. He'll call my parents, and when they find out that you found me and didn't bother notifying them, I'm sure they'll love to discuss pulling all the donations they make to your police force."

Our eyes met and I smiled, knowing I'd cornered him. "Guess you forgot that Jack's family isn't the only one that keeps you in a cushy, well paid job."

Giving my words some thought, he cursed between clenched teeth and turned to walk out the door. Before he stepped through, he cast me one last angry glare. "I'll call your parents. Not that it will do you any good."

Slamming the door, he left me alone in the room, tears welling in my eyes both from fear and anger: Fear that they would somehow pin all of this on Holden, and anger that Officer Shay hadn't been wrong.

Calling my parents wouldn't do me much good, but it would stall the process, giving Angela time to do what I'd asked her to do.

CHAPTER THIRTY-ONE
Michaela

Nineteen hours came and went before my parents finally decided to grace me with their presence. In that time, I'd been discharged from the hospital, driven back to Tranquil Falls and locked inside a room within the police station. Per the clock ticking away on the plain white wall, it was now ten at night and I had been sitting in this room by myself for four hours. I was surprised when the door finally popped open, my mother striding through in full makeup and fancy clothes, her overpriced designer heels clicking over the linoleum floors.

"What's the meaning of this, Michaela? Your father and I have been worried sick and we were dragged out of an event this afternoon to come deal with the mess you've made of this entire situation."

Lifting my head from where it had been nestled over my folded arms on the table, I blinked up at my mother, "It's nice to see you too, mom. Thanks for coming to my rescue."

"You do realize tomorrow is Christmas, right?" She practically screeched. "This is the busiest time of year for social obligations and you decide to pull a stunt like this? Where is Jack?"

The old Michaela would have cried at the blatant reminder that nobody in her family gave a damn about her. The new Michaela, the one strengthened by knowing and loving a man who'd finally opened her eyes to the injustice of this town, merely stared.

"I don't know where Jack is, mom. Aren't you concerned about why your daughter is locked in a room in a police station?"

She scoffed, one hand tossing her platinum blond hair from over her shoulder as she looked at the tables and chairs and grimaced. "I'd sit down to talk to you about my concerns, but the facilities leave much to be desired." Eyes returning to me, she scowled. "What are you wearing and what has gotten into you? I was told you've been living with that Bishop boy for the past two weeks."

Rolling my eyes, I lowered my hands into my lap beneath the table. My fingers were curling into my palms, my anger building until I could barely remain still. It was just like my mother to be more worried about ruining her dress by sitting in a chair than to be worried about me. "Is that all you were told?"

Huffing out a breath, she answered, "No. Of course not. The police said you claimed Jack attacked you, but-"

"He didn't just attack me, mom. He raped me. Does that mean nothing to you?"

Clearly, she didn't, if the disgust in her expression had anything to say for it. "I don't know what game you're playing, but I do not appreciate it. It's impossible for Jack to have done what you've claimed. You're his girlfriend, you've been sexually active for the past two years with him. And before this story you've been telling gets back to his parents, I'd like you to consider your future. Do you really think he'll want to stay with you if you're willing to throw such an accusation around? Now just tell me where Jack is!"

Shaking my head, I threw up my hands. "You know what? Screw it. Obviously, all this town cares about is Jack. And if my own *mother* isn't willing to give a damn about me, then why should I care what the town thinks? Holden was right about all of you!"

Her jaw fell open, anger a shade of crimson across her cheeks. "Tell us where Jack is!"

"I don't know," I screamed.

The door burst open again, a man I didn't recognize stepping through with Angela on his heels. Spinning to look behind her, my mother's face twisted with shock. "I'm sorry, but who are you and what are you doing in here?"

The man looked to be my mother's age with black hair silvering at the temples and black-rimmed glasses that reminded me of FBI agents from the fifties. Dressed impeccably in a grey pinstriped suit with a white shirt and burgundy tie, he pulled a silver case from his pocket, flipped the lid and extracted a card. Handing it to my mother, he introduced himself.

"My name is Jonathan Grinshaw, and I've been asked to speak to Ms. Paige regarding the current matter she has ongoing with the Tranquil Falls Police Department."

Sneering, most likely because his suit wasn't designer enough for her taste, my mother snatched the card from between his fingers and studied it. Flicking a glance back at him, she asked, "You're an attorney?"

He nodded before attempting to step around her, but my mother moved to block him from getting a clear view of me. "I'm sorry, but whoever called you to speak to my daughter must be confused. We have a family attorney who will be handling any ongoing issues."

My mother's angry gaze slid to Angela. "And who, exactly, are you?"

Mirroring my mother's disgusted appraisal, Angela answered, "I'm the confused woman that hired an attorney for Michaela and Holden. Now if you'll excuse us, we have a discussion that needs to happen and doesn't include you."

Opening the door, she held it open for my mother to step out. Mom snickered at the unspoken demand. "She's my daughter, and she will answer my questions before I go anywhere."

"Actually," Mr. Grinshaw said, "From what I've been told, Ms. Paige is twenty years old, and therefore, not a minor. It's up to her whether you remain in the room, or if she answers any of your questions."

His kind brown eyes turned to me. "Would you like your mother to stay or go?"

I didn't even know the guy, but I could tell we'd become fast friends. He wasn't the type to put up with anything. "I've said everything I need to say to my mom. She can leave."

Mom spun on her heel to pin me with her angry glare. "I will not be leaving until you tell me where Jack is!"

"I don't know," I yelled in response, "and I don't fucking care. Now get the hell out of this room so I can speak to the two people who give a damn what happened to *me*!"

Flinching at the tone of my voice, my mother opened her mouth to argue but was cut off when Officer Shay stepped into the room. "She lawyered up, Gail. You'll need to leave the room."

Angela and Mr. Grinshaw took notice of the fact that Officer Shay was on a first name basis with my mom.

Flipping her hair, mom leveled one more stare in my direction. She wasn't the type to be ordered around, but in this, there was nothing she could do. Her heels clicked across the floor as she left, each punctuated step a beat of disapproval. Shay slid his narrowed eyes over Angela, Mr. Grinshaw, and me in warning before slamming the door shut and leaving us alone.

Angela rushed to my side and took the seat beside me as Mr. Grinshaw selected a seat on the opposite side of the table, placing his briefcase on the surface.

"You okay?" Angela asked.

My eyes darted between them, noticing how Mr. Grinshaw was pulling a file from his briefcase and leafing through a few papers. "Yeah, I'm fine. I don't think I want anything to do with my mother again. But I'll live. How's Holden?"

She rolled her eyes. "Still under lock and key at the hospital, but thankfully the nurses and doctors can get to him and they're on our side. That's how I ended up here with the suit."

Laughing silently, Mr. Grinshaw flicked a glance at Angela. "This suit just chased her mother and that officer from the room. You should be more thankful of it."

"Yeah, yeah," Angela said, waving him off. It was obvious by their interaction that neither were the type to have their feathers easily ruffled. "Anyway, we're here to bust you out. The suit over there is going to pull some fancy legal stuff to get you away from the station and then we're heading back to the hospital to bust Holden loose. After that, we're all going to sit down and have a long chat, but before we can do that, you need to sign some papers."

Turning to him, I asked, "Do I need to tell you my side of the story now?"

Shaking his head, he slid papers across the table in my direction. Setting a pen on top of them, he answered, "Not now, unless you prefer staying in the station longer?"

"No, I'd like to leave and get back to Holden as quickly as possible."

"That's what I thought. These papers are the contract for you to retain me. As soon as you sign where indicated, I officially represent you, and I can," his eyes darted to Angela, a small smile tugging at his lips, "pull some fancy legal stuff to bust you out of here."

284

Panic gripped me. "I can't afford to pay you," I admitted.

"Don't worry about that," Angela said. "His bill is taken care of already."

My head spun to her. "Can you afford that?"

Laying her hands on mine, Angela explained, "I'm not the one paying the bill. It seems Holden has other friends who would like to help. But in order to do that, they need you to sign those papers."

Unease crept inside me. Angela was one of those women that is a force unto herself. No matter how, why or where, you didn't miss her. You also didn't just see or hear her, you *felt* her. Even though I'd only glimpsed a few sides to her, the angry, the skeptical, the worried, she exuded whatever emotion she was feeling. I was sure it was the same for every side of her. That's why it was unnerving how in a moment when she should have been hopeful, the only energy I felt in her was remorse. It made me wonder who Holden's other friend was.

"Who's paying the attorney's bill?"

Her expression fell, her shoulders deflated, and I knew what I felt from her was right.

"Someone at the hospital, I assume. I found the nurse you asked me to find." Sighing, Angela admitted, "Honey, Delilah isn't alive. She died three weeks after the accident that killed her parents."

It was if time itself froze in that moment while my mind attempted to make sense of what my heart had already known. Sure, I'd questioned why Delilah hadn't been in the house despite Holden's claims. I'd picked up on the subtle nuances in her bedroom that spoke of emotional turmoil and the strongest denial possible of the human mind. But I'd refused to believe the worst of a situation where logic whispered the possibility that Delilah didn't exist at all.

285

In times of grief, it is our first instinct to deny that a tragedy has occurred. We postulate and decide on alternative explanations. We beg the universe to alter reality so that the events that hurt us the most turn out to be nothing more than a misunderstanding. We become desperate for miracles with the subconscious understanding that miracles are few and far between. And eventually, we move on from that denial. We become angry. We bargain for a different result. We lose our way in such deep-seated depression that, sometimes, it feels impossible to move on. But eventually, in a healthy mind, we learn to cope and move forward. We accept the cards that reality had dealt us and we learn to live on despite them.

But what if the mind isn't healthy? What if the pain is so intense that to accept those cards is to accept the utter destruction of one's self? What happens then?

We tell ourselves lies, and eventually, we begin to believe them.

Holden truly believed his sister was alive. And I felt like an idiot not to have seen it for what it was. He'd described her *problems* to me in depth, problems that created the perfect environment for a long term belief.

A girl that never left the house. A girl that never aged beyond the date her parents died. A girl who refused to believe her parents were never coming home, refused to live on despite the circumstances. Delilah was a girl Holden only saw when nobody else was around to tell him she wasn't there.

The weight of it crushed me, and as my heart struggled to beat through the pain I felt for another person, a question echoed in my mind, one that crushed me even more until I was barely able to breathe.

"Has anybody told him?" I asked, my watery eyes searching Angela's face. "Since he's been at the hospital, has anyone-"

Shaking her head, Angela squeezed my hands. "There's more to this situation than you or I could have known. And it needs to be addressed once we figure out how to make him understand. But right now, it's not what needs our attention the most. You need to sign the papers, Michaela. We'll go back to the hospital together. And once we can get Holden free of the police that are watching him, we'll decide what to do about Delilah."

I nodded while swallowing down the knot of pain slowly crawling up my throat. My hand shook as I grabbed the pen, my signature tight and distorted as I scrawled ink across paper. Once I'd signed and initialed in all the places indicated, Mr. Grinshaw silently slid the contract away from me, tapped the papers on the surface of the table, and exchanged a look with Angela as he slipped them into his briefcase.

Just as silently, he left the room while Angela pulled me into her arms. My tears wouldn't stop falling.

"What's going to happen to him?" I asked, the sobs wracking my body breaking apart my words.

Angela tucked me closer, her own shoulders shaking with her grief. "I don't know, honey. I don't know. But whatever happens, I think it's our job to take whatever pieces break apart inside him and help fit them back together."

"This will destroy him," I whispered, my heart so crushed that I couldn't find the strength to speak any louder.

Moving so that she could grab my cheeks between her hands, Angela angled my face and locked her eyes with mine. The determination behind them was astounding.

"This will destroy him. You're right about that. In truth, it already has. It destroyed him two years ago. But Holden has something going for him now that he didn't have when the accident happened."

Blinking away the tears, I asked, "What?"

Forcing a smile, she tucked a stray bit of hair behind my ear and answered, "He has us."

CHAPTER THIRTY-TWO
Holden

With two hours left for my official police escort to clear the door to my room, I was still strapped to a bed, an IV attached to one arm and bandages wrapped over my left leg. The pain of the wound had subsided, and once the two hours were up, I'd be released from my makeshift prison and allowed to walk in order to test the weakness or strength of the leg.

Regardless of how strong it was, I was determined to walk on it, if for nothing else but to find Deli and Michaela and hopefully take them home. There was no telling what the police had found since storming the house at three yesterday morning. I'd been fortunate that the nursing staff and physicians had managed to keep Officer Shay out of my room as much as possible, however, I knew the reprieve wouldn't last once Jack's body was found.

It was obvious they hadn't located it already, only because I hadn't been placed under arrest, but it was simply a matter of time. The police knew he was in the vicinity of the servants' quarters when he went missing, but I wasn't sure how much information Michaela had given them as to where, exactly, he'd been waiting.

Resting my head against my pillow, I stared at the ceiling, wishing the drugs hadn't worn off so much that sleep became impossible. I was going crazy with boredom by the time my door opened again, an older man in a fancy suit strolling through with briefcase in hand. Blinking in his direction, I didn't recognize him, but I did recognize the determined woman marching in behind him.

"Shouldn't you be harassing people at the diner?" I asked, my voice teasing, my lips pulling into a grin.

"That's exactly where I would be if I weren't busy saving your ass," Angela snapped back. "But it is what it is and I'm busting you out of here now."

Turning to glance at Angela, the man shook his head and smiled. "Are you like this with everyone? I could use someone like you in my office."

"Get in line, pal. Everybody wants me," she answered, the tinge of pride flashing behind her eyes. "Holden, this is John Grinshaw, the attorney who'll be getting your dumb ass out of your current problem."

My gaze slid to Mr. Grinshaw to watch as he pulled a file from a briefcase and approached the bed. "You've kept me up late, Mr. Bishop. But only because you have friends in great places."

Confusion pulled my brows together. "Did Angela hire you?"

Shaking his head, he dragged a chair to sit next to the bed and pulled a pen from his shirt pocket. "No, she did not. I was contacted by Dr. Lucas Silva regarding your situation and I agreed to help. We've already met with Ms. Paige and she's signed the necessary paperwork. In fact, she's waiting in the hall as we speak. Once you agree to my representation, I'll have the police escorted from your door so that the two of you can talk."

"Dr. Silva?"

I hadn't thought about him in years, not since Deli returned home and I took the job at the diner. He was a good man. That much I remembered, but I didn't understand how or why he was involved in the problem happening now. "How did he even know I was here? I haven't seen him since they admitted me to the hospital."

Mr. Grinshaw smiled. "That's because he left the hospital over a year ago and started a private practice in a town about two hours from here. He's driving to the hospital to speak to you and Ms. Paige."

A memory flashed through my head, there and then gone again, it was a brief image that left a weight on my chest I couldn't breathe past. Closing my eyes, I attempted to chase the image, but I couldn't catch it, couldn't recall why my heart hurt the moment it was there. "Why is he coming? I was shot in the leg. He's a head doctor from what I remember."

"You're correct. He's a neurologist. But that's for him to discuss with you when he arrives. The pressing matter now is this contract. Once you sign, I have authority to request the police release this room to visitors. They haven't arrested you, Holden, and they're pushing the boundaries of what's legal by keeping you strapped to this bed and posting an officer at your door."

Not knowing what was going on, I looked to Angela. Obviously exhausted, her eyes had black smudges beneath them, concern written into the lines of her expression. "What should I do?" I asked her.

"You sign it," she answered, her voice leaving no room for argument. Trusting her implicitly, I didn't bother asking another question.

Wiggling my hand where it was strapped to the bed, I waited for Mr. Grinshaw to slip the pen between my fingers and hold the papers so that I could scribble as best as possible in the places he needed my signature. Once the contract was signed and dated, he removed the pen from my hand and stuffed the papers back into his briefcase. Standing, he stared down at me to say, "I'll only be a moment. Until I return, Angela can stay in the room with you."

His eyes slid to her. "That is, as long as you can stay out of trouble while I'm gone."

291

She shrugged. "Hey, don't look at me. I was downgraded from suspect to interfering with an investigation. Next thing you know, I'll just be a nuisance and nobody will care about me anymore." Swiping at a non-existent tear, she added, "It sucks to be invisible."

Mr. Grinshaw's laughter filled the room. "Try to stay invisible while I'm gone." With that he left and Angela approached my bed to steal the seat he'd previously occupied.

"How are you feeling?"

Ignoring her question, I asked my own. "Did you find my sister?"

It didn't matter how I felt, didn't matter what would happen to me once Jack's body was found. What mattered was Deli and Michaela, two women who didn't need to become caught in the trap Tranquil Falls has laid out for me since the day I refused to conform and join the ranks of the football team. Until the day the coach begged me to play, I'd been nothing more than a shadow, a nobody, a person as forgettable as any stranger passed on the street. But the minute I turned him down - and thus snubbed my nose at Jack Thorne and Clive Stanton - I'd been a target worthy of the smear campaign that had destroyed almost everything in life that I'd loved.

Angela's eyes glanced away, the rims stained red and swollen as if she'd been crying. "Uh, yeah," she answered, "I found her."

I wanted to feel relief at her response, but her eyes told me something was upsetting her, I just didn't know what that something was. "Is she okay? Did they hurt her?"

The volume of my voice climbed with every question, fear bleeding into anger until it was a toxic mixture pumping through my heart.

Something was off in her expression, but she smiled regardless, placing her hand on my shoulder as if to comfort the chaotic fear pulsing just beneath my skin. "She's exactly as she was before you were arrested. You don't need to worry about that. She's not scared, or in pain, or worried."

Relief weighed down on me like a heavy blanket, wrapping me in solace like the hugs my mother gave me as a child. Able to breathe again, I reached to squeeze Angela's hand in my own. "Thank you."

With that worry off my plate, I caught her eyes and asked, "Michaela? Are they giving her a hard time? She didn't do anything wrong, Angela. She doesn't deserve being harassed and -"

Her laughter cut off my words. "Are you kidding me, right now?" Shaking her head, Angela squeezed my hand before cocking a hip. "Your girl is something else, Holden. She's been holding her own. I'll admit when she first called me, I was pissed to find out you've had anything to do with her. But after talking to her, and after seeing how concerned she is for you, I may have to change my opinion. She's stronger than she looks, even if she didn't act like it while dating Jack."

Is it weird that pride surged through me at her words? I wasn't the cause of Michaela's strength. But I liked to think I was a catalyst. Perhaps truly loving a person can bring out their best qualities. Perhaps forgiveness can lift the veil of remorse to reveal the true character lingering beneath. No. Michaela's strength was hers alone, every glorious bit of it. But had love, and a few harsh words spoken to teach rather than insult been part of the breeze that lifted the veil allowing her to step into a life where she was free to reveal who she'd always been inside?

"I need to see her," I whispered, the pain in my leg returning as the effects of the medications continued to taper. The fog in my head cleared away and, without the worry for Deli holding me hostage, I smiled despite the pain, knowing that Michaela wasn't just fighting for herself, she was fighting for me.

"You'll see her as soon as your attorney gets the warden away from your door. Shouldn't be too long. He freed Michaela in a matter of minutes." Angela chuckled. "I guess the Tranquil Falls Police Department doesn't like it when people who actually know the law start talking."

My appreciation bled away to be replaced with confusion. "Why would the doctor pay for my attorney?"

Sighing, Angela took a few seconds before answering, "I'm not sure. But once the warden is gone, I assume we'll find out. Just rest, Holden. Stop trying to put the cart before the horse. At this point, we just need to the two of you away from the police. After you're free, we'll discuss the rest."

Suspicion deepened inside me, barely tempered by the pain increasing in my leg. I was ready for more pain medications, but afraid to ask for them. The hesitation I felt from Angela concerned me, the feeling that there was more to this entire situation than I understood. But demanding answers from her was as good as trying to force a mule forward. She would only dig in her heels and tell me to wait for when she ready to divulge them.

Gritting my teeth, I nodded my head and closed my eyes. I hoped the lawyer would hurry to get me released. Between the pain in my leg and the worry of not knowing, lying in this hospital bed was becoming utter torture.

CHAPTER THIRTY-THREE

Michaela

Sitting in the hallways outside Holden's door was an exercise in patience. With my head angled back against the wall and my eyelids closing with the need for sleep, I was too agitated to remain still for long, yet my body refused to allow me to pace around. Exhaustion was overtaking me, my thoughts chaotic while my brain protested the fact I hadn't seen dreamland in almost twenty-four hours.

Needing something to keep me in the present while the attorney and Angela walked in to speak with Holden, I kept my eyes trained on the police officer outside his door. Every time the son of a bitch looked at me, I smiled, mocking him for the losing battle I knew he was fighting when it came to keeping Holden for much longer. It was obvious they'd jumped to the conclusion that Holden knew more than he'd admitted. And the truth was that we both were lying through our teeth. But I refused to let Jack's parting act from this world become a crime that would lay the blame at Holden's feet.

Was it wrong to lie? Possibly. But when weighing the morality of my decision against the lack of morality in how Holden had been treated by our town since he was a child, I had to side with what I felt in my heart was the right thing to do.

After a few minutes, the attorney walked out of Holden's room and I jumped up to hear what he had to say. He simply smiled at me and patted me on the shoulder, asking me to sit back down and relax while he made a few phone calls.

Relax. Yeah, sorry. That wasn't going to happen.

Tapping my foot against the floor tiles, I leaned against a wall with the fear that sitting down again may lead to falling asleep. I had already yawned a hundred times and wasn't willing to risk missing the moment Holden was finally freed for me to check on him. It hadn't occurred to me until after his arrest how deeply he'd burrowed himself into my heart. What I felt for Holden was far deeper than anything I'd felt for Jack or other boys I'd dated in my past. My previous relationships had always been about the beginning, the racing heart when I saw them, the butterflies in my stomach that seemed to migrate away or die off once enough time had passed for me to learn that what I'd felt for those people was excitement rather than anything truly lasting.

For Holden, the butterflies were still there, but the wind generated by their beating wings was more like a hurricane than a gentle breeze. It was undeniable to me that I genuinely loved the man locked behind that hospital door, that I would do anything or be anything if it meant he could reach his true potential.

Maybe that was one of the hidden meanings of loving another person: Your life is no longer lived solely to achieve your own dreams, but to find happiness and value in helping them achieve theirs, as well.

Within love, there is no room for selfishness or self-centeredness. To love is to blend two souls, neither one able to rest until both are nurtured and given room to grow.

I hadn't learned that lesson by watching my parents. My mother and father were too concerned with their own needs to truly care if the other person was happy. And in my relationship with Jack, I'd been pushed aside for his desires, his needs, his misguided pursuit of the greatness he would never achieve.

It wasn't until Holden that I learned that in a bond where two people cared for each other, happiness could be found when they both understand that to look out for the happiness of your partner was to trust your partner would look out for yours.

I had so much trust in Holden. I could only hope that after this current problem was all said and done, I will have proven that he could trust me just as much.

Footsteps sounded down the quiet hall and I wrenched my neck to look, the hope that it was the attorney returning with good news dying as soon as I saw a man I didn't recognize. With black hair peppered with silver, the man was dressed in khaki slacks, black shoes, and a black coat dusted with snow. His eyes met mine from across the distance, kindness radiating from them as he approached.

He didn't need to check the room number to know this was Holden's room. The policeman stationed outside the door was proof enough. After glancing at the guard, the man turned to me and extended his hand. "Hello, I'm Doctor Lucas Silva. Are you Angela, by chance?"

Shaking my head, I quickly realized this was the man who'd paid for the attorney for both Holden and me. "No, Angela is inside with Holden. I'm Michaela."

His smile brightened. "I hope Mr. Grinshaw was able to help you, Michaela. He's the best I know."

Matching his grin, I shook his hand. "I wouldn't be standing here without him. He was able to get me out of the police station in thirty minutes flat."

Soft laughter shook Dr. Silva's shoulders. "Yes, well, he's a good man who loves what he does. And he's been eyeing Tranquil Falls for a while now. You and Holden happened to be the first case he could legitimately use to counter the corruption within its police force."

A throat cleared behind us, and we both turned to see the police officer glaring our direction. I scowled, but Dr. Silva merely smiled. Returning his attention to me, he touched my arm as if to lead me away from Holden's door. I resisted, at first, but when he explained he preferred to speak away from curious ears, I walked with him.

Led to another room, I walked inside the dim interior, turning just as Dr. Silva opened the door and flicked a switch to illuminate the space. Directing me to sit down, he dragged a chair over to sit opposite me. It was obvious by his expression that he was tired, but there was also a keen determination behind his eyes.

"We have several different issues occurring at the same time, Michaela. One, I'm sure you're aware of, is the biased intentions of the police investigating both you and Holden for the disappearance of that boy. Another is information I've had for several years that has bothered me since patients presented with strange complaints. And the third, and perhaps the most troublesome at the moment, is the truth about Holden and his sister. I'm hoping you can help me with all these issues, if not through legal means, but by providing me information that will help me remedy all three."

Confused where he was going with this, I asked what I believed was the most pressing question. "What happened to Delilah? And are you aware that Holden still believes she's alive?"

His expression fell, true concern floating across his gaze as the corners of his lips turned down, the perfect posture of his body slumping back against his chair. "I wasn't aware, per se, but I've had my concerns. Although I was surprised to hear from my former nurse tonight about Holden being in the hospital, I wasn't blatantly shocked when I learned that he hadn't accepted his sister's death. I'd assumed as much two years ago after she passed, but I had few resources at my disposal to help him. Unfortunately, the laws in this state make it difficult to counter mental health problems, those occurring genetically or as a result of head trauma, without a patient's consent, unless of course the patient presents as a danger to themself or other people."

Wringing my hands in my lap, I stared at him, the exhaustion I'd felt earlier all but gone as worry coursed through my veins and forced my heart to increase in pace. "I'm not sure what you mean. Are you saying Holden has mental issues?"

He crossed his legs at the knee, his kind eyes holding mine. "I'm not sure. I'd like to hear about any unusual behavior you may have observed before I can even begin to decide what we're dealing with."

A breath escaped my lungs, shaky and filled with so much tension that it was bleeding into the room, the four walls suddenly closing in and oppressive. "When I first went to Holden's house, he told me his sister was alive. She wasn't there, obviously, but he said she was visiting family for the holidays. I had no reason to believe it wasn't true. Nobody in town really knew what happened to Delilah. There wasn't a grave by her parents or anything, so I just assumed Holden was telling the truth."

"Go on," he softly prodded, the details I was giving him being logged and analyzed behind his kind eyes.

"It wasn't until Delilah came home that I noticed she wasn't actually there. Holden insisted she was, but I haven't seen her. If what I've learned since coming to the hospital is true, Delilah didn't survive the injuries of her accident, so I think it's safe to assume Holden is hallucinating. Right? Which would mean Holden has a mental illness?"

Dr. Silva gave my question some thought before asking, "Did you ever witness Holden speaking to his sister? Or to anybody who wasn't there in front of him?"

I shook my head. "No."

He nodded. "Then it's impossible to determine whether Holden is hallucinating or simply suffering from a delusion, based solely on what you've told me."

My brows tugged together. "Isn't that the same thing?"

"Not necessarily," he answered softly. "One is the inability to distinguish between what is real and what is not. Seeing or hearing something that isn't there and believing it's real would be a hallucination. A delusion, on the other hand, is a belief somebody has, despite evidence pointing to the contrary. It's possible that Holden is hallucinating, which led to a long term delusion that his sister never died. However, a delusion would not create a hallucination. Given Holden's previous head injury, I'm inclined to believe hallucinations may have played into a longstanding delusion. But without testing, I can't be sure of the exact cause. What has he told you about his sister?"

Thinking back, I remembered the conversation I had with Holden about Delilah. It pained me to remember how upset he'd been when telling me about her problems. "He said she was afraid to go outside. And that she wouldn't seek treatment for her injuries. He also said that she never matured beyond the date her parents died and that she waited for them to come home despite being told they'd died." Pausing, I tried to remember all of it, a detail floating up that I didn't think was important, but caused Dr. Silva's eyebrows to lift when hearing it. "He also said Delilah had moments where she spaced out entirely. Like she was awake, but not there, if you know what I mean?"

Scratching at his chin, he sat up in his seat. "That's interesting. It almost sounds like he's transferring his own symptoms onto his perceived sister." Dr. Silva sighed, "I'm not a psychologist, by any means. My specialty is neurology. But if there is a physical cause to his problem, I should be able to find it. I just need his cooperation."

I sat back in my seat. "How can he not know Delilah is dead? Wasn't there a body? I mean, death is a physical thing. There is undeniable evidence. How can a mind just skip over that?"

He locked his eyes with mine. "Holden never saw the body. He was contacted by phone regarding his sister's passing. Unfortunately, it happened when I wasn't at the hospital to intervene. By the time I learned of Delilah's death, Holden had already been informed and asked to make arrangements for the body. The hospital never heard from him again. I tried calling him several times and even went to his house to speak to him, but he never answered the door. After a week, I grew concerned and contacted the police for a wellness check. They did very little to confirm he was of sound mind. After that, my hands were tied. It's like I said, as physicians, we're given very few options unless a person is a threat to themselves or others. So, after the police contacted me to say they'd met with him and determined he wasn't a *legal* threat, I contacted social services. They couldn't help me either."

Tears welled in my eyes. "Do you think he snapped or something? When he learned she passed?"

His lips pulled into a thin line. "Possibly. I'm not sure. He may have suffered another seizure from the stress of learning she passed, and the seizure may have caused another head injury if he fell. Or, this could have nothing to do physically with his brain, but have everything to do with an emotional response. Unless I speak to him and conduct testing, I won't know for sure."

The tears slid down my cheeks. "What happened to Delilah's body?"

Sitting back in his seat, he scrubbed his palm down his face. "She would have been cremated and disposed of in a pauper's grave."

"A what?"

"It's a field where the ashes of unclaimed bodies are spread together as a mass burial. There are no plots or markers. I couldn't let that happen to her...or to Holden. So, I pulled some strings that weren't exactly legal and paid to have the body cremated. I've held onto the ashes hoping that Holden would come forward someday to ask for them."

"Thank you for that," I croaked. Barely able to breathe past the sorrow invading every cell in my body, I asked, "What do we do next? And what about the other issues?"

Dr. Silva sighed again, the long exhalation of air pregnant with a toxic mix of emotions. "We tell Holden. And we convince him to let me help him by testing to see what is causing the hallucinations. As to the other issues, I don't know what can be done. I've been trying to get help for years, an investigation into a town that seems to have several problems." His gaze met mine. "Do you know anything about the parties in the town? The ones thrown by the high school students."

Grimacing, I swiped a tear from my cheek and nodded my head. "Yes. I've been to many of them. My ex-boyfriend, the one whose disappearance is being blamed on Holden, he often bought drugs for the parties. Why?"

A stern line cut the skin between his eyes. "Did you see anything unusual at those parties? Anything that concerned you?"

Nodding again, I confessed, "The drugs were used on the girls in order to get them in bed. I didn't fully

302

understand exactly what was happening until I'd almost graduated high school. I thought the girls were consenting, but now, I'm not so sure. Jack and his friends started..."

My body shuddered to think about what I'd witnessed.

"His friends made it a game to pass the girls around, without their permission."

"That's what I thought. I was told by a friend of mine in the clinic that girls had arrived needing pregnancy tests and requesting STD tests. They'd admitted they weren't exactly sure who they'd slept with. My friend pushed for them to go to the police, but the girls were frightened. They didn't believe anybody would help them. I called the State Police several times to ask them to investigate, but without a girl willing to come forward, they said they couldn't help."

A light bulb went off over my head, an idea that would benefit not just the town, but Holden and me, as well. "I could come forward. And I already have a friend contacting other girls to come forward, too. But could we get it started with just me? I know a lot more than even the girls that were used. Jack would never let me do the drugs they gave the other girls, so I was always aware and saw more than they thought I saw."

He scratched his chin, a habit I noticed meant he was considering some thought. "It could be a starting point, perhaps enough to get the State Police to look into the local police. If you could find more girls that were actually victims, then that would be helpful."

Nodding, I said, "I'll work on it as soon as Holden and I are home. Anything to stop the town from hurting him more. He didn't have anything to do with Jack's disappearance."

303

Wrinkling his brow, he appeared to have more questions, but chose not to ask them. Instead, he glanced at his watch. "We should go see if Holden's been released. I think speaking to him first is the best step for us to take now."

Standing, he extended a hand to help me from my seat, and with his hand lightly on my back, he led me from the room. By the time we reached Holden's door, it was to find the police gone, the door open and Angela and the attorney standing inside quietly speaking to Holden.

Angela turned as we approached, her fingers lightly touching the attorney's arm. "I think we should give these two a minute alone."

Mr. Grinshaw glanced my direction before nodding his head.

As soon as he moved, my eyes locked with Holden's. I couldn't stop the tears that came on like a deluge of all the fear, sorrow, worry and pain I felt inside.

CHAPTER THIRTY-FOUR
Holden

Seeing Michaela for the first time since my arrest was a balm smoothed over the fire that raged inside me. Just her presence would have been enough to calm me completely, if not for the expression on her beautiful face. Part sorrow, part elation, part worry and concern. Every emotion ran behind her eyes, a constant cascade of competing thoughts and feelings that I couldn't look away from while Angela and Mr. Grinshaw cleared the room.

As they walked out, Michaela walked in, the door closing as another familiar man came into view, choosing to remain in the hall with the others and give me a moment alone with Michaela. From the brief glimpse, I saw that Dr. Silva had aged over the two years since we last spoke.

"How are you feeling?"

The moment her hand touched mine, I pulled her forward, ignoring the surprised shriek that fell over her lips as I wrapped my arms fully around her body and hugged her to my chest. Just feeling the movement of her back as she breathed was enough to send waves of relief surging through me. Just smelling the scent of my shampoo in her hair reminded me of how happy I had been in the weeks we'd spent together. There were genuine tears in my eyes as I tightened my hold on a woman who proved me wrong about her heart. Guilt raced through my veins for everything I'd believed about her before the day she shirked the costume that her family had forced on her to reveal the beauty of her soul.

"Hey," I whispered.

305

Her body shuddered with silent sobs. Her shoulders withering as her body relaxed against me. "Hey," she whispered back, her voice broken by tears.

Pressing my lips against the side of her head, I squeezed tighter, not caring if she couldn't breathe. I wanted her to know she meant everything to me, wanted her to feel the strength of my arms, the heat of my body, the beat of my heart that was only meant for her. Michaela may have been weak before the night Jack died, but she was a warrior now, a woman who had convinced me she would handle a situation that could have ended me, despite whether I deserved it.

"How are you?" I asked, my voice low, my chest vibrating with the baritone words.

Laughter infected her response, "I asked you first. And could you let me go just a little bit? I might die from lack of oxygen."

Releasing her just enough that she could pull her legs up to lay beside me, I grabbed her hips, tugging her into place until she was straddled over my lap.

"Holden! Your leg!"

"Is fine," I answered, my palm cupping her cheek as my eyes trapped hers. "Any pain I feel pales in comparison to the way I feel about you right now." Pausing, I searched her face, lingering in the beautiful light that shone from her eyes. "Has anybody ever told you how amazing you are?"

Genuine shock flashed across her features, her whispered response fracturing my heart. "I'm not amazing. I don't even know what I'm doing half the time."

Gripping her thigh, I squeezed a touch too hard. "You just stuck up for yourself and for me against an entire police department. You called in the cavalry, and if

I'm not mistaken, I assume you have another plan up your sleeve."

Her lips quirked with a smile. "Maybe, a little one."

I needed to taste her, to hold her, to smell her and love her. After Delilah, she was the first person to stick up for me, the first to have faith in me, the first to look past the labels our town had glued on me to see that, like everybody else, I had hopes and dreams. She encouraged me to be a better person. She showed me how easy it was to let go of what you'd been in the past to become the person you were meant to be.

Maybe amazing was too simple a word. She was a force all on her own. She was astounding. She was an incredible soul trapped in a world of people trying to tear each other down.

"Are you going to kiss me, or what?" I asked, my eyes refusing to let hers go.

"I shouldn't be in the bed with you like this," she teased, her expression in direct contrast to her words. Leaning forward, she swept her lips against mine, never deepening the kiss until my hand moved from her cheek to her back, pulling her closer, demanding more.

But like any beautiful moment that lifts the spirit to heights beyond reason, it had to end, both our hearts and bodies crashing down to reality, our entangled souls ripped apart by the words of a woman who hadn't meant to cause harm.

"And here I thought you couldn't live without me," Angela sniffed. "It looks like I've been replaced."

Male laughter followed her words, Michaela and I staring at each other with her long hair cascading down into a curtain blocking our view of the door.

"I swear, I just can't win. Downgraded from suspect to nuisance, and now I'm being forced to step aside for another woman. This is ridiculous."

Laughter shook my chest, Michaela's smile lighting the shadows across her face.

A deep voice answered Angela. "Normally, I wouldn't recommend two people in a hospital bed, but perhaps in this instance I can look the other way long enough for the situation to be corrected."

Recognizing that voice, I released Michaela to allow her to climb down, my head rolling over the pillow so I could meet the eyes of a man I hadn't seen in two years. He'd been a friend as well as a doctor, another person in my life who cared for me beyond what I'd believed I deserved. Scouring my mind, I couldn't remember the last time I'd spoken to him, but perhaps that was a consequence of the pain and turmoil of the accidents that had injured Deli and me, and had killed our parents.

"Dr. Silva. It's been a long time."

Michaela stepped away to allow Dr. Silva to approach my bed. He shook my hand and snuck a peek at the monitors above my head. "It looks like you're well enough to go home. As long as your pain is manageable and you can get around on that leg, I can have your attending physician begin the discharge process."

"That would be great," I answered, my eyes closing briefly as I looked forward to being back in my bed. "I can't wait to get home and help Del clean up the mess the police made of her room."

Every person in the room went still, their expressions equally unreadable as I opened my eyes and glanced between them. Closing the door softly, Angela grabbed two chairs and dragged them to my bed. She and Michaela sat down, Michaela's hand crushing mine while Angela softly brushed her palm over my shoulder.

"What's going on?" I asked, my brows tugging together, my eyes looking between Angela, Dr. Silva and

Michaela. The attorney remained in the back of the room, notably silent.

Dr. Silva cleared his throat. "We have something we need to discuss with you, Holden. And I won't lie, it's going to be difficult for you to hear and accept. It concerns your sister."

The machine above my head jacked up its pace, the beeping like a warning that a bomb would explode at any second. Dr. Silva glanced up at the machine, his eyes meeting mine again.

"What's wrong with Del?" I asked, my eyes seeing Angela's gaze. "You told me she was fine. You said she-"

"I told you she was the same as she had been before you were arrested. I didn't lie, but I couldn't tell you everything I'd learned before Dr. Silva arrived."

The beeping increased further, and Dr. Silva stood from his seat to silence the monitors. After sitting again, he breathed in deeply, expelling the air before opening his mouth to explain, "Holden, I'm afraid you have been suffering from a delusion for the past two years, and I don't know any other way to say this than to just spit it out."

Pausing, he looked between Michaela and Angela before returning his gaze to me. Angela kept her hand on my shoulder. Michaela squeezed her fingers over mine. Dr. Silva swallowed hard before finally admitting what he'd come to tell me.

"I'm sorry to tell you this, but your sister passed away a few weeks after her accident."

My head shook, the denial instantaneous. "No. That's impossible. Why are you telling me this?"

Concern flashed behind his eyes. "Holden, I have her ashes. I saved them for you, but you have to listen to what I'm saying. I would never lie to you."

What?

No.

He was lying.

I was dreaming.

Delilah wasn't dead.

I'd talked to her, laughed with her, taken care of her since she'd come home from the hospital.

"Holden...?"

She had issues, yes, but she was alive.

Why were they doing this?

Had everyone turned against me?

Reality crashed down until I understood that this moment was nothing but a lie.

Was I hallucinating?

Was this all a nightmare keeping me tethered?

Had I really been shot in the leg, or had the bullet struck my head?

"Holden, please, talk to us..."

Was I dead already?

Was this a figment of my imagination?

"Holden Bishop, you need to talk to us..."

No.

No.

No.

"He needs medical attention. Someone go get a nurse..."

Why?
What was happening?
How could they do something so terribly cruel?

"Give him Ativan to calm him down. We have to get his vitals under control..."

No.
Not Delilah.
Not my sister.
Not the little girl I'd always kept safe.

Not the girl who always made me smile.
Not a soul too beautiful for this world.
Not the only person I'd ever admired.

Hold him down!

Not her.

"NO!"

CHAPTER THIRTY-FIVE
Michaela

Even from two blocks away, I could hear the chaos erupting in the woods stretched along the train tracks leading from the servants' quarters into the main strip of Tranquil Falls. Lights flashed against the clear night sky, the winter chill still permeating the air, frosting the dormant branches of the trees that had finished shedding last spring's leaves. Like skeletal fingers reaching for those lights, the barren branches pointed toward the muted shouts between police officers.

They'd found Jack's body.

Three weeks had passed since the night Holden and I were taken into custody, twenty-one horrific days where I'd kept an eye on a man who was bouncing back and forth between reality and delusion. He'd returned to work for Angela despite the lingering pain in his leg, and I'd taken a job with her as well, if for nothing more than to keep him in my sight, always ready for the moment he broke down and accepted his sister was dead.

It was fortunate that we'd both taken tonight off for a little rest after the events that had shaken Holden to the core. And while he painted in his studio to calm his chaotic mind, I sat on the porch outside his back door staring at the lights in the distance.

Unsure what would happen now that they'd discovered Jack's body, I sipped a cup of warm tea that was cooling quickly against the night air. If not for the state police's involvement, I'd worry that Holden's house would be surrounded again, another late night intrusion that would destroy him.

As I stared at the flickering lights, and listened to the muted shouts between the police investigating the scene, I

312

thought back to the events of our lives over the past few weeks.

Dr. Silva has reluctantly released Holden from the hospital. He'd begged Holden to agree to tests, had offered to pay for each and every one, knowing Holden couldn't afford the costs. Yet, Holden had refused, his confusion burrowing deeper as his brain and heart attempted in vain to accept the reality that his sister had died years ago. After Holden had agreed, reluctantly, to consider Dr. Silva's request, Angela had driven us home. We'd stepped out of the car to walk inside, but Angela called out for me wanting a minute to speak alone.

She'd explained she called Penny, my family's cook, and that Penny had agreed to contact friends in order to convince some of the victims of the parties to come forward.

It was a secret us wealthy kids had kept to ourselves: We felt more comfortable speaking to the staff than our own families. We'd developed friendships with those considered beneath us because they alone would listen and encourage us to do what was right. Penny must have done a decent job convincing the girls, at least three had come forward with their stories despite their families demands they remain silent.

How fucked up was it that our parents preferred we endure abuse in order to continue the business ties that existed between the wealthy families? The realization sickened me, physically and emotionally.

As for me, my parents hadn't attempted to reach out to me since I spoke with my mother at the police station. And if I were to be honest, their silence was more of a relief than anything else.

Was I saddened by my family's apparent dismissal? Of course. But perhaps they were never really family to me despite the shared genetics.

Holden was my family now. Angela and Dr. Silva. They were the warriors marching in to correct the injustices of this town.

Once the girls stepped forward and admitted to Dr. Silva what they knew, we'd gone as a group to the State Police to file our complaints against not only the boys who had drugged and used them, but also the local police force that had known all along while turning a blind eye.

I'd lodged my own complaint about what happened the night Jack disappeared, and because a sexual crime was involved, the State Police had been granted jurisdiction to get involved. I was surprised it took them this long to find Jack's body, but with all the bureaucratic holdups, the local police had been barred from moving forward without the involvement of the agency investigating them.

At least, that's what Dr. Silva has explained to me. He and Mr. Grinshaw were much more educated on the matter, and I trusted them to watch over the situation and keep me informed.

With them manning the helm of the ongoing criminal investigations, I'd been left to handle a man who was spinning out of control.

Several times, I'd found Holden sitting in Delilah's room, his back against the wall, his fisted hands in his lap, his eyes closed as he struggled against the denial in his mind that she wasn't really there. I'd found him crying. I'd found him raging and destroying what was left of her room. I'd found him cleaning up the mess with the misguided belief she would return if he could put the room back together.

Most frightening, I'd found him blank. His eyes were open. His heart was beating and his lungs were breathing. But his mind had escaped, leaving him present while not actually there.

I'd cried every time I found him fighting against the truth that Delilah would never come home, but to protect him from the pain I was taking on for him, I'd hidden my tears from view, only to appear strong for him when I was falling apart right beside him.

You don't know pain until it's written plainly across a loved one's expression. You don't know loss until you have no choice but to stare it in the eyes and watch helplessly while it destroys a beautiful person. You don't know hatred until you understand that, by your silence, your weakness, and your refusal to see the truth, you had a part in the circumstances that ripped the sanity from the mind of a tortured soul.

Vacillating between blaming myself and scrambling to repair the damage, I felt helpless and bitter, while demanding I stand strong against the force of Holden's utter and complete devastation.

I had done that to him.

I could have stopped Jack before he had the opportunity to tear Holden's world apart.

A simple confession to authorities beyond the town's reach might have been enough to stop the parties, clear the drug houses and protect Holden from a fate that did nothing but force him to his knees.

Yet, I'd remained silent for far too long.

And suffering Holden's pain as if it were my own would be only a small part of my final redemption.

Not only would I suffer beside him, I would breach the shadows that kept him from moving forward, regardless if I was swallowed by their murky depths in my efforts to piece him back together.

A sigh escaped my lips, hot breath against the chill night air, and after swallowing down what was left of my tea now freezing, I stood from my seat to walk inside and

315

prevent Holden from coming outside and seeing the lights in the distance.

Dry warmth enveloped me as I stepped inside, the low hum of the central heat a white noise that lulled my mind into a calm serenity. After setting my teacup in the sink, I meandered down the hall, listening to the faint music coming from Holden's studio. His art was the only thing that calmed his tortured thoughts, our lovemaking the only thing that bled him of his eternal pain enough that he could find a few hours of sleep.

He was always awake by the time I opened my sleep dazed eyes in the morning, and I always knew where I could find him.

Letting myself into his studio, I crept quietly to lean against the back wall, watching with both sorrow and pride as he brought another image of Delilah to life, this painting revealing her laughing at something somebody said. He'd captured every minuscule detail in his memory, and stamped that precise image onto canvas with a talent that would go to waste in a town that did nothing but hurt him.

The music in the room picked up its tempo, the change in pace flicking some switch in his brain that tugged him from the tranquility of the memory into the desolation of reality.

His paintbrush fell to the floor, a scream of rage tore from his lips, and before I could stop him, Holden ripped the canvas from its easel and shattered the edge of one side over his knee. A knife driven through my heart would have hurt less than seeing him tear the painting apart, the wet paint coating his skin as pure agony tore out from his lips.

"Holden!"

Lunging forward, I gripped his arms with my hands, my strength nothing compared to the violent movements of his body. Forced back, my head hit the wall with a harsh thud, my knees giving out on me as I slid to the floor with pulsing pain spreading over my skull.

"Michaela?" He spun after realizing what he'd done, his own body dropping to his knees before me. "I'm so sorry," he whispered through heart-wrenching sobs, his forehead coming down to rest against my own, his tears dripping like a leaky faucet to wet my pants. "I'm sorry."

How many times could a heart shatter before it stopped beating? By my count, his had crumbled to dust a hundred times over.

Not caring about the paint smeared over my clothes and skin, I gripped his shoulders and tugged him toward me, my eyes meeting his as I spoke softly to soothe the chaos shredding him from the inside out.

"Shhhhh, it's okay. I'm not hurt. I promise. I just want to know you're okay."

"I'm so sorry. I'm so sorry. I'm -"

"Shhhhh," I whispered, my hand running down his hair, my tears spilling to mingle with his own. My heart shattering in time with his, the pieces tinkling against the ground in harmony with his full bodied sobs.

I didn't know if he was apologizing to me or to Delilah, to himself or to the all the people he wanted to protect but couldn't. Scouring my mind to find the answers was useless, so I simply sat there and held him, my eyes swollen by ceaseless tears, my body losing strength as I fought to hold him together.

What could I do to make him go through the testing? How could I explain that he was mentally ill? What would I do if he never got past the injuries that froze him in time on a cold winter night when the girl he'd always clung to for love and support had been lost?

There were very few options in my reach, so I fell back on the only one I knew would pull him from the

317

clutches of emotional destruction and into a moment where action spoke louder than words.

Cupping my hands over his tear soaked cheeks, I lifted his head to my own. Our eyes met, both rimmed red with heartache and sorrow as I crushed my lips to his and swallowed his sobs.

His body jolted with the force of our kiss, his mind lost to the need to escape, if only for a few hours. And as his fingers swept up my thighs to pull the yoga pants from my hips, I moaned into his mouth, willing to surrender myself entirely to anything he needed.

Love isn't just telling a person they mean everything to you, it's the ability to let go and become what they need in the moments they don't know how to can repair the damage inside them.

As heartache stepped aside to make room for lust and passion, we both continued to cry while ripping at each other's clothes. Naked, we slid to lie on the floor, wet paint coloring our bodies, as tears swept in to dilute it.

Entering me with one desperate thrust, Holden let go of the agony that had trapped him, and became lost to the rhythm of our shared desire, our minds calmed for a moment of the reality that awaited us once we woke again the next morning to find that the world had kept spinning while we'd been lost to our love.

It wasn't a solution to the problems that plagued us, but a bandage that would hold him together until I could find a way to help him accept the losses he'd suffered and teach him how to let go and live on.

I could only hope that by the time Holden was strong enough to move forward, I wasn't so broken by his pain that I'd be powerless to follow.

CHAPTER THIRTY-SIX

Holden

I'd been dead for weeks, it seemed.

Strangled to a point of labored breathing, crushed beneath the weight of a delusional life, buried beneath heaping mounds of regret that continued piling on with each new day that passed without the understanding that I was as lost as any person can become when faced with unshakeable tragedy.

Embarrassed by the idea that I'd imagined a girl who no longer spoke to me, I'd spent hours sitting in her room, staring at her on her bed, wondering how she could look back at me and smile, how she could argue that she never died, how she could reach across the room to hold my hand, and cry when I wouldn't reach back to pretend for another hour that she hadn't lost her life.

I knew the truth and yet I still saw her, my mind fighting to decide what was real and what I plainly saw. I knew Michaela cried when she thought I couldn't hear her. I knew she whispered on the phone to Angela or Dr. Silva when she worried I would never regain my healthy mind. Who knows what they said to calm her? All I knew was that I felt like a failure for not being the man she needed when my shadows attacked her, as well, and dragged her down. I should have been shaking my head of the insanity, at least enough to stand in defense of a girl who was drowning beneath the surface while trying to hold me aloft.

My only sanctuary against this living nightmare was the one place where I could take what I saw in my mind and apply it to canvas. Every brushstroke, every image, every painting I brought to life wasn't a memory of what had been, but an illustration of what I was still seeing.

319

They angered me while soothing me. They were proof of visions that others swore could never be real. They were the snapshots that clearly detailed a man's inability to make sense of his fragile mind.

Yes, I knew what I was staring at wasn't real. I believed Dr. Silva, Angela and Michaela. But despite that belief, Deli still stared back at me, her long hair trailing down her back, her smile just as innocent as it had always been, the pain of losing our parents still fresh behind her eyes.

"You're not here. Do you know that?"

Her brows tugged together, her hands wringing in her lap. "Don't be stupid. Of course I'm here. How could I talk to you if I wasn't?"

Stretching my legs out on the floor, I leaned heavily against the wall at my back. "I have to let you go, Del. I'm going to agree to treatment."

Fear flashed in her expression, panic causing her hands to move faster, her fingers to flex harder until the skin was white from the blood squeezed down. "I'll be alone?"

Shaking my head, I ignored the tears welling in my eyes, the way my heart beat in an imperfect rhythm beneath my ribs. "You won't be alone," I managed to croak in response. "Mom and dad are waiting for you. They've been waiting this entire time. You were right, Del. You will see them again. Just not because they are coming home. It's up to you to find them."

My words were logical, my conclusions sane, but still I felt a cold, cruel hand tearing my heart from my chest, felt my soul bleed from my body now that it was shredded by the claws of a reality that didn't give a damn what was fair, or deserved, or selfish about our lives.

There are different levels of missing someone, death being the most desolate and disturbing of them all. Losing a person you love is to lose a part of yourself, knowing full well you'll never manage to regain it. There would always be a hole that couldn't be filled. There would always be pain and remorse. There would always be the 'what ifs' and 'maybes' that could never be explored because time is a bastard that will never stand still. Emptiness replaces happiness. Anxiety replaces comfort. Anger comes sweeping in like a turbulent storm, wrecking every fragile wall you manage to build to block out the heartache that loss had caused.

I was enduring the storm, and I was fracturing beneath it, barely grasping on to a reality where another girl fought for me while needing someone strong to stand at her side. I didn't want to fail Michaela any longer, and in order to take her hand, I had to let Delilah's go.

My lips were quivering when I confessed, "I have to say goodbye, Del. I've fallen in love, and Michaela needs me. We're going through so much. I can't stay frozen in one moment and let her fight on her own. Please tell me you understand. Please tell me you want me to move on."

Each word ripped a piece of my soul away from me, but I knew what I was doing was right. How could I have asked Michaela to learn to be strong, only to turn around and collapse beneath my own refusal and weakness?

Whispering now because anything louder would shatter me to shards, I begged, "Please understand how sorry I am. That I couldn't protect you. That I couldn't save you when it mattered the most."

Deli climbed off the bed, her steps slow as she approached to drop to her knees in front of me. She reached to cup my face, my head hitting the wall when I flinched back. If she touched me I'd lose sight of the truth. I'd lose touch with my life with Michaela.

"She's small, you know? You told me that. Why leave me to stay with her?"

Tears streamed down my cheeks. "Michaela isn't small. I was wrong, Del. She's large. Like you. Like Angela and everybody who's fought against everything that has gone wrong in their lives. Don't you see that?"

"Holden?"

Another voice dragged my eyes toward the door, another island of safety within the crashing waves of an ocean brought to life by my storm.

"Are you okay?"

Rolling the back of my head over the wall, I shuddered to see Delilah once again on her bed, a memory and nothing more. It made sense to me in that moment, the clues exposed that I should have questioned all along.

"She never changes," I whispered. "Not her hair. Not the shadowed bruises beneath her eyes. Not her clothes. Deli looks exactly the same from the moment I last saw her sitting beside my bed in the hospital."

Without speaking, Michaela moved to sit beside me, resting her back against the wall and stretching her legs out along the floor. Her hand moved to curl her pinky with mine in silent understanding that I was coming to terms with my loss.

Soft laughter fell over her lips, not at me, but as a bit of levity to counter the weight of my pain. "I didn't mean to eavesdrop, but is she still calling me small?"

Nudging me with her elbow, she drew my eyes away from Del to look at her. A soft smile graced her lips. "You still haven't told me what that means."

Despite my tears, my lips curled in response to the teasing quality of her voice. Memories flashed through my head. The day I'd explained to Deli what the word meant to me. And the day I'd first brought Michaela to my house and reminded her that she could never be large.

322

I was wrong. So tragically wrong that I had to swallow the crow her actions had forced down my throat. "It means that there's nothing inside you worth notice. That to pretend to be something better than everybody else, you have to drag the good people down to your level instead of rising up to meet the bar they set."

Nodding, she glanced at the bed. I knew she didn't see the small girl sitting there frozen in time, a memory that never grew beyond the day I last saw her.

"So," Michaela said softly, "I assume to be large is to be the person setting the bar? The one who through natural talent or fierce perseverance becomes worthy of admiration and respect?"

My throat was clogged, so I simply nodded in response.

Her eyes locked with mine. "Delilah was large. You know that right? She had more talent on the dance floor than the entire team put together. More talent than me, even though my mother had ensured I was trained in every type of dance out there. I'd been practicing since I was a little girl, and Delilah could still dance circles around me."

My pinky squeezed hers. "You don't give yourself enough credit. I was at your practices. I saw how beautiful and graceful you were."

Soft laughter shook her shoulders. "I could say the same about you and your art." Raising a single brow, she dared me to argue. I knew better than to step up to the challenge.

Silence fell between us, pregnant with a topic that had lingered like a heavy cloud since the moment I left the hospital.

"Are you going to agree to the testing and treatment with Dr. Silva? Now that you know Delilah has never come home?"

Closing my eyes, I rolled my head over the wall, my heart beating with a slow lazy pace, like a dirge for the sister I'd lost. "Yeah. I'll call him tomorrow and see when he'd be available. I'm not sure how I'll get to the hospital or even his office now that his practice is further away."

"I'm sure Angela and Dr. Silva can take care of that."

"She does too much for me," I breathed out.

"Who?"

"Angela."

Michaela shifted, her body lifting and lowering again as she straddled my lap. Placing her hands on my shoulders, she waited for me to open my eyes and lock my gaze with hers.

"She loves you, Holden." Pausing, she swallowed, tears glistening in her honest eyes. "And I love you, too. We'll do anything it takes for you to get better."

Choked up by her sincerity, I grinned to realize that although this town had taken one family from me, it had also replaced it with another.

Fear laced my voice when I asked, "What if I never get better? What if the head injury isn't something Dr. Silva can fix?"

"Then it sounds like you're stuck with me whether you like it or not," Del answered from the bed.

My eyes clenched shut to hear her voice, a voice I knew wasn't real.

A warm palm cupped my cheek. "Holden, open your eyes and look at me. I'm real. I'm here. And regardless of what happens, I'm never leaving. Not unless you force me away. And maybe not even then."

It was my turn to laugh. Opening my eyes, I locked my stare to hers. "Oh, yeah? And how would you force your way in?"

A devious smile tugged at her lips, her response enough to shake me from my misery and force a deep laugh from my lungs. "I'll call Angela. She'll hold you down and talk some sense into you. And while she does that, I don't know. I guess I'll just show you my boobs to make you remember how much you want me."

Wiggling her brows, she leaned forward to softly kiss my lips. My hands moved to her back, tugging her closer. "Hmmm," I murmured, "I'm suddenly forgetting what they look like. I think I need a reminder right now."

Her laughter burst against my lips. "Carry me to our bedroom and I might just show you more than that."

She didn't have to tell me twice.

Lifting her up, I walked us out of Delilah's room, leaving behind a memory that refused to remain locked in my mind and moving toward a life that promised happiness and absolution for my crimes.

CHAPTER THIRTY-SEVEN
Michaela

Time couldn't have moved slower over the next several weeks, each day sinking me deeper in dread that the stress of the police investigation would hinder the progress Holden was making with Dr. Silva.

Although the injuries Holden suffered were permanent, Dr. Silva was optimistic that a coordinated effort in counseling, rehab and medication would heal Holden and return him back to who he had been before the accident that almost took his life. Already I'd noticed a difference in him, those moments when he would pause outside Delilah's bedroom door, his hand on the knob, seconds passing before he would shake his head and walk away to continue on to his studio - the best rehab of all.

We both worked to pay the household bills, but I'd made a conscious effort to save as much money as possible to keep him stocked with canvases and other supplies. The paintings he was creating were worth every second I spent working in the diner and serving a town that had come to hate me for what the police investigation had uncovered.

Sitting outside a conference room with Angela by my side, I wrung my hands in my lap as we waited for Mr. Grinshaw, Dr. Silva and the other victims from town to arrive. Today we would learn whether the State would press charges against me for not reporting Jack missing, and whether charges would be brought against Clive Stanton and the other boys involved in the parties. I hated to think it fortunate that they'd continued their activities over the Christmas break, only because the Statute of Limitations hadn't run out for criminal charges to be filed.

Laying a warm hand over mine, Angela stopped my fidgeting. "Stop messing with your hands. You're going to rub your skin off if you're not careful."

"I'm just nervous," I confessed on a shaky breath. "Not so much for myself, but for the other girls. They deserve justice in this."

Angela squeezed my hands. "They've already gotten some justice. The state police have been doing a great job of clearing out the drug dens on Holden's side of town. It's too bad the local police are only helping because a spoiled, rich asshole was murdered by one of them."

My heart fell into my stomach. I'd been relieved to learn that Jack's death has been blamed on a drug deal gone wrong, but I still felt a tiny bit of guilt for the lies I'd told to make that happen. Regardless, he'd received an expensive funeral with almost everyone in town in attendance. They'd cried and remembered him as a great man. Thankfully, I was out of reach and wasn't forced by my parents to appear and play the role of the broken-hearted girlfriend.

"Yeah, well, that's good, I guess."

"Good?" Angela clicked her tongue. "Perhaps now that neighborhood can become a decent place again. More middle income families can return and make something of it. It would breathe new life into town and balance out the bullshit power of the rich and elite. I'm also ecstatic that Officer Shay lost his job. From what Mr. Grinshaw told me, all the dirty cops who were bought and paid for are being run out of town." She paused until I looked over at her. Lowering her voice, she said, "You've done good in this, Michaela. It sucks that you had to go through hell to cause these changes, but you fought back and the town has you to thank for it."

Sighing, she wiped at her eyes and straightened her shoulders. "I'd be an idiot not to admit I was wrong about you. Over the past weeks, you've proven yourself to be a strong, competent woman. And the help you've given Holden - the hope you've given him - it's more than I could have ever asked for. I've never seen him happier, and I have you to thank for it. I know it hasn't been easy for you to stand back and watch him struggle. But you stood there regardless, like a damn rock he could cling to when he wasn't strong enough to stand on his own. It takes a real woman to handle everything you've been dealing with while also being the strength for a man as stubborn and hardheaded as him."

A smile split my lips and I couldn't refute Holden's stubborn will. Thankfully, it was that same stubbornness that helped him step away from the delusions and fight to stay by my side in the real world.

"We need to give her a funeral, you know?"

Nodding Angela agreed. "Yeah. I know. Perhaps lowering her into the ground by her parents will push Holden to let her go once and for all."

Silence fell between us for several minutes. Angela breathed out loudly to break it apart. "What are you going to do with him once everything is over? You two can't stay here. It's not good for him. He needs to get out there and away from the town that tried to tear him apart. He's a better man than working at a diner washing dishes. And quite frankly, you're better than waiting tables. Both of you need to go."

Tears slipped over her eyes to say the words. She would miss us as much as we would miss her.

I'd already considered what we would do once the criminal investigation was over. "I was thinking about taking him to Chicago or New York. He needs to be in a place where he can show his art. I truly believe that if people saw his talent, he would have people banging down his door asking for portraits or other paintings. He has too much talent for it to be hidden away in a small studio. But those cities are expensive. I'm not sure how we'd survive. I could work, I guess. Pay the bills until he got on his feet. Then maybe he could make enough on his art to support the bills while I finish college. I just don't know where we'd find the money to move."

"You could sell his house," Angela suggested. "In fact, when we leave here today, you should go home and tell him to put it on the market."

Lifting my brows at the thought, I added, "*If* I leave here today. They could still attempt to get me in trouble for not reporting Jack missing. The Tranquil Falls Police are still adamant I had something to do with it, even if it was a deal gone wrong."

Even though Officer Shay was gone, Jack's parents had been pressing hard for charges to be brought against me, suggesting that I'd witnessed the murder and run off without reporting it.

Locking her eyes with mine, she said, "Don't you worry your pretty little head about that. Mr. Grinshaw will deal with their asses. Jack assaulted you that night. You had every reason to run off. It's not your fault that rich little snot wasn't smart enough to stay away from shady drug dealers. He got what was coming to him."

Before I could respond, Mr. Grinshaw arrived with Dr. Silva in tow, three girls I recognized from school walking in behind them. Mr. Grinshaw glanced at his watch and walked into the conference room, asking all of us to wait for a moment while he determined if the police and prosecutors were ready for us to enter.

While Dr. Silva moved to stand near Angela and me, the girls gathered near the other end of the waiting room, talking amongst themselves, their eyes glancing over as they smiled shyly in my direction. I smiled back, not holding it against them that they were angry that I'd

329

known about what was occurring at the parties and had waited so long to say a word about it.

I'd be angry, too, but I'd convinced myself over the years I was in high school that the parties were common knowledge, each girl knowing what they were getting themselves into. Sadly, they hadn't understood how bad it had been. Only I knew.

Placing a hand on my shoulder, Dr. Silva quietly asked, "How are things at home, Michaela? With Holden?"

Glancing up, I smiled. "Good. He hasn't seen Delilah in over a week. I think the medications are working."

"That's good," he answered. "That's what Holden told me the other day, but I wanted to confirm. Is he avoiding her room?"

Nodding, I sighed. "He stops outside the door every once in a while, but he never goes in. He goes to his studio instead."

Before he could ask another question, the door to the conference room opened, Mr. Grinshaw waving us all inside. My stomach was in knots as I stood from my seat and followed the line of people moving in. Having Angela and Dr. Silva beside me helped to keep me from chickening out and turning around.

Walking through the door, I saw three detectives and two men in suits sitting on one side of the table, their expressions sharp and focused on each of us as we entered. We took our seats on the opposite side of the table and waited for the men to speak.

One man stood up, his shirt perfectly pressed, his badge gleaming where it was clipped to the belt at his waist.

"Thank you all for attending this meeting today, I'll make the introductions brief as I'm sure you all are anxious to know our decisions. My name is Detective

Ross Clayborn. Sitting here beside me are Detectives Winston Jones and Mark Lansk. On my other side are the two prosecutors who will be taking these cases to trial, Eric Holtz and Timothy Franks."

His eyes found mine, that grey stare driving daggers inside me. "Ms. Michaela Paige. I'll start with the charges against you. If you'll give me permission to speak frankly in front of the other attendees, I can explain our decision."

Nodding my head, I couldn't speak past the lump in my throat.

He nodded in return, his brown, short hair barely moving. "Charges will not be filed against you, Ms. Paige..."

A collective sigh burst from Angela, Dr. Silva and myself.

"Given the circumstances of the evening Jack Thorne was murdered, and given his assault against you that led to your running to Mr. Bishop's house, we've determined that you had no duty to report a murder you were not aware occurred. We've spoken with the other young women seated at the table today, and they've all given us information that makes it highly likely your story is true. Seeing that Mr. Thorne was involved in other sexual assaults and was a known drug user, it's safe to surmise that your story is truthful."

My body withered in my chair, the relief so obvious that Angela reached over to place her hand on my arm as if it would give me strength not to crumble from my seat.

Ever the professional, Detective Clayborn ignored my reaction and turned his attention to the other girls sitting at the table.

"Regarding Clive Stanton, Derrick Mills, and Rex Pritchard, you've all provided corroborating testimony that has convinced us to press charges against those young men for sexual assault. I'll ask that if any of you receive threats or any other harassment after the charges are filed and the men apprehended, to immediately contact me or the other detectives or prosecutors seated at the table and inform us of such activity immediately. We will do our best to protect you from any negative consequences that may come with your testimony against these men. Do you understand?"

Two of the girls were crying, sniffles sounding as they nodded their heads in agreement.

"I also must warn you that you will be asked to testify at trial," he turned to me, "as well as you Ms. Paige. It won't be easy, but there are advocates who will stand with you and assist during that process."

Again, the girls nodded silently, and I nodded as well.

"If we're all lucky, the men will plea and a trial can be avoided. But I want you all to understand that you may be called to testify publicly. Does anybody have any questions?"

I shook my head, as did the other girls.

"Well, then we can conclude this meeting and move forward. I wish you all the best and will be in contact should I need anything further."

Silently, we stood from our seats and walked from the room, my legs barely holding me as up as Angela wrapped an arm around me to hold me steady. While Mr. Grinshaw and Dr. Silva said their goodbyes to us and walked the girls out, Angela held me back, offering a shoulder to cry on as I finally allowed myself to crumble.

Patting my back, she spoke soft words in comfort, her hand gliding down my hair as she kissed my temple and waited for me to calm down. When I was finally strong enough, she held me at arm's length and locked her eyes with mine.

"I don't want you to worry about this anymore, you hear me? What the man just told you in that room is that you won. You get that, right? You've not only cleared Holden's name in Jack's death, but you've stopped those awful parties and potentially saved future girls' lives. That makes you a hero, Michaela. That makes you large."

Laughter broke through my tears. "Holden gave you the large speech, too?"

She grinned. "Yeah, and the first time he told me I was large, I almost decked him right there. I thought he was talking about my weight."

More laughter burst from my mouth, the tears finally drying. "Sometimes I wonder if he doesn't deserve a good smack to the jaw."

Wrapping an arm over my shoulder she led me from the room to walk outside. "Yeah, well, if he ever does anything stupid, you be sure to let me know. I have a hell of a right hook when I'm pissed enough to use it."

My smile couldn't have been wider. "Okay. It's a deal."

CHAPTER THIRTY-EIGHT
Holden

Winter had finally broken, spring sweeping in to push buds out from the tree branches, a touch of color over what had been a bleak landscape when I'd buried my parents two years ago.

It was fitting that the day Delilah was laid to rest would bring warm sun and a comforting breeze, the snow having melted away as new grass blistered over the ground. Budding flowers touched the bushes that surrounded the cemetery, Michaela walking to my left while Deli stood in the distance.

No, the hallucinations hadn't ceased entirely and I'd been honest with Michaela and my doctors that, at times, my sister still stared back at me despite having been gone for years. I didn't acknowledge her openly. I didn't believe she was actually there. But it was hard to ignore her when she called out to me, hard not to flinch at the sound of her voice begging me to promise her she wouldn't be alone.

Perhaps seeing her so clearly was a consequence of my mind, the mental snapshots I'd always used to create my art now breathing life into a memory that was far too present and visible. I could only hope that burying her ashes beneath the ground would free me of the pain and sorrow that kept her tethered to me in the moments when my mind slipped across the veil from what was real to what was imagined.

Squeezing my hand, Michaela drew my attention in her direction. She didn't have to speak to let me know she understood my sister was in view, she simply locked her eyes to mine in a show of encouragement that I would, one day, overcome. There was no room for doubt when it came to Michaela's unwavering faith in me. She was cheerleader, support system and protector all in one - a woman so dedicated to the man she loved that she would become anything just to ensure I could reach the stars.

Her astute dedication wasn't one-sided. I would fight for her as fiercely as she fought for me, our shared love not a relationship built on seeing to our own happiness, but to each other's.

When you broke it down to the most basic part of the relationships that lasted despite the odds, you found two people looking out for the other's needs, without having to worry for their own. She knew I watched her back, and I knew she watched mine, our perfect trust pushing us forward.

Where Michaela was weak, I was strong. And in the places where I fell down, Michaela was the person dragging me up again. And as long as neither of us ever lost sight of what was needed by the other, there would never come a time where one person failed while the other continued to move forward.

"Maybe she's here to say goodbye," Michaela whispered, our hands locked together as we approached the open grave. At the front, a preacher stood to lead the funeral, and to the side stood Dr. Silva and Angela, and a few friends that had been true to Deli in school. There weren't many people who'd known her well. There weren't many who were ready and willing to shirk the expectations of a town still mired in a refusal to accept the differences in others, but there were a few who cared enough to let go of past demands without caring what the town would think of them.

When I'd buried my parents, I'd stood alone. It felt right to have people with me now that it was time to bury Del beside them.

335

"Maybe," I finally answered. "But if she's just a figment of my imagination, there's always a possibility she'll never leave. Not fully."

Michaela lifted my hand to place a soft kiss on my knuckles. "Of course, she'll never be fully gone. She'll always be in your heart. In your memories. In the places that matter. I like to think when we lose someone, they live on in the people who loved them. Parents live on in their children. Siblings live on in their families. Friends live on in the lives they touched, even if it was only briefly."

We stopped walking before reaching the grave, Michaela turning to me before placing her palm against my cheek and directing my eyes down to her.

"Delilah lives on, Holden. Her legacy. Her memory. Her beauty, both inside and out. Just because she's no longer physically here, it will never mean she's truly gone."

Leaning over, I kissed her softly. "Thank you."

She grinned. "Now if you could only convince her to stop calling me small, perhaps we can just learn to live as one big, happy family."

Her eyebrow arched and I laughed, the levity easing the sorrow.

After taking our places, the preacher went through the standard funeral dialogue, the words lost to me as my eyes continued to drift to where my sister stood in the distance. She didn't appear to know she was attending her own funeral - but then a memory wouldn't know, would it?

I'd chosen not to speak at the funeral, not to risk losing my composure in front of a group of people. It wasn't that they'd judge me for the loss of control, but I still couldn't find the right words that needed to be spoken.

As the funeral came to a close and a cool breeze blew past, Delilah's eyes widened in the distance, her gaze no longer locked to me but something behind me. Turning as much as I could without drawing attention, I saw nothing that would have stolen her focus. Shaking my head, I inwardly chastised myself for even responding to the actions of a hallucination.

My eyes drifting back to the memory that wouldn't leave, I watched as her lips pulled into a broad smile, the expression stretching her cheeks as pure radiance beamed from her eyes. My brows drew together, my jaw dropping as Deli opened her arms.

I almost dropped to my knees when my parents came into view, both embracing my sister before the three of them turned to look at me.

Tears were dripping from my eyes when Michaela's voice broke through the hallucination. "Holden? Are you okay?"

Forcing myself to look away from the vision of my family, I glanced between the concerned expressions of Michaela, Angela and Dr. Silva. I hadn't noticed that the funeral had ended, the other attendees walking off while the people who mattered the most remained nearby.

Without speaking, I lifted my gaze to look out to where Deli had been standing to see that she and my parents were waving goodbye. My legs weakened beneath me, three sets of hands locking to me to keep me from falling forward.

"Holden! Talk to me!"

Drawing a breath was damn near impossible.

My family faded as they walked away, my mouth falling open to whisper, "I - I think she's gone."

Dr. Silva's deep voice sounded next. "Who's gone? Holden? Are you seeing Delilah?"

Shaking my head, I cried as my mouth pulled into a smile I couldn't help. "Not anymore, doc. At least, not at the moment. My parents just came and took her away."

Michaela gasped, her hands locked to mine. When I finally turned to look at her face, I saw that she was crying.

Releasing her hold, I reached to wipe the tears for her cheeks. Pressing my forehead to hers, I whispered, "I think Delilah finally said goodbye."

. . .

The back door of the moving van slid shut, Michaela dusting the dirt and grime from her hands as she turned to face me. Both our bodies were drenched in sweat, a black bandana tied around her head to hold her hair back and out of her face. "I think that's the last of it. We should probably get a shower and get dressed or we'll be late for the closing."

Wiggling her brows, she stepped closer and tugged me to her by my shirt. "As soon as we have that fat check in hand, we'll be heading to New York! Aren't you excited?"

It had been two months since Deli's funeral and I hadn't seen or heard from her since watching her walk off with my parents in the cemetery. Dr. Silva credited the rehab and medications, but I still couldn't stop wondering what had occurred that day. Glancing back at the house where I'd grown up, I was both excited and sad to leave it behind. "I'm happy we're leaving, Michaela. Of course, but it's just weird how much we're getting for the place. The buyer paid three times the asking price."

She wrapped her arm around my waist, ignoring the sweat that soaked my shirt. "Well, the houses around here are being bought and remodeled by developers.

Maybe because yours wasn't trashed by squatters, it's worth more?"

"Doubtful. What developer would pay more than what I was asking? It's not like they approached me."

Her face tipped up at me. "Stop worrying about a good thing, Holden. Just accept that fate was kind for once. Race me to the shower?"

The wicked grin she wore forced a jolt of lust through my body. "Only if I get to wash every part of you."

"Deal."

Michaela took off at full speed, my steps heavy as I chased behind her. We spent a good hour beneath the spray of the water ensuring that every square inch of our bodies was clean. It was a mad dash to get dressed and make it to the closing on time, but the cheap car we'd worked long hours to purchase got us there with five minutes to spare before the closing started.

Practically running to the door, we burst inside, the receptionist looking up with astonishment as we barreled through the door.

"Sorry," I muttered. "We didn't want to be late."

Staring at us from over the rim of her wire framed reading glasses, she smiled. "You must be Holden Bishop. The buyer and agent are waiting in the conference room already. Can I get you two something to drink before you join them?"

Shaking my head, I wanted to get the closing over with, return to the van I'd left at the house and start the long drive to New York. "No, we're fine. We'll just get this over with."

Nodding, she extended a hand toward a closed set of doors. "The conference room is through there. Congratulations on the sale of your property."

"Thanks," I said, tugging Michaela toward the closed doors.

Opening the door, I stopped mid step to see who was seated on the other side of the table. My eyes narrowed on the stubborn woman, my heart thumping in my chest as a question tumbled over my lips. "Can I ask what the hell it is you're doing here?"

Angela grinned, her hair pulled back in a bun and her black button down shirt struggling to remain fastened over her chest. "Buying a house? What the hell does it look like I'm doing?"

Michaela was notably silent at my side.

"Stepping in further, I closed the door behind me, held a seat for Michaela to sit before taking mine. My eyes never left Angela's.

"I was under the impression a developer was purchasing the house for *three times* what it's worth."

Her grin stretched wider. "Yeah, well, you kids need a fresh start and I'm diving into the real estate business. It's a win-win. Now shut up and sign on the dotted line."

"Actually," the older male agent said from where he sat beside her, "I believe that's my line."

Reaching across the table, the man with silver hair and a black suit offered his hand. "My name is Mark Holt. I'm Angela's agent. You must be Mr. Bishop." After shaking my hand, he shook Michaela's, their introductions being made while I continued glaring at a woman who wore a shit eating grin.

Glancing away from her, I caught Mr. Holt's gaze. "You're a horrible agent. She's buying the property for more than it's worth."

Laughter shook his chest. "Yes, well, I attempted to explain that to her, but my client is ridiculously stubborn. That being said, this closing should be short and sweet. I'll need both your signatures where indicated on several documents and then we can call the transaction complete."

It didn't take long to sign the documents, and within a half hour, we'd said our goodbyes to the agent as we walked out of the building. Turning to Angela as soon as we were out of earshot of the agent, I said, "You shouldn't have done that. We could have made the move with what I was asking for the house."

Tears welled in her eyes, her attempt to hide them pathetic. "Yeah, I know. But I want you two to have the best start possible. And I can afford it. You've been through too much, Holden. You deserve a helping hand."

Sorrow flooded me, the happiness of leaving Tranquil Falls mired by the regret of having to leave Angela behind. "We'll come and visit every chance we can. And we'll stay in touch."

She swiped the tears from her eyes. "Damn right, you will. Just know if you try to keep from calling me, I'll hunt you down."

My lips were trembling, the emotion too much. Opening my arms, I pulled her into a tight hug. My cheek pressed to her head, I whispered, "I'll miss you, Angela. Thank you for everything you've done."

Stepping out of the hug, she craned her neck to look up at me. "Just promise me you'll do something good with it, Holden. That you won't give up. You deserve more than you've been given so far. And I want an invitation to your first art show, you hear me? I'll even dress nicely for your first big, fancy event."

Nodding my head, I couldn't speak around the lump in my throat. Angela turned to Michaela and the two women said their goodbyes, the tears flowing freely as they whispered back and forth.

It was difficult to walk away from a woman who had saved me after the accidents that had shattered my life, the same stubborn woman whose tenacity had been enough to pull me from the shadows and kick my ass back into the light.

But that's how it goes when you're moving forward. You never truly leave people behind even if you'll rarely see them. I assumed this is what it felt like to leave the nest as a child turned adult. Whether leaving for college, or marriage or a job, you walk away toward a new horizon, knowing full well you left a piece of yourself back with the people who helped push you to a future they believed you deserved.

I was leaving a town that had done nothing but hurt me, but I was also leaving with a woman who loved me more than I had loved myself. A piece of my heart would always remain behind with a family buried beneath the earth, and with another kind of family that would always be in touch.

It was bittersweet to pass the diner on my way out of town. To pass the cemetery and the curve where the car accident with Jack had started the domino effect of an unfortunate life. But after leaving the town I'd wanted to escape for so long, I realized it wasn't the locations of where I'd been and where I was going that mattered the most - it was the experiences that helped shape me, and the experiences that would come.

You can live your life regretting the misfortune you'd suffered, or you could do what I was doing now: Pick yourself up from the heaping piles of suffering, dust yourself off, and fight to continue living on.

EPILOGUE
Michaela

New York was a far stretch from the lazy, pampered life of Tranquil Falls. After arriving to our new apartment, following a drive that took several days, Holden and I both experienced a culture shock like no other. It didn't feel like we'd simply left one town for another, or even one state for another. It felt like we'd left the country altogether and were trust into a life that was as foreign to us as switching planets would have been.

It took months to get used to the hustle and bustle, the constant sensory blast of a city that never slept. But as the weeks moved forward, and as we both settled into our new lives, we realized we'd missed out on the magnitude of experiences that New York had to offer.

Even now, I was attempting to navigate a packed sidewalk as I threw my arm out to call a cab. People swept around me like a school of fish, barely missing colliding against me as they passed. My feet were killing me in new heels, the chill of fall nipping at my skin where it was exposed by the strapless formal gown. But I wouldn't have asked for it to be any different. I was too excited to care about the pain in my feet, too happy to care that I'd left my shawl in the apartment because I'd been a rush to get out the door.

I couldn't be late to the event I was attending, and I was nervous that I would trip and fall, or say the wrong thing. But thankfully, I had a friend who would be waiting for me, a confidant that would stand at my side and cry with me when the tears finally began to fall.

Finally flagging down a taxi, I climbed into the backseat and gave the driver the address of the event. He pulled into traffic and my hand flew to my chest in fear of how recklessly he drove. Holden and I had considered using the car more to get around the city, but I didn't think I would ever get used to the traffic or the way people drove. For now, I was happy to travel on foot, or use the subway when the destination was too far.

The drive took a little over twenty minutes, the taxi lurching to a stop outside the large glass and metal building that lifted six stories into the sky. I paid the driver and climbed out of the car, my heart in my throat by the time I spotted Angela waiting outside. Running up to her as fast as I could in my heels, I threw my arms around her and squeezed her tight.

"It's so good to see you," I blurted out. "Was your flight okay?"

"Well, if you call being stuffed in a shoebox and having to be a contortionist to fit in the seat they give, sure, it was great." Her smile was in contrast to her words. From her expression, I could tell she was just as excited as me to be here. "Is Holden already inside?"

Nodding, I took her hand in mine. "He's been working so hard over the past few weeks. He left early this morning to get here and make sure everything was perfect. I'm so nervous for him."

Releasing my hand, Angela wrapped her arm through mine, the sequins of her gown brushing against my skin. I'd never seen her more beautiful than she was now with her hair swept up into a French twist, a crystal barrette holding fastened at the side. "You have nothing to be nervous about. The boy has more talent in his pinky toe than most people have in their entire bodies. The only thing I'm nervous about is whether we can make him proud as we're blundering about."

Pausing, she took a moment to look me up and down, her eyes widening slightly as she studied the body hugging bodice of my red gown and the long flowing skirt that swept over my legs down to my ankles. "Okay. Well, never mind. You look amazing. The only thing you have to be nervous about is whether I'll embarrass him blundering about."

Laughter blew over my lips. "Whatever. You look amazing, too." Sighing, I stared at the entrance door and the line of people slowly moving inside now that the event had started. "Are you ready for this?"

"As ready as I can be. Let's hurry and get inside before all the free champagne is gone. I need a drink or ten to stop worrying that I'll make a show of myself crying."

Nodding my head and rolling my shoulders back, I tugged her closer to my body and moved to get in line behind the people walking inside. Once we'd made it through the doors, I gasped to see the beauty of the interior. Ceilings rose twenty feet above our heads, lights shining down that highlighted the entryway where staff stood in black gowns and tuxedos to pass out flutes of champagne and small pamphlets that discussed the art exhibited inside. I knew several artists were here this evening, but from what Holden told me, his work took up the majority of the floor space, his exhibition so vast that it filled the main room, while the other artists were tucked away in smaller rooms on the left and right. To our side, a mahogany desk sat, the black haired woman behind it filling out papers for the purchases people would make throughout the event. I had to bite my tongue not to squeal like a little girl from my excitement.

Passing the drink tray, Angela slammed one flute, and took another to sip as we entered the main room. I giggled beneath my breath at the server's expression in response to her brazen behavior. With champagne in hand, I kept one arm wrapped in hers, our steps slow as we meandered inside, our breath stolen as the exhibit came into view.

It was like the faces, lives and stories of Tranquil Falls had been transported to New York, the details so precise that if you didn't know it was paint, you'd swear you were staring at photographs of the myriad of people that made up our former town.

"Oh, dear God," Angela muttered, "He has a picture of me yelling at the cooks in the kitchen." Angela's cheeks flared red, but you couldn't miss the pride in her eyes. Holden had captured every detail, down to the glint of silver of the cooking utensils, and the worry behind the staff's eyes. Even though the scene looked like an angry employer, you could see the humor in the image he'd painted, the kindness in Angela's gaze even as her finger pointed at one man who had burned several hamburger patties on the grill. I swear I could smell the food, could feel the grease on my face, could hear the low murmur of noise floating in from the dining room.

"And look," she exclaimed. "There's one of you strapping on some ballet slippers. You look gorgeous, Michaela. Look at the detail in your eyes."

A smile stretched my lips, a tear slipping down my cheek as I stared at the painting, knowing what it meant for Holden to have paid as much attention as he did to the coquettish look in my gaze. It was a memory from before Delilah had died, a snapshot of the dance studio where we held practice. The fact that he'd remembered every small detail so clearly forced the breath from my lungs.

"Damn, your man is talented with paint and brush. You were right to bring him out here. He's going to be somebody, Michaela, and he has you to thank for that."

Passing painting after painting, their surfaces illuminated by track lighting that hung above them, we listened to the excited words spoken by the other attendees of the events. Several times, I'd heard the term 'genius' or 'inspired' as they discussed the artwork they'd come to see. Several people were already discussing bids they'd make on the paintings when it was time in the evening to buy them.

Trying in vain to keep my makeup from dripping down my face, I thanked the universe that I'd remembered to wear waterproof mascara. The room was filled with people, the crowd moving and swaying as we made our way toward the center of the room.

I lost the ability to hold my emotions inside me when the crowd finally opened enough for me to see Holden standing by his largest painting - an image of Delilah spinning in place, her smile stretching from ear to ear, her soul dancing above her.

But it wasn't the painting that weakened my knees so much that Angela had to keep me from falling, it wasn't the sorrow, or the love, or the devotion I knew he'd blended together with the paint, it was the man standing before it in a black tuxedo, his dark hair swept back, his blue eyes beaming as people passed to shake his hand, congratulate him, or remind him that his natural talent far exceeded so many other artists that came to this town to make their way.

Staring at a person who had endured abuse, who'd lived through heartache, and who'd crawled out from beneath the ashes to fly again, I realized in that moment that the gorgeous man smiling at me now could never be small...

Holden Bishop was a soul that would always be brilliant. He would always be striking and large.

THE END

If you are interested in reading additional books by Lily White or would like to know when new books are being released, Lily White can be found on:
Facebook, Instagram and Twitter

Join the Mailing List!

If you are interested in receiving email updates regarding additional books by Lily White or would like to know when new books are announced or being released, join the mailing list via this link.

http://eepurl.com/Onoeb

Join the Facebook Fan Group!

If you are interested in receiving exclusive previews for upcoming novels, or to participate in giveaways, join the fan group for Lily White Books.

Follow Lily on BookBub!

www.ingramcontent.com/pod-product-compliance
Lightning Source LLC
Chambersburg PA
CBHW020521260626

47156CB00006B/2078